The
Vampire's
Seduction

The Vampire's Seduction

RAVEN HART

BALLANTINE BOOKS · NEW YORK

A Del Rey Mass Market Original

Copyright © 2006 by Raven Hart
Excerpt from forthcoming novel by Raven Hart copyright © 2006 by Raven Hart

Published in the United States by Del Rey Books, an imprint of The Random House Publishing Group, a division of Random House, Inc., New York.

DEL REY is a registered trademark and the Del Rey colophon is a trademark of Random House, Inc.

This book contains an excerpt from the forthcoming novel by Raven Hart. This excerpt has been set for this edition only and may not reflect the final content of the forthcoming edition.

ISBN 0-345-47975-0

Printed in the United States of America

www.delreybooks.com

OPM 9 8 7 6 5 4 3 2

To all who appreciate those who go bump in the night.

Special thanks to: Donna Sterling and Debra Dixon. You're simply the best.

Appearing as Jack: Susan Goggins

Time, like an ever-rolling stream,
Bears all its sons away;
They fly, forgotten, as a dream
Dies at the opening day.

—ISAAC WATTS

Savannah, Georgia
2005 A.D.

Letter from William, a Vampire

My name is William Cuyler Thorne. I have been a soldier, a scholar, a wastrel, and a womanizer. But most important, I suppose, is the fact that among the many things I have been, I remain an unwavering killer of men. A predator.

Oh, I've taken my share of women as well, in temper and in pity, in hunger or merely in petulance. I have kissed the lips of some of the most beautiful courtesans on the planet before turning to baser needs. But always the blue blood of my savage ancestry, which runs so coolly through my veins, calls out for heat and for life. For sustenance.

I am a blood drinker.

I have walked the earth for five hundred years, plus or minus a decade. For two hundred of those years I was bound by kinship to hunt with my sire—a degenerate savage who deserved a righteous staking.

I remember what it was to be human, a time so long ago that I feel the vibration of mortal pain like the desperate tug of a rope falling into a bottomless grave. The tug no longer gives me pause. I am immortal, blessed, and cursed.

In the beginning of my undeath I fed as a soldier and since have watched men uncounted meet their doom. In my bloodlust I am a nightwalker, armed with flesh-tearing teeth like the Roman war dogs and with the sharp talons of the carrion crows who circle the battle-field. I kill the weakest and find life among the dying, feeding on the wreck of man's foolish predilection for conquest.

The English and French fed me for nearly two centuries with their petty bickering; but then I set my sights on America and a bloody revolution of men wresting a country from other men. Being part Scots and part English in my parentage I should have preferred the "Redcoats," as my rebellious New World neighbors called them. But I found the blood of the revolutionaries a wilder vintage, more vital and sustaining. No, I am not an avenger or a bringer of justice. Nor am I the sadistic killer I was created to be. I am merely the last spectral face dying soldiers see on the darkened battlefield before facing oblivion.

In the winter of 1778 I arrived in Savannah, a fading flower of a city. I carried with me a welcome supply of gold and the implied support of my newly chosen British surname—Thorne. The Brits had captured the city earlier that year and I had no reason to dispute them. There was plenty of bloodshed to go around. I have remained in the vicinity of Savannah for many reasons, including other murderous wars, but I see no need to broadcast my motives. Let's just say that the city and its darker hugger-muggery suit me. As winter suits me.

Summer in these southern climes arrives with a glorious pressing heat that breeds bloodlust even in the mortal heart. Human nature being what it is, I find a steady, gourmand source in their casual bloodshed. Passions rise and humans die. There is something to be said for the term "red-blooded Americans," and I sense their fury like a shark tracks a drop of blood in the outgoing tide.

And so I've given up the wandering life of a war dog, and now I reside in this city near the sea. The sharks and I are brothers. They fear nothing and cruise the watery darkness like silent sentinels waiting for the scent of the abandoned and dying, the flashing shock of hopelessness to draw them in for the kill. I live a gentleman's life, attending evening social events, smoking cigars and drinking port in private gambling dens or exclusive bordellos, and walking the dark streets to feed my destiny.

I own all I wish to own of my adopted city. My "ancestral" home—since I am in effect *my own* ancestor—is centered on one city block on Houghton Square. The entire block belongs to me, along with a row of businesses bordered by the river. I find enterprise a mostly pleasant diversion to occupy my mind, while the riverfront assures private access to a dock near the port of Savannah.

Even monsters take vacations on occasion.

You might wish to know of my other pastimes and the small number of humans I trust. I am in no mood to speak of such things here. And I certainly do not divulge my true name or where I sleep when the sun is high and hot. My secrets are my own, as is the bounty on my traitorous, dark heart. These few scrawled lines were written only to warn that other beings walk beside you betimes. Beings you cannot fathom or interpret. Be wary of taking in strangers unawares.

Savannah, Georgia
2005 A.D.

Letter from Jack, a Vampire

My name is Jack McShane and I've been asked what I remember of being human. Of the days before William and I met.

I remember the hunger. And the fighting.

I remember a kid whose empty gut gnawed at him night and day. I dreamed of food—bread and meat piled to the sky, fruit from endless orchards, cabbage and potatoes from fields that stretched for miles. I had visions of butter and eggs to say grace over, of fat brothers and sisters and a rosy-cheeked mother. I don't even remember their faces now. Hell, I barely remember my own. All I remember is hollow cheeks, listless eyes, and dull complexions. And my mother's thin wails for those of us who didn't survive.

I didn't spend my days shooting marbles or playing tag like young boys are meant to do. My father, an immigrant dirt farmer, didn't seem to know any way to raise his children other than to treat them like the slaves he couldn't afford. Before his passage to America, he'd foraged and fought for food in the sooty, dank, urban hell of Belfast, darting up and down cobblestone alleys, dodging lines full of dingy laundry and heaps of garbage while trying to stay out of sight of bigger boys as desperate and hungry as himself.

In this new land of promised plenty, my brothers and sisters and I, the ones of us who survived, were raised on a diet of cornmeal mush and merciless beatings. All the time being told how lucky we were. My daddy beat me for not getting the milking done fast enough, for stealing an apple that could've been sold, for helping my sisters meet their measure of picked cotton. My mother was little more than a shell of a woman, without the will or the strength to challenge my father's iron hand. When I got big enough to fight back, I did. By the time I was seventeen, I figured I'd better leave home before one of us killed the other, so I ran away to the grand city of Savannah where I worked the docks as a stevedore.

No sooner had I gotten a full belly and a dollar in my pocket than a war came along to damn me to a life of hunger and fighting again. A cruel blockade dried up the work and left poor laborers like me with no other choice than to join up with the Confederacy. By 1864, we were down to bug-infested hardtack and hot water that had only a passing acquaintance with coffee grounds.

After the demon Sherman torched Atlanta, his army headed east toward the sea on the Georgia Central railroad. They ordered three brigades of us in the Georgia militia from Macon to cut off the Federals on their way to Augusta to seize its arsenal and foundry. That was when we ran smack dab into U.S. General Charles Walcott and his men, part of Sherman's right flank, not headed for Augusta, but for Savannah.

Confederate Brigadier General Pleasant J. Phillips, as poorly named a bastard as I ever came across, ordered us to charge—across an open field and up a hill—the Union troops entrenched behind a railroad embankment. Shaking as much from fury as fear, I looked around at what was left of the Georgia militia—a handful of able-bodied men like me and hundreds of old men and boys. I wanted to turn my rifle on that idiot Phillips, but when I heard the bugle call I started across the field with my comrades. I remember looking into the barrels of the Yankees' Spencer repeating rifles and thinking that I didn't survive hunger and merciless beatings just to wind up with a bullet in my brain.

Then I saw a blinding flash and felt a blow to my stomach that knocked me to the soggy earth.

The next thing I knew it was night, and I could feel that old familiar gnawing in my gut again. Only this time, it wasn't hunger but a sucking wound setting free my life's blood with every beat of my dying heart. This was it, then. All the fighting to stay alive had come down to my spilling out my life in a swampy field surrounded by the dregs of the slaughtered Confederacy. Nearing my last breath I cursed heaven as I had in my youth, not caring if it damned me to hell as it surely would.

The very next moment I sensed something near me, something both hot and cold, alive and yet not. Something evil . . . with a craving. And then it was looming over me, its eyes glowing like a hellhound's, face and fangs dripping with blood.

It was William.

"You cannot save them now," he said, gesturing to the corpses of my comrades around me. "Do you want to live?" he asked.

I did.

"Do you swear to serve me as long as you exist on the earth?" he asked.

"Will I ever have to go hungry?" I asked.

He said, "In the name of all that is unholy, you will not."

"Then, yes, I will serve."

That is the last I remember of my mortal life. The rest, as they say, is history.

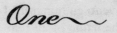

One

William

The innocent was naked, resting on an elevated table upholstered in black leather, her wrists bound, her ankles tied. A black satin execution hood had been fastened under her chin, covering her face but leaving her neck bare. Staked down like a sacrificial lamb fit to be eaten, she could not see me. Yet in the silence of the well-insulated room I could hear her breathe, see the slight flutter of the satin as she panted, birdlike. And, in the small space, I could inhale her fear.

My hostess, Eleanor, the proprietress of the house on River Street, double-checked the girl's restraints, then pronounced with a low chuckle, "Dinner is served."

"Time for me to be the vampire," I answered, making the words sound flip, yet meaning every syllable.

The lamb on the table knew my voice. She arched her back with a restless sigh, pulling at the leather, offering, wanting.

The girl would have to wait. Waiting was part of the play, and I would not disappoint her.

I turned to my hostess and held her gaze. In response,

my Eleanor, she who must be obeyed, lowered her eyes like a fainthearted human virgin. A ruse at best. She *was* human—but even if she truly feared me, she would never have shown it. Her lack of common sense was one of the things that had drawn me to her from the beginning.

"I'll be up shortly, when I'm finished with this one," I said. I used one finger to trace the edge of Eleanor's dress, then the tail end of the snake tatoo curling high on her breast over her heart. Her heartbeat fought the weight of my finger, anticipating our game.

She pulled away, turned with a swish of expensive lace, then looked back over her bare shoulder, her mouth dressed in the smile of the devil's own gypsy mistress. "Take your time. We have all night." Eleanor left the room, and the subtle musky scent of promised sex followed as she closed the door and locked it behind her.

I shifted my mind's deliberation back to the delicacy at hand. My body's hunger hadn't for one moment forgotten her. I could feel my own cool veins relaxing, warming, anticipating the feeding. Still, I resisted. Two slow steps brought me to the elevated table. "Hello, morsel," I said as I began to unbutton my shirt. No use bloodying the fabric; better to be flesh against flesh. Easier to clean up afterward—a courtesy to Eleanor's staff. I let the material slide off my shoulders and draped it across her bare thighs. She trembled at the contact.

"Hello," she answered in a faint whisper.

Lightly dragging my fingertips from her belly to her heart, I fondled her left breast. "Have you been waiting long?" I asked as I absently watched the nipple grow hard from the touch of my cool skin.

"Forever," she said in that whispery voice.

I eased my hand upward until my fingers encircled her

neck. The fat carotid artery pulsed against my palm and I had to fight my own anticipation. I was exquisitely empty—needy.

And under her pale skin . . . blood. Warm and vital. The tiniest pinprick would bring it rushing into my mouth, filling me, intoxicating me, redeeming me. I bent my head to where her left hand was tied to a metal ring and took one of her searching fingers into my mouth.

She jumped, whimpering as I bit and sucked—a teasing taste.

"Please . . ." she pleaded.

She tasted like life—dizzying. My own skin prickled with lust and I shut my eyes against the barrenness inside me, clamoring for more. *Take it all,* I heard whispered in the relentless voice of my sire. And I *could* take it all, like a greedy child, and still not be filled. But I would not—for my own reasons. I ran my tongue over the small wound to close it, ready to move on to greater satisfactions. "Just *please,*" I said. "Please what?" I asked, playing with her.

Not yet.

Humans always wish to negotiate for their pleasure, and their pain. The predators of the world are beyond negotiation. They take what they want, when they want it, victims be damned. In my case, slow was a torture for us both to enjoy.

I stretched out next to her on the table, lowering my face close to her satin-covered cheek. We were breathing the same air, two creatures who craved what the other could give but who would never know each other outside this room. Just the voices, the sighs. The heartbeats . . . *thump . . . thump . . . thump.* And the taste.

"Please what?" I taunted again, low and close to her ear.

Instead of answering, she twisted her head away from me, baring—no—*offering* her beautiful, pulsing neck. My jaw ached with the need to bite. But I licked instead, from collarbone to earlobe, making her jump in surprise. I could see the faint scars from other nights, other offerings. No need to lull this one with sweet distracting visions. She expected pain, wanted it, would bargain for it. She would risk even death for her perverse pleasure. But this was my game, and I would oblige in my own time.

And the time had come.

Finally, I would give us both what we wanted. I placed my cold right hand flat over her heart and pressed her down. Her gasp quickly turned to a moan as I bit hard, holding her fast with my teeth. In her world of pain she made a gurgling sound then bucked against the weight of my hand as her sweet flowing blood flooded my mouth. Rich. Intoxicating. If she knew how delicate the line was between life and death, and how easy it would have been for me to suckle until her empty heart stilled—obsolete—I could not say. If she knew death had come to visit, would she plead for me to stop? Or beg me on?

As any gentleman would, I held myself back. While the thick living essence gushed into me, I concentrated not on the changes in my body, but on the lamb's.

Blood for pain—our corrupt bargain.

I scraped my fingernails across both her breasts, raising welts and a long bleeding scratch just under one nipple. Her tears, leaking from under the satin hood, mixed with tiny splatters of blood and ran into my mouth. It made me want to sink deeper and longer, knowing she would never, ever ask me to stop.

Blood for pain and pleasure.

Nearing my own self-imposed limits, I shoved downward, pushing my hand between her thighs, sinking damp, warming fingers into her sex.

Her muscle-clenching orgasm sent one last tantalizing shudder of blood into me as payment and—I withdrew, licking the punctures to gather the final drops before leaving her. Replete, too weak to move or call for help, she remained still. Only the satin of the hood fluttered as she whispered, "When may I return?"

"When I call for you."

"I'll do whatever you want . . ."

"Yes, morsel, you will."

Have I mentioned that this river city, Savannah, is mine? My home, my sanctuary. The enduring connection between my existence and the empty darkness beyond. Savannah is rightly called the most haunted place in America. Blood has been shed here—some of it by me. To be fair, however, humans have needed no help in the bloodletting. They have proved by war after war that they are up to the task. The spilled blood of the past lies thick and moist over the cobbled streets and savage gardens of Savannah like the heavy mist covering a grave. The effect can be . . . suffocating. The residents here are used to the unusual, however. There are times— at equinox or All Saints'—when spirits brazenly walk the streets and unseen worlds open their invisible doors under the dark of the moon.

Then again, perhaps it's all rubbish. Humans can be so fanciful at times. Myself? I'm a realist. I see beyond the charm and the glamour, the human and the not-so-human. I pace the darkness, moving through the city's stick-at-nothing history in perfect step with the invisible ones. Ghosts don't hinder me, for I am death wearing seven-hundred-dollar shoes.

But tonight, now that I am fed, my interest is—excuse the pun—*firmly* set on sex. Up these stairs, my Eleanor awaits. She who has sworn to kill me, if she can. Without knocking, I turn the handle and open her private door. We have six hours until dawn. *Let the games begin.*

Candles are lit around the room, giving off the scent of magnolia. Still, I can smell her. And I do not need candlelight to find her. I would recognize the distinctive rhythm of her heartbeat in the dark of a dungeon. Tossing my shirt over the Queen Anne chair placed strategically opposite the bed, I hesitate before sitting down to shed my shoes.

Someone likes to watch. But not tonight.

The fluffy cloud of a bed has shed its usual satins and silks. On this night, for me, Egyptian cotton bleached to a snowy paleness. Frankly, a splash of red blood spilled on pristine white still turns me on, as you moderns say. Especially when the blood is my own.

We all have our kinks—even the undead.

I flex the warm muscles of my back, offering the perfect target before standing to shed my pants. It's too soon, I know. But perhaps she'll surprise me tonight. It's downright difficult to surprise a being who has lived for five hundred years; however, I always like to give Eleanor a head start, just in case. After that, I depend on her enthusiasm.

Naked, I take my time stretching out on the boat-size bed—my body humming with energy, lust. Sleeping is the last thing on my mind.

"Eleanor . . ." I whisper. "Come out, come out, wherever you are . . ."

In the silence I hear her breath catch, yet she doesn't move. In a feigned expression of boredom I slide my arms behind my head, baring my chest, my immortal black heart exposed to her whim. The room grows quieter—my Eleanor holds her breath before rising like an exquisite, tattooed viper from the floor beside the bed. Her lovely body is bare except for the artwork and the long beaded strands of her black hair. Mesmerized by the look of hot promise in her dark eyes, a man might not notice her concealed hands. But I'm not a man—haven't been for a very long time—and I notice. It doesn't stop me from beckoning her with my eyes and my will.

Slowly, in an act of submission, she brings her hands forward and shows them palm out. They are hennaed and empty of weapons. Then her fingers are on me, teasing, tantalizing. Then her mouth. She knows her business after all. And we both know the game. Her skill at seduction is legendary; but there is more than just that for me, and only for me.

Balanced over me, she slides sinuously, the length of our bodies matched—the smoothness of chest to breasts, the heat of sex to sex. When her mouth reaches mine, her tongue darts in, following my own tongue, touching teeth, fangs, and I feel her surge of excitement. She tastes blood and wants more. She would be mine across the shadowy future if I called her. But she knows I will not. I have an ancient hate, which I must starve and defy. Besides, permanent death holds even odds against the hope for immortality, and I will not take that chance—for her sake. Possibly for my sake as well. Being already damned doesn't mean I don't have a conscience.

When she flicks her tongue against the sharp edge of my fang, I taste her blood, her ultimate tease. And the flavor of her intent sizzles through my bloodlust like a firestorm of promise. If I'm not very careful, she'll succeed, with my blessing, in killing me. Either that, or in forcing me to kill her.

I suck her tongue, pulling her essence into my already dizzy senses. She presses into me, harder, then shifts her lower body, taking me inside her. We are locked together in a silent, primal dance of sex and death. Both of us drawn to the edge.

She stares boldly into my gaze. Most humans don't have the backbone to look death in the face. She calls me beautiful, and in her view I must be, yet I don't remember my own face—have not seen the otherworldly glow of my soulless gaze. My reflection was lost on the night of my making. "My beautiful, green-eyed, killer angel," she whispers.

Then she teases with a wistful smile. "Or are you the devil wearing a movie star's face come to steal what's left of my soul?"

That's when I feel her concentration shift, her hands move. One slides through my hair, dragging sharp fingernails along my scalp, while the other leaves me little time to prepare. In reflex, my left hand tightens around her throat as I shove her upward. I could kill her by squeezing my fingers, yet even as she straddles my hips, her tight warmth surrounding me, her arms are in the air above her head, holding an ornately carved ash stake. Meant for my heart.

With our gazes locked, I see one nearly my match. Not because she's stronger or smarter than most humans, but because she's done what few others over the centuries have managed. She's found a weakness in my defenses. Eleanor has discovered my fascination with wanting to die. To trade one undead version of hell for another.

Her chest rises and falls as she struggles to draw

breath through my grip on her throat. In the candlelight the snake tattoo seems to slither to life on her skin. Cleopatra clasped a snake to her breast . . . and it killed her. I pause, enjoying the killing lust almost as much as how it feels to be hot and hard inside her. For the first time in our game my excitement exceeds hers.

With a scream she plunges the stake downward.

To me, her movement unfurls in slow motion—in dream time. Those few seconds become like minutes in my altered perception. That lovely ability allows me to enjoy every facet of the action, from the small smile preceding the scream to the way the muscles of her chest shift, making the snake look as though it is striking as she moves.

The stake penetrates my skin and strikes my breastbone before I knock it from her grip. Both of us breathe as though we've run a race. The pain from the wound is minimal, and the tremor that shakes me to the core has more to do with yearning and loathing. I loathe the weakness that causes me to yearn for death—the final sum of my rebellious equation. And this woman understands both.

Eleanor's gaze is brilliant with triumph as she takes her now empty hand and runs a finger through the blood welling from my chest. Still the seductress, she brings the finger to her mouth and sucks the evidence of my weakness. She knows what comes next, as do I.

Fury, sex, and something akin to submission on my part, since now I can't stop. I won't allow her to drink from my wound, only from my lust. With a flip of my wrist she's on her back. Trapping her under the cage of my arms it's my turn to tease with a few long strokes inside her until she is crying out for more. As I feel her orgasm build, feeding my own, I lower my mouth to her neck, catching her skin with my teeth. The scream this time is louder and mindless. Death or life, either seems to be pleasure at this point. She and the lamb have more in common than they realize.

As I hold my Eleanor down, filling her without feeding, my hands ripping the sheets to ease the spasms tearing through my very much alive body, I feel almost human. Not a particularly elevating thought since humans have so many . . . flaws. But human I once was, and for that brief time, I was happy.

Jack

I rolled down the window of the wrecker and let the cool wind whip my face, flooring the accelerator and wishing the rig was as fast as my '65 Corvette convertible 327. I cranked up the radio tuned to classic country. Merle Haggard was turning twenty-one in prison, doing life without parole. Life. What a concept.

I was towing a car that a client had left broken down on the side of the road a few miles outside of town. He'd already hightailed it back to hearth and home, having called a friend on his cell phone for a ride. I didn't blame him. You never know what kind of monsters you might meet up with while stranded alone on a dark night outside of town. Especially a town as alive with supernatural shenanigans as Savannah.

I leaned my head back, wishing for even more wind in my hair. Like a lot of southern good ol' boys, you could say I have the need for speed. I reckon I'd be on the NASCAR circuit by now if I could show my face in the light of day. Instead, I have to be content with amateur night, racing by the light of the moon on the dirt tracks of southeast Georgia and the blacktop roads on the outskirts of Savannah. I'm somewhat of a legend among the shrimpers and river rats who have lived for generations in shacks dotting the edges of the piney woods. They think I'm a spook and the 'Vette is a ghost car.

Who can blame 'em? Their daddies and granddaddies have passed stories about me down through the years. Before there were cars, they'd see me dressed all in black, with silver spurs, riding a huge black horse. The horse's tack was studded with Mexican silver, and the way it flashed in the moonlight scared the very devil out of anyone unlucky enough to be traveling the roads at night. Nowadays they see me blaze by 'em on four of Goodyear's finest as they fish by lantern light along the intercoastal waterways. They don't bother to call the cops, though. The cops couldn't catch me during the years when I made a fortune running moonshine whiskey—and they can't catch me now.

Almost on cue, I heard a siren coming up behind me. Dammit! If I'd been in my 'Vette, I could have left 'em eating dust. Cussin' a blue streak, I pulled over onto the sandy shoulder and waited.

"Evenin', Jackie," came a honey-coated voice, and I relaxed and let it flow over me.

Officer Consuela Jones of the Savannah PD came to stand beside me. She played a flashlight across my face as if she didn't know full well who I was. I squinted and hoped she didn't notice the very unhuman way my pupils turn to oblong slits in bright light.

I'd known Connie since she first came to Savannah. Met her one night when she showed up to work the accident site where I'd wrecked one of my other convertibles. I'd swerved to avoid hitting an alligator out on the road to Tybee, rolled a few times, and been thrown from the car. She got there before the paramedics and was so convinced I was dead, because of the unhealthy angle my neck was in, that she didn't even check me for a pulse. Lucky Jack. Fact is I *never* have a pulse, and it would have been hard to explain why once I came around. As it was, explaining how I snapped my neck back into place had been dicey. I'm usually not so careless, but I had my back to her when I sat up. In the weirdness of the moment, I hadn't sensed any humans around, so unbeknownst to me, she saw me grab my head and straighten my neck. Kinda like you'd fix a finger you jammed during a pickup basketball game.

I realized she was there only when I heard her gasp. When she asked me how I'd done that, I told her I got the idea from that *Lethal Weapon* movie where Mel Gibson fixes his own dislocated shoulder. She wasn't convinced and has had her eye on me ever since. She knows I'm *different*, but she can't quite put her finger on what the difference is. Since she works the night shift, she drops by the garage now and then to check up on me, and sometimes just to hang out. I like to think we've become friends, although I still hold out hope for hotter and closer, if you know what I mean.

I'd ask her out, but I can tell she doesn't trust me. She knows something is up with me, something abnormal. I don't think she knows that something's up with her, too, though. It's weird how I can't sense or smell her humanness, like on the night I first met her. And yet she doesn't exactly smell like a shapeshifter either. Maybe she's a half-breed of some kind. Whatever the mix, she doesn't realize she isn't 100 percent human. It's probably just as well. It's strange that she works only at night. There's got to be a reason for that, but around these parts it's always best not to trade too many questions.

That night she looked particularly fine, wearing her long black hair in a braid down her back. And, as always, she looked damn good in that uniform, especially the fitted shirt. A standard service revolver rested in its usual place on her right hip and her badge winked a silvery blue in the flashing lights of the patrol car. A woman of authority. Be still my inhuman heart.

"If it isn't my favorite patrolwoman."

"Sweet talk will get you nowhere with the law." She gave me a lazy smile and a slow, sexy blink, showing thick lashes. "I'm going to have to write you a speeding ticket." She took a pen out of her breast pocket and leisurely moistened a forefinger to flip to a new sheet in her ticket book.

I gave her a wink. "Are you sure you don't want to frisk me?"

She leaned her head down as she wrote, thinking I couldn't see her grin underneath the patent leather bill of her hat. "That won't be necessary."

"Strip search?"

"I wouldn't dream of violating your civil rights."

"I meant you."

"Careful, I might run you in for sexual harassment."

"I thought that was a civil matter."

She tore off the ticket and reached into the cab to tuck it into my shirt pocket, tickling my chest a little through the fabric with the finger she'd licked. "Oh, I'm sure I could find something to charge you with. Drive safely, Mr. McShane." With that she turned her back and treated me to the sight of her walking away. I laughed and pulled back onto the blacktop. She could put a charge in me anytime.

Human females are kind of troublesome, but feminine vampires are nonexistent from what I can gather, so hey, what's a boy to do? The human variety think I'm the ultimate commitmentphobe. It's ironic because if things were different, I wouldn't mind settling down. But with my little . . . affliction, long-term relationships are out of the question. It's hard enough keeping my true nature secret from the outside world. I could never manage to hide the truth and nothing but the truth while living with a woman. *Don't mind me honey, I sleep all day and prowl all night. Not to mention drinking blood and never getting old.* So my relationships are always short and sweet. Intense (probably because I know they won't last), passionate, even—but brief. Maybe that's why I haven't pushed things with Connie. I'm afraid if I started seeing her, I'd never want to stop. I guess I'll just have to stay a love-'em-and-leave-'em guy with the kind of women who don't expect till death do us part.

A one-woman man in an undead womanizer's body. Ain't love grand?

Ten minutes later, I pulled the wrecker into the garage and hopped out. Rennie was rummaging in the cabinet over the coffeepot.

"Jack, there's no more coffee."

"Look in that grocery bag by the sink."

My partner at Midnight Mechanics, Rennie, wears Coke bottle–thick glasses that are always so smeared with grease I wonder how he sees anything. He's short, buzz-cut, and barrel-chested, and he can rebuild an engine in nothing flat. At the moment he was in the middle of a game of poker with some of the regulars.

"The regulars" is what Rennie calls them, and they're a collection of oddballs—not even close to regular as far as I can tell—who for some reason enjoy hanging out at an all-night garage. I wonder about them sometimes—what they do for a living, where they go in the daytime, and, well, just what they *are* exactly. But none of them ask me any questions, like why can I lift a car by its front end without a jack, so I return the courtesy. I guess that's why they feel comfortable hanging out at the shop, where there's almost always a pot of coffee on and a card game under way. I know for a fact that some of them aren't altogether human. I can smell a shapeshifter at twenty paces. Like Rufus, who never comes around when the moon is full, and Jerry, whose ears look a little too pointy whenever he takes off his Braves cap to scratch his bristly head. Exactly what kind of shapeshifters are they? Who knows and who cares? As long as they don't try to eat the customers, who am I to judge?

Even though I'm a loner, I don't mind a little company now and then. Especially company who can tell me what's going on in the city after the lights in the windows of the mansions along the squares have gone out. After the gentry have tucked themselves into their antique four-posters and asked God to deliver them from evil. From the likes of me.

A vampire can never be too careful. When I walked into the garage, a wormy-looking slip of a fellow named Otis was sitting down at the card table next to Huey. Huey detailed cars and acted as a general go-fer around the place. I wouldn't say he was simpleminded exactly, but he wasn't blessed with an overabundance of brain cells either. While he might be at a loss when it came to ciphering up a bill, he was a cheerful, pleasant soul who greeted each customer with a smile and a greasy handshake, and they liked him.

Otis flinched a little as I sat beside him and motioned

Rennie to deal me in. Otis never looks directly at me, but always just a bit off to one side. I think he's a little afraid of me. In fact, there are about three or four regulars who won't come into the shop if I happen to be the only one there. Can't say as I blame them. Us guys who are not rightly human always seem to know a weirdo when we see one. Or smell one.

"I detailed both hearses from the funeral home today," Huey announced while studying his hand. "It was kind of weird."

"Why's that, Hugh-man?" I held up two fingers and Rennie slid me two cards.

"Because that's what they ride dead people in," Huey said. "Dead people creep me out."

Rufus, who'd just taken a sip of coffee, nearly choked, spraying it all over his cards. The others were trying really hard not to look at me. The corner of Rennie's mouth twitched. "I reckon we're all going to die one day, Huey," he said. "I reckon we'll all take our last ride in one of those long, hatchback Cadillacs."

Speak for yourself, I thought.

"I just want to be buried in my car," Huey said, brightening. His face was so shiny with grease, I could almost see the reflection of his poker hand in it.

"You go and die," Otis said, as he took a pouch of Red Man out of his pocket and stuffed a wad of shredded tobacco into his cheek, "we'll see to it that you and that car get buried together." He wore greasy Dickies and a work shirt with a patch that said BUD. No telling who the hell Bud was. "You know that antiques warehouse down by the river?" he asked around his chaw.

That antiques warehouse belonged to William. I wondered what William's business had to do with Huey riding off to glory land in a Chevy Corsica.

" 'Bout an hour ago they tugged a boat into the docks and the warehouse guys were runnin' around screamin' at one another. I thought I heard one of 'em, well, you know how when you overhear a conversation and just a word now and then jumps out at you?"

"What was the word, Otis?" I asked warily. He spat a stream of tobacco juice into a Styrofoam cup through the space between his front teeth.

"Um, 'coffin.' " he said. "You think someone wanted to get buried on their boat? Kinda like Huey here?"

This got my attention. That would be William's boat. Running and screaming and talk of coffins. I folded my cards—only had a pair of eights anyway—and went to call the warehouse. What the hell could be going on?

On the sixth ring someone finally picked up. "Jack. Praise Jesus, you're there."

"Praise Jesus" was not a sentiment I was used to hearing in the same sentence with my name. I recognized the voice of one of William's warehousemen, Al Richardson. What he told me next made my blood run even colder than usual. "I'll find him," I said, and hung up. I muttered to Rennie that I'd be back soon, jumped into my ragtop Corvette parked in the last bay, and put it in gear. I had to find William fast because all hell had just broken loose. Literally.

I'm usually easier to find than William, seeing as how his tastes in nightlife activities are a mite more peculiar than mine and he completely refuses the whole concept of a cell phone. It's not in his DNA to be available to anyone—no matter what the so-called emergency. Seems like I'm always chasing him 'round town for something.

And William ain't easy to chase down. He could be at a black tie charity event, rubbing elbows with the high society folks, or he could be stalking a pretty art school coed who'd wake up the next morning on a stone bench in Colonial Cemetery, pale and wan, with a couple hours' gap in her short-term memory.

Among his many enterprises, William has a sweet little import business involving antiques bought for a song from down-on-their-luck European aristocrats. William turns around and sells the items to the new-moneyed here in Savannah—those social climbers who don't have any expensive old family heirlooms of their own, since most of them only acquired pots to piss in relatively recently.

But the antiques business is just a cover for the really important European cargo—vampires. I have no idea why they leave their castles and châteaus in Europe to come over here, but there seems to be a pretty steady stream of old, rich vampires that William brings over in his yacht, always one at a time. Vamps don't always mix well with one another. And you don't want some pissing contest about who's older and richer to turn into a full-fledged vamp war at sea. The crew is nervous enough dealing with one coffin at a time.

The imports have to be rich to afford what William charges them. These Old World vamps go first class all the way. It's like a Carnival cruise for carnivores. William provides all the conveniences, complete with hot and cold running blood. Hell, they might even play shuffleboard in the moonlight for all I know.

And the deal comes with an introduction to Savannah society. After a while they usually go off into the sunset for parts known only to them and William, who has contacts in the vampire communities all over the country. Every once in a while he gets in a Eurotrash bloodsucker, but for the most part, they're real high class. And get this. They even bring their own dirt with them.

I don't know what's so special about settling their coffins on that damn European dirt. Give me good old red Georgia clay any day of the week. But there's something about that old dirt that must have some kind of power. William won't tell me what it is. I have a sneaking feeling that William doesn't tell me a lot of things. Damn him.

Oh, yeah, too late. He's already damned.

He tries to treat me like his personal field hand. In the last couple of weeks, he's had me helping him prepare for this big party he's throwing for his latest imported vamp. Planning parties is women's work if you ask me, but at least he doesn't ask me to park cars at his shindigs anymore. Not since I threatened to whup his ass. I may have sworn fealty to him 150 years ago (give or take), but I'm through being his lackey. Thankfully, he just laughs at me when I call him out. I guess I'm lucky he's in a good mood most days. He's old, real old—although you'd never know it to look at him—and in the vampire world that means power. He could squash me like a bug and I know it, but a man has to take a stand once in a while, you know? He treats me with more respect than he used to, but I'm still at his beck and call, and it surely grates at my soul. Or it would if I had a soul.

William puts on the dog like nobody else, and all of Savannah society will be at his so-called retro charity ball. We're building a new wing on the hospital and a state-of-the-art blood bank. That takes money. Better to suck their money than their blood, as William always says. There'll be the most sumptuous banquet these blue bloods ever saw. And the most expensive liquor will be flowing like water down the Savannah River. There's only one problem.

William's warehouseman had informed me that the guest of honor had up and vanished.

I took the last turn on two wheels and parked under a live oak behind the wrought-iron gate of a respectable-looking antebellum mansion. I say "respectable," but looks can be deceiving. Even though his black Jag wasn't there, I knew that *he* was. Unless William blocks me, I can smell him out wherever he is, like a bloodhound. I don't know if he has the ability to block me out because he's the vamp who made me or what. Like I say, William doesn't fill me in on a lot, but it doesn't work that way for me with other vamps. I jumped out of the convertible and caught sight of motion on the back veranda. Two of the house girls swung languorously on a porch swing, the chains creaking like the shackles of the ghost slaves you can hear some nights out in the swamps.

"I just love the way you get out of that 'Vette, Jackie," cooed a baby-faced prostitute with fine blond hair. "Why don't you take me for a ride sometime?"

"I'll take you for a ride all right, darlin', but not just now." I thought her name was Sally, but I wasn't sure. I winked at her and the other one, who was thumbing through an issue of *People* magazine and trying to look as demure as a high-priced whore can.

I walked in without knocking. I'm not what you'd call a regular, but I must admit, I've partaken of these ladies' wares from time to time. William comes for blood and sex. I just come for the sex, since I don't have much of a taste for the kind of suffering you inflict when you bite into live human flesh. Even if the victim is willing. Since I'm a mechanic, I'm happy to negotiate services taken out in trade, especially if they're *really* good services. Not that I *have* to pay for sex, you understand. Last time I saw my reflection, 140 years ago now, I remember a shock of thick black hair and eyes the color of blue gas flame. Black Irish they used to call looks like mine, a product of the Frenchies (probably smugglers and pirates) mixing with Irish blood. I'm not saying I'm good-lookin', but I usually don't scare off many women—unless I decide to flash my fangs.

In fact, I have a rep as a womanizer and a heart-breaker. How can I help it? Running an all-night mechanic shop and a wrecker service means a never-ending supply of damsels in distress. Sometimes they can be really, *really* grateful. Not that I'd ever take unfair advantage. Being a vampire means always having to say good-bye.

William's romances are a mite more complicated. I didn't want to think about the things William did inside the mansion. I had my suspicions he let 'em think he was one of those kinky goths, the type who likes to pretend he's a real vampire by playing blood games. Not my scene, but if that's the way William gets his fang freak on, its none of my business. I did ask him once why he never shipped in female vamps, but he just gave me that ask-me-no-questions-and-I'll-tell-you-no-lies look and changed the subject.

Maybe, I thought, there *aren't* any female vampires— a mightily depressing notion.

As I entered the parlor, I found a few of the girls chatting up some flushed and panting businessmen, probably out-of-town conventioneers from some of the big hotels farther down Bay Street. Other patrons had the relaxed look of regulars, right at home at the ma-hogany bar as they negotiated for services over drinks. The furnishings and fixtures conveyed the appropriate image—money and privilege. A brothel dressed up in the expensive respectability of a gentleman's club.

A nicely dressed young woman turned away from the tooled leather appointment book she was thumbing through and rose from the antique writing desk just past the foyer. "Jack, how nice to see you again. You don't get by here nearly enough these days. What kind of party are you interested in this evening?"

I shook her proffered hand. Her slender fingers felt as smooth and soft as a rosebud in my huge, callused paw. Her perfume assaulted my keen vampire senses in a not entirely unpleasant way. It was a shame I was there on urgent business. "I'm not here to party tonight, darlin'. I have to see William. It's urgent."

Ashley rolled her eyes upward as if she could see through the ceiling into the boudoirs in the floors above. "I'm afraid you might be interrupting him at an inopportune moment."

"Let me worry about that." I started up the stairs and met William on the first landing, a pristine white shirt in his hand as he mopped blood from his chin, neck, and chest with a monogrammed linen handkerchief. He'd picked up my vibe, so to speak, as I had followed his.

"What is it?"

"It's the ship. Your cargo has disappeared."

A flicker of annoyance rippled across his smooth features. "The antiques were stolen from the harbor?"

"No. Your latest Euro—I mean, *shipment,* has vanished into thin air along with the entire crew. The *Alabaster* was floating loose up the river near Lazarus Point. Some of your boys found it and tugged it in. It's a ghost ship, William." I lowered my voice before continuing. "The coffin's empty. And no human bodies. You'd better come see this."

He brushed by me, but not before I saw the murderous look on his face. If a mortal was behind this, he'd soon be nothing more than a dry husk. But I didn't believe this was the work of a human.

I followed him to the car, matching his long strides as he buttoned his shirt. "A human, or even several, couldn't have done this, could they? Taken out a whole crew and an old, powerful vamp?" I asked.

"No," William said as he vaulted into the passenger seat.

"It must have been the import vamp himself. But why would he eat the crew and skip the welcoming party?"

William stared straight ahead with a look like he could spit nails. "I have no idea."

William was plenty mad, but that was okay as long as he wasn't mad at me. He was at his best and sharpest when he was mad. "We've got a rogue vamp on our hands, don't we?" The words sent a chill up my spine as soon as I'd said them.

"Stop asking questions and drive."

Two

William

It was one thing to be robbed, quite another to be rudely interrupted in the middle of an interesting evening. Eleanor and I had just been getting to the truly exciting part of our kill-or-be-killed game, and I would've thought Algernon Rampsley—the missing cargo—owned better manners. Ah, but vampires, like humans I suppose, grow selfish over the years.

I myself am more prone to anger than selfishness. I have to work to control the frequent bursts of rage that can nearly blind me. A migraine of the soul, my old human friend Tilly called it. She refused to believe me incurable, however, and over the eighty-five years of our acquaintance had tried out several remedies. Lately she'd charmed me into watching a taped television speech by a so-called Doctor Phillip. He'd lectured on anger management.

I tried to recall how Doctor Phillip proposed I manage my anger. It would have been counterproductive to take it out on Jack or the men who worked for me. *Missing cargo*. I'd find out the true culprit soon enough. If it turned out to be Algernon himself, then he was destined to feel my displeasure. My little import/export business had become more urgent in the last five years, and we needed to do it better and faster. Instead of the devil being in the details, hell waited for each of us in the wings.

My meditation on anger came to a skidding stop as Jack cut off a slower car before maneuvering around Johnson Square at a pace that made the Spanish moss in the live oaks sway. I momentarily longed for my Jag. I've never been fond of loud, roaring contraptions. In my opinion, the invention of the automobile was a grave mistake. Give me a sound, warmblooded Thoroughbred any day. But Jack loves his machines.

"If I were mortal, I'd be in fear for my life," I said.

Jack grinned with a flash of fangs. "What can I say? I love to wake up these old farts sleeping on top of their piles of money." He downshifted as he ran the red light on Bay Street. I decided to leave off. In the unlikely event he attracted the sleepy local police, that would be his problem. And the sooner we arrived dockside, the sooner I could get out of his vehicle.

Four of the night crew were waiting as we roared through the opening gate of Brampton-Thorne Marina, named circa 1902 in honor of one of my putative ancestors. I must admit that being my own ancestor is a unique way to view history. The term "grandfathered in" has its rewards as well. One of them being prime, *private* riverfront property bought and paid for in the 1700s and beyond the control of the current state authorities. As long as they have no cause to believe anything illegal is afoot, they completely ignore my small, exclusive shipyard. After all, it has been owned by one of the oldest, wealthiest families in the city—that family would be *me*—for more than two hundred years. Longer than any of them has been alive.

I've accumulated five houses, two plantations, and several aliases since my arrival in the Savannah area. Moving from one home to the next every forty or fifty years, changing names and affiliations, altering my appearance with the help of a series of housekeepers when warranted. It has gotten easier over the years, due to the increased population and decreased interest in social structure. As always, anyone with sufficient money is welcomed into the inner circles without too many questions.

The nature of my shipping business would be cause for a great deal of alarm if the facts were widely known. I was not eager to face that eventuality.

A cloud of dust, mixed with a muddy whiff of brackish river water, surrounded Jack's beast of a car as we came to a halt. In human legend vampires only smell blood—tracking the living for food. But our sense of smell, enhanced like so many other formerly human traits, is heightened beyond their imagining. Not only can we inhale actual odors, but we smell other things as well, like emotions and histories. The Savannah River has moved along these banks since before the English arrived, before even the Indians—and the smells have changed accordingly. But the original odor of ancient mud, brackish water, and millions of water creatures living and dead remains.

"This way, sir," said my foreman of fifteen years, Tarney Graham. He turned toward the dock. Jack clapped one of the other men, Richardson, I believe, on the back and followed.

The *Alabaster*, an eighty-foot top-of-the-line sailing yacht, stood securely tied to the outer dock. The hatches were thrown open but there were no lights on in the cabin. It looked as though the vessel had been abandoned in a hurry. I wondered why Tarney and the crew hadn't brought it into one of the private slips as usual.

Tarney handed me an industrial-size flashlight. "If you don't mind, sir . . ." He motioned for me to go first. He was afraid; I could smell it and see it in his eyes. He'd done his job by bringing the ghost ship home. Now it was up to me.

"Jack? With me," I said. One of the others gave over a light and stood back as we moved across the gangplank onto the ship.

As soon as my foot touched the deck I understood why the men were afraid. The boat had an unnatural feel, a sizzling presence I recognized. For a moment, even I was loath to take another step.

"What the hell is this?" Jack mumbled. He had to feel some part of what I was feeling, but he wouldn't know the source. For his own good, I wasn't eager to enlighten him.

There was blood on the forward deck near an open hatch, and there was more near the wheel. But that was nothing compared to the seared fiberglass and blackened ashes of what could only be a vampire lying amidst the anchor chains on the stern platform. The remains of a stake, which had been driven through so hard that part of it had survived the fire, stood embedded in the smooth, scorched surface of the deck. I leaned over and yanked it free.

"Jaysus, Mary, and Joseph," Jack said under his breath. He'd started life as the son of an Irish Catholic, after all, and had seen a great deal of human bloodshed before he became a vampire. But seeing the remains of one nearly impossible to kill must have been a cruel surprise. Most immortals tended to forget about their peculiar vulnerability. I, on the other hand, played games with mine.

Holding the blackened shard of English oak, I put up a hand for quiet. I let the awareness of evil guide me, and it spoke in a harsh, stinging voice, an old forbidden tongue. I recognized its blasphemous language. And I recognized the presence of an old enemy. Reedrek.

The final time I'd seen my beloved Diana, she'd been in his presence, too. Screaming . . . and dying. Reaching out to me with pleading hands.

"William! For God's pity, do something. Help us!" she'd wailed as Reedrek worked, tearing at her clothes, her neck.

Then he'd turned on our son.

And I, awake but unable to speak or move, hadn't been able to save her, or Will, or myself. I would've killed them both with my own hands rather than have their last moments end so savagely.

My life for theirs, I'd offered, stupidly making a gentleman's deal with a monster. Rather than keeping the bargain, he'd acted with the sort of cunning that can only be summoned by pure evil. He'd not only killed my family, but by making me immortal, he'd gleefully planted the memory of their agonizing deaths in my brain for eternity.

I wore a feverous hatred like a cloak from that day forward. And I bore anger at life itself—because in making me, Reedrek had gained a barely human protégé while protecting himself. For, no matter now much rage and hatred runs through my cursed veins, a blood offspring can never kill its sire.

Now old fury rose within . . . crawling through my heightened sense that something very much worse than death had visited the *Alabaster.*

I wrapped the scorched wood of the stake in my hand-kerchief and slipped it into my breast pocket, close to my unbeating heart. I had to remain focused. When I touched the rail in the gangway, the screams inside my head increased, ringing through the polished brass like a tuning fork.

Reedrek.

My maker, my so-called sire, my reason for existing, and the object of my death grudge. Not my mortal father, yet Reedrek's black blood ran in my veins. His treachery had blighted my heart forever. If he'd set foot on this continent, then it was certain he was looking for me, calling me out. But how had he gotten on my ship?

It was dark below. I moved the light over the galley and past the living/dining area. The door to the forward customized cargo hold stood ajar. The strongest inner hatch, built to withstand any normal calamity, had its double safe-quality locks ripped and broken.

"Whew! What a god-awful stink," Jack said.

That's another advantage vampires have over humans—other than being harder to kill, that is. In death, vampires burn clean—to ash. Humans are too juicy to burn; they must rot.

I shoved aside what was left of the hatch and entered the cargo area. The hold could've been called spacious, if not for the seven-foot-long, ornately carved mahogany coffin resting on a raised, dirt-filled trough. The screams in my head were receding, a testament to my tainted but potent New World blood. I handed my light to Jack before bending to run my hand along the gold inlay grac-ing the heavy lid, which was resting on its side. Beautiful handwork. Algernon always had good taste. Before ris-ing, I gathered a handful of dirt. It had been more than a lifetime since I'd set foot on English soil. Even in the stuffy, evil-smelling hold I brought the dirt close and drew in the lingering familiar smell of Derbyshire, of family, of home. I've lived long enough to realize that as humans our birthplace is somehow etched into our cells. Even living for more than five hundred years couldn't erase it from my memory.

"Do you suppose old Ambrose went ballistic from being locked in?" Jack asked. "Surely he wasn't scared of tight places?" Jack knew as well as I did that it had taken more than average vampire strength to do such damage to the door. "Or maybe his appetite got ahead of his contract with you."

There would've been no reason for that. The cabin was equipped with several glass cages containing live animals. Jack called them the three Rs—rabbits, raccoons, and rats—and there were enough to keep a vampire quite happy for a month or more. Then there was the refrigerator, which was routinely stocked with at least ten pints of human blood when it left the Irish coast. Jack opened the door. There were only four remaining.

I dropped the dirt and dusted my hands together. "His name is Algernon . . . not Ambrose." Even as I said it, I knew I should've said *was* Algernon. The remains of the vampire on deck were surely his. But what had happened? Who had staked him?

Not a human—or even four humans, for that matter. In my opinon that left only Reedrek. It seemed my successful little smuggling enterprise had been compromised.

"Find the smell," I said.

It took only a moment. "Bingo," Jack said from the other side of the room. The highest cabinet was stuffed with what looked like butchered beef. A human hand protruded from the slaughter, still wearing a wristwatch. "One of the crew accounted for," Jack added.

Damn.

I returned to the deck with Jack following. Any discernible evidence of a presence ended when my foot settled on the dock. No wake to follow, no rhyme to the riddle. If Reedrek had stowed away and was bound for Savannah, he could've left the boat at any time during the night. More than likely near Lazarus Point. "There's nothing more to do here," I said to the small group of men waiting for instructions. "I want you to tow the ship out to deep water and sink her."

Tarney looked like I'd asked him to commit murder. "But sir, we can pull her into the slip and give her an overhaul."

I thought of the grisly cargo hold and what the men's logical reaction would be.

"I want her blown up." Out of the corner of my eye, I saw on Jack's face a mixture of shock and excitement. Reading his emotions, I knew that he would mourn the *Alabaster*'s loss as much as I. But the little boy in him would be pleased to make something that big go *ka-boom*, as he would put it. Doctor Phillip would probably say Jack had never lost touch with his inner child.

"And what about the law?" one of the other men asked.

"They might be interested, if I invited them to stumble around in my business. Which I'm not inclined to do."

"What of the crew?" Tarney asked. "There were four men on that boat when it left here."

One of whom was still aboard. I turned to face the empty, forlorn hull of the *Alabaster*, one of my favorite toys. The rest of the human crew were surely as dead as Alger. Reedrek would only be getting his cold heart warmed up to the slaughter. "Yes, the men . . ." I faced Tarney once more. There was nothing more to be done. The police would be no help in solving this particular crime. "Report them missing after the ship is destroyed."

"But—"

"They read and signed the contracts, just as the rest of you did. Mourn their loss, open their lockers, and pay their debts. It's all we can do." I'd made it a practice to hire unattached men who kept to the shady side of the law. No families, no roots. No one to search for them if they dropped off the edge of the ocean. My employees were paid very well and protected by my reputation. In return, they kept their mouths shut about any business involving the marina or myself. None of them knew, however, that by signing those contracts they'd come very close to selling their souls.

To me.

"I'll find out who did this."

Tarney nodded but I could see he was unhappy. Well-paid loyalty might not be enough if anything like this occurred again.

My anger boiled up a few degrees. The maker of this mess was truly getting on my more dangerous nerve. Then again, there had never been any love lost between me and my unholy *father*. If he'd found me I needed to prepare. Reedrek wouldn't be after my heart; he'd be after my equilibrium and my sanity. There are things worse than death, and Reedrek was a master at finding the perfect enduring torture for his enemies. I had defied him for three hundred years after my apprenticeship and had no intention of being his victim again.

Out of habit, I tugged out my pocket watch—an heirloom of my supposed ancestors—and checked the time. I didn't actually need it, for I could feel the movement of the earth turning, the approach of another day. Four hours until dawn. "Jack, you know what needs to be done. Pull the security tapes and any paperwork you can find, along with the charts, GPS, and computer hard drive. I'll pick you up at the river walkway at Lazarus Point in three hours."

For once, Jack didn't argue with me—until I asked for the keys to his car.

"No way. You'll leave chunks of my transmission all the length of Bay Street."

I hated when Jack quarreled with me in front of others. The man had no sense of place or decorum. But then, what could you expect of someone whose greatest desire was to become a race car driver? Sometimes he was more human than I ever remembered being. That was one of the things I scrupulously protected about him, without his knowledge, of course. There were times when I regretted keeping him ignorant on so many dark subjects. This wasn't one of those times. I held out my hand for the keys.

He tossed them to Richardson. "Let Richey drive you home. He can bring my car back and leave it here."

Richey, as Jack called him, looked like he'd rather board the *Alabaster* and climb into the empty coffin than be shut up in a vehicle with me. Unable to utter a refusal, he took one quick glance in my direction, then took two full steps backward.

I wasn't in the mood to coddle any more humans. "Get in the car," I ordered under my breath and permitted Richey to feel a small dose of my anger. He immediately trotted toward the Corvette.

"How do you do that?" Jack said, shaking his head.

I allowed Jack more than a glimpse of my displeasure. Of the few things I needed at the moment, Jack's little rebellion didn't qualify. "Practice," I answered, then, "Three hours."

He wisely nodded.

After a silent and somewhat safer drive from the marina to my home on Houghton Street, Richey left me with a petrified nod and a squeal of tires. An action Jack would've admired, I'm sure. I paced up the walk past ivy-covered walls and the massive concrete lions guarding the stairs. As I reached the door it swung open, revealing one of my guardians, Reyha, in her long-boned and graceful human form, standing just inside the threshold. If she'd had the tail associated with her daytime form, it would've been wagging. She smiled as she twined herself about me in greeting, pushing her cheek into my coat.

"It's lonely here without you," she whispered near my ear before bouncing away toward her brother, Deylaud, who seemed perfectly engrossed in reading a book. "Aren't we lonely, brother?" she asked as she propped her arm along the back of his chair. Deylaud rumbled something inaudible but pushed to his feet to give me a brief embrace.

"Some of us are lonelier than others," he said, awarding his sister an arch look. "Why won't you let me teach you to read English books?"

Reyha rolled her wide eyes heavenward. "Pah! Books. There is no life in books, only the dreams of others." She sashayed toward me once more. "I have enough dreams of my own."

"And I have no time for you tonight, sweet." I ran the fingers of one hand through her long silken hair. "I have to leave again shortly."

She hung her head in disappointment for a moment, then brightened. "May I go with you?"

"No, you must stay here with Deylaud. You've the whole house for roaming. I'll be back in a few hours, before dawn surely."

Knowing she would only continue her wheedling, I walked away. I had business to attend to before joining Jack at Lazarus Point. With a sniff of disappointment, Reyha retreated to the divan and sat on the cushions, curling her legs beneath her.

I headed for my basement office, tapping the wall sensor as I descended the final three steps from the landing. The electronic wizardry of high-end computer systems sprang to life and the heavy metal shutters covering the floor-to-ceiling windows of the house whirred open. I hate to be shut in after dark. Nights are my speciality, you might say. There are few enough sunless hours for my pursuits.

Out in the courtyard a breeze rustled through the stand of bamboo that guarded my privacy, and the waxing hunter's moon winked from its reflection in the Japanese mirror pond. The image wavered like a small white ship on ocean waves.

The *Alabaster*.

I heard the roar of the ocean—the voices of the shells calling me.

Out of habit, I felt for the hidden drawer in the antique wall unit. It slid open with a touch, and the pads of my fingers brushed along human bone. The box and the ancient shells within knew my name, my blood. Carved by an African voodoo priest out of the skull of his own father, the box of bone was one of the few things I owned that was older than I was. The shells were a gift from the venerable man's great-great-great-granddaughter, Lalee. She'd given me something else as well, the gift of her power, of her bloodlines. I'd drunk it in, along with her rich blood—the ancient practice of voodoo. After stepping through the door to the courtyard, I sat down on the stone bench overlooking the water. I used my thumb to push open the lid of the box and stared at the eight white shells within. As I watched, the shells seemed to change size and shape, increasing their call. The roar of an agitated ocean pounding on a rocky shore filled my ears. From my pocket I withdrew the remnant of the stake from the *Alabaster,* unwrapped it, and held it in my hand. I shook the bone box until the shells rattled and dumped them on the stone at my feet.

The cool breeze feathered through the courtyard, then stilled. The mirror pond flattened completely to reflect the moon and the stars. Then the night went entirely dark, as though a velvet black hole in the sky had opened and swallowed all light. Instantly I found myself night flying—fast and low over moon-touched waves. In the distance I saw the twinkling running lights of the *Alabaster.*

I heard a long low sound, a sigh or hiss as my feet touched down on the deck. It was a sorcerer's trick I rarely used, this visioning, this stepping into the netherworld. Tonight, however, the shells would not be ignored. In the distance I could see the coastline. The ship rocked under my invisible feet, the moon rose low on the eastern horizon, and new blood reflected wetly in the light. Someone had already died. I drifted down the stairs toward voices.

"Running away like a coward won't save you," a familiar voice said.

Reedrek.

A shudder of hatred and revulsion shot through me. Reflexively my fingers tightened on the shard of wood in my hand. I had to force myself toward the compartment door.

This would be the true test of my mutated blood: whether I could face him without being distracted by fury and whether Reedrek would be able to sense my presence.

Then Algernon Rampsley spoke. "What delusion made you think you can rule the world? Do you think humans will ignore indiscriminate slaughter of their kind? Will the other clans overlook what you did in Amsterdam? I'd rather face the fires of hell than bow to you and your group of tyrants."

I stepped through the door. I could see them both now—Reedrek seated comfortably on a chaise with Alger standing near the head of his open coffin.

"Really, well . . ." Reedrek lost his concentration for a moment, turning his attention to where I was invisibly watching. I could feel his power like a blind man's hand searching for a hold. It passed over me and moved on. "In that case, hell is what I've brought you—without the fire." Reedrek rose from the chair. "Do you know what I did to Lyone? I boxed him up and had him frozen in a block of ice before shipping him to the Arctic. He's buried in a glacier like some hoary old woolly mammoth." Then Reedrek smiled. "Six months of light, six months of darkness. He'll sleep—for half a year at a time, growing weaker. But then he'll wake up and spend the other half lying there in that terrible cold, knowing the long night can't save him. And knowing he can't save his offspring. They are mine to do with as I wish now. I've killed the two strongest males and set up two females in a dungeon in Amsterdam to serve my friends. You'd be sickened by what odd and depraved acts other vampires dream of doing when nothing is denied. Things only an immortal could survive."

Reedrek gave Alger an arch look and rested one hand

on the coffin. "I would send you to the moon in your own hand-carved time capsule if it wasn't so much trouble. Perhaps later, after we have the American clans more in hand. For now, I believe I'll sink you in the ocean to be the newest member of the fish clan. If you're lucky, I'll forget all about you. I won't, however, forget *your* offspring." Reedrek's body moved faster than a thought. He shoved the lid of the coffin to one side and gripped Alger's neck, lifting him like a child. It was obvious he intended to seal him inside. While I stood there helplessly, Alger fought for his life. The boat rocked as they battled from one side of the cabin to the other. But Reedrek was stronger, older. And Alger had always been a gentle vampire, if that was possible.

As I watched, Alger gave a terrific last ditch heave, breaking Reedrek's grip and shoving him backward. "I'll see you in hell," he said as he raced right through me and the door. Reedrek flew after him, his feet barely touching the floor. I followed them upward and when I cleared the companionway hatch I watched in horror as Reedrek pulled out the very stake I held and killed Alger before he could find water and escape. I had already known he couldn't get away, and now I knew what he'd avoided in forcing Reedrek to kill him.

I did not wish to stay to see him burn.

An insistent tapping jarred my senses and when I opened my eyes, I was staring at the moon in the mirror pond. The shells had returned to their box. I opened my hand and, aside from a dusting of ash, the stake had disappeared. I was left with the undeniable truth.

Alger was dead and Reedrek had apparently discovered my whereabouts. How many more of his cronies were on their way?

I looked toward the glass office door and saw Reyha

standing just inside. She was watching me expectantly. I needed to find out how my sire had gotten on one of my boats. I also had to send the bad news about Alger to his people, not family per se, but his retainers and blood kin. No doubt they'd already felt a change of fortunes in the air. And I had to alert those closest to Amsterdam to mount a rescue of Lyone and his remaining offspring. I rose from the bench, feeling older than my five hundred years. After placing Lalee's gift box and shells back in their cubby, I settled in front of my computers—my one concession to modern times.

Most humans are unaware that amidst the Anne Rice devotees and the vampire wannabes, actual vampires use the Net.

Stealthy yet familiar footsteps on the carpet announced Reyha's approach. Leaning over the back of my chair, she snaked her arms around my neck and pressed her face into my hair. She snuffled once, as if she could smell the otherworldly energy I'd collected as I'd spun through time.

I ignored her and she seemed content to be close to me.

First I had to alert the clan. I wrote directly to Alger himself. Someone in his employ would be monitoring his mail.

> *Alger,*
> *Shipment is lost. Best look to your safety. Please contact me as soon as possible.*
> *Cuy*

Only my very old acquaintances ever used my boyhood nickname. Alger had been one of the few vampires I considered a friend.

Next I entered the chat room for bloodygentry.com.

Do you have any contact with A.R.? I am searching for kindred.

I drew an immediate response. *A is missing?*

He is not here. Need information.

Will get back to you.

Also, must send out abductors. Have closest to Amsterdam contact me immediately.

Will ASAP.

I still had allies and contacts in Europe, after all. And a pact to deny Reedrek and his kind any kind of support.

I picked up the telephone and dialed the shipping office I owned along the Irish coast. It would already be morning there.

The shipping manager, Regan Andrews, had no helpful information. According to him they'd loaded the cargo under the dark of the moon as usual. The warehouse and shipyard were under lockdown and surveillance until the *Alabaster* sailed.

"Any employees fired, or anyone who failed to come to work?" I asked.

"No. But there was—"

"What?"

"Well, I don't see how it's related, but one of our men, James Dugan, was killed in an accident the day after the ship sailed. He was riding his motorbike to work and got run down by an automobile."

"Did you see his body?"

"Well, no. But I was told he was pretty wrecked."

"Who told you that? Who saw him?"

"The constable, sir. They had to determine he was dead so he could be cremated."

Cremated.

Rather than telling him my suspicions—that the worker had been compromised and killed—I told him to shut down the shipping operation. Until I found out just how much Reedrek knew, I couldn't risk another vampire shipment. "Pay your workers for the month and send them home. Lock down the warehouse and keep both eyes open. Call me with word on anything unusual."

"Yes, sir. You can count on me, sir."

Reyha sighed and tightened her grip on my neck as I ended the phone connection. I patted her forearm. "I have to go pick up Jack, sweet."

She snuggled closer, if that was possible, and sighed, "Stay . . ."

I levered her arms away and stood. As graceful as a member of the Bolshoi, she twirled and slipped an arm around me, snuggling against my side. Rather than hurt her feelings, I pulled her close and moved up the stairs. When I reached the door to the garage, I plucked the keys from the counter and called to Deylaud.

"No one is to be invited in while I'm gone," I said. Not until I ascertained whether Reedrek was in Savannah. The thought gave me a twist of anger and, truth be told, left me uneasy. It would be painfully ironic if my wishful weakness of wanting to die had drawn one of the few beings who would happily accommodate me.

"No one comes in." Deylaud nodded, then raised a hand beckoning to his sister. "Come, let him be," he said.

After a slight hesitation, Reyha gave me an obligatory good-bye kiss on the cheek, then flounced away in disappointment. By the time she reached her brother she was smiling again. "Will you play with me instead of reading those horrid books?"

He slipped an arm around her shoulders. "All right."

Deylaud held his place, staring at me, waiting for permission, I suppose.

I nodded and left them to their games.

Jack

I watched William get in my 'Vette with Richey, sorry to see him go. It's hard to spook a vampire. I mean, I'm usually the spook*er*, not the spook*ee*, if you catch my drift. But I had to admit I was spooked right then.

I headed for the secret supply area in the cellar of William's warehouse. That's where we kept the emergency items our human helpers were better off not seeing—a selection of coffins, samples of earth from foreign lands, a refrigerator stocked with frozen human blood, and even hard-to-find ingredients for Melaphia's charms and potions. I had to laugh when I stepped around a couple of "shake-'n'-bakes"—special bags designed to help forest firefighters avoid death from wildfires sweeping over them. William had wanted me to test one out to see if covering myself with it could keep me from catching fire in the daylight. I'd told him I'd get back to him on that.

I stuffed a duffel full of explosives along with wiring and an electronic detonation device and headed topside. I seldom got to use the demolition skills I'd honed many years ago as a moonshiner. (Blowing up stills ahead of revenuer raids was part of the job description.) Of course the art of making things go boom had changed through the years, but I managed to keep my skills current. You never knew when you might have to blow something up real good.

Tarney was preparing to tow the *Alabaster* out toward Lazarus Point using a small fishing boat. The human was good company but not much use if whatever had broken the lock on that hold came back. We'd searched the boat thoroughly, and whoever or whatever had done it was long gone.

So why were the hairs on the back of my neck standing up? And what was that smell? I was convinced it was more than the human carcass. More *feeling* than smell, it was impossible to describe. None of my five senses, as sharp as they were, could tell me what was crawling over me. It was suffocating, cloying, maddening, and . . . familiar. Not familiar as in something in your memory, but familiar as in something in your bones, something that's part of you. That was what gave me the creeps.

As Tarney was busy steering us downriver, I went back to inspect the remains of that staked vamp. It's not often I'm reminded that even though I'm technically immortal, I can still die. And unlike mortals, when I die, it's a done deal. It's "go straight to hell" for Jackie-boy. No passing Go. No collecting two hundred dollars.

I poked around in the ashes of my distant blood kin, searching for my usual dead-people connection. Nothing. Zip. Nada. Wherever he'd gone was dark and deep. Deeper than I could go . . . until my time came.

I shivered, wiped my hand on my pants, and went to the compartment where the coffin was. After filling it with explosives, finishing the wiring, and setting the detonation device, I took the empty duffel to the bridge to collect the material that William wanted. Tarney had collected the charts, ship's log, and some other paperwork that he said William might need. I stuffed all of the papers and the GPS gizmo and the notebook computer into the duffel bag. My work done, I went belowdeck again to the guest quarters, as William called it, straight to the small bar across from the wired coffin. Did William know more than he was telling about what went on here? I tore into one of the remaining blood bags with my teeth and poured it into a tumbler, followed by a healthy splash of Dewar's.

He was certainly taken off guard, that was clear. Whenever William was mad, I mean *really* pissed off, he actually levitated off the ground without ever realizing he was doing it. He did it ever so slightly when he first got to the boat. The humans didn't notice, but I did. He was barely able to keep his temper under control. Something in William vibrated when he was that mad, and I could usually feel it from ten paces.

I downed the thick red cocktail and wiped my mouth on the back of my hand. William also wanted the surveillance tape from the hidden camera he kept in here. I had to shift the dead body to reach the compartment door for the tape. I hated the smell of dead food. As a newly minted vampire during the War of Northern Aggression, I sometimes had to follow William, walking right on top of the corpses of soldiers killed in earlier battles. It had always sickened me.

I don't know what William expected to get from the tape since it erased itself every day. By the smell of that carcass, whatever happened had been at least a few days ago. William's high-tech computer setup had the capability to monitor this cabin via satellite, but had he done it if he wasn't expecting any trouble? I knew it was possible to capture video digitally on a computer. Had

William done that? Or was the evidence of what had happened here gone for good?

Evidence. Why hadn't I thought about that before? I grabbed the body jammed into the cabinet and hauled it out onto the floor in the little space in front of the empty coffin. Rigor mortis had come and gone and the body was fairly easy to handle, if nasty. I checked the dead crewman's neck. Yep. There they were—two bite marks, deep and savage, widely spaced. Suddenly that faintly familiar reek I'd experienced on deck became stronger. It thrummed through me, nauseating me.

It smelled like . . . hell.

I stuffed the three remaining bags of blood (no sense wasting it) in my jacket pockets, threw the tape in the duffel with the other stuff, and left. The *Alabaster* was a beautiful boat, but I would be glad to see it blown to smithereens if whatever presence lingered here would sink into the sea forever along with it.

An hour later the sight of the *Alabaster* blowing into a zillion pieces in the distance didn't give me the clean-slate feeling I'd hoped for. It looked cool, though. And the sound was thrilling even though it hurt my oversensitive ears. By the time the Coast Guard got wind of it, any debris would be scattered by the Gulf Stream from here to Nags Head.

Another job well done.

Some of the nagging foulness subsided but was replaced by a hunch that I was being watched. I looked over my shoulder for the hundredth time as I treaded water near the dock at Lazarus Point. The Point was deserted and William hadn't arrived yet. After securing the duffel full of papers and the computer on the raised walkway, I'd jumped in to try to lose the stink of carrion as well as the mysterious funk that enveloped me on the ship.

I wasn't prone to paranoia. (That's one good thing about being a vampire; you're sitting pretty much fat and sassy at the top of the food chain.) But even though the *putt-putt* of Tarney's outboard had long since died off into the distance, I had the definite sensation that I was not alone. Maybe the explosion had attracted the attention of the Coast Guard sooner than I'd expected and there was a boat full of New Age revenuers lurking somewhere nearby.

I had to laugh when I thought about the possibility of Tarney's little Noah's Ark being stopped by the authorities. When I insisted we take the remaining live animals with us, even the rats, the look on his face was priceless. I'd made one more trip down to the customized cargo hold and brought the animals out in a makeshift sack I'd fashioned out of the cabin curtains. When I kill an animal for food, I make it quick and painless for the critter du jour. Of course, with us vampires, the real craving is always for blood from live humans. But if you're not a monster, you learn to keep your baser instincts under control and live on animal blood. Every now and then I get a craving for live flesh, but mostly I survive on blood from butcher shops. There's enough voodoo activity in Savannah that one blood ritual or another is going on in some cemetery almost any night of the week. When someone comes into your butcher shop wanting to buy a quart of pig's blood, you don't ask questions. The customer is always right. Especially a customer who could turn you into a zombie.

So, anyway, I couldn't stand to think of the fuzzy things blown to bits or drowning. Not even the rats. Since there was really nowhere to put them out at the Point, I insisted Tarney take them to shore elsewhere. If the Coast Guard did catch him, what could he say? "It's such a pretty night, I thought I'd take my rabbits, 'coons, and rats for a little boat ride. Doesn't everybody?"

But I didn't think that would happen. Tarney was making for the boatyard like his hair was on fire. And only silence remained. If it had been summer, the marsh all around me would be noisy with the sounds of wildlife. There would be insects buzzing and gators bellowing and everything in between chirping, croaking, or singing. But now the reptiles and amphibians were hibernating in the mud and muck underneath me, and everything else had gone wherever wild things go when the autumn cold creeps in.

I bobbed in the water waiting for William and looked over my shoulder again. Maybe the sensation of not being alone was caused by the unquiet souls that inhabited this place. The quarantine station for the slave trade had been right here at Lazarus Point. I tried not to think about the hundreds, thousands, who'd crossed the Atlantic but never made it into Savannah. I could feel many of them that night, wandering in search of a homeland they would never again see.

I concentrated instead on what we'd found out. To a coldblooded creature, the chill water felt particularly bracing, but the waving of the marsh grasses in the night breeze soothed me.

It helped me think.

As I was saying before, I almost never kill humans. Unless they really need killing, that is. The regulars keep me informed of any particularly bad characters who come into town. If an all-too-human serial murderer or rapist winds up dead I reckon that's one less criminal the police have to deal with. Savannah is usually a peaceful little town. As a taxpaying citizen, I consider it my civic duty to aid the police in keeping it that way. But if you're a vampire you have to be discreet. If too many bodies with two neat puncture wounds rolled in with the high tide on the beach at Tybee or floated up out of the river, it could spell trouble. That's why William and I do some policing of our own.

William and I are the only two permanent vampire residents of this river town. We've worked too long and too hard to keep our noses clean (Well, I've worked hard. Nothing seems to stick to William. He's the boss, after all) to let a trespasser threaten our peaceful dealings with the community. So when the occasional blood drinker passes through town to check out the pickings, we make sure he knows to mind his manners. Leaving a drained body where it can be found by the authorities will get any vamp playing fast and loose a quick escort out of town, usually being dragged by a chain behind my Corvette.

But this situation was different. The vampire who had broken into that cargo hold was a lot stronger than I was. Possibly even stronger than William. It had killed the vampire on board and undoubtedly the crew as well, throwing three overboard and leaving the other body behind. Was that body and its teeth marks meant as a calling card of some kind? Why were there two vampires aboard, and what was their beef with each other? Why had the strong one sneaked his way aboard rather than come out in the open? And where had he gone?

Questions and more questions. Would William have the answers? And if so, would he share them with me? Fat chance. They say knowledge is power, and William won't give me any more information about our way of life than I need to survive. He keeps me under his thumb by using my ignorance about exactly what I am and what I can do. The idea that he might be afraid I'd challenge him makes me feel a little better, but not for long. You'd think that after three human lifespans of loyal service, I'd have earned his trust. You'd be wrong.

I heard the purr of William's Jag in the distance, hauled myself from the water, and fetched the duffel. I figured I must look like the Creature from the Black Lagoon.

"You can't possibly be thinking of getting into this automobile dripping with mud," William stated. The top was down, as usual, despite the chill.

I slung the bag into the back and hopped into the passenger seat.

"I'll get one of the boys to detail it tomorrow." William glared at me briefly and then gunned the engine. With one undecipherable glance back toward the *Alabaster*'s watery grave, he steered the Jag out of the parking lot and back toward Savannah. "So, have you figured anything out yet?" I asked him.

"I've made some inquiries. There was an accident with one of the Irish dockworkers before the *Alabaster* sailed, but it seems unrelated to what happened on board. I'm waiting for more information."

I settled back in the soft leather bucket seat, waiting to see if William would ask me if I had a theory as to what happened or at least if I'd found any more evidence on the boat. He didn't. After a few minutes, I said, "I examined the body stuffed into that cabinet in the hold. Found bite marks, deep and wide. It was a vamp, all right. We're looking for a big boy."

"I thought as much from the looks of that broken hatch."

More silence. Hell, you'd think he'd be ranting and

raving. He'd just lost a seven-figure yacht and a powerful rogue vamp was stalking his territory. And yet I felt nothing from him, not even the rage I'd sensed at the docks. He was deliberately blocking me out of his mind, cutting off the communication of the blood, as he called it. We couldn't read each other's minds exactly, but we were definitely on the same wavelength. It had something to do with him being my sire. But if he didn't want me to follow the direction of his thoughts and read his emotions, I couldn't.

Then again, there was always the direct approach. "So, boss, what are you not telling me?"

"Nothing you need to know at this point."

"Dammit, William, there's a killer of vampires on the loose, and in case you haven't noticed, *we're vampires*!"

"I'll find whoever did this and I'll deal with them. End of story."

"There has to be more to it than that. What about—"

He turned in the seat so I could see his fangs. "It's been a long night. I've suffered losses you can't imagine. We'll talk about this when I have more information. Not before."

I settled back in the seat. There was no use in provoking William too far. We rode the rest of the way to my sleeping place in silence except for my call to Richey to have my 'Vette dropped off at the garage. When we reached Bonaventure and William stopped the Jag, I got out and started into the cemetery on my shortcut home.

"Jack," William said. When I turned, he was staring straight ahead, not looking at me. "Watch your back." With that, he roared off, scattering gravel and bits of tabby in his wake. "Gee, thanks, Dad," I muttered under my breath as I walked into the cemetery on my way home. Bonaventure was right next to the storage rental facility I owned as a side business, one of the units being my daytime resting place.

Bonaventure never failed to take my breath away with its beauty. Its statuary angels stood solemn guard over their dead masters, silent sentinels looking toward the sea. Live oaks, their beards of Spanish moss waving gently in the breeze, pushed up their knotted roots among the tombs.

Remember that movie where the kid said he saw dead people? Well, I hear dead people. And they hear me. After all, I'm one of them. I can feel them stirring underneath my feet sometimes, the unquiet ones. Not just here and in the other cemeteries, but everywhere. If you're walking in Savannah, you're walking on dead people—the dead from two wars who were often buried where they fell, yellow fever victims whose remains were burned and whose ashes were scattered like the petals of dandelions on the wind, pirates who lived and died by the dagger, brigands and murderers of all kinds, as well as the slaves and other innocents who were victims of cruel times when life was cheap. I felt them all when I let myself, heard them sometimes in words, sometimes just in emotions.

Tonight they warned me I wasn't alone. That what I'd felt onboard the *Alabaster,* at Lazarus Point, and now here at Bonaventure wasn't my imagination. I hurried along, ignoring their pleas for me to sit and talk a spell, for once comforted by the slight lightening of the eastern sky. I'd make it to my resting place before the sun's rays could burn my flesh. And I'd put money on the bet that the rogue vamp would find a resting place as well. Bonaventure was full of tombs covered by concrete slabs a powerful vampire would have no trouble lifting. Yep, we'd all sleep the day away, soundly.

It was tomorrow night I had to worry about.

October 2005

Letter from Olivia, a Female Vampire

My human name was Olivia Margaret Spenser, and yes, I was/am distantly related to the former Diana Spencer, the ill-fated Princess of Wales. You might wonder that I make the distinction of being female right "up front" as the modern Americans say. Because it's necessary. At one time, back when I was a girl, *we* were called the moderns. The twenties being our wild response to the Great War and death by influenza on the Continent.

We were determined to live.

We had such fun, reading about American gangsters, hiking our skirts over our knees, chopping our hair into caps of boyish rebellion. Drinking and screwing as we saw fit. But all of that was before I met Alger.

Oh, he was a posh cit if there ever was one. And gay as a picnic basket by his own account. I loved him at first sight. He was my Oscar Wilde and I his George Sand. Unwilling to let him ignore me, I dressed like a boy and followed him whenever we crossed paths, egging him on to bed me at least once. It was during that bloody, long-awaited bedding that I finally found out what else he was besides rich and bored, and beautiful.

A bloody vampire.

I wanted to be just like him—or, more exactly, to be a female version of him. A blood-drinking, headboard-banging, endless party girl. I promised I would dress in men's clothes and allow him any sort of sex he craved. But sweet Alger didn't wish it. He said that if he made me a blood drinker that he wouldn't allow me into his bed ever again.

Then he told me two things. One, that we females very often didn't survive the process. And, two, that if we did survive we became more than hunters living off human blood. He then patiently explained the meaning of *succubus*. When a female is made into a vampire she loses the ability to give birth. What she gains is the ability to take strength—life force, you might say—by having sex with male blood drinkers. They might feed from us and get their pleasure, but we keep part of them and can call on them in need.

Being such a shy and retiring girl with an absence of anything like the natural feminine urge to please the males around me, I doubled my wheedling and whining until Alger relented. I think he made me to shut me up.

I kept my word. Since my making, Alger has had me in any and all the ways he could dream up—even loaning me to his friends on occasion. Making me obey and yet giving me his power. And I loved every minute of it. But I also planned for my far-spanning future by organizing my "sisters in blood." I took it upon myself to track down each and every female vampire on the planet—their lineage and connections. Their homes and their lovers.

After all, us girls must stick together.

Three

William

I awoke with the familiar warm weight of Reyha along my side. The day had not fully waned, so she remained in her dog form, her head resting on my chest, her breath warm on my neck. She was snoring slightly. I opened my eyes and waited for the rest of my body to animate. There was no rush. Right then the sun would be sinking, gold through the purple sky, setting the clouds and Spanish moss aflame with a fiery farewell to the day.

I don't remember my final sunset. Had I known it was to be my last I might've paid more attention. But there had been others before I'd lost the daylight, and like a painter without hands I'd composed the memories of all my sunsets into a fine, flaming image that pleased me. I have found that one should pursue the many small pleasures in each day; otherwise the relentless unpleasantness of long life can be overwhelming.

I heard movement outside my coffin. Footsteps, human and canine, and a low voice speaking. That would be

Melaphia, greeting Deylaud, both of them waiting for me to rise.

Reyha squirmed, coming awake. I shoved open the lid of my coffin and stretched my arms above my head.

"Good evening, Captain," Melaphia said. Although I no longer went to sea with my ships, Melaphia called me "Captain" as her foremother Lalee had in our years together.

Beautiful Melaphia, straight-backed and proud, stood with her hands clasped in front of her, looking very much like her ancestor, the dusky beauty of their bloodline straight and true. Next to Melaphia, her eight-year-old daughter, Renee, another budding charmer with a queenly manner, though still a rascal by all accounts, stroked the arched neck of Deylaud in his form of an Egyptian sight hound. A hound who had been bred to watch over the tombs of the pharaohs. Spotting him, Reyha leaped over me to playfully greet her brother.

"Take them outside before it grows darker," Melaphia said to her daughter.

With an impish smile in my direction, Renee whirled and, with the two dogs nearly as tall as she, raced down the underground hallway. It was their favorite game, hide and seek, although the dogs invariably won. That is, until full dark when they transformed back into human form. Then all bets were off.

"The sky ended gray and green tonight," Melaphia said as she dusted a few stray dog hairs off my jacket. "Trouble coming."

"Yes, trouble . . ." *Reedrek*.

"I'll cast a warning. No one with bad intentions will dare step foot on the property."

I had learned long ago that Lalee's voodoo was a strong ally—that, and her family's unwavering loyalty.

"Thank you." I owed Melaphia and her ancestors more than I could repay. Two hundred years ago, when Lalee had refused my offer of immortality, I'd had no idea how fortunate that refusal would be for me. But Lalee had known her own mind and her own destiny.

"Make it a strong one," I said, not wishing to go into too much detail. Melaphia stopped fussing with my clothes and looked up at me. "Is he that powerful?" she asked.

No use hiding the unpleasant truth. "Yes, I'm afraid so. He's my sire."

"Has he come to kill you?"

"No, he's come to destroy me—a subtle difference."

She dropped her gaze to my cuff, which she'd been busy straightening. "I'll need to call upon the bones and blood of Maman Lalee."

This was the first time in Melaphia's lifetime we'd discussed using Lalee's personal powers, but I didn't hesitate. Melaphia knew best about these things. "Yes, of course. Go; fetch your key."

The vault within a vault was set into the wall behind the smooth stone near the mantel. The two matching keys that unlocked the secret locks were made of the purest gold. In the mortal world a lock requiring golden keys would seem to hold treasure beyond description, much like a pharaoh's tomb. But my most valuable possession was not golden or jeweled.

It was blood.

After a chant of reverence, Melaphia brushed away the cobwebs and removed the ancient vial with the care of one who'd been entrusted with the Holy Grail. Lalee's gift to me and her descendants looked innocuous enough: a vial filled with brown liquid. It was an old piece, surely, but nothing more. Yet in the right hands this living legacy could harness the power of the voodoo *loas* into a formidable weapon.

"I believe we'll need all the help we can get," I said.

Melaphia nodded. "I will see to it."

I placed my cool hand over her warm one, feeling a strum of power from the vial. "I know you will."

Jack showed up within the hour. I'd just come upstairs from the office with my now human companions when he walked in bold as you please and demanded the keys to my Jag. Deylaud glanced at me for permission before handing them over.

"Huey's outside. He'll take it to the shop and give it the once-over."

"Make it a twice-over," I said. "The leather smells like a swamp." I nodded to Deylaud and he tossed the keys to Jack. "Tell him to go straight there and back. No joyriding. And make sure they don't use any imitation scent. You know how I hate that."

Jack gave me a mock salute. "Back in a sec."

Reyha was waiting just inside the door when Jack returned. As he stepped over the threshold, she flung herself into his arms like an amorous linebacker.

"Ooof!" he huffed, teasing her. Then he swept her up, holding her against his chest. "I think you're getting fat," he added as he carried her into the study ahead of me. It always amazed me to watch the two of them together. Around me, Reyha was graceful and timid . . . submissive, but let Jack show his face and she became a hoyden who demanded to play. I hoped Jack's unruly nature wasn't catching on, for even Deylaud always looked happy to see him.

Jack dumped Reyha unceremoniously on the leather

couch, shoving her over to sit next to her. She immediately twisted around to rest half in his lap.

"I should be careful if I were you," I said. "After all, the two of you are from different species. People will begin to talk."

They looked at me as though I'd spoken in a foreign tongue. I guess it had been awhile since I'd tried to make light of anything. Of course Jack took me seriously.

Pushing Reyha upright with one hand, he said, "I'd like to meet the human who had nerve enough to look in any of your grand windows. Or are your neighbors investing in night-vision goggles?"

I shook my head. No use trying to explain. That I felt the need to joke at a time like this was unusual to say the least. And for the first time in several centuries, I was experiencing fear. Reedrek had finally come and I needed to face him alone.

Reyha, with a subdued look of guilt, left Jack and moved across the room to me. I slipped an arm around her and whispered in her ear, "It's all right, sweeting." With my permission to play with Jack granted, she held on to me harder for a moment, then danced away. Having soothed her feelings, I stepped over to the sideboard and poured a brandy. Through the years I'd cultivated a taste for brandy. In many respects it was as rich and dark as blood. A complicated, ancient taste that could placate my ever-present hunger. For Jack, I opened the wine refrigerator and withdrew an IV bag of human blood. Jack needed to feed, for both our sakes.

"Would you like a glass?"

Jack had been busy pinning Reyha down for a good tickle. He glanced up and shoved mussed hair out of his eyes. Instead of answering, he kissed both of Reyha's

smooth cheeks. He was like some Italian playboy, and
he caused a gale of pleased giggles from Reyha. Then he
pushed up from the couch.

"Yep, a glass. And a splash of Dewar's to boot."

Of course I already knew what he liked to drink. I
knew everything about him, but I didn't want him
aware of that. "I remember now," I said, handing him
the bottle before pouring the blood into hundred-year-
old crystal. "It makes such a pretty combination, alco-
hol and blood."

"Hmmmm," Jack acknowledged in a noncommital
sort of way. I could practically watch his mind calculating, waiting for the right moment to announce the real
reason he'd shown up so early after sunset, before I had
even called him.

"I need to know what you're planning," he said as he
accepted the drink. "And if you aren't gonna let me in
on it, I at least have to know what you want me to do."

Plans. That was the crux of it. Right then my only
plan was to wait. Reedrek would come in his own time.
If I'd left Savannah, it only would have extended the sus-
pense. I couldn't avoid him forever.

"We wait."

"Wait? Sit back and let some monster do who-knows-
what in *our* town?" Jack held the fragile crystal in his
hand but didn't take a drink. He swallowed back his
anger instead. "I swear, I think I felt him in Bonaventure." He looked uncomfortable, like a sinner at confession. "The sleeping ones were singing, saying he'd walked
on their graves."

I used my power to project a calm facade—to hide my
alarm. Yes, Reedrek would find Jack and follow him to
me. But Jack had to be left out of it as much as possible.
For that reason, I'd purposely kept him ignorant. He

had no clue what he was up against and no training to counter what Reedrek could do.

"I want you well out of it," I told him firmly.

He almost choked on his disgust. "You won't even tell me what you know? You're so almighty strong you don't need my pitiful help? Well, I sure as hell have a stake in this, too—no pun intended. And if you expect me to stay out of it, you're gonna have to lock me in a box somewhere deep and quiet cause I'm not leavin' here until you fill me in." With a smirk of bravado, Jack added, "Here's blood in your eye," then knocked back the cocktail in his grip before handing the empty glass back to me. "Maybe if we wait long enough, he'll come knocking on your door to say hello."

He was closer to the truth than he knew, and I was just about to award him a good dose of my temper when someone actually did knock on the door.

Jack laughed out loud as Deylaud moved to the solid river oak panel and stared at it, evaluating who was on the other side. Reyha stood a few paces behind him.

"I don't know this scent," Deylaud said. Both he and Reyha looked to me for orders.

The being was unfamiliar. Not Reedrek, not a human.

I motioned my faithful guardians to the side as I grasped the doorknob. Jack took up a position on my right, determined to face whatever fate waited on the landing.

I swung the door open.

An extraordinarily beautiful woman with cropped silver-white hair and wide gray eyes stood facing me. Dressed in supple black leather pants and wearing a matching designer jacket, she looked like a female pop diva without her entourage. Only a large leather duffel bag sat at her feet for company.

The most amazing thing, however, was that she wasn't just a beautiful tourist lost in the historic district.

She was a vampire.

Jack let out a low whistle. Before I could speak, the woman dropped to one knee and bowed her head.

"I can't believe I'm standing before you," she said, her voice low and intense. She looked up at me with those mesmerizing eyes. "William Cuyler, the legend." Her voice contained such awe that it held me silent for a second. A second is a long time to be speechless in my world.

"Get up," I ordered. "And here you should add Thorne to my name."

She straightened then and waited for my invitation inside. She still seemed a little starstruck. "Yes," she managed, "I'm sorry. William Thorne, not Cuy."

"You are Algernon's kin, then?" It had to be so since she knew the name of my human heart. But how in hades had she managed to get to my door so quickly?

"Yes, I'm Olivia. Alger is my sire."

"Aren't you gonna ask her in?" Jack prodded with the same besotted tone he'd used when he first set eyes on that beast of a car he loved.

Slightly bewitched myself, I'd almost forgotten he was there. But he made a point. I rarely conducted business out in the open for the world to see. And Miss Olivia would not cross the threshold unless she was invited.

I found my manners. "Come in, please."

Jack

Great googly-moogly, a female vampire. I felt my face go slack. There was no doubt about it. Vampires can always recognize one another. Somehow we can just *sense* another blood drinker. I had never, ever sensed a female vampire before now. William had always told me the females of our species of undead were rare, but he never said why. And here one was, a real, live—sort of— lumpy-in-all-the-right-places female bloodsucker.

As she stepped through the door, the Rin Tin Twins, as I called them, were on the alert, their noses up in the air to pick up any scent of trouble, ready to react to any threatening motion. Reyha edged closer to the woman, trying to catch a better scent. She bared her perfect white teeth, and William gave his favorite pet a warning look.

Big as life, Olivia reached out and gently cupped Reyha under her chin. "Aren't you a beauty, then," she said. The sound of her voice made parts of me want to stand up and howl, if you know what I mean. Then William ruined it all.

"Jack, see to the lady's bag."

I couldn't help but scowl at him. Probably the only female vamp in this hemisphere shows up on his doorstep and without saying a word, he's already got her on her knees. A blond bombshell in black leather—just exactly my type—lookin' at William like he was Frank Sinatra, Prince William, and all four Beatles rolled into one. And what does he do? He treats me like a servant. Whatever kind of "legend" William turned out to be, how could his lackey—meaning me—compete with that?

But I could try. "Deylaud? How 'bout you get the lady's bag? I'll pour Miss Olivia a drink." I crossed my arms, daring William to order me away.

Instead he opened the library door and gestured to the beautiful stranger. "Miss Olivia, won't you please make yourself at home?"

She proceeded into the room, and William shut the door behind her like she was a precious jewel that needed watching, but not by me. The front door stood open, and since Deylaud wouldn't cross the threshold without permission, William nodded in his direction. "Get the bag." Then he came close to me. "I have to tell this young lady that her beloved sire is dead." He kept his voice low. "She's going to be very upset . . ."

"So you want me to clear out."

"Would you be so kind? I know you have other things to do." It was true I didn't spend much of my time hanging around William's mausoleum of a house. I took pride in having my own life and my own friends. But in this instance he was humoring me. That was suspicious right off the bat.

"You can leave me outside with the dogs for now, but I'm not going anywhere. I'll wait until you're through talking to her. Then I'd like some answers, like what does this chick Olivia know about you that I don't, Mr. Legend."

William gave me one of his looks. The one intended to scare me, all fangy and intense. I stood my ground.

"We'll see" was all he said before he turned his back on me to open the parlor door. "Oh, and Jack?" he said, pausing. "Don't forget that drink."

I went to the wet bar in the den, Reyha at my heels, Deylaud pacing behind me with the duffel. Good thing the highball glass I picked up was made of heavy lead crystal. I was so hot that if it wasn't, I figure it would have shattered in my hand.

"Do you like her? I don't like her," Reyha declared.

"Too soon to tell, pet." I filled the glass with blood. Then, for the hell of it, I splashed some liquor into the mix and added some ice. I sure as hell liked the *look* of her. I wondered how it would feel to have those long, cool legs wrapped around me.

Deylaud appeared at my other elbow. "I think it's about time we had some excitement around here. By the way, she's from the island. Won't like the ice."

I glanced at him. The island? He must mean England. "Are you a guardian or a bartender?" I frowned at the drink and realized he was probably right about the ice. After all, he spent most of his time with his nose in a book. What the hell. I downed the drink myself in a couple of gulps and started fresh with a new glass.

"She smells funny," Reyha said.

"It's the leather," said Deylaud. "It's Italian. I don't know why that makes a difference, but—"

I walked down the foyer to the library door and knocked. William opened the door, thanked me (ever the gentleman, that one), took the drink, and closed the door, but not before I got a glimpse of Olivia sitting in a high-backed wing chair in front of the fireplace. She looked devastated. What if something happened to my sire—to William? I didn't want to think about it. I had my problems with the guy, but damn. Could I survive without him if it ever came to that? I honestly didn't know. Did I want to be the only vamp in town? Not really.

I went back to the den and poured another drink, which I sipped while pacing back and forth in front of the bay windows. Autumn leaves were drifting down into the park in the square. The streetlights had come on and the fountain gracing the center of the green looked like a nightwalker's postcard. *Alger, old boy, wish you were here.*

The twins were giving me some space, but they were still on alert. I could feel their gaze on my back as I looked out the windows, as if they expected me to turn around and throw them a stick to fetch or something. What was William telling her in there? I was pretty certain he'd already told her that her sire was dead. What else was there to say?

I turned around and my gaze fell on the duffel bag on the sofa. With a glance toward the still-closed library door, I set the half-empty glass on the bar and walked to the bag. What if this woman wasn't who she said she was? Maybe she'd been in Savannah all along. She might even be the one who'd been watching me. "Deylaud, stand over there near the wall, look down the foyer, and cough or something when the library door opens."

He moved in that direction. "What are you going to do?"

"What does it look like?" I unfastened the flap on the duffel.

Reyha moved back to my side and put her slender hand to her mouth. "Ooh, naughty."

Right on top was a big zip baggie of ordinary-looking dirt. That figured. All those imported vamps had it. The soil of their native land. But Olivia didn't bring her own coffin, and I happened to know that William didn't keep a spare. So where would she sleep? I felt my jaw tighten just thinking about the possibility of her bunking with William. Two in a coffin was mighty cozy.

Deylaud looked over his shoulder from his watching post. "The obligatory soil, I see. What else?" He didn't comment on the rightness or wrongness of what I was doing. It wasn't his place. But his curiosity came just as naturally as his sense of servitude.

The bag had obviously been packed in a hurry. The clothing was balled up and stuffed in willy-nilly along with some scents and powders. "Here's something," I said. Deylaud slowly crept toward me and Reyha, caught between interest and his job of watching the foyer. "It's a book. An old one." So fragile I was almost afraid to open it, but I had to see what was there. The pages had oxidized to a dark brown, but the names were in bold indigo ink. Just names. Many, many names, with indentations and lines drawn from some to others, like somebody was trying to show some kind of hierarchy or relationship. Something about it gave me a sizzle of the creeps. There was a lot of that creeps stuff going around.

I was putting the book back when I realized that Reyha's curiosity had gotten the best of her and she'd reached into the bag. I grabbed her wrist just as she brought out a wisp of red silk.

"This is all that goes between the legs?" Reyha gasped.

Deylaud was at my other elbow, having forgotten his lookout duties. "It's a thong. I saw one on television."

"You've been watching that naughty channel again."

I grabbed the thing out of her hand. "You guys calm down."

"Aren't you going to sniff it?" Reyha asked innocently. "You need to memorize her scent in case you ever have to track her."

"No, I'm not going to sniff it!" Whoever thought of creating half-dog/half-humans ought to have had his spell-casting head examined.

"I'll sniff it," Deylaud offered.

"No, you won't. I—"

I looked up just in time to see Olivia and William standing in the opening to the foyer. Olivia's face, dewey with tears, started to pucker a little around the cheeks and finally broke out into a grin, complete with the cutest little dimples I ever saw.

William, on the other hand, looked like he wanted to

sic the dogs on me. Once, during Prohibition, a stupid jerk had beaten one of William's workers to the point of death over a quart of moonshine. William, the twins, and I found the jerk drunk on the waterfront right before daybreak one morning. William and I left. The twins stayed. I heard that after sunrise they'd had to hose what was left of the guy off the docks. I stuffed the thong back into the duffel and closed the flap.

"Olivia, I apologize for Jack's behavior. He can sometimes be a bit . . . uncouth."

"He's only trying to protect you," she said simply. "I can tell."

I found myself wondering if I could fit the tip of my tongue into that dimple. A couple of seconds later, my tongue finally said, "I'm sorry. And I'm sorry for your loss."

"Thank you. And since you're wondering, I don't have anything to hide."

William seemed to relax. "Please sit down, Olivia."

Deylaud moved the duffel to the floor so Olivia could sit in the middle of the sofa. William sat on her right side, and I sat down on her left. The twins took the matching leather chairs. Olivia shook her head when William asked her if we could get her anything. "Now, tell us, how did you manage to get here so quickly?"

"When you called, Alger's human staff came to wake me. It was day there, of course. Some quick inquiries at the nearest airport led us to a pilot of a private jet who was willing to fly a body out of the country. So our workers brought my coffin, which was locked from the inside, and loaded it onto the jet—and off I went."

"Any trouble with the pilot?" William asked.

"We gave him enough money so that 'no questions asked' was strongly implied. I doubt if he ever really thought there was a body in the coffin. He probably just assumed it was filled with some kind of contraband." She waved her hand as if mortal questions weren't important. "Anyway, we refueled at Greenland, hung a left, and here I am. When we got to Savannah, the private airstrip was dark. I let myself out right after we landed. I was waiting when the pilot came into the cargo area." She smiled at me. "I was wearing that red thong and little else. After we *came* to a mutual . . . satisfaction, I fed off him to the point where he most likely doesn't remember the flight. Then I strongly suggested that he take the coffin back to an address in Greenland. He won't even know what he did or why he did it."

I had plenty of questions, but I could see William was getting mad, so I decided to keep quiet. One of the things William wouldn't tolerate from itinerant vamps was carelessness about the secret of our existence. And this vamp had not only broken a few thousand rules, she'd made a beeline for William. We'd see how she and her dimples would stand up to one of William's conniption fits. He got to his feet, his eyes glittering like hell's own demon. His voice, however, was calm, almost quiet.

"Any number of things could have gone wrong along the way. What were you thinking?"

His quiet tone made all the hair on the back of my head tingle. I'd seen William shout an order, but I'd never heard him sound so deadly. He was beginning to levitate. *Oh, lawsy.*

I gave Olivia a sympathetic look. Might as well take advantage of a chance to play good cop. After the duffel bag fiasco, I needed all the Brownie points I could get if I ever wanted to see that red thong again. Even the twins looked uncomfortable. If they'd had tails on the night shift, they'd have been firmly between their legs.

Olivia lost her smile but didn't fall apart under William's gaze. She calmly said, "My sire was missing. I decided the risk was worth it. I'm sorry you don't agree."

William, a good foot off the carpet now, stared at her, eyes flashing. "How do you know you weren't followed?"

"How could I possibly have been followed?"

"You—you . . . *child.* You haven't been undead long enough to understand the power of some of the old sires. Now you've endangered the whole operation and every lost soul in hiding."

Old sires? Lost souls in hiding? What the hell? I'd opened my mouth to ask what the Sam Hill he was talking about when my cell phone rang. Reyha yelped in surprise and William transferred his angry stare to me. I snatched the phone off its belt clip and flipped it open. It was Rennie.

"Jack, where's Huey with Mr. William's Jag? I was expecting him an hour ago."

"Shit," I muttered.

Now, this was a fine howdy-do. Me driving my 'Vette and William sitting in the other bucket seat with a blond vamp on his lap. And Huey missing. Just damn, damn, and damn.

"Maybe he stopped at a pub for a lager," Olivia offered.

"Not Huey," I said. "He didn't drink. He used to, but his wife had a voodoo queen put the juke on him. If he ever drinks again, he'll puke his guts out."

"That's what happens to a lot of humans when they drink too much," she said.

"He'll puke his guts out, *literally.* I believe her exact words were 'crows will feast on your entrails.' Problem is, his wife died about ten years ago. Now he's stuck with it."

Olivia thought about that for a moment. "Brilliant," she said.

William was showing signs of impatience. I couldn't imagine why—he was the one with the gorgeous vampire babe in his lap. "Are you sure this is the route he would take?"

"Yeah. I told him to go straight there and back. Wait a minute. What's that?"

Up ahead, a town house was under renovation. One of those Victorian affairs being restored to its former glory. A large, professionally painted sign in the yard read FUNDED BY THORNE HISTORIC TRUST. One of William's little projects. What I saw on the front steps sent a shiver up my spine. There was a handwritten sign that said WET PAINT tacked to the porch post. Underneath it was Huey, his chest bathed in blood.

I stopped the 'Vette in front of the house and we all vaulted out. "Oh, no." I muttered. "Poor Huey." He was sitting on the top step, leaning against the porch post, his throat ripped out, viscera gaping, startled eyes wide open as if looking into the great beyond, which I guess they were at this point. I reached out and gently closed them.

Olivia bent down and ran one of her elegant fingers through the blood that was still oozing from Huey's neck. Then she tasted it. "Not more than thirty minutes, I would say."

"Leave him be!" I ordered. It made me sick to think of anyone eating Huey. I couldn't even look at her.

I heard Olivia whisper to William, "Jack befriends many mortals, does he?"

"Yes," William said softly. "This is a calling card directed at me." He put his hands on my shoulders as I knelt in front of Huey. "We've got to move him, Jack. Now."

I nodded and walked back to the car to open the trunk. William was right behind me with Huey cradled in his arms. He laid the body carefully in the trunk, then looked at the keys in my hand.

"Can you drive?" he asked.

I must have looked stunned. I sure felt like it. I wiped a sleeve across my eyes. "Sure, I can drive in my sleep." Even through a nightmare.

"Good, I want you on your way."

"William, what about you? We have to find the creep who did this. He's got your Jag."

"Yes, I know. But right now you need to look after Huey."

Four

William

How typical of Jack to worry about my car. Blast the car. It was Jack I was worried about. I could feel Reedrek's unholy gaze on us. The sensation so strong it made my blood itch. The challenge so loud I wanted nothing more than to search the darkness until I found him. Or almost nothing more. I wanted Jack safe first.

Olivia was in danger as well, but at least she had some idea of what we were facing. If we split up, I was fairly sure that Reedrek would be more tempted to follow Olivia and me.

I rested a hand on Jack's shoulder, again using all my persuasiveness to get him to follow orders without an argument. "Take Huey home," I said. I glanced toward the nearest street sign. "We're only a few blocks from Eleanor's. Meet us there with some sort of transportation when you're finished. And, Jack, remember that old beaded charm I asked you to keep for me? The one from Lalee?" I didn't wait for him to answer. "Bring that with you when you come."

Jack's gaze shifted to Olivia. "You're taking her to Eleanor's?"

"Yes, now go. And don't forget the charm. Find it. Put it on."

It was a testament to his dazed condition that Jack simply nodded and got in his car. As the sound of the red beast faded in the distance, I signaled Olivia to silence; then I made a slow 360-degree turn, searching for my own personal boogieman. There was movement in the bushes near the half-built foundation of the house, but it turned out to be a sleepy guard dog, too tired even to bark. Reedrek was more elusive—well hidden or long gone. Since this was his game, he would make the rules. And he would take his own good time to reach the conclusion.

I slipped a protective arm around Olivia. If my blood held any charm it would hide her as well. "This way," I said, and pulled her along with me.

She seemed more entranced than worried. "This city is actually quite lovely," she said. "Nothing compared to London but still . . ."

"There is probably a rogue vampire watching us right now. Aren't you even a little worried for your survival?" I asked. It was painfully clear to me that Olivia was young and still in the discovery stage of her vampirism. Alger had obviously spoiled her. Fascinated by the exploration of her own feast of powers and her inability to die, she didn't know the meaning of *reckless*. After all, she was half Jack's age and Jack sometimes slipped back into his own version of adolescence. Yet another reason I felt compelled to protect him, even using his own ignorance when necessary. Back at the mansion, I'd ordered Olivia not to tell Jack anything she knew about me—or about being a vampire in general—especially how she'd been able to travel so far from the land of her making at such a young age. I had to remain the only rebel in the family for now.

Olivia gazed at me with admiration. "I'm not worried. I'm with you. You'll find a way for us to deal with Alger's killer."

"Oh, yes, right, William the *legend*. Is that correct?"

She seemed confused. "Well, yes. Alger told me about all the times you've defied the old ones. That you formed the Abductors. He told me that you're the strongest, smartest of the lot. That on several occasions you've stolen slave offspring from their sires and set them free." She stopped to face me. "He said you were special. He wouldn't have lied about that."

How was I to tell her that Alger loved me in his own way and that he saw me with flawed sight because of that love? That in stealing offspring, I was trying to set myself free. That my strength, rather than being based on the number of my offspring, was instead based on my fury. Explaining would serve no purpose other than to confuse her more than I already had.

"No, I suppose not. He was a terrible liar, anyway. I remember once, when we were visiting Paris, he vowed to bring me Napoléon's head as a souvenir. He brought me a head all right, but it looked nothing like Napoléon—it turned out that he'd snuck into Josephine's bedchamber intending to find the great man busy with her charms and had ended up stealing one of her lovers instead."

Olivia smiled into my eyes as though I'd given her a blood gift. In those few seconds I saw an offer of paradise, or the closest thing to it I'd seen in centuries.

"Keep walking," I managed, and moved away. The very last thing I wanted was someone else to care about.

She fell into step next to me. "Where are we going?"

"To a friend's. I need to think and you need to feed."

"I'm fine, thank you," she answered, but her voice had slowed and deepened. I could feel her bloodlust warming at the mere mention of feeding.

"I want you as strong as possible. I may require your help." What I needed most was for her to be able to defend herself so that I could concentrate on Reedrek. I myself would not be able to feed. Since he was my sire, any increase in my own strength would benefit Reedrek—making him even stronger. In starving myself, I starved him.

I looked ahead to the next cross street—and as the light turned red, I saw my Jag cruise across the intersection headed for the river.

Even across the threshold, I could smell Eleanor's confusion. She couldn't quite cover her surprise at seeing me, especially in the company of a woman. I usually called beforehand to arrange our evenings, and I always arrived alone. Eleanor was dressed demurely in what looked like a business suit with tailored pants and jacket, her tumbling gypsy hair drawn back into a smooth chignon. She looked expensive and competent.

"I'm sorry to show up unannounced," I said before she could speak. "We seem to have had a bit of car trouble and I wonder if you'll humor us until Jack returns." I kept my voice formal, without any of the sexual undertones Eleanor and I usually traded. "May we come in?"

"Of course, William," my Eleanor said, recovering. "You know you're *always* welcome here."

"This is a . . . friend of mine," I said. "Olivia, meet Eleanor—this is her house."

"Hello," Olivia replied as we stepped through the door.

Briefly, she sized up Eleanor before her gaze moved on to the parlor where several scantily clad women amused the well-dressed men among them. It looked like a private party.

"What is this place? A whorehouse?"

Eleanor drew herself up, and the recent memory of her—naked, driving a stake downward—assailed me. Her voice was perfectly calm. "We prefer to call it a gentlemen's club. But if you must get down in the gutter you could describe this as a house of pleasure."

Olivia returned her full attention to Eleanor.

"Or pain," Eleanor added with a slight smile. Again, I had to admire her lack of fear, although I wasn't sure whether Olivia, child of a vampire, would shrug off the "gutter" insult or shed blood.

I stepped between them, moving close to Eleanor's ear. "Might you arrange a swan for my friend here?"

"I might," Eleanor answered softly, then lightly nipped my ear. "Will we get to finish our game?"

Her words set off my own heated reaction. I'd conditioned myself to her pleasures. "No," I managed.

She pushed back to look at me. I could see disappointment in her eyes, and although she'd never admit it, I could tell she was hurt. "Why?" she asked. "Is she—"

"It has nothing to do with Olivia," I assured her.

Eleanor held my gaze, looking for a lie. She had no idea how easily I could lie if I wished to. But in this case, I let her see the truth.

"Follow me," she said.

She took us to a comfortable sitting room, although we chose not to sit. "Wait here and I'll make some calls." Then she looked at Olivia again. "What's your preference?" she asked. "A man or a woman?"

Olivia licked her already swelling lips, which were

warming and changing in front of us. She was becoming the predator. Her moist pout was more than any mortal could resist kissing, risk dying for. Watching her, I wondered if I had that effect on Eleanor when she offered me her blood. Olivia put out a pale hand and slowly slid her fingers up Eleanor's bare neck, gliding along her jaw as though she meant to draw her forward for a kiss. Instead, she ran the soft pad of her thumb over Eleanor's mouth.

"I love pretty bitches like you," she purred, teasing Eleanor's lips apart. I felt my Eleanor tremble under her touch. Even I was not unaffected. I had controlled my appetites for so long that this primal overload made it hard to breathe.

"I see why William likes to play here," Olivia exhaled.

The three of us stood transfixed for a moment. I had the uncanny feeling of being touched, and had to clear my own throat and swallow against the urge to bar the door and drag both of them to the carpet. Then Olivia reluctantly released her hold on Eleanor. "But I also like to fuck my food, so I suppose a man would do."

Eleanor nodded, perhaps unsure if she could speak, and disappeared through the door.

Had I thought of this upstart as a child? If so, she was proving to me that she could run with the big dogs, as Jack would say. What would he think if he saw her now?

Olivia laughed, her eyes bright with mischief and lechery. "You must satisfy her well. She's all about you." When I didn't respond, she moved closer, rubbing herself against me like a cat. "You know I said I wasn't hungry, but suddenly I'm *famished*. I hope your friend Eleanor hurries." She smiled up into my face, running a knowing hand downward, caressing the arousal I could not hide. "Otherwise, I might have to take matters into my own hand."

Jack

I drove back to the garage, trying to figure out how I was going to tell the guys about Huey. At least there was no next of kin to notify. Huey's wife was dead, and he had no kin that he knew of, or would admit to. The passenger seat was loaded with a couple of twelve-packs of beer and some chips I'd picked up at the convenience store. I'd never planned a wake before, but I figured there had to be refreshments.

When I pulled into the garage bay, I could see all the regulars there. Rufus, Otis, and Jerry were playing cards, and Rennie was working on a transmission. Rennie, who knew me best, sensed immediately that something was bad wrong.

"What's up, chief? Did you find Huey?" Rennie asked cautiously. Jerry and Rufus, who I'm convinced are not 100 percent, grade-A human, each put their noses in the air, their nostrils flaring slightly. They obviously could smell fresh kill almost as well as I could. Otis looked back and forth between the two of them as the card game halted.

"Yeah, I found him. Something got him. Something bad. It's new in town and William and me are going to catch it."

I paused a moment to let this sink in. Huey, who'd detailed cars, changed oil, and did odd jobs around the shop, had been popular with the regulars. He didn't have two good brain cells to rub together but had been pleasant company and hadn't asked questions. In the poker game of life, it wasn't that he'd been canny enough to bluff about the weirdness of his compadres; it's just that he hadn't been blessed with a curious nature. If I'd wanted, I could've filleted a drug dealer in here, roasted him on a spit over the oil pit, and Huey would never have made a peep. You had to admire that in a human.

Finally I opened the trunk and the boys shuffled over to see their friend, who looked fairly peaceful now that his eyes were closed.

"Don't he look natural?" Otis mused.

"Not with a hole in his throat you could drive a Mack truck through, he don't," Rufus pointed out.

"It's just what folks say," muttered Otis.

After a pause, Jerry spoke up. "Can we help find the guy who did this?" Wiry and strong-looking, Jerry would probably be pretty handy in a fight. Out of respect to Huey, he removed his Braves cap, and once again I noted that his ears were a little too pointy for a regular human. If the going got rough, I figured he might be able to shapeshift into something real useful. But this wasn't his fight, and when William and I finally did find whoever murdered Huey and Alger, I didn't know if even the two of us would be powerful enough to stop him.

"Thanks, but me and William have to handle this."

Rufus bent his two index fingers and brought them to either side of his mouth. This was his way of saying *vampire,* a word which was never uttered in my presence. Better to waltz around the truth than to know for sure.

"Yeah," I said. "It's our kind of business."

They were silent for another moment, contemplating the seriousness of a new and vicious blood drinker in town. I had more to fill them in on later, but right then, we had to see about Huey. They continued viewing Huey's body as if gathered around a proper casket in a funeral home, and I put the beer and chips on the card table. They each took a cold one, and I raised my can of Budweiser, the king of beers. "To Huey," I said.

"To Huey," the others chimed. We all popped our tops at the same time, sounding like a redneck funeral's version of a twenty-one-gun salute.

Otis said, "Remember the time before he got cursed when Huey got drunk and fell into the oil pit?"

"Do I ever. I had to pay his hospital bill," I said. "He 'bout broke every bone in his body. Even had his jaw wired shut."

"That wasn't the worst of it," Rennie said. "He had to sit around for a couple of months in a body cast listening to his old lady bitch at him for being so dumb. And he couldn't answer her back because his jaw was busted. Couldn't get up and walk out either. He just had to sit and take it."

Rufus put in, "Drove him crazier than a shithouse rat."

We all laughed, and it felt good. A little guilty maybe, but good. It was fitting to share the bad times as well as the good with mortals. Their feelings were so real, so in-your-face. I forgot sometimes that I wasn't one of them.

"It was right after that when his old lady had the curse put on him," Rufus said. " 'Course he tried to have it took off. He wore a *gris-gris* around his neck twenty-four/seven, but he was still afraid to drink."

"Yeah," Jerry said. "A man can't do without his guts."

This was a sobering thought. As sober as a thought

could be after the thinker had downed a few Buds, anyway. "That's a fact," Rufus agreed solemnly.

"What are you gonna do with him?" Rennie asked.

"I thought we'd take the backhoe and bury him out back in his Corsica like he wanted."

"He loved that car," agreed Rennie.

"Seems a waste of a perfectly good Chevy," Jerry said.

"It's a *Corsica*," I said, thinking perhaps he hadn't understood.

"The transmission's on its last legs," said Rennie.

"Oh, well, then," Jerry acquiesced, and cracked another beer.

The shop is several blocks away from the nearest residential area, so nobody was annoyed by the sound of a backhoe digging a car-size hole out back. After we'd finally gotten the car situated in the hole, I positioned Huey behind the wheel, his head at a jaunty angle, his left hand on the steering wheel, and, at Otis's insistence, a cold Bud in his right. I guess it was the least we could do.

"Maybe we shoulda bought him some new clothes," Rufus said. "You know, a suit or somethin'. That's how they do it down at the funeral home."

Jerry looked at Rufus like he was a black cloud just waitin' to rain on our funeral parade. "Well, Rufus, you *dufus*, just where exactly do you think Huey is goin' that he can't go in his coveralls?"

Rufus scratched the back of his neck like something had bit him. "I told you not to call me that," he mumbled, then fell silent.

As we stood looking down at Huey, Rennie said, "I guess somebody should say a few words." Then everybody looked up at me.

On the one hand, it seemed kind of inappropriate for a creature damned for all eternity to preach a graveside funeral service for a human. But, on the other, I was Huey's employer and friend, so I guessed I should rise to the occasion.

"Here lies Huey." I glanced around at the four of them, all sad-eyed and getting soggy around the sinuses. Rennie's eyes swam, magnified behind the thick lenses. "Please, er, Lord, receive him into heaven and take good care of him because he was a good ol' boy and never hurt a fly that I know of."

"Amen," the others muttered.

Afterward, as I watched the boys sitting around the card table finishing off the rest of the second twelve-pack, I cursed myself for what I had to do. Humans, and even semi-humans, seem so frail to me. Their lives, which are short enough to begin with, can flicker out like a candle flame in a stiff wind when you add a little danger into their day-to-day routines. I couldn't let what happened to Huey happen to them.

"Boys, I'm going to have to close the shop for a few days. Just until me and William can find the thing that killed Huey and deal with it."

They began to protest, as I knew they would. Rennie especially had good reason. He was my partner in the business, which was his livelihood. "What about the customers? We've got four cars in there we're working on."

"Three. I've finished with the mayor's car and I'll take it to him tonight. You call the other three customers and tell 'em it'll be a few days longer on the repairs. Tell 'em you'll tow the cars elsewhere if it's a problem."

Rennie, having worked with me for years, knew me well enough not to push the matter. The others didn't.

Jerry stood up. "Jack, we can take care of ourselves. We'll keep an eye on Rennie, make sure nobody bothers him. It's not fair to close the shop."

Jerry thought he was tough, and maybe he was by mortal standards, but in the nonhuman world he was way out of his league. Through the years I'd called many humans my friends, and a few, including these boys, had figured out my special situation, more or less. Hell, I had to hang with humans or be a hermit since William wouldn't let me within spitting distance of other vamps. But every now and then, when someone you hang with gets too big for his britches, you have to show 'em who's the big dog. It's not an ego thing, honest. It's for their own good.

"You wouldn't know what we're dealing with if it came up and bit you on the ass. Hell, I don't even know if I can protect you. I don't even know if I can protect myself. If this thing goes after me, it might not be picky about what it does with whoever gets in its way—like Huey. Until further notice, I don't want anybody hanging around here. I'm serious."

"Dammit, Jack, we—"

Jerry's train of thought came to a screeching halt as I set my mouth to show off my fangs. I let my eyes dilate and leveled a deadly stare on him. "Drop it."

Jerry sat down immediately. I'd never shown them my game face before. I sighed, seized by an overwhelming sadness. The regulars would never look at me the same way again, I knew it. The little scare was for their own good, but it made me feel like an outsider in my own home. I liked humans. I liked the rosy look of their skin, their musical voices, their genuine human smells, their normalness. The way they went about their business oblivious to the things I could see, smell, and hear that they couldn't. Like the movement in a corner of the eye, the scent of old, dead things, the sound of lost souls stirring. They would never be troubled by any of that. Sometimes I longed to be one of them again.

Rennie broke the tension by saying, "All right. We get it. You're bad."

After the regulars went their separate ways, Rennie patted me awkwardly on the arm and told me to take care of myself. I could tell he was worried. Hell, so was I.

Alone at last, I went to the small safe I'd had poured into the concrete floor in the corner of the garage. I kept one of the tool cases parked above it, so that it was pretty much invisible. I'd installed the safe because some of our more eccentric customers liked to deal in cash. It's tough to get credit cards and checking accounts when you're not human. Me, I applied for a Social Security card when that system was established, so I have everything I need. Been drawing benefits for a good number of years now, and I pay my fair share of income tax just like your average human Joe. You know what they say. Nothing is certain but death and taxes. I have them both covered.

I fished out the tacky little necklace William had asked me to keep for him years ago. He called it a charm, but it wasn't very charming. It was pretty ugly, in fact. Just a bunch of shells and beads strung on old, stained leather that looked like a kid's "what I did last summer at camp" project. I wondered what was so special about it besides the fact that it smelled like blood. Just more of William's mysterious shit. I tucked the stupid charm in my pocket, relocked the safe, and closed up the garage.

I took the mayor's vehicle and headed over to Eleanor's. Through William's connections, I happened to know that his honor was at some kind of mayors' conference out of town and wouldn't be back until the night of William's party. I figured William might as well continue to ride around in style while his Jag was missing. Something domestic wasn't really him, but the Escalade was big and roomy and would do in a pinch. At least I wouldn't have to drive 'em around and watch Olivia and William getting cozier and cozier in a bucket seat made for one.

My bucket seat.

I parked the car on the street in front of Eleanor's, got out, and started up the steps, expecting to feel William's usual impatience with my timing. I stopped on the landing halfway up and had to get a grip on the rail to keep from falling on my butt. Bloodlust and just plain old *lust* lust hit me like the lead car at the Daytona 500. Pleasure and pain so intense I could barely draw a breath. Was this what William had been hiding from me? He must have been so involved he'd forgotten to shut me down. That was a first. Unable to move, I looked down at the basement floor foundation. William was down there. No telling what kind of kinky party he was having with Olivia and Eleanor. And guess who wasn't invited? Not that I had much stomach for that kind of thing. Tonight anyway. I stumbled down the steps, opened the door to the Escalade, hung William's charm around the rearview mirror, and walked away.

Having nowhere to go and nobody to go to, I sat down on a stone bench in the square and waited for my temperature to drop to normal. I couldn't remember when I'd felt more alone. Cut off from my human friends and kept at arm's length by William and the few other vampires I got to meet, I felt like a man without a country.

Hell, I might as well be one of those aliens people were always yammerin' about. Add to that the fact that a fierce, kick-ass creature was out there somewhere looking to kill all of us and it just wasn't one of my better days.

I heard human voices and looked up. One of those ghost tours was coming across the square. The tour guide, dressed in a Civil War–era getup complete with petticoats, was regaling the tourists with some supposedly scary story about one beastie or another who was rumored to haunt the antebellum house on the corner. As they approached me, I felt drawn to reach out to them but stopped myself. Humans for the most part don't cotton to being stroked by strangers in public places, at least not when they're sober.

Instead I bared my fangs at them, just the barest glint, not the full-out vamp face. The guide froze in mid-spiel and her customers gaped. She pulled herself together quickly, though, and straightened the bill of her bonnet. "We get all kinds here in Savannah," she declared. "Halloween is just around the corner. I'm sure this gentleman is just rehearsing for a party."

Halloween? She thought I was a Halloween vampire? Now *that* pissed me off. But it just goes to show you, humans have an uncanny knack for explaining away what they can see with their own eyes and hear with their own ears. It's a terrific skill for holding on to their sanity. As an ultimate survival skill, however, it sucks. William once told me that when humans first see a vampire, they choose to squander that crucial instant to search their minds for a concept that would explain away their instinctive sense of danger. It's in that instant, even more so than in the bloodbath that follows, in which they lose their lives. Humans are nothing if not predictable. When they had passed by me, I muttered, "I got your party right here, lady." When they couldn't see, I extended my fangs full-length, pulling my lips back as far as they would go. I hate to say it but the effect must be pretty gross. Think of a snake unhinging its jaw to swallow a rabbit whole.

They might have been able to explain away my little flash of fang, but if I had showed them the full game face, it would have made 'em scatter in all directions, screaming like a bunch of banshees with toothaches. In my mind's eye, I could just see the guide with her hoop-skirt hiked up, running like a wide receiver. The fantasy was amusing but not as satisfying as it would have been to actually do it. It would almost have been worth the risk to see them scatter like bowling pins.

I was alone again. Or maybe not. That same feeling was creeping up my spine, spreading along my neck, and making my arm hairs stand on end. The feeling that I was being watched.

William

The man was on his knees as all good swans should be, blindfolded, naked, with hands tied securely behind his back. Helpless. Eleanor had outdone herself. Asked for a snack, with true southern hospitality she'd served up a banquet certain to keep Olivia busy for a while. Not only had Eleanor found a willing male donor in record time, he came damned close to being handsome—or at least he had a handsome body. No pale goth club rat this one. This swan was broad-shouldered, long-limbed, and the proud owner of impressive *equipment,* so to speak. Most likely an out-of-towner, perhaps a college footballer here for a bit of naughtiness. A big bite of naughtiness was more like it. If he'd had the opportunity to look Olivia in the eyes just once, he might have been a bit more careful about volunteering.

We were in one of Eleanor's viewing rooms, seated behind mirrored glass. Comfortable chairs and a long leather couch had been placed so that watchers could have a full view of the proceedings. The swan waited on the other side of the glass, in what humans nowadays call a *dungeon*. Funny that. I'd seen the original versions, which consisted more or less of a hole in the ground with a heavy wooden lid. Eleanor's dungeon resembled the operating room at a local hospital, or perhaps an epicurean's shiny chrome kitchen. There would be no cooking here, however. The stainless steel and leather tools so carefully arrayed around the soundproofed room were meant to restrain or to cause pain. From bullwhips and cat-o'-nines to chains with cuffs and locks, the chamber held a little something for everyone's preferred torture. It couldn't rival the deviant dens of Amsterdam, Paris, or even New York, of course, but in this small corner of the world it was obvious Eleanor had spared no expense. The tray of scalpels and custommade knives alone had cost a small fortune.

Eleanor had removed her suit jacket and now she wore a silky white blouse, open at the neck. She escorted Olivia into the room. There were no formal introductions. Olivia slowly warmed her hands on the swan's quivering shoulders and back, sizing up the merchandise. Eleanor, satisfied she'd done her job, turned to leave. Olivia, however, grabbed her hand.

"Why don't you stay," she said, the persuasion in her voice palpable. "We could both play. I don't mind sharing." Then Olivia kissed Eleanor, teasing her mouth open, their tongues meeting, exploring, accepting. After one very long moment Olivia released her.

Eleanor's wary eyes searched the mirrored glass—she was looking to me, whether for help or permission I could not tell. I waited, as interested in her answer as Olivia. The kiss had been exquisitely tempting.

"I'd rather watch." She barely managed to get the words out, held in the gaze of Olivia's compelling eyes.

Olivia brought Eleanor's hand to her lips but paused before kissing it. She laughed when Eleanor startled at the touch. "I could show you a whole different world," she said.

Eleanor removed her hand and stepped away, anxious to leave. The lack of common sense in her dealings with the only vampire she knew—me—had fled her with a vengeance. My Eleanor was *afraid* of Olivia. "I'm sure you could," Eleanor responded in a subdued tone. Then to my further surprise, she paused, as though waiting for permission to go.

Olivia transferred her unnerving attention to the swan, and Eleanor slipped out of the room.

Then Alger's child-woman began to slowly strip off her clothes. I watched as she raised her arms and tugged the gossamer silk blouse over her head before dropping it to the floor. Her breasts were high and full, the nipples the palest pink. Looking straight through the mirror as though daring me to watch, she unzipped the leather pants and slid them down off her hips, stepping out one leg at a time, until she stood naked but for a red scrap of lace covering her sex.

She had the body of a goddess. No, of the huntress—Diana.

Diana.

The emergence of the name in my mind brought back a rushing tumble of memories.

My Diana, running with her skirts rucked up through a field of barley. Laughing, daring me to chase her down. And I did—both of us tumbling to the ground, out of breath and as horny as any two creatures in rut. With the sun warm on my back and the golden bed of barley beneath us, I'd felt more than heard her sigh as I sank between her welcoming thighs. Then, with her urging, I rode her until we both were well satisfied.

"My own sweet William, my heart." She'd smiled, eyes closed, lying back among the crushed barley like a fair bird fallen from the sky.

"I'll naught get any fieldwork done if you keep tempting me," I said, out of breath and completely happy. "Married or not, if the priest catches us here in the broad light of day we'll be damned." The memory brought as much pain as pleasure. If I had died in that moment, I would've been a fortunate man. Instead, I've been made a damned one who lives in the dark.

A living hand touched my back, jarring me out of the painful vision of the dead. Eleanor's voice whispered my name. The image of my lovely Diana evaporated.

Beyond the barrier of glass, Olivia, perhaps sensing my distance of mind, reached down and with little effort dragged the swan to his feet.

"You're very strong, mistress," he said in a low voice.

"Are you afraid?" she asked, running her palm over his chest then downward to cup his balls in her hand.

He drew in a quick gulp of air. "Yes, mistress."

"You should be." It came out as a purr, but more tiger than kitten.

On my side of the glass, Eleanor's hand was moving, pushing under my shirt. I had a vague notion of stopping her . . . but then Olivia, busy like a spider in her dungeon, wrapped herself around the swan and bit.

Whether by savage kinship or the magical properties of my tainted blood, I could taste him—warm and bloody in my mouth. I could feel the well of wetness sliding over my lips and down his neck. Without thinking I drew Eleanor into my arms, allowing her to nuzzle my warming skin. A soft sucking sound filled my head with the powerful intensity of a train engine. Eleanor squirmed as I clasped her closer.

Just as I reached an almost dangerous level of sensual attunement, Olivia released her hold. As blood trickled down from the wound, she wiped her fingers through it, wetting her hands. The swan stood, panting, with an erection to rival a bull's.

"My, my, my," Olivia said as she slid her hands over the length of his penis—lubricating it with his own blood—and pumped, once, then again. The swan moaned. I stood mesmerized, unable to stop Eleanor as she slid to her knees, working the fastenings of my pants.

Olivia smiled, her lips and teeth red with new blood. She seemed to be orchestrating her play for my benefit rather than her own, or even the swan's. She pumped his length again and I felt Eleanor capturing my organ in her greedy mouth. I leaned forward, placing my hands flat on the mirror, my face close to the glass as Olivia squeezed until the swan whimpered in pain. Before she let go, the identical sound rose in me. Gracefully, she removed her red lace underwear and stuffed it into his mouth.

I could taste her.

Shoving her now eager volunteer backward until his thighs were pressed against the leather-covered table, she ordered, "Lie down on your back." With a muffled reply, the swan complied as quickly as he could with bound hands. Impatient with his performance, she selected one of the knives from the tray and cut his bonds. He made the mistake of relaxing too soon, however. In a lightning-fast movement that only another vampire could see, Olivia sliced down with expert precision and opened a vein in his wrist.

She stared at me as she sucked, as Eleanor sucked. The experience was like none in my long memory. I had lost all control and felt myself inexorably drawn toward a staggering orgasm. My breath had warmed enough to fog the glass as I groaned and came. Moaning in response, Eleanor sucked harder, taking all of me.

Olivia, however, looked like the cat who'd swallowed the canary. With a sly smile, she mounted the swan and with little or no fanfare rode him until he was quivering and twitching. Dragging Eleanor to her feet, I pinned her between my chest and the glass. At the mutual moment of orgasm, Olivia bit the swan, sinking her already bloodied fangs into the other side of his neck.

I felt a second erection filling and hardening. I heard the sound of ripping silk as I tore Eleanor's clothes from her body. The urge to feed had grown so urgent that I found my bared fangs poised at her neck. Her heart was fluttering like a trapped bird. She gasped and leaned into me, offering . . . anything . . . everything.

The scent of her blood teased my ever-present hunger. Blood meant life, blood meant power.

As if awaking from a dream, I looked down at Eleanor writhing against me, begging me to take her. A sudden cold wash of reality slid over me before I did any further damage. And as odd as it might seem in that moment, I thought of Jack. Some nagging worry. But first I had to pleasure my sweet Eleanor—something I could accomplish with a physical fucking. Jack had Lalee's charm. He would have to take care of himself for a little while longer.

Jack

"Come out wherever you are, you murdering sonofabitch!" I hollered after the last of the humans had disappeared around the corner. I can see pretty well and hear even better. Nothing. Whoever was stalking me was not going to make himself known until he was good and ready. I was starting to hate surprises.

I'd managed to alienate all the human beings I'd come in contact with that night, and my fellow vampires were playing bloodsucking sex games without me. I figured I might as well see if I could commune with some dead people, the kind who couldn't get away from me—a captive audience for my self-pity, you might say. So I headed off to Colonial Cemetery a few blocks away. When I got there I easily vaulted the iron fence, avoiding the spikes on top.

As soon as my feet hit the spongy earth, I felt them. The dead in Colonial were as restless as they were at Bonaventure. I closed my eyes and opened my senses. Yes, they were disturbed, all right. I walked around the perimeter, getting a feel for their mood, trying to gauge the depth of their agitation. I'd never felt anything quite like it. They seemed to be warning me. Things had come to a sorry pass when I had to depend on the long dead to give me advice. But I couldn't count on my own sire. William had been so damn busy in that whorehouse, he'd forgotten to block my thoughts. Too bad he'd had his mind on nookie instead of the killer, or maybe I'd have picked up some information I could use. Instead I'd gotten a jolt of such raw sexual energy that I needed a cold shower.

As I walked through the center of the graveyard, over the usual rustling and scuttling animal sounds in the night, I heard the unmistakable whine of a Jaguar's engine. It was moving away from me, going east toward the ocean. The gradual settling of souls underneath my feet told me what I'd already figured. It was the rogue vampire in William's ride. He'd probably been hiding under one of the concrete slabs covering a crypt.

I sat down near the garlanded headstone of one Gerald Hollis Jennings, a victim of galloping consumption a couple of hundred years ago, or so he'd indicated the first time I'd visited him. His soul was always quiet, so he was a good listener. Believe it or not, sometimes people die with no unfinished business.

"Gerald, my man. Have you sensed any evil here recently? I mean, *big* evil? Not the usual suspects lying around here."

I'd never known him to actually speak out loud. There was a groaning and a little vibration, which I took as a yes. When the dead communicate with me, it's usually sort of indirectly. It's all in my head, so to speak. I closed my eyes and words formed in my brain, almost shouting: *Danger, Jack.*

I had known I was in danger, of course, but this coming from Gerald startled me. How bad was this mess if a codger as old as Gerald here could feel it?

"Is there anything else you can tell me?"

I sensed a frustrated thrumming, as if he was using all the psychic energy he possessed to work up another message, but I also got the feeling he'd petered out with that last all-out brainstorm. What could you expect from a guy whose brain had been dust since before I was born? Maybe a more pleasant subject would charge him up again.

"Do you remember sex?" I asked.

The image popped into my head of a blushing house-maid smiling shyly, chest heaving. I felt Gerald reach under her kerchief for a handful of red curls as he pulled her against him. She closed her eyes to receive a kiss. Then she raised her skirts with one hand.

Of course I'd had to ask. Now I needed another cold shower.

There was a pause as I sensed laughter, and I laughed along with him. I stopped laughing when I heard a cry.

"Errrmmmph," someone or something said.

"Gerald?" I asked. But this voice sounded human. Kind of constipated, but human.

"Aaarrruh," it said.

I followed the sound a short distance to the scrawny and squirming contents of a black leather suit. It was caught by the collar on one of the spikes of the iron fence circling the cemetery. *Dammit!* Humans should have better sense than to sneak around cemeteries at night. They just aren't equipped to handle what they might come across, such as the likes of me. I got in the struggling stranger's face and demanded, "What are you doing up there?"

A pair of brown eyes as wide as headlamps peered out from beneath a thatch of spiky ink-black hair. Multiple earrings studded both ears and one nostril of his blade-like nose. Because of the way the fence was holding him by the collar, he looked neckless, like a turtle afraid to come all the way out of its shell. I grabbed him by the shoulders and shook him, which made his collar swallow even more of his head, like he was disappearing bit by bit into the quicksand of his all-black clothing. "Answer me, you little twerp!"

"My name is . . ." His voice broke and he started again, trying to compose his face even as he trembled. "My name is Lamar Nathan Von Werm, but the underworld knows me as the Prince of Misfortune. I'm pleased to make your acquaintance." He extended a slender hand, which was sporting a large silver ring in the shape of a skull. *Geez Louise.* I didn't shake his hand—some things can creep out even a vampire. "The underworld? The Prince of Misfortune? What kind of freak are you, and what do you want with me?"

If he took offense, he didn't show it. In fact, his face took on a rapturous look. "Bite me," he said.

What the—"Bite you? Bite *me*!"

"You don't understand. I want to be one of you. I want you to initiate me into the brotherhood of the blood. I want to be a vampire!"

To say I was stunned would be an understatement. Never in my existence had a human being confronted me like that. Sure, a handful of humans sorta knew what William and I were, all of them trusted longtime confidants like the regulars. Even if the ones who worked for us hadn't been well paid for their silence and loyalty, they would have been too terrified to ever betray us. Or to come right out and ask. As I looked at the pathetic little weasel I figured I had two choices on how to deal with him. I could tell him he was being crazy and insist there was no such thing as vampires, or I could skip denials altogether and just scare the bejesus out of him. But first I had to know how he knew.

"What makes you think I'm a vampire?"

"Two years ago my mom and dad and I were driving back from my violin recital and the Caddy broke down in front of Melfrey's department store on Houghton Street. The one with the big picture window right in front. While my dad talked on his cell phone and my mom went over her appointment book, I watched the reflection of the car being loaded on the tow truck with that hydraulic thingie. Only you weren't in the picture. I had to turn around to make sure you were really there. It was so cool. Besides, I saw you on the street a little while ago, full-fanged."

Oh, shit. The little weirdo had been following me. I couldn't believe I'd been so careless. And I was usually pretty damned careful about mirrors: I'd accidently/on purpose broken the rearviews on my truck. But there I'd been, going about my business in front of a picture window that reflected the whole street. The kid had made me for a vampire, fair and square. The denial option was out. It was showtime.

With one swift motion, I lifted the kid off the fence and held him in the air. "Listen, pal, believe me when I say, you don't want any of this." I slammed him up against the fence hard enough to make him see stars, and then I unsheathed my fangs and bent near his face so that he could see my pupils dilate. It was an involuntary reaction to letting down my fangs, a vampire adaptation that helps us hunt at night. At least that's how I'd got it figured. Anyway, the fangs coming out and the eyes going reddish black never failed to scare the absolute crap out of any human. He might have seen the show from a distance, but it was a whole other animal up close and personal.

And it didn't fail this time. Von Worm, or whatever his name was, was going all swimmy-eyed like he was about to pass out. Of course that could've been due to the death grip I had on the front of his jacket. But then, remarkably, he rallied and poked his chin out. "Yes, I do. I want to be one of you," he wheezed.

"No, you don't."

"Yes, I do."

"You don't know what you're saying. Have you noticed I'm sitting in a cemetery alone?" *Telling my troubles to dead people because they're the only ones who'll listen.* "Trust me. You don't want this kind of life."

He took a deep breath and looked me squarely in the eye. "Yes," he said in a stronger voice, "I do."

I let go of his collar. As he slid to the ground, I rubbed my chin. "Okay, so you've been following me because you want me to make you a vampire. Just why do you think you want to be a blood drinker?"

He straightened his jacket and relaxed a little. "When I saw what you did that night, after you'd driven us home, I sneaked out of the house and over to your garage. When you thought nobody was looking, I saw you lift up the car by the bumper without a jack or anything to see what was wrong with it. Right then I knew it was true what I'd always read in vampire stories—the parts about how strong vampires were. I figured there couldn't be many more vampires in Savannah, or else bodies would be showing up everywhere. So I just assumed you must be the only one. That would make you the baddest guy in town."

"Yeah, well." I wasn't about to tell him about William. If he didn't already know, he'd probably never guess. William didn't make the kind of mistakes I'd obviously been making. William didn't make any mistakes at all.

"Ever since that night, I've studied everything I could get my hands on about vampires. Of course, most of it's fiction, but even in fiction, sometimes there's a grain of truth. I followed every piece of information I could, wherever it led me. The more I found out, the more I wanted to be a vampire."

I looked him up and down by the light of the moon. He was naturally pale but had enhanced his look with white pancake makeup in the usual goth manner. Underneath the leather jacket would be skinny arms and a flat, boyish chest. The other boys at school must have beaten the shit out of him every day of the world, just on general principle. No wonder he wanted to be a badass. He might be a freak and possibly a pansy, but he'd had the guts to look me in the eye without wetting himself when I was giving him the full-tilt boogie vampire treatment. Whatever else he was, he was no coward.

I sighed. "Listen, kid. I'd like to help you out. I really would. But I'm telling you this *brotherhood,* or whatever you call it, is not all it's cracked up to be. Besides, making somebody into a vampire isn't easy. I've never done it before. I'm not even sure I know how."

"You remember how it was when you were made a vampire, don't you?"

Actually, I didn't. Not completely. The last thing I remember of my mortal life was lying on a muddy, bloody battlefield when William came toward me with bared fangs. Then the unimaginable pain-pleasure. There's no other description for it. Then nothing for a while. Then I was back again, with all new hungers and thirsts. Sounds, touches, tastes, and smells were all enhanced—bigger, deeper, somehow more real than they'd been before. "It was a long time ago," I told him.

The kid leaned forward and lowered his voice. "It's the blood exchange. That's all. Of course, most people don't survive the limbo stage, but—"

"Huh? You make it sound like a luau."

He was looking pretty exasperated by this point. "You know, you really should know this stuff."

He was right. Damn William. He'd never let me in on the fine points of how to be a vampire. He'd just told me the minimum of what I needed to know to stay alive. It was entirely possible that this pimply shrimp in front of me, with his two years of book learning, knew more about vampires than I did.

"I know plenty," I said. "In fact, I'm going to test you. If you know so much about vampires, tell me what it's like to be one. First off, how do you spot one?"

"Okay, you might be a vampire, if . . ."

"Very funny."

". . . you were afraid of garlic," he continued.

I snorted. "I love me some garlic." The only thing I actually ate, in addition to drinking blood, was red meat. I had no idea if I was afraid of garlic. Why the hell should I be afraid of garlic?

"You might be a vampire if you can't go out in the sun."

"Check."

"You can only be killed by fire, wooden stakes, and silver bullets."

"Yeah, yeah. Silver's mostly for werewolves, but technically, yeah." I waved him on to the next topic.

"You might be a vampire if you can fly."

"Kid, are you on drugs?" If I could fly this whole time and William didn't tell me, I was going to stake him myself.

"Not lately. Anne Rice's vampires can fly."

"Oh, crap. Is that what you're basing that on? Anne Rice's vampires can't even have sex. Screw that."

"So you can have sex?"

"*Hell* yes." I swear I could feel Gerald laughing again.

"Good." The kid seemed to perk up a bit at this piece of news. I'd bet my fangs he'd never gotten laid in his life. Hope springs eternal, I guess. Maybe that was the real reason he wanted to be a vampire—to get chicks. Or dudes, I thought, looking at his earrings again.

"What else?" I demanded.

This went on for a while. He got the part about the coffins right. Also crosses (can't go near them). He said holy water would hurt us, but water's water, as far as I know. He also knew you can't cross a threshold uninvited. He did come up with a number of things that I'm definitely going to have to experiment with. You just never know. I figured I might quiz him some more some other time, but it was getting late—or very early depending on your sleeping habits.

"What exactly is a Van Worm anyway?" I asked.

"Von Werm," he corrected. "W-e-r-m. My family's old Savannah. Former plantation owners, now bankers."

Now I remembered. The Von Werms were one of the high-society couples who were regulars at William's parties. I'd just bet they were thrilled by how their sprout had turned out. In fact, that was probably why he went around like every day was Halloween. Just to get under his folks' skin.

"So what do they think of their little boy wanting to grow up to be a vampire?"

"I don't tell them anything. They're barely aware I'm around. I'd have been better off being raised by wolves."

"Is that why the getup? To get attention from Mommy and Daddy?"

"When I first became aware of you, I was fascinated with the world of the dead. Goth culture was the perfect outlet. I made them my tribe. I flunked out of SCAD after a year and needed to be able to work and play at night and sleep during the day, so I took a position in retail."

I raised my eyebrows.

"I went to work on the night shift at Spencer's in the mall, okay?"

"How old are you?"

"Twenty." He plopped down on the nearest crypt and was about to apply some black lipstick.

I grabbed his hand. "Oh, no, you don't."

"Why not?"

"That's not the vampire way," I heard myself say, like I was the Roy freaking Rogers of the vampire world. By now it was clear that I had no idea what the vampire way was. I just knew this kid creeped me out. And, like I said, I was a vampire. Not only did he look weird, he talked weird. One minute he was talking like a normal kid and the next he was saying things like "pleased to make your acquaintance." The poor kid had indifferent parents, a spindly body, and a funny-looking face and was saddled with a name like Lamar Von Werm. Shit, no wonder he wanted to be a vampire.

"Okay. So why should I make you into a vampire? What's in it for me?"

"I'll be your servant. Just like Renfield in *Dracula*. And after I've proved my worth, then you can convert me into a blood drinker."

I remembered Renfield in *Dracula*, the Coppola version. Who would have thought of Tom Waits as Renfield? Now that's what I call casting. Maybe Werm could be useful. On the other hand, he might just be in the way. It was not like I needed any complications in my life just now. "I don't know."

"I can be an informant. I hang out with some pretty tough people. They know things."

I laughed. "What things? Like what store in the mall has the blackest jeans?"

His dark eyes took on a kind of gleam. "Like who's the new vampire in town."

He had my attention. Since he thought I was the only vampire in town, who was he talking about? William, Olivia, or the killer? "Okay. Who?"

"Don't you know?"

"Would I be asking if I knew?"

"Promise to make me one of you and I'll tell you."

This kid was as stubborn as a mule. I figured I could rough him up a little, but he'd probably made a career of being roughed up. I had a feeling it wouldn't faze him. Besides, there was no time. Morning was coming soon and I had to get back to Eleanor's to get a ride to the warehouse. I'd have to sleep on a way to get him to talk. And on his offer to serve me. Would he have to serve me like I served William?

"Okay, you little pissant, if you're so good at following me, come and find me tomorrow night. We'll talk about this some more."

"Make me a vampire now!" he demanded, his voice rising. "There's time. I want to be like you!"

I grabbed him by the shoulders again, lifting him off the ground. He was starting to piss me off. I jumped over the fence with him and hung him back onto the spikes by the collar. He'd be safer on the outside. "I'm going to leave you hanging here until daylight. Then you can call somebody over to help you down. In the meantime I want you to spend the rest of the night thinking about what it really means to be a vampire." I remembered Algernon's charred and staked remains on the deck of William's boat and my mouth went dry. "Think about what would happen if you were a bloodsucker and some stronger vamp kicked your ass and left you here to burn to a crisp when the sun came up.

"I want you to think about what it would mean to have to live in the world of humans but never really be part of their world again, never to be able to share their warmth and the spark of their souls. To feel the heat of a human woman surround you but never be able to wake up with her. To never again feel the sun on your face. To be trapped by cold and darkness for eternity, cut off from everything good and decent, always on the outside looking in."

"But what about the brotherhood?" he whimpered.

When I laughed I heard the bitterness in my own voice. "You think that once you become a vampire, you'll be in some cool fraternity or something? Let me tell you, kid. Just because you're a blood drinker doesn't mean you're going to stop being the last one picked for the team. If you think you're lonely now, if you think you're an outcast and a freak, just wait until you become one of the undead. Then you'll really know what isolation feels like."

I left him then, still trapped on the fence, his mouth gaping, eyes wide. I didn't hear another peep out of him as I walked back to Eleanor's.

Someone on their way to work would find Werm and help him down. But not, I hoped, before he'd had a chance to reconsider his career choices. Being a vampire was a long leap from selling Halloween masks at the mall.

In a few minutes I was back at Eleanor's. Olivia and Eleanor were resting comfortably in the porch swing. William stood at the top of the stairs like a sentry. When they saw me, the women got to their feet, and William gave Eleanor a chaste kiss on the forehead before he and Olivia came down the steps.

"Jack, does this vehicle belong to who I think it does?" He didn't wait for me to answer. "Why the hell have you parked the mayor's vehicle in front of a house of ill repute?"

"It's not like it's not parked here twice a week anyway," Eleanor said, sounding a little peeved.

"Oh," William said. "Very well, then."

William walked to the SUV and his face turned dark with anger. "Why the hell did you leave that *collier* here? You were supposed to *wear* it. Keep it with you all the time, do you understand?"

"No. I don't understand. Why don't you explain it to me? Why don't you explain everything while you're at it. You know who this guy is, don't you? You know who we're looking for." We were nose-to-nose now. I expected him to haul off and slug me—wished he would, in fact. Then I'd finally have an excuse to at least try to whip his ass once and for all. But instead of getting angrier, William's face took on a look of sorrow. Like instead of making him mad, I'd hurt his feelings.

Most of the time I didn't think he had any.

"This charm—*collier*—has been blessed by the Voudoun. It will protect you as much as you can be protected at this point. I can't say how right now. It's too complicated." He tried a stiff little smile. "Please wear it. For my sake."

Olivia came down the steps, smelling like sex on a stick. Part of that smell was human. She had fed, in addition to who knew what else. She reached into the car and took the charm off the rearview mirror. "Be a good boy, Jackie," she said as she put it around my neck. "Wear the pretty necklace." Her soft pink tongue slid out from between her bloodred lips and she licked my cheek like a child would lick an all-day sucker. "Nice lolly," she purred. For the third time that night, I needed that damned cold shower.

"So I take it now that Algernon's dead you're lookin' for love in all the wrong places," I said to cover my reaction.

Something in her eyes cooled. "I'm always looking, sweet cheeks. Besides, Alger was my muse, not my mate."

William stepped between us. "Is Huey taken care of?"

"Hmm?" I was starting to feel bewitched. It took me a second to realize that William was talking. "Yeah, he's . . . right where he needs to be."

I got into the backseat. William and Olivia got in front. Olivia blew Eleanor a kiss as William put it in reverse. Hell, even a human—and a female to boot—got more attention than me. The thought of Olivia's mouth made my gut tighten. I decided not to clue William in on my meeting with what's-his-Werm. After all, William didn't tell me anything to speak of, so why should I keep telling him about everything? Little Werm might prove useful.

Since I wasn't in the mood for small talk, I kept my mouth shut on the drive out to the warehouse. William gave Olivia a whole travelogue's worth of information about Savannah. It was like he wanted to make sure she didn't do any talking about herself and her situation within earshot of me. When we got to my sleeping place, I got out and slammed the door a little too hard.

"See you tomorrow night, Jack," William said. "Remember what I said about the charm."

"Yeah," I responded without looking back. As I unlocked the door to my room, I noticed that the SUV was still there. William was waiting until I was safely inside.

He'd only do that for a reason. He definitely knew more than he was telling me about what we were up against. I just hoped what I didn't know wouldn't kill me.

I couldn't wait to find out whatever I could talk, or squeeze, out of my new friend, Werm. I thought again about how badly the little dude wanted to be a bloodsucker, wanted to be strong and fearsome. If I made Werm a vampire, maybe I'd have someone I could really tell my troubles to. But if I did, would he be in as much danger as William and I were? As I'd told him, I'd never made another vampire before. And it was probably a bad time to start.

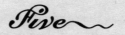

William

As Jack disappeared into his night quarters, Olivia shifted in the passenger seat to face me. Well fed and free of any sexual temptation, she looked almost human again. Dead but beautiful. "You're going to have to tell us something sooner or later," she said, inclining her head toward the whining electric gate.

My hands tightened on the steering wheel as I turned the car toward home. "I know. The question is 'what?'"

"Why not everything?" She smiled. "As far as help goes, we're pretty much all you've got."

"You and Jack are too reckless. Knowledge is the only kind of power with any leverage in this situation—not immortality, or strength, or even loyalty."

"Jack would face a dragon for you, if you asked him."

"Yes, and the dragon would very likely eat him for breakfast." The comparison of Reedrek to a dragon was an apt one. He was as ancient, as dangerous as the fabled coldblooded, fire-breathing beast, and he killed without any trace of humanity. Perhaps the legend of

Vlad the Impaler as the original blood drinker was untrue. Perhaps when the last dragon fires had gone out, the remaining beasts had learned to walk on two legs, and to live on blood.

Wouldn't Jack love that story? A grandsire who was a dragon. He'd be asking the girls at Eleanor's to search him for scales.

Poor, guileless Jack was going to have a surprise when he awoke the next evening—the arrangements had already been completed.

"I'll tell him as much as I feel necessary. But I'm going to have to sleep on the matter."

"Speaking of sleeping . . ." One of her hands caressed my arm.

I allowed the touch but kept my distance mentally. "You'll sleep with me tonight, then I'll arrange delivery of your own temporary coffin."

She seemed pleased but not surprised. "Mmmmm, what pleasant dreams we'll have . . ."

When we arrived home, Deylaud met us at the door. I immediately recognized he'd been up to something he wasn't supposed to be doing. Rather than pressing him, I waited for a confession. It was impossible for him to lie to me, not because of any punishment or spell-binding but because he loved me above all others, except perhaps Reyha. With that love came honesty and a ferocious willingness to do my bidding.

I could feel dawn tingling just over the horizon in the east. No more time to work the puzzle of my killer sire.

"Reyha, show Olivia to my quarters and help her get settled. I'll be down shortly." I might have smiled at the gruesome face Reyha made to show her displeasure, but it wouldn't do to encourage her. "Go now, please," I added. "And take her bag."

Ever obedient if pugnacious, Reyha shrugged, yanked up the leather duffel, and led the way downstairs. That left me with Deylaud. I took up a pen and a pad to write Melaphia a note. We would be receiving a very special delivery that very evening. Plus, I needed to remind her to go over the checklist for the charity event on Saturday night. Although I let Jack think he was doing most of the work, the reality was that he had no clue how much organization it took to host the top social movers and shakers in Savannah. The hospital fund-raiser had had the triple purpose of supporting the blood bank, introducing Alger as Lord Something-or-Other to pave the way for his escape into this country, and providing cover for a meeting with the usually far-flung leaders of other American vampire clans. To cancel now would raise too many questions—Olivia would have to do as a replacement for Alger. As I anchored the note with a glass paperweight, I noticed that Deylaud had disappeared into the front of the house.

I followed and found him seated on the oriental rug in the parlor, next to a lump where something had been shoved under the carpet. I flipped back the edge of the rug and found a book—a very old book.

"Why are you hiding books here? You know where they go." I pointed toward the library. He didn't answer, he just looked guiltier.

As soon as my fingers touched the binding, I received a jolt. The pages seemed to whisper and warn. *Not yours. Not for your eyes.* Obviously, it was not part of my collection. I picked it up and let it fall open in my hands.

Names—female most prominent—with lines connecting. Some sort of genealogy. "Where did you get this?"

Deylaud ducked his head. "From the bag."

"What bag?"

"Miss Olivia's," he answered, looking miserable. He held up his hands and his fingertips looked slightly scorched, as if he'd gotten too close to a burner on the stove. "I read it. I'm sorry. I—"

Suddenly Olivia was standing in the doorway. "I've been looking for that," she said. She held out her hand for it.

"You'll have to excuse Deylaud," I said as I gave it over. "He's fascinated by books. I think his first master must have been a writer or a librarian."

"Papyrus," Deylaud whispered, keeping his gaze on Olivia's feet.

"This one belongs to me," Olivia said. "Leave it alone." With a tight smile she retreated.

I had the distinct feeling she'd been warning both of us. Another puzzle to ponder. With Deylaud at my heels I followed Olivia downstairs, through the short underground passageway flickering with candles at each altar, and on into my bedchamber. I waited, allowing Olivia to settle herself, her book, and her bag of dirt in my coffin. Then, after soothing Deylaud's guilt by giving him a quick hug and offering a kiss to Reyha to appease her annoyance at being relegated to sleeping with her brother, I stretched out next to the only woman I'd slept with in five hundred years.

Olivia was an unfortunate distraction. Deylaud closed the coffin lid over us, and the sweet, safe darkness blanketed our bodies. I'd planned to concentrate on how to fight Reedrek, at least until the growing sunlight outside lulled me to sleep, but my female coffinmate wouldn't be still. I heard a hiss near my ear as she slipped a hand inside my shirt and angled her thigh over mine. She was a worse bed hog than Reyha. I pushed her hand away from my bare skin but it came back without hesitation.

"Do you mind?" I muttered under my breath.

The only answer I received was a pleased sigh. She was obviously already asleep. Her natural affinity, even when unconscious, for sleeping close to another made me wonder what connections she'd left behind in England.

England.

I felt around in the dark until I found the bag of soil she'd brought. Home base as it were. Slowly I raised the bag to smell the contents.

Home.

Images streamed through my mind. My gruff but loving human father, dying in my arms after falling from his stallion. My mother throwing herself on his grave and refusing to move, forcing me to have her carried to her bed where she'd stayed. Both of them buried in English soil. And, as always, Diana. Holding a candle, round with our son inside her. Crying with joy at his birth. Crying with horror as Reedrek killed him before our eyes.

I pushed the bag as far away from me as was possible in the confined space. It took several moments to catch my breath. No, I'd been right to stay in the New World, in Savannah. Going home would only bring more pain.

And now the maker of my pain had followed me here.

Jack and Olivia were depending on me for protection. With the help of Lalee's blood, I could block Reedrek, I could hurt him. But because I was his offspring, his existence wasn't mine to end. That left a gaping hole in dealing with him. Our only chance would be for the three of us to combine our strength and work together. But I'd kept Jack from finding his potential—and now it might be too late.

I should've known Reedrek would find me sooner or later. No matter how low-profile or humanlike I stayed. Truth be told, immortal or not, I had never thought I would exist long enough to have to face him. Here was my opportunity to find an end to everything—my monstrous memories, my night-prowling half life, my unsalvageable black heart, and most of all my anger. Yet it was the anger that had kept me going, and even now it rose in hot waves to resist the idea that Reedrek should decide any other part of my destiny.

I wouldn't allow him the satisfaction of killing me.

Although killing might not be what he had in mind. With the help of the shells, I'd seen that he'd meant to trap Alger, not kill him. Once trapped, Alger's offspring would be fair game. Without protection . . .

I knew I must not be trapped.

And I would kill Jack myself rather than let Reedrek have him. Jack might thank me for the favor. But he wouldn't thank me for keeping him in the dark any longer. He already believed I thought him stupid or unworthy, and I regretted not being honest with him. I'd told myself I'd been protecting the both of us by refusing to teach him. Each time I considered releasing him from his apprenticeship, I found a reason to postpone.

Jack was no fool. Some things he'd figured out on his own. I could only hope that he wouldn't use any knowledge he gained against me. At least I could tell Jack about his tainted blood—a blessing and another curse. Not as powerful as my own, but potent just the same. If we were very lucky, I'd have time to teach him to control some of the blessings of his origin. I would have to act fast before the curse—Reedrek—caught up with us both.

I woke to the touch of Olivia's tongue roaming along my neck. She wouldn't dare bite me without permission, or so I thought. The vision of her biting the swan played through my mind. Better be safe than be forced to subdue her natural aggressiveness by killing her.

"Leave me be," I said.

My words seemed only to amuse her. She chuckled and slid over me until we were face-to-face, body to body. She teased my lips with her own and breathed into my mouth. "You know you want to. I saw how you watched me last night." She moistened her lips before sucking at mine. "We would be so good together," she sighed. "Count on it."

My blood stirred. Not only was my body waking up, but the promise in Olivia's voice, the friction of her mouth moving over mine, brought parts of my body to rapt attention. With a slow grinding of her hips, she brought my erection to full staff.

"Mmmmmm." Busy hands moved to shove away my clothes.

She was right. I had watched her the night before, and I'd wanted her with a crazed vengeance. I had more than half a mind to let her take me, to see just how good it could be. If nothing else, it was sure to be a novel experience.

A loud banging on the lid of my coffin made Olivia jump and hit her head.

"Fuck!" she grouched, sliding off me so that I could push the lid open.

Jack's angry face greeted me.

I gave him an evil smile. "Surprise!" I said, then levered myself out of "bed." Better to be on my feet to face Jack's righteous anger. I knew I'd been high-handed again. Jack should have been used to it, but the look on his face indicated otherwise.

"Just what in—" He glanced at Olivia, her beautiful nakedness enough to stop any normal human's heart. "—*blue blazes* is going on around here?" he demanded.

Rather than answering, I made a great show of helping Olivia out of the coffin. It wouldn't do to accept Jack's challenge too quickly. As soon as Olivia's feet reached solid stone, she gaped at the other coffin in the room, Jack's coffin. It hadn't been there the night before.

"Good morning, Jack," she said almost as an afterthought. "And, yes," she purred, "what *is* going on?" She moved to the smooth metal surface of Jack's "ride" and ran a hand along the black paint. "What does the number three stand for?" she asked him.

Jack, torn between wanting to impress Olivia and, I imagine, wanting to tear me limb from limb, stood glaring at me. Finally, he turned to her. "It's the number of Dale Earnhardt's race car." When she didn't react he continued, "He was the best NASCAR driver in history."

"NAS—" Olivia shook her head. "Does that mean he's famous?"

"Well, yeah," Jack answered, hiking his hands on his hips like he'd been insulted. Then he remembered me.

"Of all the low-down dirty tricks. What's the idea of stealing my coffin—and with me in it?"

I shrugged. "I didn't want you to go off half-cocked and endanger us all. So I arranged for the dock crew to move you here—lock, stock, and coffin."

"Did it ever occur to you to ask me?" He threw up his

hands. "But what the hell? I guess slaves don't have any say-so in their own lives."

Melaphia, flanked by Reyha and Deylaud in their human forms, entered from the well-hidden door to the outside courtyard. Ignoring me, Reyha immediately went to Jack and slipped her arms around him. Another little rebellion. Jack flung an arm around Reyha, but otherwise ignored her presence.

"The captain doesn't have any slaves," Melaphia said, looking insulted. "He has those who love him."

"And those who don't," Jack finished.

His declaration stung a bit more than it should have. What had I expected? Gratitude? "Love has never been a requirement," I said. "But you *will* do as I say." Melaphia opened an armoire and came forward with a blue velvet jacket. As I held out my arms she helped me into it.

"What about it, Melaphia? Don't you get tired of taking his orders?" Jack persisted.

Melaphia paused and awarded Jack a long look. "Stop acting like a fool. I serve out of loyalty and love," she said, as though nothing else existed. She continued to adjust the jacket. To me she said, "The blue has been blessed—the offering placed."

The vial of blood . . .

"Thank you."

Olivia, having pulled on her leather and lace, moved to stand on Jack's other side. She slipped her hand into his, causing Reyha to bare her teeth. Olivia ignored the warning. "Don't be angry, Jackie. He's promised me he'll tell us what's up. That should be worth a trip across town."

"It's not the trip," Jack groused. "He *never* asks, he just does what he pleases."

"I would be pleased if you would stop acting like a petulant child. Let's go upstairs to talk." I raised a hand to indicate the way. As Olivia pulled Jack along, Reyha, feeling left out, trotted over to give me a belated morning kiss. She, at least, wasn't holding a grudge. I stroked her hair. "I missed you last night." Her usual good humor returned as though she'd forgotten any slight. We moved into the connecting passage, arm-in-arm, only to find Olivia and Jack blocking the way. They'd stopped between the first and second altar carved into the rock wall.

"What is this?" Olivia said, picking up one of the handmade dolls lined along the wooden shelf below the ever-lit candles. "I saw these last night but didn't think to ask."

Before I could reply, Melaphia plucked the doll from her hands. "It's an offering to one of the *loa*. It's been blessed by a sacrifice and shouldn't be touched by a non-believer."

Olivia glanced toward the other eleven stations along the corridor. Each contained an assortment of candles, dolls, and items of food or drink. She turned to me. "Believer in what?"

"The *hounsis canzo*," I said, knowing the words would be of no help. "*Les invisibles* spirits."

"Voodoo," Jack said, sounding amazed at my admission.

It pleased me that he knew something about it. I hoped that would make it easier to explain that his blood called out to any manifestation of Lalee's craft. "It'll make more sense later." I ushered them forward. I looked back as we reached the far end of the corridor and watched as Melaphia knelt before the altar that had been disturbed. She was beginning a chant to appease

the *loa* for Olivia's indiscretion. Just my luck she'd dese-
crated the altar for the *loa* of death. Oh, well. I would
leave the problem in Melaphia's capable hands.

Darkness had not thickened in the outside world yet
so all the curtains in the house remained drawn. Our little growing family took up positions in the parlor while
I poured blood drinks at the wet bar. Jack accepted his
in silence but I could see he was on his last bit of patience. After serving the drinks I sat in a leather arm-
chair facing the couch. Reyha sat on a pillow at my right
hand, Deylaud in a chair to my left. I chose my words
carefully.

"As you know, there's a rogue vampire in Savannah.
He's already killed Alger and several of my employees—
our friends." I nodded toward Jack to indicate his little
friend Huey. Jack nodded back but looked ready to leap
to his feet if I didn't get on with it. "What I haven't told
you is that he's one of the old, violent sires. And I believe
he's here to kill me."

Jack settled a bit but leaned forward, his drink un-
touched in his hand. "Why you? Because of the shipping?"

He was closer to the truth than he knew. I figured I
might as well take him the rest of the way. "Yes, in part.
That is what Olivia meant when she called me a legend.
I've been smuggling vampires away from their sires so
that they might live more independent lives." The rami-
fications for Jack rang so loudly in my mind that I
almost couldn't continue. Jack had a good life, a fine
life. The other offspring had been beleaguered and
threatened. The distinction obviously wasn't clear enough
to Jack, however.

"I can relate to that," he said. Then, as though to prove
he was tougher than any other offspring, he knocked

back his drink in one gulp, then belched to punctuate his contempt.

"The rogue vampire is called Reedrek, and he is my sire."

Olivia sat up straighter. "We must call for help then. I've heard of Reedrek and his bully boys."

She knew what I didn't want to tell Jack. She knew I couldn't kill my own sire. It was physically impossible for me to do so. In the wonderful world of vampires, sires could kill their offspring but not the other way round. My long-ago decision to keep Jack in the dark twisted like a fist in my gut. But what would Jack do if he knew how very vulnerable I was to Reedrek? Probably something stupid. He might even try to save me.

I hoped Olivia would just assume that Jack knew the facts of our offspring/sire relationship and not say it out loud. I also hoped my decision to trust Olivia wasn't a tragic mistake, because I was about to disclose to her one of my most guarded secrets. "I have something I can use against him," I continued. "You saw the altars in the passageway. Well, more than two hundred years ago, I met a woman named Lalee. She was a *mambo*, a voodoo priestess." My memory fell back through two centuries, tripped by the indelible image of the first time I'd seen Lalee—at midnight out among the freshly dug graves of yellow fever victims—glowing in the dark like a lantern through smoked glass. She was one of the most beautiful humans I'd ever set eyes on—fine dusky golden skin, black shimmering hair like strands of jet beads hanging to her waist. Afterward I wasn't sure if I'd found her in the graveyard or whether she'd summoned me there. Whatever the case, I'd had to come to her, speak to her, touch her.

"She knew me for what I was," I went on slowly.

"And we struck a bargain." I didn't say it was she who offered. I didn't want to admit how powerless I'd been in the face of her faith. The faith in her spirits and charms. The faith that could spin a chant to wing penitent sinners to heaven or whisper a dirge to transport the damned quickly to hell. "Jack, you're wearing a charm she made for me. A protection. But the real protection is in the gift of her blood—my mutated blood and, hopefully, yours as well, since we are blood kin."

It was too soon to explain how powerful a charm Lalee's blood in my veins might be, mainly because I hadn't had to plumb the depths and invoke its unbridled nature. I'd only used it to innoculate the offspring who wished to escape their masters. Reedrek would be the first and most powerful challenge to my borrowed magic, and possibly the last.

"I'm not sure how the magic will serve me, but I plan to test it tonight. I'm going to find Reedrek, or let him find me, and see what occurs."

There was a long silence in the room. Then Jack said, "So that's it? That's the plan? You're gonna walk up to this monster and see what he can do to ya?" He rose to his feet and headed for the bar. "That's the stupidest plan I've ever heard."

"I'm afraid I have to agree," Olivia said. "Reedrek might not be alone."

"It's the best I can do for now. Until I face him and know what I can do, I can't make a better plan." Jack stared at me, his anger clearly rising. "If Reedrek kills me, the two of you have to run. Leave Savannah by any means. As a matter of fact, you should probably leave tonight anyway."

Jack slammed his glass down on the bar, hard enough to crack the mirrored top.

"Oh, for cryin' in a bucket! I never thought I'd see the day when the biggest badass in the city would tell me to pick up my skirts and run like a girl." He glanced at Olivia. "No offense."

"None taken," she answered. "And I can't believe I'm hearing the great William Cuyler—a being idolized in England and Europe—speak in this manner."

I shook my head. "You're going to have to trust me as I trust Lalee. If there's a way to stop Reedrek, it has to come through me and indirectly through her. But mark my words, if Reedrek wins, he will come for you. And you don't want to know what he's capable of."

Images of the tortures that Reedrek's twisted mind could conjure made my skin crawl—I'd already had a taste of his cruelty. The thought of him breaking Jack's still in many ways human heart tore at me like claws. And Olivia, she of the wicked willfulness, would soon find her manner tamed. A shame on both counts. But, if I had to force Reedrek to kill me rather than take me, at least he might be put off Jack's trail. What's the fun of torturing the offspring when the sire is dead and unable to writhe in concert? Alger must have appreciated that sentiment.

"Hell, I don't even know what *I'm* capable of," Jack grumbled.

"If it's any consolation, neither do I," I admitted.

He gave me an incredulous look. "You mean you can't even tell me how to fight him?"

"I can't let you try."

"Can't, or won't?"

"A little of both, I think."

"Well, I'm not going anywhere until this is settled," Jack declared.

Olivia stood and literally moved over to Jack's side.

"Neither am I," she said. "If you leave us here and go off to face him alone, I, for one, will follow you."

"Me too," Jack added. "And after this is over, you and I are gonna have a long overdue sire-offspring talk. I'm sick of being left in the dark."

I could feel the solid intention behind the threat. I could block Jack. But Olivia?—I wasn't so sure. Better to keep them in my sight, I supposed. But having Jack and me in the same place—the same unprotected place— would be too much temptation for Reedrek to resist. After all, one of his triumphs had been to kill my first family in front of my eyes.

"You seem rather optimistic that when this is over we'll all still be here and in undamaged condition."

"Yep, my mama used to always say the boogieman you see is less scary than the one you dream about. Problem was, she lived with my old man, her own personal boogieman, until she died of a broken heart."

I rubbed my hands together. "Well, on that optimistic note, I would say we have an agreement."

Either Melaphia had been listening or she had the uncanny timing of the supernatural because she entered the room carrying a file folder.

"Before I leave, I need you to sign some things. And according to your computer, you have e-mail."

"Thank you," I said. I took the folder from her as though we were conducting business as usual. Most of the papers had to do with party preparation—the contracts for the food and drink. I signed without reading them, knowing that no one would dare cheat me. Grateful for the interruption, I left Jack and Olivia alone to lick their wounds or plot their plots while I went downstairs to my office.

I had a message from the Abductors. They reported

that they were searching three separate locations in Amsterdam and felt sure they would succeed in freeing the two trapped females. Their whereabouts had been rumored for months, and now they had solid information. Three other messages detailed the present political situation on the Continent with regard to Reedrek. A tale was circulating that my volatile sire had had a falling-out with his collective of Eastern European henchmen. Apparently there was—pardon our vampire humor—bad blood between him and a protégé named Hugo.

If I'd had more time and fewer concerns I would have investigated the European news further. As it was, I needed to deal with Reedrek in Savannah no matter what had driven him to me. And I needed to do it before the leaders of the American clans arrived for the party.

The last two e-mails were from Alger's people. One questioned whether Olivia had arrived safely and a second, which was puzzling indeed, read: "In the past, Alger forbade Olivia to contact you. Be aware she has her own agenda."

It was obvious I had to keep a close eye on her. It wouldn't be safe to leave her with Jack for any extended time. No telling what the two of them might cook up.

What's the best place to call out a rogue vampire? Where the odd and the odder gather. Where the willing and not-so-willing blood is. In Savannah that would be a suitably dark goth club called Nine.

Jack

"God*damn*!" I banged on the door with both fists. "Fuck you, William! I'm not some snot-nosed kid you can just lock up until he does his homework or cleans his room!"

"No?" I heard him say. "What is it the young people say nowadays? 'Chill out?' Why don't you do that for a while. Get some rest and I'll be back later."

"What if you don't come back later? What if you have a showdown with this Reedrek guy and he kicks your ass? What if he stakes you and sets you on fire like he did Alger? And what about Olivia? Where is she?"

There was a pause before William responded. "Melaphia's here. If I don't return before daybreak, she will unlock the chamber at sunset tomorrow night. Use the time while I'm gone to figure out how to get yourself and your coffin out of Savannah as quickly as possible. This is your opportunity to leave me and my rules behind. If you decide to have yourself shipped somewhere, avoid my docks. Reedrek evidently knows about my shipping operation. I would advise you to avoid Europe. You might try South America, or maybe—"

"Stop it! I'm not going anywhere. Let me out of here so I can go with you. Between the two of us—"

"I'm taking Olivia with me. Good-bye, Jack."

I screamed at the sound of his retreating footsteps and threw my back against the door as I sank down onto the top step of the passageway. Deylaud was covering his sensitive doggie ears with his slender, human-looking hands. There was no way out. I knew the door to the courtyard could be locked from the outside. I rubbed my temples and tried to think.

My head was spinning from everything that had happened in the hour since sunset. As if being literally uprooted, coffin and all, wasn't enough of a shock, come to find out that my sire was in danger of getting snuffed out by his own daddy dearest, that we both were tainted with some kind of wonky blood, and that he was depending on voodoo mumbo-jumbo to save the both of us. I was tempted to get the bottle of Jack Daniel's that I knew was in the bar beside the blood and spend the night on a blood-and-booze bender. But I had to keep my wits about me, such as they were.

Deylaud looked as nervous as a cat, if you'll pardon the expression. He knew his master was in danger and he loved William more than life. And he'd been left to guard me. I hated to make him feel worse, but I had to exploit every advantage I could think of to get out of this tomb. Ordinarily, he wouldn't go against William's wishes for a dozen top sirloins and a bitch in heat. But since his master needed help, maybe I could persuade him to get us out.

"Deylaud, come here." Immediately he sat down on the step beside me. I gave his shoulder a reassuring pat and looked deeply into his eyes. This set him even more on edge. You don't look an attack dog—even one in human form—in the eyes unless you want to rile him up. "You know that William is in trouble, don't you?" Deylaud looked like I'd stabbed him in the heart. A whiny little moan escaped him and his eyes welled up. He nodded.

"Don't be upset, buddy. I think I can help him. And I'd die trying, just like I know you would."

The tears fell faster than old number 3, and he wiped them away with his thumb. "I don't know a way out, Jack, honest. I can't even get Reyha to help us. I don't have any sway with her while she's on the other side of that door with Melaphia."

I looked along the passageway at all the little recesses that held the voodoo crap. I'd never much believed in it myself. Huey was the only one I ever knew to fall under its spell. But there was no telling if he was really cursed into sobriety because he was too afraid to ever drink again anyway. But William and Melaphia certainly believed. "Have you read any of those books upstairs about voodoo?" Deylaud had a photographic memory. Not only could he tell you word for word what he'd read in any book, he could tell you the page number.

"Oh, yes."

"Of all the little doodads in those little altars, can you tell me what the most important thing is?"

He rubbed his eyes with his fists, like a little boy waking from a nap. He stood up and went over to the wall where the altars were and looked them over carefully. I joined him. "It's this, I think. But I don't know that from anything I've read. I just have the sense this is important. All these things have Melaphia's scent, this one most of all, but it's more than that. It kind of . . . vibrates." He pointed to a small vial so old that the glass had turned milky. You could barely see through it, but it looked to contain some type of brown liquid. The tube itself looked hand-blown, not manufactured, and the top was sealed with black wax.

I picked it up and felt a jolt. Like when you ground out a car battery, only worse. I nearly dropped it, and Deylaud yelped. "Easy, pal. I've got it," I said.

"What are you going to do?" He was wringing his hands now. "Don't get us in any trouble."

"Don't worry, I'm not going to rat you out to William for helping me. We'll tell him I figured it out by myself."

Deylaud blanched. "Figured what out?"

"How to get Melaphia to let us out. Watch this." I took the vial and stood by the door. "Melaphia! Come here!" In a few moments I could hear two pairs of light footsteps on the carpeted floor outside. Reyha was with her.

"Forget it, Jack. I'm not letting you out," she said. "William would kill me. And besides, I'm busy with paperwork and laundry. So why don't you just cool your jets, because—"

"What's the dark stuff in this little glass vial in the last altar?"

"Don't touch that, Jack."

"Too late."

"Put it back."

"Hmm?"

"I said, put it back. You don't know what you're getting into." Melaphia was starting to get annoyed, which she almost never did.

I could hear Reyha whimper. She was sensing the usually unflappable Melaphia's displeasure.

"How much is it worth to you?" I asked.

There was a pause as if my implied threat was starting to sink in. "A defense chant has been cast. You need to stay put. I'm serious, Jack."

"So am I. Let me out, or I'm going to knock back this little potion to see for myself what it'll do."

Melaphia issued a string of obscenities that almost made me blush—and I've spent some time around longshoremen. It was enough to make Deylaud put his hands over his ears. I could hear Reyha running around in a tight little circle on the other side of the door. Finally, Melaphia took a deep breath and spoke in a calm but murderous tone. "Listen to me. If you drink a drop of what is in that vial, it will bring harm to you, me, Renee, William, Olivia—everybody. In fact, it will probably kill you."

I took my own deep breath at this. Renee, Melaphia's

eight-year-old daughter, was the apple of all our eyes. William and I didn't get to see her much because she had to go to bed early for school, but we all, the twins included, doted on her. I had hoped to see her grow up as I had seen Melaphia grow up and her mother before her. I'd bounced them all on my knee, the closest thing I'd ever have to children of my own. I stopped to think about how Melaphia's and Renee's lives might change if anything happened to William. Reedrek had already killed some of William's other human employees. Was Melaphia in danger, too?

"Then let me out so I can go and help William for all our sakes," I said.

"Do what the captain has told you to do. He knows what's best. And when it comes to that vial, *I* know what's best. What it contains is more powerful than you can imagine. It might be the key to getting rid of this evil creature. That's what William has gone to try and find out."

"What the hell is it?"

"I can't tell you that right now. William will tell you when the time is right."

"It's now or never, darlin'." Melaphia unleashed another round of cussing. As bad as the situation was, I had to laugh. She cursed my whole family up one side and down the other. "Seriously," I said when I could get a word in edgewise. "On the count of five, I'm going to drink it."

I paused for effect. "One!"

"Damn you, you ignorant cracker!"

"Two."

I heard the door handle start to rattle. "You're just dumb enough to do it, aren't you, you stubborn bastard."

By the time I could say "Yes, ma'am," the door opened. Melaphia stood there, her golden brown skin mottled with rage. I handed her the vial on my way past. "Damn you," she muttered.

"Too late."

I left her and the twins chattering at me all at once as I took the stairs two at a time.

I walked all the way from William's to the garage, as much to clear my head as to retrieve my 'Vette. I had a lot to think about. I wanted to go and rub myself on the rocks along the river like a water snake, to shed all the unwelcome feelings weighing me down. I was still spittin' mad at William for moving my coffin without asking. But at the same time I had to wrestle with the idea that he did it because he was so afraid for me.

In all the years of my existence as a vampire, I'd never known William to feel fear. Now, not only was he feeling fear, he was letting me feel it, too. *Wanted* me to feel it. That was the scary part. Us vampires, we're like your ultimate guys' guys. If you think a regular guy doesn't want to show you his emotions, you should know some of us undead types. Creatures of the night can smell fear. Literally. Smelling fear on somebody can get your predatory juices all flowing if you have the upper hand. If you're the one shedding those kind of weakness vibes, you'd better learn to run. That was what William wanted me to do: to run. And that went against every fiber of my unholy being.

Now that I was in the Corvette, I had the need for speed. I wanted to get out on the open road and floor that Stingray for all she was worth. Get some wind in my hair and bugs on the windshield. But there wasn't time for that, and you couldn't get up any decent speed passing through the Savannah squares. I had to find William. Where would he go to confront Reedrek? Hmm, if I was an ocean-hopping, offspring-murdering, extra-evil blood drinker, where would I be?

I drummed my fingers on the steering wheel. So William wanted to scare me. And I *was* scared, dammit, for the first time since the days when I was a human. Actually, that's not quite true. There was that one time I went parking by a marina with Jeannie Sue Gribble and woke up with the sun about to break over the water. I had to climb into the cargo hold of a shrimp boat with a FOR SALE sign on it. I got back home an hour after sunset the next night, hungover from spending the day outside my coffin, smelling like a half ton of rotten shrimp. William nearly killed me, not to mention Jeannie Sue.

I was ruminating about Jeannie Sue, the silkiness of her hair, the suppleness of her skin, when I heard a loud thumping noise. The whole car shook like a dogwood in a hurricane. From out of nowhere, someone had fallen into the other bucket seat, just like in one of those old rental car commercials. Somebody was ready, whether I was or not.

Once I got the car under control again (I think I jumped the curb and plowed through a couple of garden club flower beds) I looked to my right and saw my new passenger. If I'd had a working heart, it would have been pounding right then. This was the guy. This was definitely the guy.

He wore a dusty black suit and a white shirt with a string tie. Not a western-style string tie, but the kind you see guys wear in old European paintings. He had a hairdo to match the same time period, kind of mid-length and wild, swept back from a high forehead. He smelled like the grave, probably because he'd been tomb-hopping since he'd got here. He smelled of something else, too. Yeah, that was the same odor I'd smelled on the boat, that sickening, ancient but familiar reek. *Damn,* this dude was scary. It was hard to imagine him passing for human like William and I did. He was just too damn creepy. All of a sudden, there he was, grinning at me with a mouthful of yellow teeth, except for his fangs, which were gleaming white.

He knew me. The realization hit me like a ton of manure. I decided to say something, try to test the issue.

"Nice of you to drop in, Grandpa."

His eyes went dark. "How dare you speak to me with insolence, you sniveling mongrel!" He reached for my neck so fast I could barely see his hand, but as soon as it got within six inches of William's charm, a blue spark arced off of his long, filthy fingernails. His whole body drew back and, for a second there, he looked shocked. Then that predatory stare came back. He growled like he could eat me whole and pick his fangs with my bones. I was beginning to wish I'd stayed in that vault like Melaphia had advised.

"So William has learned a trick," he said. "I'm glad he has not entirely wasted his time in the New World."

"He's going to kill you," I said with as much bravado as I could muster.

He laughed a nasty, cackling laugh. "You ignorant pup. William could not kill me with an army of undead at his side. But there are ways in which I could kill William that you haven't even dreamed of. Death is not what William fears from me. When I eventually do kill him, he will beg for death's sweet release. But you know none of the ways of torture because William hasn't educated you. I taught William more in one day than he has shared with you in more than a century. You have no idea what you are capable of."

I felt my gorge rise. This guy, this *thing,* knew me all right. Knew me enough to go to the heart of my resentment of William. "How do you know what William has taught me?"

"I know everything about you, my child." His tone softened and he sheathed his fangs. "There is so much I can teach you."

"About what?"

"You ooze power, yet you do not know how to use it. I'll wager you've never even made another blood drinker."

He was fishing. I could feel it. "No, I haven't."

He looked away quickly, but not before I saw his face harden with rage. When he looked back again he'd composed himself. "My son, let me teach you what it is to be a true sanguinarian. I can show you how to hold sway over every creature in your world, mortal or immortal."

"What kind of sway?"

"You can enthrall those weaker than yourself. You'll command and they'll do your bidding."

His beady eyes twinkled and he smiled like he had a great secret to share. If what he was telling me was true, well, I had to admit it would be pretty cool. I let the idea sink in for a moment as I continued weaving down Bull Street. Then I heard a siren. Shit. Maybe my passenger would make himself scarce if I let the cops into the picture.

I pulled the Corvette to the curb and turned around (no rearview mirrors for me, remember). It was Connie. *Double shit.*

"Hello again, Mr. McShane. My, but you're getting

careless. This is twice in one week," she drawled. "Do you know how fast you were going?"

I glanced at Reedrek. He'd put on a guileless expression. Surely he'd be cool. It was me and William he wanted, not the local citizenry. Although Connie *was* important to me. What a time to realize *that*. I needed to start being one of those sensitive Alan Alda types who's always in touch with his feelings. If I got out of this mess, maybe I'd take a class or something. But the pressing matter was whether Reedrek would sense she was important to me.

"Good evening, darlin'. Aren't there enough criminals out there burgling or armed robbing to keep you busy without stopping piddling little speeders like me?"

"I'll always go out of my way for you, Jackie. And by the way, you just incriminated yourself."

"I could never lie to you anyway, baby."

She reached into her back pocket for her ticket book. "Where's the fire?"

"Uh, nowhere. I was just talking to . . . to . . . my uncle . . . Fred, here, and I kind of lost track of how fast I was going."

Reedrek looked at her sweetly, not a fang in sight. "How do you do," he said, all pleasant-like.

"Nice to meet you," Connie said.

I didn't know what to do next, but I knew I wanted to get out of there. "Go on ahead and give me that ticket, then. I'd hate to take up any more of your valuable time when there are muggers and murderers on the loose."

I gave the old bloodsucker a sideways glance. Speak of the devil . . .

"I'm not in any hurry. Where are your manners, Jackie?"

"Uncle Fred, this is Officer Consuela Jones, Savannah's finest."

They nodded at each other, and Connie said, "Don't you mean *one* of Savannah's finest?"

"I mean just what I said, sugar."

"Well, aren't you sweet?" She flipped open her ticket book and took the pen in her hand.

Reedrek spoke to her. "You don't wish to issue that citation." I stared at him. What in the Sam Hill was he doing?

Connie looked puzzled but not angry. "I don't?"

"No, you don't. Come to the passenger side of this vehicle."

I twisted toward Reedrek, ready to spring if he made any threatening move in Connie's direction. She walked calmly to his side, as if waiting for some instruction from him.

"Bend down toward me, my girl," Reedrek purred. She did. He reached up to cup her chin in his awful hand, running his fingers along the side of her cheek. He leaned upward as if to kiss her. Then I saw those awful fangs grow down and out. He was about to bite her, and she wasn't trying to get away. She was going to let him.

I reached over Reedrek and, in one swift motion, swept the charm from around my neck and dropped it over her head. I shoved Connie's shoulder, just enough to make her straighten and take a step back. I put the 'Vette back in drive and stomped the accelerator before she had time to come to her senses. "That's enough."

"Do you believe me now, young one?"

"Yeah." The implications of what I'd just seen were exploding in my head like so many multicolored fireworks. What else hadn't William taught me about vampires?

"Let us go and see William," Reedrek said.

I knew instinctively that I couldn't refuse, especially since I didn't have the charm anymore.

"Yeah," I said.

I followed Reedrek's directions until I pulled up to a dingy goth club called Nine. To say I was freaked out would be an understatement. Whatever happened when Reedrek and William came face-to-face, I didn't want to be within biting distance. Besides, I was starting to get really pissed at William again. If I let dear old Grandpa teach me the stuff he wanted to teach me, what would he want in return? William's head on a plate? I was getting to the point where I could almost consider it.

Reedrek headed for the door and I followed. Several dark figures loitered near the entrance, smoking cigarettes—young goths, all dressed in black just like . . . I stopped in my tracks as Werm came forward out of the gloom. He looked back and forth between me and my grandsire, and a rapturous look came over his ferretlike features. I knew he'd made Reedrek for a vampire. He met me a few steps from the entrance and I grabbed him by the arm. Reedrek sensed I was no longer following him and stopped.

"Get as far away from here as you can," I hissed at Werm.

"Why? What's going on?"

"You don't want to know. Now, *git*!" I shoved him away from me.

Werm's eyes widened. "Who's he?"

"Never you mind. Move your ass or I'm going to beat the shit out of you."

Werm seemed mesmerized by Reedrek. "No way."

Some badass I am. I fought the urge to slap the little

weasel. But that would have further drawn Reedrek's attention. It was best to get the blood drinker into the club, where at least Werm could fade into the crowd. Something told me he was good at that. I turned my back on Werm and marched toward the entrance with Reedrek.

God have mercy on us all.

William

The music was infernally loud. Jack's human obsession for noisy mechanical things would've been tickled by the racket. It never failed to astound me when humans purposely assaulted their ears with blaring sounds that in no way resembled music. True music came from finely tuned instruments, not electronic distortion boxes.

Jack would simply say I was old fashioned and out of it. As if I wanted to be *in* anything so annoying.

The only redeeming part was the beat—a driving, pulsating base line that pushed through the air like a pounding heart. Loud and hard. A primitive sound very near and dear to my own impulses. And to Olivia's. She'd taken to the dance floor like a fish to water, swirling and swimming among the pierced and pale mortals like a shark sizing up a school of tattooed mullet.

I kept my back to the wall. The mortals, doing their best to look scary in their own right, gave me a wide berth. Good for them. Their innate sense of danger served them well. I was in no mood to mix with humans. I had other, more pressing matters on my mind. I could feel Jack's sense of betrayal and his anger like a sharp ache. But I refused to feel guilty for protecting him. I'd become accustomed to his anger, although there were times I wished I could gain his friendship, if not outright love. At least I'd been able to depend on his loyalty. Locking him up would severely test that loyalty, but it could not be helped.

A human touch on my arm pulled me from my dismal thoughts. A pretty blonde with amber eyes gazed up at me—as if she was a night creature and I was her moon. As though she'd been caught spying, she quickly looked away. Although I'd never seen her face, I recognized her immediately. The smell of her blood was familiar to me. She'd been my dinner of nights past.

I grasped her chin and forced her eyes to meet mine, searching for any conscious remembrance of me. There was nothing. Just the animal recognition—body to body. Her skin, muscle, and bone had retained the sensory memory of pleasure, and she had found the giver—me—in this room full of people.

"Hello . . ." She looked down again but her hand moved along the velvet softness of my jacket. "My name is Shari."

"Hello, Shari," I answered.

At the sound of my voice she stepped in closer until our clothes were touching. She raised her chin and whispered into my ear. "Will you dance with me?"

Any normal human would not have been able to hear her. I heard not only the words but the longing in them that even she didn't fathom.

"No," I said, although I allowed her to lean against my chest. As though her body had turned to water, she slid downward. I clasped her with one arm and held her next to me before she fell to her knees. Then I gazed into her eyes again. "You don't know me."

"I want to," she said slowly.

In spite of the loud music, I could hear the beat of her heart and feel it pumping as though we were back in Eleanor's secret room, skin to skin. I lowered my face and smelled the hair that spilled over her collar, hiding my favorite spot on her neck. For a few seconds I wasn't sure who had bewitched whom, because my hunger rose like the head of a cobra sensing prey.

Not here, not now.

To divert my greedy thoughts, I concentrated on a group of three men and one woman watching our little tête-à-tête. Two of the men were nodding with lecherous, knowing smiles. How would Jack put it? They thought I was about to score.

Little did they know I was thinking more of lunch. The thought nearly brought a smile to my face.

"Some other time," I promised, recovering my control.

"Let me stay." She sighed and slipped her arms about my waist, nuzzling my neck, snuggling closer. Her sweet sexual arousal billowed around me like an earthy perfume.

I had to send her away, but not without reward. I bent over her and captured the edge of her ear with my teeth. With a whimper, she went still like every good little swan, waiting breathlessly for the bite. I increased the pressure without breaking the skin and her well-trained body spasmed into an orgasm, coming swift and hard. I held her securely as she curled toward me, moaning into the front of my jacket. No blood, just a little discreet pain and then pleasure.

Feeling pleased with myself, I looked up in time to see Jack—he who should've been behind locked doors—walk through the entrance of the club. I felt his fear like a knife in the dark. Then in an instant Reedrek was standing next to him.

In the space of a single heartbeat, Reedrek crossed the room and loomed in front of me, close enough to touch. I pushed my little human swan away so suddenly that she stumbled into the arms of the nearest clubgoer. Then I drew my speechless hatred about me like a cloak. The human world receded, leaving us in our own supernatural dimension. Even the music hushed.

Reedrek looked well pleased with himself as always. A few hundred years had not softened his manner—nor my hatred toward him. The air around us crackled with malice and enmity. Thanks to the magic of Lalee's shells, my sire's appearance didn't shock me as it might have. I'd seen him with Alger. I'd known he was coming.

"You look old," I said, just to annoy him. Inside I was rapidly barring the doors to my mind, shoring up every defense. *You will not take me.*

"I *am* old," he admitted. His nasty smile bared long fangs polished by a millennium of blood. He looked out over the crowded club, which appeared to be moving in slow motion. "So this is the pinnacle of society in this backwater town. I made you for better things than this."

"They do well enough." I wasn't about to debate the merits of Savannah with him. I would much rather teach him to hate and fear it, since his absence would improve the city immeasurably. He'd taken my true life and everything I'd loved, and the tomblike smell of him made my skin crawl. "What do you want?"

I could feel him searching for fear, for weakness. "You've been a detestable disappointment thus far," he said. "It's time you fulfilled your potential."

I decided to remain deliberately obtuse. "My potential?"

"Yes. You could be king of your own empire here, and yet you do nothing."

"Ah, and I suppose the disappointment lies in the fact that I haven't made you stronger through our blood ties."

A roiling cloud of anger darkened his expression. "It's true; in doing nothing to further your own power, you've contributed even less to mine. But that is about to change."

I cocked my head like a fascinated student and let him continue.

"You will feed tonight and every night. I've come to make certain of it. And I've come to put an end to your little underground escape venture." He paused for effect, I suppose. "Or I'll rip out your heart and stake you to a tree in the center of one of these lovely squares you seem so fond of."

Death or submission—those were my choices. No great surprise there. Unfortunately, in the world of dominance and submission I was what would be called a natural top. Dominant in every way. Submissiveness went against my nature. A true son of my "father." And death—death was my fondest fantasy. Time to find out what other hells awaited me.

"Why did you kill Alger?" I ventured, leading him into what I hoped would be at least an intellectual trap.

A slight hesitation gave evidence of the lie to come. I wondered at my ability to see it. "I killed him because he was a failure, a coward, and a disgrace to his lineage."

"And you had no grand plans for him?" I persisted.

"No. He was supremely unworthy."

"Are there no others you have killed?"

"Only Alger—he had to be extinguished."

I let his insults pass. There would be time to avenge Alger later. I moved in for the check. "What of Lyone?"

Reedrek leaned back as though he'd been shoved.

I'd surprised him—a feat I hadn't thought possible. I used that success to spin my own half truth for, as Jack might say, the hell of it. "You'll be happy to know he's been located. A polar expedition has been mounted to free him." I savored the final blow. "Frederica and Gaelan have been released and moved out of Amsterdam as well."

There, I'd truly stunned him, and he let it show.

"How did you—"

The tight lid I kept on my fury rattled inside me as I drew myself into my finest killing posture. A human would have been struck dead by the sight of my pure intent. I felt my feet leave the floor as I rose into the air. Reedrek took a half step away from me.

"You were there. I felt it. How could you have been there?" he asked, unbelieving of his own senses.

"Do you imagine I will tell you any of my comings or goings? Have you discovered yet that you don't own me, that you never did?" I waited for the leap, the fatal blow.

"No. But I made you and I can end you." He rose to face me, his hair floating upward like a nest of writhing snakes. His clawed hand shot forward but stopped just millimeters from my neck. The air disturbed by his sudden movement caressed my skin, but the blow did not land.

He smiled and I knew I'd somehow made a mistake. Instead of stepping into me, however, he turned. The blurred world of humans came back into sudden focus, and Jack's face stood out most prominently.

It was clear to me that he intended to kill Jack; but first he would use him to make me obey. Reedrek reached into the lingering crowd and dragged my little swan Shari to his chest. With his pointed glare trained on me, he bit into her neck like a savage. Blood splattered the front of my jacket and she whimpered in surprise before Reedrek silenced her with his poisonous mind.

I'm not completely sure what happened next. My vision blurred and a bloodred mist began to rise out of me. Then with the sound of a gunshot, the fury I'd kept inside for so long exploded outward like a sonic boom, trailed by the red mist. Immediately the human crowd around us changed. Half the mortal occupants of the club seemed to fall on one another with fists and chairs— punches were thrown, tables overturned. A hand gripped my arm and I focused on Olivia's face, her pale skin splattered with tiny drops of blood. She drew me down until my feet once again were solid on the floor.

"Where's Reedrek?" she shouted over the noise.

Only then did I notice that Reedrek had disappeared with Shari. It was too much to hope the ground had opened up and he'd fallen into hell. "Where's Jack?" I said.

A chair sailed toward us and Olivia pushed it away. Bodies were tumbling, and at the center of the largest pile stood Jack, one hand keeping the fists at bay and the other dangling a pale, skinny human arrayed in black leather. The anger rolled and reverberated through the crowd like waves of booming sound.

"Do something!" Olivia shouted.

Fury was my consort. I was constantly drawn to it and repulsed by it at the same time. In this case, my own pent-up anger seemed intent on the destruction of this place and every human inside it.

So I took it back.

I tore open my shirt, shoved it, and the lapels of my

blessed blue protection aside and called to my constant companion, my life force. Faster than a human eye could detect, the destructive mist gathered into a spinning spiral as it was sucked back into my heart, my well of hate.

Perfect silence followed the tornadolike roar.

I looked down at the sheen of blood on my chest as the last of it slowly disappeared through my skin. I heard Olivia's voice as if from a distance. "I'm going after him."

When I looked up, the entire room seemed to be staring at me and I realized that Olivia had vanished as well.

Six

Jack

I dropped Werm and went to William. "Where did Olivia go?"

"I didn't see. She said she was going after Reedrek." William leveled on me a gaze so full of anger that I took at step back.

"Let's go. We've got to find her," he said.

He made for the door and I followed him. By that time, Werm had caught up with me.

"What the hell just happened?" He was about to shake out of his shoes. He reminded me of one of those nervous little dogs, a Chihuahua. I expected him to start peeing on people's feet at any second.

"Never you mind. Just go back into the club and forget what you saw."

Werm lowered his voice. "You've got to be kidding me. That was some serious undead special effects in there. I can't forget that! I've got to know more."

"Not now."

"Aren't you at least going to introduce me to your friend?" he asked.

"No."

"Come on."

"Get lost."

When we got outside, William stopped and swore viciously. "He's taken the mayor's SUV."

"Damn. Not another one." In addition to being one scary sonofabitch, dear old Granddad was a prodigious car thief. If I was of a mind to open a chop shop, we could start a family business. "The Corvette's over there," I told William.

"Can I go?"

I wheeled on Werm, incredulous that he was still following us. What good is being a vampire if you can't even scare away a five-and-a-half-foot pissant? "What part of 'get lost' did you not get? I'm *busy* here."

"I—I felt a force in there."

"Yeah, well you're about to feel the force of my foot in your ass."

"Seriously, Jack, I've just got to know what's going on."

"No, Werm, you just don't."

William was in the passenger seat by this time. I jumped into the driver's seat and cranked the engine.

"Let me go with you."

"Do you see an empty seat here?"

Werm clasped the top sides of the car in a death grip. This was insane. I was tempted to drain him right there.

"Get rid of him, Jack," William said.

I looked at Werm and could tell by the thin, tight line of his mouth that he wasn't going to budge. He'd found himself a real, live vampire, by crackey, and he was hanging on like a leech. About then I remembered what Reedrek had done to Connie. How did he do it? In desperation (I hated it when people embarrassed me in front of William) I looked deeply into Werm's eyes and concentrated as hard as I could. "You want to go away now."

His mouth twitched and he blinked a couple of times. "I do?"

"Yes. Go back into the club and hang out with your friends."

Without another word, or the worn-out explanation that he didn't have any friends, he took a couple of halting steps backward, then made a robotic turn toward the building and walked away.

"Well, I'll be a . . ." I muttered to myself. I put the 'Vette in reverse and backed out of the parking space, but not before catching William's expression in the corner of my eye.

"What else did he teach you?" The iciness in his voice could have frozen the balls off a brass monkey.

I bristled immediately. "Where do you get off using that tone with me? At least he was willing to teach me something about what I'm capable of, which is more than I can say for you, *Dad*!" I only called William that when I *really* wanted to piss him off. I think if I wasn't driving, he would have slugged me.

"Everything I've ever told you and everything I've ever *not* told you over the past century and a half has been for your own good. I hope I live long enough to see you realize that."

"You lay a guilt trip on me and expect me to be grateful to you for manipulating me? For keeping me in the dark? Even for locking me up tonight, for cripes sake? Are you out of your evil freakin' mind? Maybe I *ought* to break ties with you and go with this Reedrek guy."

William grabbed the steering wheel, and I swore and stomped the brakes to the floor but not before I ran over the nearest curb. It's a good thing I do killer front-end alignments.

He let go of the steering wheel and gripped me by the neck. "Don't say that. Don't *ever* say that. You have no idea—"

"That's right! I have no idea! No clue what this guy is about, what he's come for, or anything else that's going on because you won't tell me. Give me one good reason why I shouldn't let him teach me everything you won't."

William sat back wearily. "Jack, you've trusted me all these decades, and you've stayed safe and done quite well for yourself. I only ask that you continue to trust me. I have every expectation that before too much longer, you're going to know everything there is to know."

We stared at each other for a moment. I owed him everything I had. If it weren't for him, I'd be pushing up daisies at the foot of a cold marble cross in some Confederate cemetery who knew where. I sighed. "All right, but you'd better spill before too long."

William stared at the place where he'd released my neck. "Jack, where's Lalee's charm?"

"I gave it away."

"You what?"

I backed the Stingray off of the curb—changing directions and changing the subject. "Where are we going, anyway?"

"We have to find Olivia. Drive to Colonial Cemetery."

"What makes you think she's there?"

"I have no idea where she is, but if she's following Reedrek, perhaps he's leading her to his resting place. And you didn't answer my question. Why did you give the charm away? And how did you get out of my vault?"

"Holy hell." It was going to be a long night. "I broke the door down."

"No, you didn't."

"I'm not telling you how I got out of the vault in case you ever lock me in again. As for the charm, I gave it to Connie." I told him about Reedrek dropping into my car, how the charm worked, and about Connie stopping us.

"So you used influence on that youth after seeing it demonstrated only once." William's eyes lit with interest. "Very impressive. I think we may have discovered another of your many talents, Jack."

"That's what it's called? Influence?"

"The ability to 'dance in the mind' of humans and other weaker creatures vulnerable to our powers. It usually takes years for a vampire to master. Some are completely incapable of learning the skill. And yet you did it on your first try."

I bit my lip to keep from screaming. "I could've been going around all this time making people do what I tell them to do just by thinking about it real hard. And you didn't tell me about it. Great. That's just great."

"You've always been able to charm people, Jack, just by using your amiable personality."

"I guess it runs in the family. So what are my other talents?"

William ignored the jab and answered my question with a question. "What else did Reedrek tell you?"

"Nothing. But he *promised* to tell me everything."

"I'm sure he didn't inform you of what he wanted in return. My head, perhaps? Or Olivia's? I understand why you gave that charm to Officer Jones, but you shouldn't have. Now she's more vulnerable than ever because he knows you care for her." William gave me a calculating glance and I shrugged. "That's why he took my little swan; he could smell my touch on her. That's the problem with making connections, especially human ones. Rogue vampires kill family . . ." He paused as though he'd said too much, then continued, "You must get the charm back."

"How can I do that? You just told me that Connie is in danger from him now. Besides, he was in the car with me, as close as you are. He could've killed me anytime he wanted." But then I remembered he might have tried when he almost grabbed me. Before the charm had stopped him.

"He made his intentions clear during our little confrontation. He's more likely to go after you to get to me than he is to go after Consuela to get to you. I've told you, we're the ones he wants. Just get it back."

I stared straight ahead.

"Jack? Give me your word!"

"Okay. Okay." Of course, I had no intention of getting it back. But I did need to talk to Connie as soon as possible to convince her to wear it. When she came to her senses and found that nasty-ass thing around her neck, she'd probably toss it in the nearest Dumpster.

By that time we were at Colonial Cemetery. We vaulted the fence and did a quick sweep, arguing the whole time about the relative merits of voodoo and why it wasn't important that I know the whole story of the charms. There were no other vampires in the cemetery. If there had been, we probably would've scared 'em off with our bickering. "Where now?" I asked when we got back to the car.

"Bonaventure," William said.

We jumped into the car and headed toward my own backyard. "What do you think he's going to do with Shari?"

"I feel sure we'll find her in much the same condition as your friend Huey."

"What about Olivia? What if he catches her?"

As if I didn't already suspect how much trouble Olivia was in, he then said something I never thought I'd ever hear from him.

"Step on it."

William

Bonaventure turned out to be a dead end in more ways than one. Jack and I paced down each avenue but Reedrek's scent was diffused. He'd been there, no doubt, and might return, but I couldn't feel his presence.

We did find my Jag, however. It was parked on the grass at the easternmost boundary where the venerable old cemetery gave way to river marsh. It would have been the perfect place to watch the sun come up. Jack checked inside for the keys while I tested the air for a trap.

"No keys, but I can hot-wire it. I'll need the tools in my 'Vette."

I watched Jack walk away in the darkness, then turned to gaze at the water. The moon had risen and was flying, almost full. I studied the wavering reflection in the water among the saw grass and did my best to reach out without the aid of Lalee's shells.

Other beings heard my call and, out of curiosity, I suppose, floated toward me. Faded faces, bloodless shapes tired of being abandoned under cold stone or abiding in tombs. They gathered in small knots near statues of angels and hovered among the swaying beards of moss in the trees. I ignored them—let them have their fun.

Come home, Olivia. Come back to us. We are stronger together.

I did not sense her here, but I hoped she would feel my call on the breeze. But instead of Olivia, it was Jack who returned in his rumbling car and set to work on the Jag. In less than two minutes he had it purring.

He opened the door for me to get in. "It stinks like the old man but there's no damage that I can see."

When I touched the door, I had a sudden vision of little Shari. "Open the trunk, Jack."

He looked at me as if I was joking. "I'll have to punch out the lock—in case you didn't notice, we don't have any keys."

"Open it."

Grumbling, Jack retrieved a crowbar from his car and placed the end of it against the lock. "It's a damn shame to vandalize a fancy ride like this," he said as he hit the bar. The lock popped inward and the trunk opened partway. Jack shoved it up. "Now what exactly—" He stopped when he saw the body. "I'll be damned." He dropped the crowbar and gently rolled her over.

Her skin looked so pale under the moonlight it seemed like milky glass. Blood was still seeping from the wounds in her neck, yet she had what could only be called a look of contented bliss. At least she hadn't died screaming.

"Hey," Jack said, pressing a hand to her neck. "She's still alive."

It was then that the true horror hit me. Reedrek had sworn to make me feed, he'd sworn to force me to increase my power and in turn his. I could only do that to any significant degree by making more of our kind. I could either allow Shari to die, or I could make her.

"Put her in the passenger seat," I ordered and got in the car. It was better if I didn't touch her, less dangerous. But the smell of her blood seemed to swim around my head.

I stripped off my blue velvet jacket. When Jack returned I thrust it at him.

"I want you to wear this jacket at all times. It gives us a slight advantage with Reedrek, probably temporary, and it's not as strong as Lalee's charm, but it's better than nothing."

He rebelled, of course. "You expect me to go around Savannah looking like a fugitive from the gay pride parade? No way is that happening. Or in vampire-speak—not on your immortal life." He put his hands behind his back like a child refusing to eat his vegetables.

"Jack—"

"You can't make me."

I really didn't have time for this. As usual, he knew how to pluck the strings of my anger. In order to get through Jack's pigheadedness I had to resort to threats. "Do you think I cannot?"

He looked at me steadily for a long moment. "You might just have to go ahead and kick my ass, then. Get it out of your system."

Bloody hell! Without the calming effect of the jacket and on the heels of the night I'd already had, I could feel my blood rage rising. As my feet left the ground I grasped Jack by the throat and brought him up with me, pushing him against one of the massive oak trees sprouted from the moldering dead.

Jack looked too stunned to fight. I'd never touched him in anger before and didn't wish to now. But I had no choice. His eyes bugged out slightly at the sight of blood oozing out like sweat, soaking my shirt.

"How does the jacket work?" he hissed through his trapped throat.

"It's been blessed," I said, holding my anger somewhat in check. I knew Jack well enough to know he wouldn't simply acquiesce. He had to come to his own decision. "Voodoo blue—the color of the sky, the color of your damnable stubborn eyes. It's to keep evil from passing over a threshold. As your sire, I order you to wear it until you retrieve Lalee's charm."

Fluttering like a banner on the breeze, the ghostly face of a young woman materialized next to the heavily mossed limb of the oak. She looked from me to Jack, then smiled her eagerness to see what would happen next. Jack kicked his feet against the solid mass of the tree, searching for the ground.

"I can hold you here for what little remains of the night. And all the while, your Consuela will be in danger, along with Olivia—" I angled my head toward the Jag. "—and that dying girl. We'll just stay here until you get over your fashion snit."

"All right," he said in a strangled voice. "Let go of me. I'll wear the freakin' thing."

"As you wish," I said, and released my hold on him. I heard a colorful curse as he hit the ground. Ghostly laughter echoed around us like the clacking of dead branches in a cold wind.

I tossed the jacket to him and waited until he put it on before leaving. I'd done all I could for my reluctant ally. Now I had to attend to Shari—either ease her death by taking the last dregs of her lifeblood or perform the ritual to make her a blood drinker. *My* blood drinker.

Jack

I didn't need a watch to know the sun was about to come up. I was getting tingly all over. And not in a good way. I'd been pacing in Connie's hallway for half an hour. I'd forgotten that since she was on the night shift, she wouldn't get off work until seven A.M. Right around sunrise. Good thing her apartment came off an interior hallway, or I'd be a crispy critter any minute.

Just as I was about to give up and beat it back down the hallway to make it home before I was toast, Connie came around the corner, still in her cop's uniform. The charm was no longer around her neck. Oh, Lord.

"Do you have some blue suede shoes to go with that?" She pointed to my jacket with the index finger of the hand that held her door key.

I looked down at the damned blue velvet jacket. "I lost a bet, so I have to wear it until Halloween," I blurted.

"Hmm. You must be going as the ghost of Elvis. Where'd the blood come from?"

I brushed at one of the bigger splotches. "Uh, I agreed to wear the jacket, but I had to kick the guy's ass first, just on general principles."

"That's not very sportsmanlike. You lost fair and square, didn't you?"

"Yeah, well, it's a long story. Hey, can I come in for a minute? There's something I have to talk to you about."

"Sure." She unlocked the door and I followed her in. "Have a seat. Want some coffee or anything?"

"No, I'm fine." I'd never been in her apartment before. The only place we ever hung out, if you could call it that, was in the garage and usually with at least a couple of the regulars present. Not what you'd call romantic. It felt strange being alone with her in her place. Good, but strange. Her decorating style was more feminine than I'd expected. She had a few nice antique pieces that didn't match exactly but still managed to look right together. Everything was neat and tidy, though, just like I'd imagined it would be. I'd mostly imagined her bedroom to tell you the truth (bloodred satin in my fondest dreams) but I couldn't see it from here.

I was too nervous to sit down, so she didn't either. While I was waiting for her to arrive, I'd tried to think of something to tell her about that damned charm, but everything I'd come up with sounded incredibly lame. "Do you still have that necklace I gave you?"

"You mean this?" She put her purse down on a pedestal table and opened it. She fished out the gnarly thing and held it out to me. "Um, are those what I think they are?" She pointed to two chickens' feet strung next to some seed beads on the ancient-looking leather thong.

"Yuh-huh," I said. What could I say? Chickens' feet are chickens' feet.

"You know, I hate to sound ungrateful, but it just doesn't match anything in my wardrobe. Do you want it back?"

"No. I want you to keep it. In fact, I want you to wear it." If this mess wasn't so serious, I would have doubled over laughing at her expression. As it was, I felt like an idiot. "I want you to wear it all the time."

She gave me a long, incredulous look. "So does this mean we're going steady?"

I smiled at her hopefully. "Want to?"

"Be straight with me, Jack. I didn't just fall off the turnip truck. This is a *gris-gris*. I wouldn't have thought you believed in black magic. What's going on here, and why do you think I need to wear a voodoo charm?"

Well, there went the medical experiment cover story, the make-believe niece's college anthropology assignment cover story, and every other cover story I'd thought up while I was waiting. All that was left was the truth. Or something close to it. I took a deep breath. "Do you remember my uncle Fred?"

"From this afternoon? The one who was flirting with me?"

Is that what she'd thought he was doing? Boy, he'd really done a number on her. "Mmm, yeah. Well, he's kind of a bad dude."

"Bad in what way?" Her eyes narrowed. All of a sudden she was a cop again.

"You see, he believes in all that black magic stuff, and we're not on very good terms right now. There's sort of a family feud going on."

"That's why you seemed so tense earlier." She nodded slowly.

"Yeah, that's right." She was sensitive to my moods, and I realized how much that pleased me. I stood up a little straighter. "Anyway, I don't really believe in that voodoo hoodoo, but I try to keep an open mind, you know?"

"Hmm," she said, an unreadable expression on her face.

"So I want you to wear it."

"But it's you he's feuding with. Not me."

"Yes, but . . . he thinks I've . . . got the hots for you." I looked away from her, feeling the "hots" rise to my face. When my gaze fell on the shuttered window, I realized it wasn't just from embarrassment. Razorlike beams of sunlight were oozing between the slats. I stepped back toward the door. As long as the beams didn't actually reach me, I should be all right. "Does this apartment building have a basement?"

Now Connie was looking at me like I was an escapee from the state mental hospital in Milledgeville. "It has a cellar." She took a step closer to me as I backed toward the door. "Three questions for you now, Jack. First, why does your uncle think you have the hots for me? Second, what does that have to do with the charm?" She put her hands on my shoulders. "And last but not least, *do* you have the hots for me?"

By this time, my back was against the door, and the sunbeams were sliding my way. To hell with them. I slipped my arms around her waist. "Answer to the first question—I guess it's obvious. Answer to the second— I'll tell you in a minute. Answer to the third—" I pulled her to me and kissed her. Her lips were soft and tasted like strawberries. I pressed her firm, vibrant body against my cold, undead one and bathed in her living, breathing warmth. She hugged me back, molding me to her until, if it wasn't for the hardness straining my jeans, I wouldn't have known where she left off and I began.

I broke off the kiss, dragging my mouth away from hers, feeling like I'd been drugged. Damned sunbeams. "Answer to the second question—he's a mean son-ofabitch, that Uncle Fred. Now that he knows that I . . . have the hots for you . . . he may try to hurt you just to get to me. If you see him again, run the other way. And *please* wear the charm. I know it sounds silly. But do it for me. Promise me, Connie." I took her hand and brought it to my lips. I could feel the pulse in her thumb beating right beneath my fangs. I fought the urge to nip her there, to get myself just a taste for the road.

"That's so sweet," she whispered. "But it's not regulation."

"Wear it under your uniform," I said.

"Those chicken claws look awfully scratchy."

"I'm not kidding." I looked deeply into her cola-colored eyes. "Promise?"

She cocked her head to one side. "I promise."

I put my hands on her hips and pushed her away gently. "I've got to go now."

"Wait a minute. You're going to declare your undying . . . hots . . . for me and then just walk away? Just like that? No 'I'll call you sometime' or 'Want to go out for dinner and a movie?' "

"Yes, all of that stuff." Hey, this was working out pretty good. Alan Alda had nothing on me. "But I've got to get this situation with Uncle Fred worked out before something bad happens."

"Something I'd have to arrest him for?"

I closed my eyes against the image of the kind of havoc a rampaging vampire with Reedrek's strength could do inside the closed space of a police station. "I pray it doesn't come to that."

Connie looked at me for a long moment. "I want you to know something. I never would have let you kiss me just now if I hadn't sensed that you were being honest with me. But I also know you're still holding back. As soon as this trouble with your family blows over, if you really do want to get close to me, you're going to have to tell me everything. And I know that you know exactly what I'm talking about." Her delicate dark brows arched toward each other in a way that told me she meant every word.

I swallowed hard. "It's a deal," I said, and hoped she didn't also sense that I had my fingers crossed behind my back. "I'll talk to you soon." I'd turned to go when I felt her hand on my sleeve.

"Wait," she said. She moved to the corner of the room, to a little shrine I hadn't noticed before. I started to follow Connie and then shrank back. A cross was nailed high on the wall over a sconce that held a statue of the Virgin Mary, a rosary, and a few other small items.

"If I'm going to be wearing the charm, I want you to have this for protection. One of the sisters took a trip to the Holy Land and got this vial of water from the Jordan River. She then had it blessed by a bishop that she met on the trip. For protective properties, I'll put my holy water up against your voodoo charms any day of the week."

She held it out to me. As far as I knew, holy water didn't hold any special powers over me. I was convinced that the lore about holy water and vampires not mixing well was just the stuff of Dracula movies.

I took it. And it immediately turned hot.

She didn't seem to notice as I passed it quickly from hand to hand, afraid it would start boiling any second. "Gee, thanks," I said. What the hell was I going to do now? I looked down, remembered the jacket, and popped the little vial in the pocket before it blew like Old Faithful. I patted the pocket, as if for security's sake, and immediately felt that it had cooled. *Well, I'll be a suck-egg mule.* It worked. They *both* worked. The holy water against evil entities (yours truly), and William's voodoo blue jacket.

I planted a kiss on Connie's forehead and she gave me a smile that weakened my knees. "I'll call you," I said, and backed out of the apartment, closing the door behind me. I headed toward the door to the stairs humming the tune to "Blue Suede Shoes" and wondered if Elvis's eyes were as blue as mine.

Seven

William

Limp in my arms, Shari seemed to weigh no more than a winter woolen topcoat. There was very little warmth left in her, very little life. If I tossed her in the air I wouldn't have been surprised to see her float away—a loose flag in the wind. I had to do something soon or her spirit would very quickly follow the direction of my thoughts.

Would it be punishment or paradise I offered? Did my sweet swan want to become a giver of pain rather than the grateful recipient? I would have to revive her to find out. It was possible the choice had already been taken out of my hands, although I was sure Reedrek knew what he was about when he'd brought her to the brink of death. After all, he'd proven to be a master at changing fates.

Deylaud opened the garage door and held it for me to enter the house. "You found your car," he said. Then he sniffed. "It smells like death. Is this one dead?"

Reyha, seeing yet another female in my arms, flounced out of the room, only to return with Melaphia close behind her. Everyone looked unhappy to find one more stranger in the house.

"She's not dead yet. Did Tarney deliver a coffin for Olivia?" I asked as I headed past them toward the back of the house. Close to the stairs and my own sleeping place.

"Yes," Melaphia answered. "It's in place with the others." She followed me down the hall.

"Has Olivia returned?" I asked.

"No, Captain. Neither has Jack."

I hoped I knew where Jack was. All I could afford to do was hope, since I literally had a life balanced in my embrace.

"Draw a warm bath and help me get her out of these clothes."

As I lowered Shari into the bath, her eyelids fluttered. As the warmth returned to her body she sighed and slipped away again. Keeping her face out of the water, I carefully rinsed the blood from her skin and hair, paying special attention to the ragged puncture marks in her neck. She'd been used ill, and not only by Reedrek. My fingers traced the long scratch—made by my own hand—that marred her breast.

"I'm sorry about Jack," Melaphia said from behind me. "He—"

I held up a hand to stop her. "I know. I left you as a safeguard, not as a jailer. Next time I'll seal him in his racing coffin and be done with it."

"As you say," she said. "But I've already worked up an *abide* chant that would make a man on fire sit still."

The comment wasn't lost on me. One might easily offend a backyard dabbler in the occult, but it didn't do to make voodoo royalty mad.

I moved on to the problem at hand. "Shari?" I whispered close to her ear. She moaned and tried to turn her head in my direction but I held her still. "Shari, open your eyes." Her eyelids fluttered but the tiny drops of water in her lashes seemed to weigh them down. I shook her slightly and put more force in my words. "Look at me."

Ever obedient, she gazed up at me, blinking once to clear her vision. Her pretty amber eyes were pale, the color faded. Instead of normal white, her left cornea floated in brilliant red blood, courtesy of a broken vein. From the struggle with Reedrek, no doubt. My hunger stirred.

"Please save me. He said you would save me."

Anger, my ever-present partner, reared up in me. Reedrek had set me up well and fully—teaching the girl to plead for her life in my name. "Do you wish to give up the light forever and live like me, in the dark?" I asked.

"I want to stay with you." She arched her back upward, pushing her breasts out of the water—to tempt me, I suppose.

"Do you know what I am?"

She relaxed back into the water. Confusion crossed her face. "What do you mean?"

I bent closer so there would be no doubt; then I bared my fangs.

"No!" she struggled weakly. "Don't let him hurt me!"

So she remembered Reedrek's evil after all. I composed myself and made the offer. "If you become one of us, I'll do my best to protect you." Even as I said the words I knew she would be better protected by remaining human and taking her chances with death. The process of making her a vampire might kill her anyway, since the odds were against female making. I forced her to look into my eyes. "Do you want me to let you go, to leave you in peace?" I hoped she would say yes.

"I want to be with you," she said, her voice fading. Her eyes closed. She was slipping away again.

Damn.

"I'll need a blanket now," I said to Melaphia. "Then a preparation table and candles for the ceremony. As soon as Jack returns we'll begin."

To thwart Reedrek, I'd decided to let Jack make Shari. Were I to make her, then Reedrek, as my sire, would benefit—and that irked me to my angry black heart. If the girl survived, Jack would receive the lion's share of the power. My share would be of a lesser degree. There would be little left over for Reedrek.

Melaphia returned with a blanket and I lifted Shari once more—wrapping her against the cool air.

"Come with me," I said to Reyha and Deylaud. I took Shari to the closest bedroom, waited for Rehya to pull back the bed covers, then placed my unconscious swan on the sheets. "Get in and keep her warm," I ordered, holding up the covers so Reyha and Deylaud could lie close to her.

Then we waited.

And waited.

An hour later Melaphia moved into the parlor. "The sun is rising," she said as she began systematically closing the heavy second set of curtains that hung from each window.

I had already felt the itch of it on my skin, the weight of the sun pressing down. Melaphia approached and stood in front of me, her hands folded. She didn't speak the question on both our minds. *Where the hell was Jack?* Had Reedrek been waiting for him? Had Jack just dawdled the time away instead of doing what I'd asked of him? Having used up my meager portion of perseverance, I walked into the bedroom where I'd left Shari.

Rehya and Deylaud remained curled next to her, but now they were in dog form. Without moving, Rehya's gaze followed my progress as I tested Shari's pulse. Weak but still there.

I pulled back the covers and carefully scooped her into my arms. Then I carried her down into the vault, past the flickering altar candles, past the table where she would be killed only to eventually be called back to life. Melaphia arrived and opened the black-and-chrome coffin meant for Olivia. She fluffed the pillow and I placed Shari on the cushions.

I patted the cushion next to Shari. Reyha leaped into the coffin and curled up next to our fading swan. "Deylaud, with me." If Jack couldn't return on his own, then I would go and find him. Reyha whined once as we left the room.

Have I mentioned that Savannah is my city? I know it better than my own veins. I've tasted and tested every dark corner, every secret. Many people don't realize that the older part of the city is basically a second incarnation built on top of the original streets and alleys. You see, the river that brought prosperity to the city turned traitor at times, flooding the streets, taking lives and ruining commerce. Spoiled goods meant lost money. So the enterprising merchants built a wall—a bluff, they called it—from the stone brought in on ships as ballast. A wall so high that come flood or hurricane, the river would never again threaten the heart of Savannah. When they reached a proper height, they hauled in river sand and filled in behind it, raising the level of the city by twenty feet in some places. Then they simply built a new city. Even now you can look into a few of the storm drains and see abandoned machinery or cobblestone streets from bygone days. Pirates took advantage of the secret spaces left behind, digging new burrows to hide contraband to be loaded later in private.

I've walked the streets—now more like tunnels—of the city below. I maintain a door to underground Savannah in my cellar. It's the only way for a night dweller to safely move around the city during daylight.

Yet darkness is not the only thing to be found in the city below. Through the years since piracy failed there have been others who've found uses for shadows and secrecy. Let me just say that the homeless who huddle inside the known openings to fresh air are the least of the dangers. There are tunnels so close to Colonial Cemetery that occasionally one might have to step over a moldering thigh bone or face an empty skull grinning from the crumbling wall. Or one might meet the restless ones who won't accept their fate and refuse to stay in their graves. There are sounds human ears aren't meant to hear. Faces like my own hidden by darkness that humans are better off avoiding.

The true length and breadth of the tunnels was another secret I'd kept from Jack. The havoc he caused on the surface with his thundering automobile was enough to warrant my silence. I had enough to worry about without setting Jack on the underworld during daylight hours. But it couldn't be helped now.

I unlocked the heavy iron door, opened it, and, with Deylaud at my heel, I stepped into the cool dark. A fine shower of shifted dirt sprinkled downward as Deylaud raised his head and drew in a breath of tomblike air. "Let's go find Jack," I said.

Jack

Now this was a fine howdy-do.

I'd found my way to the cellar of Connie's building and managed to squeeze myself into a corner to keep out of the shafts of sunlight coming in through two ground-level windows. I shoved all the castoff flotsam and jetsam of the tenants' lives into a pile and still didn't have enough room to stretch out for a nap. Screw it. I'd have a hangover from sleeping outside my coffin anyway.

With nightfall so many hours away, I figured I'd just have to while away the time reliving that kiss. Hmm. What a woman. She was soft and firm in all the right places. And warm—living, breathing, mortal human warm. I could still feel the thrum of blood pumping through her veins. I closed my eyes and leaned my head back against the plaster wall, recalling every curve of her all over again, tasting her salty-sweet mouth.

I was settling into a more or less comfortable slouch when I heard a snuffling noise on the other side of the plaster wall. Rats. Shit.

I remembered a time right after World War I when I got locked for two days in a storeroom inside a hospital full of Spanish flu victims. I was looking for their new-fangled blood depot, stumbled into the wrong room, and had to hide when someone came in. They locked the door on me and I was alone with my thoughts—and about half a dozen wharf rats as big as 'possums and just as mean. I had to eat those suckers before they ate me. And let me tell you, it wasn't what I'd call four-star cuisine.

The snuffling turned into loud scratching. Geez, those rats must be as big as wiener dogs.

Quicker than you could say "Houdini," a long-fingered fist came through the wall and grabbed me by the scruff of the neck. Before I knew it, I was being pulled through an opening in the plaster like a rabbit yanked out of a hat. Was this what it was like being born? Holy crap, no wonder everybody on the planet suppressed the memory.

The next instant I was nose-to-nose with William, dangling from his beyond-human grip. I put my feet on the ground and he released me.

"For cripes sake, haven't you ever heard of 'Ready or not, here I come'?" I sputtered. "You could've at least given me a three count. I would've heard you on the other side of that wall, ya know."

"Why didn't you come back like I told you to?"

I dusted plaster off the shoulders and chest of his blue velvet coat and mostly told the truth. "By the time I got a chance to talk to Connie, it was daylight already. I decided to hole up here until dark." Deylaud sniffed earnestly at the knees of my jeans. I scratched his head, and he lolled out his tongue. At least someone was glad to see me.

"Did you get the charm back?"

"I told her to keep it and wear it for protection."

"Jack!" William glared at me, showing his fangs, then looked upward as if he could see into Connie's apartment to where the charm was. For a moment I thought he might levitate and get it himself. He was not a happy vamper. "I should have known you would give up your protection for her sake." He looked at me and his expression softened into resignation. "I suppose threats won't influence you to go back upstairs and get it now."

"Yeah." I braced myself for another choke-and-dangle routine like the one when I'd defied him in the cemetery earlier. Instead he just sighed. I could tell he was mightily stressed, and then I remembered Olivia and Shari. And my old buddy Reedrek.

"Have you heard from Olivia?"

"No."

"How's Shari? Is she going to make it?"

"That's why I came for you. I need your help with her. Come."

He started off down some sort of tunnel, Deylaud at his heels, and I noticed my surroundings for the first time. "Hey, what is this place?"

"This is part of a labyrinth of tunnels beneath Savannah."

I stopped in my tracks and looked around me. I was standing on a cobblestone street with the stone front of a colonial-era building on one side of me. An antique piece of machinery, a hand cart of some kind, had been abandoned on the other side of the passageway. Just the right size to transport a body or two. William side-stepped a shaft of light coming through a street grate above our heads. I could hear the sounds of morning traffic from the streets overhead. I felt myself go all whomper-jawed.

"What?" I asked feebly.

I jogged to catch up with William and Deylaud. "This is the perfect way for us to get around the city in the daytime!" I said.

"Yes," William said.

It took a second for the full impact of his tone to register. Of course, he had known that all along. Had known it for hundreds of years probably. I stopped walking and watched the back of William's pompous head. I charged at him just as he sidestepped another shaft of light, missed him, and ran right under the grate. A stab of pain knifed through my scalp.

William turned to glance at me briefly, but he didn't slow down. "Your hair's on fire, Jack."

"I know that, goddammit!" I slapped myself on the crown of my head with both hands as I jogged to catch up with him. I'd never been one to use much hair product, but what little gel I had was obviously flammable. I decided to adopt a more natural look from now on.

"Why the hell haven't you told me about these tunnels all these years? I mean I knew there were a couple of pirate tunnels along the river. We used to stash a little shine in them. But this—" I flung out my arms. "—this is something you should've let me in on."

"What would you have done with that knowledge? Gone on daytime shopping trips? Lunch with your cronies, perhaps?"

"Hey! Real men don't shop," I said, indignant.

"I was being sarcastic."

"And vampires don't do lunch."

"That's right. We're vampires, and we need our sleep for rejuvenation. I've only had to use these tunnels for emergencies, perhaps just a handful of times over the centuries. You needed to use them today, and now you know about them." William dismissed the discussion with a wave of his hand.

I was torn between wanting to throttle him and being fascinated with my surroundings and the freedom of movement they represented. If nothing else I had to remember the way back to Connie's cellar. The possibilities were absolutely exhileratin'. We came to an intersection; William kept on in the same direction, but I paused to peer off into the darkness of the side tunnel, wondering where it led.

"You can explore some other time, Jack. We have to see to Shari."

It had been a very long time since we'd found Shari nearly drained. She was evidently still alive. "Shouldn't she have a transfusion or something? Why didn't you take her to the hospital?"

"And tell the doctors what?" William finally did stop then. He wheeled around to face me. "Here's my friend, doctor. Pay no mind to those two large puncture marks. Notice the fact that she's completely drained of blood and yet there's not a drop on her body or clothing. And, by the way, I'd love to stay and chat with the police but I really must be going before the sun rises."

"Oh, yeah," I muttered. "I see what you mean."

"She's been marked by Reedrek. She'll have a better chance with us than at any hospital."

William resumed his long strides with a raspy, humorless laugh. "For pity's sake, it's as if you were mortal only yesterday. After all these decades you still think like a human being and not like a vampire."

Sometimes I think that's why William kept me around. It was like I amused him or something. Like I kept him close to his humanity. It really didn't make any sense, though. I mean, he had Melaphia and Renee for human companionship. They were the real humans. Maybe I was William's missing link.

"What are we going to do with her?"

I was walking at William's side now, and he looked over at me gravely. "We're going to make her."

"Make her?" I thought for a minute, and then the gravity of the situation hit me. "Make her into a vampire?"

"Yes. But I'm not going to do it." He looked straight ahead again.

He was talking crazy talk. We couldn't make a vampire. It was against everything he stood for. Why, I was the only vampire he'd ever made and that was because I . . .

. . . was going to die anyway.

Then the rest of what he'd said sank in. "What do you mean, *you're* not going to do it?" I asked.

We'd reached the end of the passage. A steel door with a round, chrome handle was set in the rock. William wrenched it open, revealing a wooden panel, which he shoved inward. It swung away from us noiselessly.

"Just as I said, Jack. I'm not going to do it. *You* are."

Candles flickered from every wall, swirling like fireflies in my tired vision. How was I supposed to make a vampire when I could barely keep my lids open? I watched as William lifted Shari from yet another coffin I hadn't seen before and placed her on the table.

Naked.

Any other time I might've enjoyed the view. I've never been one to pass up the opportunity to admire the female form, if you get my drift. But staring at an unconscious, half-dead girl wasn't sexy or fun. It was creepy. I know I'd said I wanted to know all there was to know about being a vampire, but this was shaping up to be one of those TMI situations. Being told is one thing; doing is a whole different kettle of fish. Even Melaphia had deserted us on the excuse that she had to get Renee off to school. And Melaphia wasn't scared of anything, living or dead.

I looked at Shari lying there, exposed and vulnerable, her arms hanging limp from her shoulders. She looked like some kind of primitive, ungodly sacrifice, and maybe she was. What were we doing exactly? This was a human being with a soul. And we were about to take it away.

"Are you listening?" William demanded.

The seriousness of what we were going to do hit me like a Freightliner in tenth gear. "Huh?" I said.

"Focus, Jack. We have only a short window of time to perform the ritual. Her existence hangs in the balance."

"Are you sure about this? I mean, do you think she would want to be one of us? What happens to her soul?"

William's expression softened and he took a deep breath. "I asked her before she lost consciousness. She wants this. Reedrek told her we would save her. And for your part, you can only do your best. The rest is in the hands of fate."

That didn't exactly answer my question about the soul business, but I figured that's all I was going to get. "So what do I do?"

"You must drain her completely of blood . . ."

That shouldn't be too difficult. I hadn't fed in a long time, so I was beginning to feel weak anyway. I was about to ask William if I could start when he finished his thought.

". . . by biting her in the heart," he said.

Now that was just waaay too creepy. "Why not the neck?"

"Because she's female. Go on. You can do it." William slid his hands underneath Shari's shoulders so that her chest was elevated. "It's time," he said. "Do it."

"Her heart," I muttered. Slowly I bent down to her, giving William one more uncertain glance. As my lips got closer to her creamy flesh, I could feel the ebbing life faintly circulating through her body. Her heartbeat was thready, rapid, and weak. I closed my eyes and let myself feel the hunger for human blood.

It was a hunger I took pride in denying myself, like a priest denies himself sex, or is supposed to. Sure, I'd fed off humans from time to time, even killed more than a few over the past hundred or so years. But never had I fed off an innocent just to satisfy my thirst for human blood.

Make no mistake, human blood is different from animal blood. As I've said before, I keep myself alive on blood from butcher shops, but a vampire is made to drink human blood, and human blood is what makes our blood, bone, and sinew sing. For lack of a better description, it makes us high. The hunger can drive you if you let it take over. But there's room for only one driver in my skin.

As my lips met her flesh, I felt my fangs extend, almost painfully. A sexual rush I wasn't proud of brought my body to alert. The vampire in me knew instinctively just how deep the heart was, and I bit down and down until blood rushed over my fangs and filled my mouth. She whimpered like a trapped animal without hope. I drank, thirstily, heartily, and long until—with my last swallow— I felt something inside her let go. Her heart stilled and began to cool. She was now truly dead. But not, hopefully, for long.

I felt dizzy, sluggish, like I was drunk on some sweet wine. I teetered on the edge of both nausea and euphoria. King of the world. Hot damn. Every artery in my body seemed as if it was bulging. I felt the holy water in my pocket begin to warm again as a reaction to the unholy action I'd just taken. That really sobered me up. I'd just taken a life, and now I was about to take a soul and forever cut it off from the grace of God. I'd never felt so damned, so evil, and yet so alive. I understood, for the first time, what it was to be a vampire.

"Focus, Jack! Now you must call her back to you. Take some of your mingled blood and make the sign of the four winds of spirit on her flesh. That is the blood benediction." William touched Shari on the heart, the forehead, and each shoulder.

Busy enjoying the wild spurt of energy shooting through me, I gave him a fangy grin. I felt like I'd grown a foot taller, so I looked down to see if I'd actually levitated.

A huff of annoyance came from William's direction as he grasped my wrist and plunged his thumbnail into my skin.

"Ow," I yelped, my euphoria level dropping like a car slipping off the blocks.

He dipped his thumb into the blood that was rising from the wound and touched Shari's forehead. "Call her, Jack," he ordered.

I thought briefly of saying "Jack" but decided against it. William might not appreciate my humor at a time like this. And I was pretty sure Shari wouldn't get the joke. I looked down at the girl I'd just killed.

"Shari?" I shook her shoulder. "Shari, wake up!"

William frowned, but instead of giving me more orders, he bent down, sliding his face next to Shari's ear. "Shaaari?" he whispered.

The hair on my arms rose. I recognized the power of that call. He'd once called to me in the same tone. I pulled my hand away but William grasped it, forcing my palm against the wound in Shari's chest.

"Shari? Come back to us, love. You are ours now." He kept his voice to a whisper but I felt the same vibration I'd felt back in Bonaventure when William had called to Olivia. Scrabbling noises in the darkened corners made me want to look and close my eyes at the same time. There were dead people in the room—I could feel them. Restless bees drawn by William's honeyed voice.

William pulled me down close to Shari's other ear. "Say it, Jack. Tell her you want her."

I swallowed. One thing I wanted for sure was to get this over with. I did my best to imitate his tone. "Shari, darlin'? Come on back now. We're—um, I'm waitin' for you." I felt a breath of air move against my skin.

"Shari?"

Her body trembled slightly. Her heart fluttered feebly against my palm.

William straightened. "Now you must let her drink of your blood. Tear the artery in your wrist and put it to her lips. Let her drink until you begin to hear her pulse pounding in your ears. Then stop. Don't let her weaken you too much."

Time to share. I patted my jeans and couldn't find my pocketknife. Aw, screw it.

I bit savagely into my own wrist. "Sonofabitch!" I yelled to anyone within ten feet. Shari was way past caring. "That hurt like a rat bastard!"

I tilted Shari's head back and let my blood flow into her open mouth. Her mouth filled almost to overflowing. "Swallow, punkin," I coaxed. "Swallow for Daddy Jack." Just as I had begun to worry, she did just that.

She coughed enough to spray the blue jacket with another dose of blood and then swallowed again. Her eyes flew open. They were amber, almost yellow. Like a feral cat's. You could tell she didn't know who, where, or what she was. The only thing she knew was that she was thirsty for blood and for the life force it offered. Her hands locked around my forearm and I was afraid I'd need a crowbar to break the vacuum seal she had on my artery.

When I started seeing spots in front of my eyes, I put the heel of my free hand against her forehead and tried to pry my arm away. And not a moment too soon. It took every bit of my strength to loosen her grip.

"All right. What else?"

"Put her in the coffin I had delivered for Olivia. In fact, lock her in. She must sleep for the remainder of the daylight hours. During this time, her transformation will take place. It's a time of agony. She may cry out to you, curse, scream, perhaps. But whatever she says to you, *do not let her out of that coffin.* To do so would cause death to her physical body and unimaginable suffering to her spirit. She must be restrained until the agony has passed. Do you understand?"

"Yes. I understand," I said. "So that's the end of it? She wakes up and presto chango, she's one of us?"

"There is one more step you must perform to ensure the survival of a female."

"Lay it on me," I said.

"You must have sex with her, immediately after she rises."

"Huh? Why? I never laid eyes on this girl until tonight."

William smoothed blond curls away from Shari's pretty, pale face. It was a small gesture of affection for a girl clinging to life but on the brink of eternal darkness. "It's all about power. A woman's power, her essence, is her ability to create life. That is taken away when a female becomes a vampire. When that reproductive power is lost during the metamorphosis, it creates a vacuum. Nature abhors a vacuum. And even this unnatural process is ruled by nature. The loss must be filled by the power of the maker through the act that in mortals creates life. That's why makers of female vampires must be male. This is the female's compensation for their loss of the ability to conceive—instead of taking the seed of the male to make life, they take the strength. Thus the balance of nature, to some degree, is restored."

"That's all well and good, but is giving my power to Shari going to make me weaker?" I tried not to sound suspicious, but I was starting to wonder why I had to be the one to make Shari a vampire instead of William. I could see the wheels turning behind William's eyes. He knew what I was thinking.

"No, Jack," he said wearily. "Having sex with Olivia will make you weaker. Any strength you lose temporarily this first time with Shari will be more than compensated for by the power you get from making her into a vampire. I, as your sire, will share a portion of that strength, but the benefit to Reedrek in a single making will be insignificant. That's why you must make Shari and not I."

"Oh," I said. "Yeah."

I lifted Shari off the table and carried her to Olivia's coffin. I set her in it, none too gently as she'd locked her arms around my neck and began to nuzzle for the artery there. She was half vampire already. I guess I'd done a pretty good job. I closed the coffin lid and latched it.

I collapsed over the coffin, silently congratulating myself for a job well done.

Then she started to scream.

Eight

William

"You may as well get some rest, Jack. Shari's making is out of our hands now. The keepers of the dark will either help her or take her to them . . ." *to wander, soulless and alone.*

A panicked, scratching noise came from the coffin. Jack winced but thankfully didn't ask any more questions. Frankly, whether Jack agreed or not, there are many things in this world one is better off not knowing, the process of making a vampire being one of them. The only comfort I'd found in my sweet Diana's death had been the knowledge that she hadn't had to suffer as Shari was suffering now. As I had suffered. And my son Will, thank the gods, had been too young to be useful to Reedrek as anything other than food.

Always, Reedrek.

I left Jack to his own choices. I was proud of him for doing what must've been distasteful to one so attuned to humans. But there was no time to congratulate ourselves; I had to check for messages from the Abductors. And I had to find Reedrek and Olivia. As I opened the door to the house proper, I nearly stumbled over Reyha and Deylaud waiting just inside. Another scream echoed down the hallway behind me, causing the candle flames at the altars to flutter and sputter. A cold gust of air wafted around us. Reyha dropped to the carpet and clamped her paws over her ears. Deylaud watched me with sad eyes as though he wished to help. I slid a hand over his head and he pushed his face against me. "She is on the journey. There's naught we can do now but wait."

They followed me to my office, whether to comfort me or to escape the terrible sounds rising from the vault, I couldn't tell. It didn't matter, I'd grown to appreciate their silent company. I had my own dark business to attend.

My computer said I had mail.

> *Frederica is out of Amsterdam—safe although damaged. She is in Lillith's care.*

So my words to Reedrek were only partly untrue. Good. Vampires did not take captivity well. There was no imagining the horrors Frederica had faced alone and at the whim of Reedrek's imagination. Best to leave her to the females. Lillith would know what had to be done. If she couldn't save poor, tortured Frederica, she would kill her and end the suffering.

As I queued up a box to answer, I considered whether to inform my network of New World friends that Reedrek was in Savannah. They would want to know, want to help. It could mean all-out war. I wasn't ready to bring my web of contacts out in the open just yet. Their representatives would be in town soon enough—at our All Hallows soirée. Better to see what I could do to throw a hitch in Reedrek's plans before they arrived.

To accomplish that, I needed to find him.

"Go find Miss Olivia's bag and bring me something she has worn," I instructed Deylaud. He returned with a lace camisole that looked as fragile as blue ice crystals.

The bone box seemed warmer than usual, as though it had anticipated my touch. The shells had led me to Reedrek before; I trusted that they would do so again if I asked the proper question. But first I would find Olivia. I sat down and rubbed my eyes to clear the dust motes of fatigue. It was three hours past sunrise and I hoped my lack of sleep wouldn't interfere with my connection to Lalee's gifts.

I held Olivia's undergarment to my face and breathed in her scent. Then I shook the box and tossed the shells out on the polished wood at my feet.

Olivia? Where are you, Olivia? They tumbled and then righted themselves into their own magical code.

Immediately the view of my office shifted sideways, and I found myself back in the tunnels of the city below. Flying. Whispers like the flutter of bats hurtled by me in the dark. Damp cobwebs of displaced time brushed my face and hands. A right turn, then a left. Dead faces watching me from the gray air.

Olivia . . .

I found them in the deepest tunnel. One that even I rarely visited. Too much like visiting a grave. A coffin was comforting, but being buried in the damp, wormy loam reeked of a smothering-hell kind of eternity. Deep scratches marred the stone wall of the tunnel, and dirt had been flung out to make a space inside. A shifting morass of hibernating snakes filled the corners. I hesitated on the threshold. The place even smelled like death—old bodies and decay. I wondered what had prompted fiery Olivia to visit a place so devoid of warmth.

Then I saw her, the bright patch of her silver hair

glowing through the gloom like a beacon. She was curled up, sleeping like a babe, in the arms of my immortal enemy—Reedrek.

Olivia . . .

She shuddered in her slumber, then raised her head. Her gaze searched the dimness for a moment but the weight of day in the world above pressed her down into the safe darkness. She snuggled closer to Reedrek's side, giving in to slumber once more. I watched as his fingers closed gently around one of her wrists. I felt more than heard his voice.

Stay.

Then I realized his eyes were open. He was staring at the empty air, waiting. He must have been expecting . . . something. Could it be possible that my monster of a sire was actually a little afraid of me, his rebellious kin? The prospect gave me a surge of pleasure.

A pity I couldn't find a way to strike him dead using my invisible essence. Could my shattered molecules float into his lungs with the musty air and strangle him from the inside? I might have smiled at the thought but Reedrek's warning hiss brought me out of my pride. Any of the real snakes couldn't have been more clear about their intentions. Yet he didn't move. He wasn't sure. One thing seemed certain: We'd lost Olivia. If he hadn't killed her by now, he surely meant to keep her, to use her. The idea struck like the slice of a sword.

I am stronger than that, her mind whispered.

Foolish, foolish, Olivia. By my life you are not. I have failed Alger and you under my protection. But, in any case, I am coming for you.

I took one step forward, intending what, I couldn't say. In midair above them I reached for Reedrek but ended up with a fistful of empty air. It was a familiar feeling. In one form or another I'd been striking at him most of my vampiric life and had yet to land a serious blow. With that dismal thought a *whoosh*ing sound filled my ears and without warning the tunnels around me were moving, flashing by like the march of trees outside a speeding train.

The shells guided me, and my destination turned out to be darkness. The silence stuffed my ears very like wads of cotton.

I knew my eyes were open but the total absence of light confounded even the superior quality of my vampiric night vision. Effectively blind and most certainly alone, I waited. This then was the borderless, barren realm of the dark ones. A place for damned souls and lost entities. A ferocious rustling sound followed the realization, then a rolling wave of whispers and curses. I had no wish to explore. I needed to believe Lalee would not draw me into the perilous darkness without cause.

A tiny flash of light blinked in front of my eyes, then another off to the left. Soon a sparkling array danced before me, swirling and coalescing into a bright ball of light. The light took the form of an image. I squinted into the sudden radiance.

It was Jack. But not the familiar, friendly, bent-for-hell-raising Jack I knew. This Jack was a master wearing my blue coat, king of all he surveyed, and in that particular moment I stood as his servant. He held my life in his hands. He even had the nerve to smile as he betrayed me by giving the vial of Lalee's blessed blood to Reedrek. I struggled against the cruel invisible bonds pinning me down and knew we were, each of us—Jack, Reedrek, and me—for his own reasons, waiting for the sun.

Jack

"Goda'mighty!" I yelled in alarm and jumped away from the coffin like it had caught fire.

The horrible screech seemed to go on forever—keening, beseeching, wailing. The moans I'd heard from gutshot soldiers on the battlefield had nothing on this girl. I put my palms flat to my ears, but it didn't help. Had I done something horribly wrong? Taken too much blood? Not taken enough? I guess William had said it would be like this. Sort of. I checked the latch on the coffin. Coffins aren't normally made to lock—I mean, think about it—but this box was a custom job, as were all our coffins.

What had William said exactly? Panicked, for a moment I couldn't remember. Right. He'd warned that she would freak out somehow and that I was not, under any circumstances, to let her out of the coffin no matter how much she might scream and beg.

The screech ended only long enough for her to get another lungful of air and then she set up a sustained howl that made my fangs vibrate. I staggered over to the wet bar and mixed myself a drink. Half blood and half Dewar's. *Here's blood in your eye.* I downed it, took the rest of the bottle back beside the coffin, and drew up a chair. It was going to be a long night. Or day. Or what the hell ever. It was easy to lose track in William's underground lair.

A string of vicious curses followed by another loud wail cut through the still air of the chamber. I took a swill straight from the bottle. I was startled again when the coffin started to shake and vibrate. Damn. I'd be a monkey's uncle if she wasn't actually turning over and over in that coffin. Talk about spinning in your grave.

At this rate, what kind of shape was she going to be in by sundown? What kind of wild woman was I going to be expected to get it on with? I'd heard of guys—sumo wrestlers—who could draw their own genitals up into their body cavities. Damned if it didn't feel like that was happening on its own right about now. I pictured the most scary, hysterical female I could think of and came up with a mental picture somewhere between the Bride of Frankenstein and Courtney Love. Pucker up, buttercup.

I kid you not, the gyrations she was going through were enough to put you in mind of the caterwauling, spinning, levitating, and head rotating that Linda Blair did in *The Exorcist*. Only worse. I had a clear picture in my mind of how much she was suffering. I wondered how I could actually know, what with her being on the inside of that box and me on the outside. Maybe it was that connection with the dead I had, the way I can communicate with spirits. Then it hit me.

I had been through it myself.

That realization sent another chill through me and I took one more pull on the bottle. I closed my eyes tightly as Shari continued to scream. Yes, I was starting to remember. It was so long ago. I could recall the smell of the earth, loamy and rich with the blood of all those dead soldiers. There was no coffin for me, since I was made right there on the battlefield. I earned my fangs the old-fashioned way. In the earth.

I remembered. Oh sweet Lord, I remembered. When the agony started I tried to claw my way out of the ground so I could run from whatever demon had ahold of me. But I couldn't. Something kept me down. It was him. It had to be him. That toothy, red-eyed devil who'd asked me if I wanted to live. Who'd said he'd save me. What had he said—that I'd never be hungry again?

But there was a price to be paid. I of all people, who'd never gotten a break in my life, should have known that nothing ever comes free. I'd felt like I was turning inside out. My guts were on fire. My skin was burning. My nerves and sinew were turning to concrete. My bones were turning to stone. The pain was unbelievable. I begged for someone to take it away. I flopped this way and that but could only move an inch at a time in any direction. Finally, I managed to free two fingers on my left hand. I felt the air on them—the warmth of the sun. Warmer and warmer until . . .

They caught fire.

I remember withdrawing them, extinguishing the fire in the soil. What was happening? What was I becoming?

Then there was thirst, unbearable. But thirst for what? I needed—no, *craved* something. But I didn't know what it was. The longing seemed to go on for days, years. My body was converting into something else, something strange and foreign. I didn't recognize the feel of my own flesh.

Then the night came. I felt it, knew it inside me— inside my new, thirsting self. The weight lifted and I literally sprang from the earth like some evil planted thing that was ready to be harvested. Or maybe ready to do the harvesting. I was a vampire.

William stood facing me in a clean captain's uniform, looking so different from the way he'd last appeared in my human existence that I didn't so much recognize him by sight as by smell. The blood had been wiped away. His boots were shined. He was the very picture of the gentleman officer.

"Private McShane, are you ready for your new life?"

I looked around me. It was night but I could see right well. And it wasn't just the moonlight illuminating the ghostly landscape. It was a new *kind* of sight. Unfamiliar smells wafted to me on the breeze, and new noises from the woods and the earth cut through what should have been silence. I peered back at William, who continued standing tall, watching and waiting to see what manner of creature he had wrought upon the world.

"Yes, Captain. I'm ready," I heard myself say.

A particularly plaintive wail brought me back to the present. I was getting more than a little drunk now, but it hadn't dulled my horror at the long-suppressed memories brought on by Shari's suffering. I knew exactly what she was going through.

"Heeeeelp meeee," she shrieked.

Now she was using actual, understandable English. That had to be good. I patted the top of the coffin and crooned, "It's all right, darlin'. I'm right here and I ain't going anywhere. You're not alone, okay?"

"Let me ooouuut!"

"Can't do that," I slurred. "That would not be good. Trust Uncle Jack. There's nothing worse than a half-baked bloodsucker. Or so I've been told." I belched for emphasis.

She broke into an unladylike braying sob and cursed a little more. She cursed me and my lineage back to the Stone Age. The womenfolk in my family came out very badly indeed in Shari's estimation.

"Now, now," I cooed. "In a little while, you'll be as good as new."

"Nooo! I want out nooooow! It huuurts!"

"Tough it out, sweetheart. In just a few hours, it'll be all over and you won't remember a thing. You'll be extra strong and you'll live forever, and you'll have great . . . teeth. So sit tight." It's funny. When pressed—or maybe when drunk—it was hard to think of the benefits of being a vampire. Now what did that say about me?

There was another long shriek from inside the box. Then she said, "Let me out or I'll kill you!" Her voice had changed considerably. She was grunting and pounding on the coffin like a professional wrestler.

"Now, now. You know that's not possible," I told her. "Besides, I'm dead already. Tough it out, sweetheart."

"It hurts, and you're a bastard asshole son of a bitch!" she said.

"Well, that about covers it," I said, and contemplated the empty Scotch bottle. I neglected to tell her that she and me would be bumping uglies in a few hours. She'd find that out soon enough. This wasn't shaping up to be what you'd call a romantic encounter.

If there was anything I was terrible at, it was comforting hysterical females. But this was different from all the other times. And not just because she was in a box and couldn't throw things. I sensed that I was in touch with the girl's spirit as she teetered on the edge of two worlds, one darkness and one light. I hoped for her sake that she'd make the right choice, and I cursed William for not taking her to the hospital and facing a different set of consequences.

I didn't think like a vampire, he'd told me a number of times. Truth be told I didn't really feel like one either. Not before this, at least. I'd wanted to know what it felt like to be a real vampire.

Be careful what you wish for.

"Jack? Isn't that what you said your name was?" Her breath was coming in ragged gasps, like she was workin' to control the pain.

"Yo."

"Do you think he likes me?"

"Who?"

"The sexy one with the green eyes."

Oh, geez. She was one of William's play toys, and she didn't even know his name. "I'm sure he likes you just fine, honey."

"What is his name?"

"William." I sighed. I remembered how Olivia had practically kissed his feet when she'd arrived on the doorstep. Now he had another groupie. I was officially in the middle of an undead soap opera. *Young Vampires in Love.* Could you stand it?

A new wave of torment must've hit her because she began to bawl almost as loudly as before. I staggered over to the bar again and rifled through the little drawer underneath until I found two old wine corks. I used my pocket-knife to whittle them down a bit, then fitted one into each ear and made my way back to the chair by the coffin.

I patted the lid again and felt myself slipping into drunken oblivion. "There, there" I heard myself say.

William

I woke up on my office floor with Reyha's cold nose prodding my ear. A wave of dizziness held me immobile. I felt drunk. The image of Jack swam through my mind on an unstable wave of confusion that soon turned to anger.

Why would Jack betray me? Had I somehow warped him into an oath breaker? I couldn't believe it. Or was the lure of Reedrek too strong for any of us—even with the aid of voodoo blood—to resist for long?

I pushed Reyha away and sat up. I listened intently but no sound floated through the still air. It felt as though

I'd been away for hours. Yet I could still feel the early-morning burn of the sun scratching the inside of my skin. I had to sleep, rest for the fight to come. I needed to save Jack from what he might be about to do; forget trying to save the vampire world. But it wouldn't happen that way. With Reyha following, I went in search of Jack.

I found him looking dead, dead to the world. Seated on a ladder-back chair he'd pulled up next to Shari's prison, he was slouched over onto the cushioned surface of the ottoman passed out, his lax fingers trailing possessively over an empty bottle of Dewar's that was lying at his feet. Two other empties rested against the chair legs. I shook his shoulder and called his name, but he only moaned and tightened his grip on what must have been the final bottle.

Shari stirred then, feeling my presence. She began to twirl and shriek.

"William! Help me!" Somehow she'd learned my name. I should've been angry but the least I could offer her at this point was my acquaintance.

"Be at peace," I said.

"Wi—Will—William?"

I didn't speak to her again. Her suffering would go on for a while yet. I checked the lock on her coffin, then gently disengaged Jack's favorite mode of oblivion before lifting him into his own racing coffin. I straightened the blue velvet lapels of Melaphia's protective jacket and shut the lid.

There would be no rest for me this day and no time to dwell on when or if Jack might come to the decision to allow Reedrek to kill me. The future was not set, no matter what the shells showed. I intended to keep Jack busy and out of the way while I faced Reedrek, my own sire, my own destiny. Perhaps I could at least save Olivia.

I stripped off my shirt and threw it into the trash. Opening the armoire, I selected a fresh one along with a dark blue tailored jacket. The jacket wasn't blessed like Jack's, but it was Armani. Nothing but the best for what might be my last stand.

I sat down to write a brief note to Melaphia.

> *Dear One,*
> *I have business to attend and I'm not sure how long I'll be away. I leave Jack to handle things in my stead. Tell him to finish what we started downstairs, and try to clean him up to act as host for the All Hallows gathering. Tell him I'm depending on him.*
> *Yours,*
> *William*

I made one last trip upstairs. Deylaud followed me step for step. I placed the sealed note on the kitchen counter before returning to the vault with Deylaud trailing behind me.

"Guard," I ordered him, and waited until he took his usual position near the passage leading back to the house. I opened the tunnel door and stepped alone into the cool darkness.

The tunnels seemed deserted. I moved through them swiftly, as I had in the voodoo dream. Quite suddenly, I knew I was close to Reedrek.

He sat up as I entered the stone doorway to his hidey-hole. I ignored him as best I could. I kept my gaze on the shifting mass of snakes half filling the room. Several had twined close to Olivia's head, making her look like an ancient Medusa in the dim light.

"Wake up, Olivia."

She stirred, combing a clinging copperhead from her

bright hair. Reedrek was instantly next to me, hovering within striking distance. I could smell ancient tombs on his breath. This would be the ultimate test then—to stand before him weaponless, no jacket, no charm. No blessings except for my mutated blood.

I kept my concentration on Olivia. "Are you all right?" *Are you his yet? Will you come at me, too?*

"I'm fine," she said, working to hold my gaze, folding her hands together in a portrait of submissiveness. What remained of her will I couldn't tell. There was no time to test where her loyalties rested.

"Go home, Olivia," I said before turning to Reedrek. "Whew! You smell worse than a rotting corpse. Have you taken to cannibalizing the dead to stay alive?" Olivia rose to her feet but seemed uncertain. I shifted my gaze to her once more. "I said, go home."

I expected Reedrek to dispute my order. Instead he smiled. "I suppose people never truly change. You would trade yourself for a female as you did the very first time we met. How gallant. How pointless." His gaze swung to Olivia. "That's right, child. Go home. My chivalrous offspring and I have things to discuss."

Without any further hesitation, Olivia disappeared through the door and into the dark tunnel. Having her out of harm's way provided me with some slight relief.

I nudged a snake with my well-polished shoe. "What a perfect place for a coldblooded reptile like yourself to hide."

He casually dusted the dank soil off his coat sleeve. "Shall we adjourn to a more hospitable place, then? One that more suits your delicate sensibilities?" he asked. "This is your city. Surely you know of other, *cleaner,* accommodations."

I led him in the opposite direction from my home.

Whatever happened between us, I wanted him as far away as possible from the ones I cared about. We ended up in a spot I knew well. A cavelike room near the river, with a steel barred door and smooth dry walls—a chamber that had most likely been built by pirates to store their booty and hide from the law. A table made of heavy rock stood in the center and two equally substantial benches sat on either side. Someone or something kept the dirt floor swept clear of debris and the corners free of cobwebs. A single lamp burned from a shelf carved into the wall. In all my time in the tunnels, I'd never seen a human there, nor a vampire for that matter.

With a lulling sense of normalcy, Reedrek removed his coat, shook out a lingering snake, then put the coat back on before taking his place on one of the benches. I sat on the one facing.

He got right to the point. "Now what is this I hear about voodoo blood?"

I felt myself flinch inside, although I know my features remained impassive.

"What do you mean?"

"Don't play games. I already know about your mixed blood. Olivia told me."

Olivia—I should have been more careful—

"She's mine, you know," Reedrek said on a huff of laughter. "You traded yourself for nothing. I sent her to bring Jack to me."

"She doesn't know anything. Do you think I would trust someone who showed up on my doorstep like a stray bitch?"

He shook his head sadly. "No, I suppose not. But you trust Jack, now don't you?"

In my darkest moments I had pictured Jack being tortured or killed by Reedrek in revenge. With the help of the shells I'd seen the true danger—the blackest possibility. That Reedrek would turn Jack's fledgling vampire mastery into something more traitorous. Closing my mind to that possibility, I drew in a long breath. I had to save Jack, and I had to stop Reedrek. But it wouldn't do to fight him in any obvious way.

"You know, Jack didn't turn out as well as I'd hoped," I said with a sigh. "I thought to form him into something closer to my equal but he remains more than half human." I allowed myself a pained expression. "As a matter of fact, no one on this side of the pond has given me a moment's true pleasure."

"Tsk, tsk. Poor fellow. Did I not tell you what a backwater hole this Savannah is? For all that it has in"—he waved his hand around—"ambiance. It lacks any true class or even intrigue. I mean, pirates and drunken Irishmen—have you forgotten England? Or Elizabeth? For pity's sake! You've bedded a queen."

Yes, I remembered Elizabeth. She'd been my equal in many ways. Not vampiric—no, she'd never craved my sort of half life. She'd been after her own immortality— as the God-appointed monarch of England. But I'd been her night counselor, confessor, and lover for many years. She'd even sent me to the Tower, to her cousin Mary, but not in love.

"If you'd taken her, she would've made us invincible," Reedrek whispered. "Instead you entertained her with your cock—"

"While you killed her courtiers. She never liked you, you know. She put up with your presence because of me."

Reedrek chuckled. "That's because I never rode the 'virgin' queen half so well as you. I had more patience with your sport then."

Elizabeth had always enjoyed the company of men,

flirting shamelessly with half the ruling class. In an instant, she was there like a bright angel in my mind, standing before the fire with her halo of glorious red-gold hair, bundled in pelts of ermine to keep her safe from the cold English winter. She looked pale and fey in the firelight, as though the fairies had deposited her in the center of the English court. Her voice music to my desolate heart.

"Tell me of my cousin Mary. How does she keep in her confinement?"

I brushed my fingers along the fur, caressing her smooth, warm cheek in the process. I watched her skin pinken with excitement, and decided I would only lie a little. "She is angry and fearful. And the effort ages her." A small satisfied smile tilted Elizabeth's mouth. "But still quite lovely," I added. The smile disappeared and she pulled away from my hand.

"Walsingham will not be swayed by beauty. He wears his duty to a Protestant England like the cross of our Lord."

"Mary wears a rosary as well, in the place of breast-plate armor." I didn't bother to mention how I'd been disinclined to get close enough to touch the Catholic relic. Elizabeth had sent me to frighten her, and that I accomplished with very little effort. Climbing through the high, unscalable window of her Tower room had been enough—and a show of fang had been more than enough. But her anger had drawn me in. She had tasted of heather and hopelessness.

Elizabeth turned on me then, inexplicably defending her cousin. "She is a queen, after all. And Walsingham would have your handsome head if he knew what we do together." The English were eager to burn witches; what would they do with a creature like me? When I responded to her threat by casually pouring a cup of mead, she sighed. Tired of the game, she drew herself up and stepped close enough for me to feel the warmth of her body. She was naked under her fur wrap. She took the cup out of my hand and drank from it first. "I am your queen. Are you not here to please me?" I saw vulnerability in her gaze. It disappeared as quickly as I discovered it.

I smiled. "Aye, that I am." Without warning I tossed the cup away, snatched her up in my arms, and threw her on the bed. I stifled her surprised scream with a kiss—deep and demanding. She fought me like a man until both of us were breathing hard. When I relinquished her mouth she grimaced. "You taste of blood," she hissed.

"Aye, the blood of Queen Mary." I thought she might scream again, or push me away, but as always she managed to surprise me. She licked her lips, then pulled my head downward for another taste.

Reedrek's voice called me back to the present. "Yes, I let you have your fun. Then I taught you to hunt."

After Elizabeth's death, a death as natural as being born, I'd been more than half-crazy, uncaring. Lost in grief, with anger as my true love once again, I had hunted London with Reedrek as if we were lords of the realm, as though mayhem was our God-given right.

But God had nothing whatsoever to do with it.

One evening we'd boarded a merchant vessel, recently arrived from the southern climes, that was loaded with slaves and spices. Just remembering it brought back the scent of cinnamon, curry, and pressed olives. I'd spent most of my time killing the crew above decks while Reedrek relieved the slaves of their chains and their blood below. I'd watched in numb fascination as he'd decapitated this one, then strangled that one. Rather than pin them down, he'd held them aloft, off the slippery deck, as he'd sucked their arteries, seeming to enjoy their kicks and screams. Afterward, we were so bloody and bloated we could barely make our way back to our coffins. And I still felt no satisfaction or peace.

"Don't you remember how it used to feel? Feeding at will? Walking the streets and reaping the juicy meal of the misguided?" He gazed at me and I could feel his mind searching for a weakness. "How long has it been since you've fed? And I mean truly fed, until you were satisfied?"

Possibly never, but at least longer than I intended to admit. I'd become a master at self control when it came to most things—especially hunting. With Eleanor's help I'd gathered a stable of willing victims—my swans. A workable if not-so-sweet compromise.

"I find satisfaction in a different way," I said, deflecting the true question.

"Show me," he said. "Be my guide to this New World way of death and dining."

He was challenging me in order to read my thoughts and habits. Humoring him, I blocked his vision of Eleanor and any reference to my mixed blood. If I could convince him that he might have the power to turn me into what he desired, I might have time to find a way to kill him. At least I might keep him busy and away from Jack.

"Where did you leave the mayor's SUV?" I asked.

"In the parking lot of one of your churches. The one with the gold cross embedded in the window glass. A rather good joke, don't you think? Why do you ask?"

"Because we'll need it," I said. "As soon as the sun sets, I'll take you hunting."

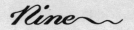

Jack

Someone was knocking on the door. "Five more minutes," I muttered.

"Jack," came a muffled shout from somewhere nearby. It was Deylaud.

I groaned. It all came flooding back. Making Shari. Listening to her suffer for hours. Too much whiskey. I didn't even remember getting in the coffin.

"Jack, it's sundown. Melaphia says to remind you that you still have work to do, whatever that means. William told her you'd had too much to drink and that I was supposed to make sure you didn't sleep in."

"That William thinks of everything, don't he?" I raised up on one elbow, wondering why the hell my wrist hurt so bad. Then I remembered that too. I raised the lid and blinked at Deylaud. "Yeah. Yeah. I'm up."

He looked relieved. "I'm going upstairs to work on the household accounts. Let me know if you need anything." He turned and disappeared up the passageway.

I looked over at Shari's coffin. She wasn't banging away like a marimba band anymore or screeching loud enough to wake the dead. There was only silence. Dead silence, if you'll pardon the expression. I sat up and climbed out of my box. When my feet hit the floor, the jarring sensation felt like somebody hit me upside the head with an iron skillet. If you don't think vampires can get hangovers, think again.

Not only did I not feel so good, I was sure I wasn't looking all that great either. This was one of those days when I was actually glad I couldn't see my own reflection. I probably would have scared the living shit out of myself. I looked down at my clothes. My jeans were dirty, my shirt was wrinkled, and the magic sport coat was rumpled and bloodstained. Shari would probably take one look at me and start screaming again. Especially when I explained the final step in the manufacturing of female vampires.

I thought I'd better put the jacket somewhere for safekeeping. It was getting to be in rough enough shape as it was. I patted the pocket and felt that the holy water was still there. What could the stuff do to me?

I could bump up against something in public, break the vial, and spill some on myself. I could just see the steam coming off me as I boiled away. "Excuse me, y'all. Mind if I smoke?" I considered pouring it down the sink of the wet bar, but who knew if it might come in handy someday. At the very least I could get it back to Connie when this Reedrek thing blew over. If I survived it, that was.

I walked over to the passageway and inspected Melaphia's little altars along the wall. As quickly and carefully as I could, I took the holy water out of the jacket pocket and placed it behind a little statue of some saint or other. I watched it for a couple of seconds to make sure it didn't start bubbling. It looked like it was going to be fine.

I hung the blue jacket in the closet behind the bar and returned to Shari's coffin. I smoothed my hair down as best I could and wondered if I should take a shower. Better not. William was specific about the wild thing needing to happen as soon as she woke up. I tapped lightly on her coffin, feeling as awkward as a teenager knocking on his girl's door for their first date. I remembered that Shari was stark naked. Well, that would certainly save time. I also remembered that she'd been braying like a wild animal and whirling like a dervish a few hours ago.

"Anybody home?" I called. I reached out and disconnected the fastener.

The lid of the coffin flew open with such force that it bounced against the hinges and nearly flipped closed again. But the creature inside was so fast, she still would have made it out. She sprang up and over, landing in front of me, her knees bent in a crouch like she was ready for a championship wrestling match. I shouldn't have been surprised. Hadn't I sprung out of the grave at William in just this way? Well, maybe not in *exactly* this way.

"Hello again," I said, rubbing my hands together. "How're you feeling? Fit as a fiddle and ready for love?" She stared at me, round-eyed and waiting, her arms out to her sides, fingers flexing. Her skin had a leathery and sallow look. I hated to be critical at a time like this, but this was not a good look for her. Her hair looked lifeless and dry, her breasts shrunken, eyes dull. There was nothing about her that seemed like it had ever been alive. An animated corpse, something out of a zombie movie, the living dead is what she looked like.

"Not too talkative this evening, huh? That's fine. Now, you understand what's happening, right? I mean, William said he talked to you about being made into . . . one of us." I paused for a response, or at least a reaction. Nothing. She just kept on staring.

"Okay, well, there's one more step you have to go through and that's—"

She shoved me so hard I staggered backward until the back of my knees struck a giant ottoman. I fell back on it, my arms splayed out to my sides. Shari was on me like an animal, straddling my hips.

"Hey, now," I said. This was going to be interesting.

"Hey, yourself." She grabbed either side of my shirt and ripped it open. I heard the buttons ricochet off the opposite wall.

At least she could talk again. That was a relief. "I'm glad you've found your tongue."

"Yeah? Now you're about to find it." She leaned over me and pressed her mouth to mine. Her tongue teased my lips apart and went to find my tonsils. Her hands went to find something else.

I managed to get my mouth disentangled long enough to say, "Let me help you, hon. Now, don't rip that belt. It's real alligator and that NASCAR belt buckle is brand-new. I had a friend pick it up at the last big race at Hampton." I wrestled her for control of the belt and finally got it open. I planted my boot heels against the rug and raised my hips off the ottoman before she could rip my jeans apart. They had just gotten nice and worn, the way I like them.

She thrust my jeans down to my knees, and I somehow managed to slide out of my boots and shake the jeans off completely. Then she made a grab for my privates. I caught her hand in my fist. "Be gentle with the jewels, girl. Simmer down, now." The way she was going, I was afraid she'd crush the old meat and two veggies like walnuts.

In one swift motion, she twisted her hand in my fist, gripped my wrist, and pinned both arms above my head, bringing her breasts against my face. By this time I must admit I was getting interested. There's nothing like a pair of nuzzling nipples to get your attention. She gyrated her hips against my johnson and it responded. As soon as she felt it get hard, she mounted me in one swift, hard stroke and began to ride me like a stallion.

Gasping for breath, I looked up at her. She was changing before my very eyes. Her skin was becoming rosy, her lips moist and dewy, her breasts full and round. Her hair bounced in a most attractive way as she thrust her hips. She leaned her head back and the flesh at her throat seemed to plump and become soft and supple-looking. When she tilted her head back down to me, her eyes were alive and dilated.

She pressed another needy kiss on my lips, opened her mouth, and sucked on my tongue. I thought about my earlier kiss with Connie and felt guilty, but not guilty enough to stop kissing Shari. After all, it was part of the job now. That made me think of something else, though. As much as a man could think at a time like this. What would my relationship with Shari be like? What would I be to her? Would she have to do what I told her—the way it was with William and me? The possibilities made my head spin even more than it was twirling already. Maybe there'd finally be someone who belonged to *me*. Maybe I wouldn't have to be alone anymore. I hoped she was nice. I hoped she'd like me.

I wrenched my mouth free. "Do you like NASCAR?" I asked.

Still pumping away, she looked at me like she was trying to make sense of the question. Finally, she said,

"Isn't that sweet. You're trying to make it last, aren't you?"

Now it was my turn to be puzzled. "What?"

"I've heard of guys making themselves think about baseball. But I guess thinking about racing would do just as well."

"No, that's not it. I mean—oh, never mind." Plenty of time to get into turn-ons and turn-offs later. I thought about Connie again. I really dug her, but if she and I got together, she'd eventually find out what I was. And she probably couldn't deal. I mean, who could? It was for the best. Really.

I took one breast in each hand and kneaded them gently. Oh, yeah. This was more like it. She was coming alive, in a matter of speaking, right on top of me. She seemed to be enjoying it, too. She ran her fingers over the muscles of my chest, tugging none too gently on the short curlies there. Hey, why hadn't I been making female vampires for years?

She began a little keening cry. It wasn't the same as the noises she'd been making in the coffin. Not atall. This was the sound of a vital human female in the throes of passion, not of everlasting torment. I put my arm around her back and lifted her enough to flip her over. Then I plunged into her again with a moan of my own. We were both getting close to the brink. She wrapped her legs around me and arched her back.

I picked up the pace and she urged me on and on until we both came at the same instant. Think colored lights, bells, whistles, thunder, lightning, the Daytona freakin' 500, the whole nine yards. Her body bucked and writhed. Way to go, Jackie.

She relaxed, deeply and completely. Isn't that what good sex will do for you? I held her against me, catching my breath. Then I realized she didn't have any breath at all.

Something was wrong. Very wrong.

"Shari? Darlin'?" I raised myself above her and looked into her eyes. The beautiful honey-colored irises were gone. They were still dilated, but now they were fixed and staring. This was not post orgasmic relaxation.

This was death.

I put my hands underneath her shoulders and shook her. "Come back!" I pleaded. I stood above her, panicked. What was I to do? I tilted her head back, pinched her nose, and gave her mouth-to-mouth resuscitation. There was no response. Heart massage? I punched her sharply in the chest with the heel of my hand. What was I thinking? A heartbeat didn't animate vampires. What *did* animate vampires? Whatever it was, I would've given my life force to Shari right then if I could have, but I had no idea how.

I stood over her, pulling at my hair with my hands, wracking my brain. This wasn't supposed to happen. Five minutes ago, she'd been vibrant and lifelike. Now I could see her flesh starting to dry out. The color in her cheeks was gone. She was dying all over again. That was something you should only have to do once.

Where the hell was William when I needed him? What had he said? All coherent thought left my brain. And even as I panicked, I knew it was no use. Even if I figured out that I'd zigged when I should have zagged, nothing was going to reverse what had just happened. As usual when the chips were down and I really had to think hard, my brain did what it does best and kicked out a useless piece of trivia. I thought about that old line from *The Wizard of Oz*. She wasn't merely dead. She was really most sincerely dead.

I sank to my knees and bellowed in rage and pain. In the name of all that was unholy, what had I done? A couple of days ago, this beautiful young woman had been going about her life. And now thanks to a couple of evil bloodsuckers, she was dead, a husk, decaying before my eyes. I helped kill somebody who didn't deserve to be killed. I was well and truly a vampire. Bully for me.

I realized I was sobbing and rubbed at my eyes with the heels of my hands. I couldn't remember the last time I'd cried. Was I crying for Shari or was I crying because—after more than a hundred years—reality had finally hit me?

I was a monster.

Somewhere in my just discovered deviant consciousness I became aware that a human had entered the vault.

"Jack! I heard you scream. What happened?" It was Melaphia.

"She died!" I looked up at Melaphia from the edge of the ottoman. "Is there anything you can do? Say a chant or a prayer or . . . something?"

Melaphia went to Shari's body, put her thumb and forefinger against her throat, and looked into her eyes. She laid her fingers gently onto Shari's eyelids and closed them. "No, Jack. There's nothing I could have done even if I'd been right here."

She stood in front of me and took my face in her slender brown hands. I'd known Melaphia since the night of her birth, helped to raise her. We were both untroubled by my nakedness, but I reached for my jeans anyway, dragging them into my lap. "What did I do wrong? Why did she die?"

Melaphia sat down next to me and put her arm around my shoulders. "I've heard that this happens sometimes. I don't think anybody knows why. Many people die in the process of becoming blood drinkers. Men and women, but especially the women. It's nothing you did wrong. Believe me. I know it's hard, but don't blame yourself."

I leaned my stubbly cheek against her smooth, fragrant one. Melaphia knew everything there was to know about the mysterious twilight space between life and death. She was fluent in all things unearthly and unfathomable, comprehended things that humans weren't supposed to. Knowledge and power that should have belonged only to divine beings were her birthright. Wisdom beyond age was her legacy.

I looked down at her hand holding mine. One of my tears fell onto her fine skin. The tear was tinged pink with the blood that animates my body, and I felt revulsion that it had touched her. For the first time I was ashamed of what I was. I hung my head and wiped at my eyes with the back of my other hand. To think I'd been silly enough to fantasize in those few exquisite moments about having another creature like myself to call my own. Stupid, stupid Jack.

"Don't cry. Please don't. This too shall pass." Melaphia brought her palm to my face again and kissed my cheek lightly. I could smell her clean, perfect humanity. I shrugged away from her touch, not wanting to soil her.

I cleared my aching throat. "What are you doing here at this time of night?" I asked hoarsely.

"I was worried about you and William, what with Reedrek on the loose and Olivia gone, so I came to check on you."

"Where's Renee? Isn't it past her bedtime?"

"She's upstairs with Deylaud and Reyha, doing her math homework. She's fine."

I felt ashamed all over again, knowing that I'd just had

wild, evil vampire sex under the same roof as Melaphia and her precious little daughter. An aching tenderness for those two crushed my chest and sent more tears rolling down my face. I'd lose them one day, just like I'd lost Melaphia's mother, grandmother, and great-grandmother. For all their power and glory, they were not immortal as I was. I'd known each of the women in Melaphia's lineage, going back as far as when my existence as a vampire first began. I'd held them just after they'd come into the world, and I'd stood broken-hearted by the side of a weeping William as they'd died in his arms. They were as close as I'd ever come to a family, and yet I was not of them and they were not of me.

"You should take Renee home to bed now. I'll be all right."

"I'm not leaving you here to deal with this alone. Besides, there are things I have to do." She inclined her head toward the corpse. "For her."

"What do you mean?"

"It's complicated. Long story short, I have to do my stuff—say some incantations over that poor girl so her body won't be inhabited by any spirits that happen to be floating around."

"I don't sense anything. I'm pretty good with the spirits too, ya know."

"Does that spirit happen to go by the name of Jack Daniel's?" She ruffled my hair.

"Very funny. I mean spirits as in ghoulies and ghosties and long-legged beasties and things that go boo in the night."

"That's 'bump' in the night."

"Whatever."

"I know you're sensitive to the dead, but all the same

I'm going to do the spells. It's the least we can do for her, isn't it?"

"The least and the last," I mumbled. "Can I help?"

"You can put Shari in that extra coffin. Who knows if Olivia will come back. If she does, we'll get her another one. You can't help with the rest of it. I have to go upstairs and consult some texts and prepare some ointments. Then I'll come back and take care of Shari a little later tonight."

"Is William out looking for Olivia?" I pulled on my jeans and gently lifted Shari's body into the coffin.

Melaphia took a moment to cross Shari's arms over her torso. Then she made the sign of the cross. I had to look away as she closed the lid. "Yes. He left me a note saying where he was going. He also had a list of things to do for the party. And there were instructions for you, too."

"What now?" She knew I hated William's damned shindigs and all the extra work it took to put them on.

"You're not going to like it."

"I don't doubt it." I picked up the rag that used to be my shirt, inspected it long enough to make out that it was a total loss, and flung it into the fancy trash can against the wall. "So? What did he say?"

"He wants you to quit drinkin' and help me with the party preparations."

"Crap. As if I don't have enough on my mind already."

"That's not the worst of it."

"Oh, no."

"He wants you to take his place as the grand host."

I could feel my head throbbing again. "What the hell? Why?" If vampires could get hangovers, you'd think they could at least get relief from an aspirin or sex or something. There was no justice.

"He said he had business to attend to."

"Geez Louise, what is he thinking? I can't run this party! I can't be William—standing around in a monkey suit, remembering all those society jackasses' names, making high-class small talk without putting my foot in my mouth. It'll be a nightmare! Besides all that, some of those Eurovamps he's been importing are coming in from all over the Americas. What am I supposed to do with them? I've never been invited to mix with those other vampires. I know next to nothing about being a blood drinker. I feel like somebody's redheaded stepchild all the time. It's embarrassing."

"Look, I'll be there to help you. But that's the least of our worries right now. I think the real reason William wants you to host the ball is that he's afraid he might still be tied up with this Reedrek, maybe even still trying to get Olivia back. Or worse." For the first time I could see how worried Melaphia was.

Worrying about William was something new for both of us. Nobody, and I mean nobody, had ever been a threat to him. He was king of the jungle as far as Melaphia and I were concerned. Ten feet tall and bulletproof. Now I was sorely afraid that nothing was ever going to be the same.

It was my turn to comfort Melaphia. I took her gently by the shoulders. "Try not to worry. I'm going to go out and find William. Together we'll beat this guy, this—thing. Everything is going to be all right. You'll see."

"You're not going anywhere. You've been through hell tonight already and you were up most of the day. You've got to rest. I want you to get in that coffin until William gets back. You don't have any idea where to look for him anyway, do you?"

I started to protest, but I realized she was right. Looking for William now would be like looking for a painted minnow in the Savannah River. Besides that, I was feeling really strange. Strong, but strange. "You're right, my sweetheart. As usual." She let me hug her to my chest. Her fuzzy hair tickled my chin. I let her go and tugged one of the twisty dreadlocks that she had pulled back in a scrunchie. "You take such good care of us, ya know."

"Yes, I do. And I will for a long time. I'm going to send Reyha in to keep you company so you won't be alone. I'm sure William will look in on you when he gets back. Now, get in that box. By the time I've made my preparations and come back down to work with Shari, you'll be sawing logs, or killing hogs, or whatever you vampires do in your sleep."

"You're the boss. Kiss Renee for me."

"I will. When all this settles down I'll bring her by, as long as it's not a school night, and you and William can spend some time with her. Take her to a movie or something."

I figured the happy talk was to reassure the both of us. Might as well hope for the best while you're planning for the worst. "I can't wait to see Renee," I told her.

We squeezed each other's hands before she turned to go back upstairs, and I watched her until she was out of sight. I went over to the bar and mixed another blood-and-booze cocktail. My headache was waning but I still felt really weird. On one hand Melaphia was right; I could tell I needed to rest. The undead body clock is a funny thing. You have to get that beauty sleep or you really feel the effects. But at the same time I also felt . . . strong somehow. Like I could bench-press a cart horse.

As I finished my drink, Reyha entered the vault, wearing something slinky and pink. I set down the glass and she linked her arms around my neck.

"Melaphia said I should keep you company," she said.

"That would be nice. I've had a hard day's night." I stroked her long, pale hair over and over for several long moments. Then I climbed into my black coffin and she settled down beside me, nestling her head against my chest.

"Say goodnight, Reyha," I said.

"Goodnight, Reyha," she replied.

William

Reedrek sang under his breath. "A-hunting we will go, a-hunting we will go, hi-ho the dario, a-hunting we will go."

For the immortal life of me I couldn't figure out why he'd become so cheerful. I was sure he had my destruction in mind—sooner or later. But now that he held my attention, he seemed perfectly content. I didn't trust him for what the moderns term a nanosecond. I blocked his good humor from my mind and concentrated on my own anger . . . and on fear in the world at large.

My particular dinner bell.

With me at the wheel of the mayor's vehicle, we were cruising the streets of one of the more unfortunate areas of the city. It was probably the first time this particular SUV had been down these streets of run-down houses, every third one abandoned. Hopeless street dwellers wandered in the darkness, ever the bait for one monstrous killer or another. Tonight would be our turn. I searched deeply for my anger. Feeding on that eclipse of the heart would serve me better than the blood of innocents.

I kept my mind on business. I couldn't afford the luxury of worrying about Jack or what might be happening between Shari and him in my absence. Jack was a big boy now—it was time for him to act like one.

Finding the dark emotion I'd been searching for, I shut off the vehicle lights and coasted to a stop in front of a dilapidated three-story flophouse. Huge oak trees hung over the yard, blocking any view of the upper levels. The door was boarded up, along with the first-floor windows, but there were humans inside, scrabbling around like rats. And someone was drunk and furious.

I stepped from the car and let the wave of fuming rage wash over me, drawing it in with my breath. I'd spent a long time resisting my anger fetish, only setting it free during my darker days. Tonight I would free it out of necessity, in order to lull my sire into thinking he had me back again.

Reedrek smiled. "Shall we?"

I nodded my assent. Before we reached the porch stairs, a gunshot sounded from somewhere inside.

"Even better," Reedrek said. "It amuses me when they fight back."

As easy as plucking peeling paint, I cleared the boards from the front door. "After you," Reedrek said with a courtly bow. I didn't bother to argue the social niceties of guests going first. The anger was tugging at me like promised sex.

A long, dark, dank-smelling hallway split the house in two. A termite-rotted stairway dangled stairless on our right. Down the hall, several floorboards were missing and as we entered the less-than-human things scurried through the thicker darkness below. I could see several pairs of small red eyes blinking from corners, from holes in the walls, and I could feel the faint warmth of their beating blood. This was not a place for man nor beast; yet here we were, a bit of both.

Shouts echoed from one of the rooms at the far end of the hallway. Then another gunshot blast sounded. Before one more conscious thought, I found myself standing in the doorway of the last room. The dim kerosene lantern and the small fire in the hearth seemed bright after the gloom of the hall. There were a few pieces of broken furniture and a spoiled mattress. The room stank of sour clothes, urine, and wine. There were other bullet holes in the walls, from other nights, I suspected. The man with the gun was too drunk to realize we had even entered the room. His staggering attention was set firmly on the woman and two children huddled next to the fireplace.

"I tol' you to fix me some supper, bitch!" The man waved the gun in their direction and kicked at the crushed cardboard box at his feet.

The woman pulled the children closer, shielding them with her body. "There's nothin' to cook," she managed in a low voice.

"Find somethin!" he ordered, making an attempt to hold the gun steady. "Or I'll—" Suddenly he noticed me. "Who the hell—"

My sire's eyes were already on the children. He had a predilection for the young and innocent. I looked at the woman. "Run!" I hissed, and bared my fangs. The woman, realizing she had one slim chance, grabbed the children and disappeared into the doorless dark.

With a look of regret, Reedrek turned on the man. The drunk managed to get off a final, ineffectual shot before Reedrek took the gun from his unresisting hand and tossed it over his shoulder.

I was surprised at how quickly the killing instinct returned to me. Hunting by twos is very much like dancing or having sex. No need to rush. There is a giving and a taking, with polite pauses for the other to find the perfect bite. Then, the sucking. Reedrek settled on one side and I took the other, spinning the victim up in the air. The man managed one last gurgling, angry scream as our mouths nearly met in a bloody kiss—fang to fang—with only his throat holding us apart. Then there was sucking and silence—no muss, no fuss. One of the victim's shoes deserted him, hitting the floor with a plop. The smell of fresh urine wafted around me. I blocked everything from my senses except the lure of blood. There were other humans upstairs, more gushing warmth if I chose them. I could feel their quiet fear. But no anger, only resignation.

Then I heard the sirens. Some Good Samaritan had called the law.

It takes a solid five minutes for one vampire to completely empty a body of blood. Two can do it in less than half that time without wasting a drop—presumably because competition makes the hunger sharper and showing off is ever a dangerous temptation for the undead. We finished just as the police lights flashed down the hallway. I thought it rather brave of them to face those dark rooms and someone with a gun, being that their mortality meant they could pay for their jobs with their lives. If they had known that we—unkillable with their weapons—were there, they might have turned back. To live another day.

Reedrek shoved the boards out of the window and vaulted into the dark shrubbery. I was left holding the victim, staring at the very obvious puncture wounds in his throat, feeling the rush of the kill. An old habit of self-preservation rose through my blood euphoria. Savannah was my city, after all, and I'd spent a good two hundred years protecting my place in it. There would be no time to make the body disappear. Even if this night was to be my last, I would not deliberately cause a public uproar over the rumor of vampires. Jack at least had to go on in Savannah. Or so I hoped. So, out of necessity, I tossed through the few cooking utensils near the hearth until I found a piece of a knife. It was missing the hilt but it would do nicely.

As a policeman yelled down the hallway, "Everybody out!" I pushed back the victim's head and slit his throat ear to ear, cutting through the fang marks. A human coroner who knew his business would notice the absence of arterial blood on the victim but he wouldn't easily attribute it to vampires. It was the best I could do on such short notice. I dropped the victim and the knife, picked up a relatively clean piece of discarded clothing, and followed Reedrek outside.

My heart hummed like a lover who'd been stroked one step away from orgasm. The hunger for human blood had been mitigated by the almost druglike after-feeding euphoria. Sucking away an actual life added extra power to the already pleasant sensation of feeding on human blood.

More, my body whispered. *More please.*

With what turned out to be a child's shirt, we cleaned up and watched the drama unfold from further down the street. The mayor's car had been blocked in by four cruisers. A few of the neighbors—if you could call this a neighborhood—came out to see if they knew any of the dead or jail-bound. That's when I saw Officer Consuela

Jones. As she was interviewing a witness, she suddenly stopped, pivoting to look directly at me—as if she'd felt my gaze on her back.

I turned to Reedrek. "I think we'd better move on before they want to ask us questions."

"What about my car?" he said with a smirk.

"It was never yours. Besides that fact, there's someone there who knows me."

Reedrek zeroed in on Officer Jones. "Ah yes, Jack's little girlfriend. A pity we didn't run across her with fewer—" he glanced at the knot of neighbors close to the police "—witnesses around."

"As for *your* car—" I nodded in the direction of the SUV. "One of the officers seems very interested in it." A policeman with a notepad was writing down the license number. It was only a matter of time until they found out who it really belonged to. The mayor would not be very happy.

An ambulance raced from the far end of the street. "Our new friend has his own transportation," Reedrek said. When he smiled his teeth were still pink with blood.

The power of feeding shot through me again, like electricity. My cock thickened, hard and insistent. The habit of sex after a feeding was coming back to haunt me. There would be no time for sex tonight, and, more important, I had to keep the memories of my games with Eleanor out of my thoughts—or Reedrek was liable to reverse the order and have her for sex, before eating her heart. He was still staring at Officer Jones.

"Come. We have other places to hunt," I said. Without looking back, I turned and headed toward the next street. We could find more victims before the police even finished their paperwork.

On foot now, we paced down the broken sidewalks, barely touching the ground. Playing the part of tuning fork, I caught snatches of conversation behind windows and walls: a baby crying, a man sighing into a drug-laced stupor, a couple having lackluster sex. That nearly stopped me. But even as I broke many of my time-tested rules, I clung to some. Anger was my affliction and my lure. And it took less than ten minutes to find another sample.

Jack

I'd barely gotten to sleep when I heard the eerie sound of brokenhearted sobs—sort of disembodied and creepy. I opened the coffin and crawled out, over Rehya and her sleepily murmured protests. At first I thought the cries were coming from Shari's coffin, so I flung open the lid, hoping that the horrors of the last day and a half—geez, how long *had* it been anyway?—had been a mistake or a bad dream and that she was alive after all.

But her body was in the same state as when I'd last seen her, so I closed the coffin again.

"Over here," said a small voice.

I should have realized what it was. Ghosts love me, I tell you. And the feeling is not mutual. Yes, they creep me out as much as they do anybody else, okay? She stood wringing her translucent hands in front of her, shimmering with that weird light they sometimes have.

It was the ghost of Shari.

I know it sounds silly, but ghosts kind of look like Princess Leia in *Star Wars* when she appears in that hologram and says, "Help us, Obi Wan. You're our only hope." I had a feeling that Shari had come back looking for help from me, and Obi Wan I wasn't.

I put up my hand in a feeble little wave. "How you doing?"

She shimmered a little harder in answer to my question and gave another squeaky little wail.

"I was afraid of that." I ran one hand through my hair. "Can't you sort of go toward the light or something?"

Her eyes got bigger and rounder. "There's no light here. It's dark and scary. There are frightening noises everywhere. Things are moving in the shadows. Dead things, evil things." She rubbed her arms. "And it's cold."

"Look. I'm really, really sorry. I did everything I could to keep you around here as a vampire, and something went wrong, so you died. I don't have any idea how to help you now. Can't you just stay in this dimension with us even though you don't have a body anymore? Just, well, hang out or something?" I was trying really hard to be helpful, but I've never understood the big picture afterlifewise. Who does? I mean, it's not like anybody hands you a map or anything. It's also not like anybody ever gets to tell about it—except for when the dead talk to me, that is.

"I'm not really there with you anymore. I'm stuck here. There are scary things and I don't know what they are." She began to sob again, real hopeless-like, and looked over one shoulder and then the other. Poor little thing. It was enough to break your heart. "I think some of these . . . these . . . animals or creatures or whatever are after me."

"What do they look like?"

"I can't see them. I can only hear them—feel them. Every now and then something slimy will reach out and touch me."

Damn them, whatever they were. I wished I could protect her. I felt helpless. "So there's no light at all to go to and there isn't anyone there to help you find your way to a better place?"

"Nooooooo! Please help me!"

Talk about your king-size, grade-A guilt trip. I decided the next time I got the bright idea to make somebody a vampire, I'd just go and stake myself. Not like it *was* my idea or anything. William should have just left this girl alone—but no, he had to make out with her at that club and get Reedrek to fang her.

That idea made my blood go cold . . . colder. I realized I'd made the same mistake with Connie by letting Reedrek know I cared for her. I just hoped to hell that Connie would wear the charm like she promised me she would.

As I was wracking my brain for how to help Shari, Melaphia came back in with a tray of ointments and herbs. Under one arm she had a really old-looking book.

"What are you doing out of that coffin? I thought you said you were going to get some rest."

I pointed in Shari's direction. "Do you see that?"

Melaphia narrowed her eyes. "No. But I can feel something—a spirit. Is it Shari?"

Melaphia's way with the dead was almost as good as my own. "Yeah. She says she's in a dark, scary place and that there are things in the shadows making her nervous. There's nobody there to help her."

Putting the tray and book down on the straight chair by Shari's coffin, Melaphia spoke to the little ghost. "If you feel something bad approaching you, move away from it as fast as you can."

"Oo-kay," Shari whimpered. "Which way should I go?"

"I heard her!" Melaphia answered the question before I had a chance to ask. A look of profound sadness came over Melaphia's face. "I've only heard about the place where you are," she said to Shari. "None of us who walk the earth have ever been to that dimension and come back to tell the tale. All I can tell you is to move away from anything that troubles or frightens you."

"That's pretty much everything here, but all right. Is there anything *you* can do?"

"Yes. I'm going to try to fix things on this end so the evil entities that are there—and here—can't . . . take you over."

Shari issued another otherworldly moan, as if she hadn't understood the danger she was in until Melaphia spelled it out. She hugged herself harder and shimmered some more.

"I want you to go back inside yourself now," Melaphia said. "Make yourself as big and strong and brave as you possibly can."

Shari nodded and slowly began to fade out until there was nothing of her left to see. At least here on earth.

"Thank you," I breathed to Melaphia. "Again."

"You're welcome, Uncle Jack." She favored me with a tired smile. She hadn't called me that in years. It comforted me somehow, as she knew it would. "Now, you get back in that coffin. And don't come out even if the devil himself tries to wake you."

"Don't jinx me. The way this night has gone, he might just show up." I climbed back in next to Rehya.

Would I ever rest again? We vampires sleep pretty soundly. We are dead, after all. But even though we're the stuff of nightmares, don't think for a New York minute that we don't have nightmares of our own.

Ten

William

We headed for the river, avoiding the area of well-lit bars and restaurants. Instead we sought out the darker parts, where the underbelly of the city gets scratched in its own favorite way. We walked the turf of small-time drug dealers. We moved through streets occupied by ever-present pimps, sitting like fat tomcats, waiting for their girls to return with the cream. We slipped through night air that was growing cooler, making the damp, cloying breath of the tunnels seem springlike. But winter was almost here. The nearly full hunter's moon was rising from a bank of clouds to the east. It was still early yet. Plenty of time for hunting.

A disagreement had broken out on a dark street corner a block away. We moved toward it, following several other curious bystanders.

"You owe me money, man. Don't come around here beggin' for somethin'. You hear me?"

"You cheated me last night. You gave me some squirrelly shit!"

The dealer smiled, but it didn't change the hard look

in his eyes. "You can't cheat somebody who don't give you no money. *Comprende?*" He slid a knife out of his pocket and twitched it open. "Now get away from me." He glanced toward the small but growing group of witnesses. "Or I'll cut off your limp dick and feed it to the rats."

"The doomed," Reedrek whispered. "They never cease to entertain me. Cutting off body parts . . ." He chuckled as he stepped forward into the light, causing two of the bystanders to turn and stare in our direction.

At the center of the argument, the two participants didn't seem to realize that death had arrived.

"I told you to get the fuck away from me!" the dealer bellowed at the smaller man.

Rather than backing down, the disgruntled customer showed poor judgment when he pulled what looked like a household butcher knife out of his jacket. Instantly, the dealer grabbed the arm of the junkie and pushed upward. Then he plunged his own knife into the man's stomach.

"Damn crackheads don't ever listen!"

With a gasp of surprise, the wounded man crumpled. Reedrek and I stepped into the circle of onlookers.

"We'll handle this now," I announced to the witnesses.

"Who the fuck are you, man?" the dealer asked. He looked me up and down, his fingers moving on the knife hilt. "You ain't no tired-assed cop," he laughed.

"No, I'm not."

He raised his weapon. "Then get out of my face and off my corner." I could smell his fear under the bravado. When I didn't move, his grip on the knife tightened and, after a moment's hesitation, he sliced it in an arc across my chest. Blood seeped from the cut, dyeing the edges of my white dress shirt. I could have easily prevented the contact, of course, but that urge to stand on the edge of immortal life and unholy death kept me still. In some ways I was more like my sire than I wanted to admit. I liked it when they fought back.

I ran one of my fingers through the welling blood and brought it to my mouth to suck it clean. "Damn. Now look what you've done. You've ruined my new shirt." I heard Reedrek chuckle, but I kept my eyes on my next meal. In a movement too quick for the dealer to follow, I removed the knife from his hand and flung it away so hard that I heard it splash into the river fifty feet away.

"What the fuck—"

My grip on his throat didn't allow him to finish the sentence. Both Reedrek and I gazed around the group of people who'd gathered for the fight, soothing their minds and sowing forgetfulness until they began to melt away, back to their own dark business.

"Time to go," I said, and led my attacker by the neck like a recalcitrant dog, down in the direction of the tunnels, allowing him to struggle just enough to hold my interest. Reedrek followed, dragging the mostly dead junkie by one foot.

In the dark tunnels, away from inquisitive eyes, I allowed a scream from my hapless meal before I silenced him. Death at least was quiet and peaceful.

We hunted until well after midnight, until we were drunk with blood. My head was spinning with sheer delirium. I needed sleep, but I needed sex more. All of my body wanted Eleanor—she would understand this thrumming energy running beneath my blood-hot skin. She would soothe my mind and take part of this restless power inside her. Then she would play the game of death and undeath. But these were thoughts that I had to block from my sire.

Reedrek was actually staggering under the frenzy of our blood gorging. We stumbled back through the empty streets and squares, arm in arm, like two of the drunken Irishmen he held in such disdain—Reedrek searching for sleep, and I half-crazed with lust. Somewhere near Colonial we came to the conclusion that we needed to lie down, if only for a while. We set our spinning heads on finding a tomb to use as a resting place.

We'd just decided on an ornate tomb with room for two when I smelled a sweet smoky odor and heard low voices, then a coughing laugh. Reedrek smiled like a tipsy card player who'd been dealt four aces. He wasn't finished with the night just yet. By the startled looks on the faces before us, we'd appeared among the tombs like wraiths stepping from thin air.

Eight surprised teenagers stared at us in silence.

Then they burst into uncontrolled laughter. The laughter stopped when I reached forward and snatched the cigarette, or joint, as Jack would say, from the hands of one of the boys.

"Don't you know that smoking this stuff will make you stupid?" I suggested with a fatherly smile.

"Nah," one of the boys protested. "The worst thing it'll do is give you the munchies. Go ahead, dude, try a hit."

"The munchies?" Reedrek repeated, barely able to contain his mirth. "And pray tell, what does that consist of?"

"Wow, you guys really are old." More laughter. "Smoking pot makes you starvin' hungry—gives you the munchies. Get it?"

"Offering us this *pot*, as you call it, would be very unfortunate then."

"Why? You old dudes could at least afford some waffles at Denny's."

"Because they're vampires," a voice from the other side of the circle said.

After a moment of silence, all the teenagers except the one who had spoken burst into more unrestrained laughter. One of the boys laughed so hard he fell back against a convenient headstone, gasping for breath.

"Vampires—yeah, right."

The boy who'd spoken stood up, but even he was smiling. It took me a second to place him—he'd followed Jack as we were leaving Club Nine. Werm, he'd called him.

"I'm afraid your friend Werm is correct. You should listen to him," I said.

Reedrek bowed like an inebriated showman. "Evil vampire at your service."

More laughter.

Werm moved closer. "You know my name," he said, staring at me, sounding awestruck. "That's so cool."

I handed the joint to him. "Yes, and since Jack isn't here, might I suggest that Colonial, at least tonight, is not a *cool* place for you and your friends."

Three of the boys were literally rolling on the ground. "You dudes are already stoned out of your gourds," one of them said, causing the others to laugh harder.

Reedrek leveled his full attention on the boys. I could feel his mind probing their inebriated thoughts.

I dug in my jacket pockets until I found a folded sheaf of bills. I had to do something before Reedrek exhibited his appetite. Too full to argue, I assumed, he remained leaning against a tomb wall and watched as I handed the money to Werm. "Take your friends away from here," I said, bending his mind with my own.

"But I want to stay," he mumbled, looking toward Reedrek. A truly bad inclination when one is in the presence of a vampire.

"You're too hungry to stay. You'll starve to death if you don't get to Denny's right now."

I'm not sure these mortals had ever felt the kind of hunger I planted in their minds. I certainly had—the belly-scraping-backbone need of a body for sustenance. In my case, a whiff of blood. Right now, however, my hunger had been more than satisfied, and I hoped that Reedrek felt the same. However, that wouldn't stop him from killing for sport.

"Go!" I ordered, and one by one the boys stood up and, still giggling, walked into the darkness.

Reedrek leered at me. "Just as I expected. Why do you bother saving the helpless? They're all dying one day at a time anyway."

"Frankly, I'm too tired and too full," I lied. "Now that the cemetery is quiet, I need sleep."

Reedrek, still wobbling on his feet, was little help in lifting the ten-foot concrete slab that covered the opening to a family crypt. I, on the other hand, felt as if I could stack the automobiles parked along the street into one glorious pile if I chose.

Under no circumstances would I be able to sleep.

Reedrek crawled down next to the dusty bones of the other long-dead occupants. He passed out as soon as he achieved a prone position. The sight of him so helpless brought back my hatred, and I thought I should kill him then and take him to hell myself. But first I had to see Eleanor a final time. If Reedrek killed me on the morrow, I would have had one last grand night of living.

The least I could do, however, was to leave the tomb open in hopes the sun would catch him unawares. As my lust pounded with new urgency, I upended the massive slab of stone, leaving my not-so-loving sire under the stars. Then I practically flew down the sidewalk to Eleanor.

I took a seat on the chair next to Eleanor's bed, thankful that she was alone. I'd already done more than my share of killing for the night. I needed a different sort of exercise. Besides, killing Eleanor's paying customers was bad for her business. Not part of our oh-so-civilized arrangement. Heat radiated from my skin in such thick waves that I thought surely it must wake her. It did cause her to sigh in her sleep and push the covers off, baring her body to my gaze. It surprised me that she wore a man's long-sleeved dress shirt. I would've thought a woman in her profession would sleep naked. Then, with an even more surprising jolt of pleasure, I realized the shirt was one of my own. Lucky shirt. Not a problem; she would be naked soon enough.

As I rose from the chair intent on waking her, she startled and sat up as though I'd already touched her from across the room. Perhaps my mind had called out since my body had been so preoccupied by thoughts of her.

"Who is it?" she asked, then coyly pulled the sheets over her bare legs with her left hand. Her sleepy vulnerability heightened my wanting.

You've already guessed, I whispered in my mind, *have you not?*

"William?" she responded. Then she flicked on a light. Eleanor gasped when she saw me. "What—what's happened to you?" She actually sounded afraid. Although she'd always been a good actress, this seemed real.

I moved over next to her, doing my utmost to keep my

feet on the floor. I sat down on the bed. Instead of sliding into my arms, she leaned away from me, staring. "You look so different—and the blood—" Her empty hand fluttered toward my chest.

"Do I? Look different?" Without the sometimes handy advantage of a reflection, I couldn't tell. I knew I felt different. My arteries were singing through heated muscles, my hard-won control balanced on a knife edge.

"Your eyes, they—" She looked away.

I brought one hand up to cup her cheek and noticed that I had blood under my fingernails. There'd been no time to mimic respectability by cleaning up. No telling what I looked like—or smelled like. My senses were overrun with the scent and taste of new blood, and now of sex.

Now, my body howled.

"I'm here to play," I said, pushing my fingers into her hair.

She tentatively placed her hand over mine, looking uneasy. Perhaps my appearance made our game all too real. "Why don't I draw you a bath? Fix the cut on your chest—"

I pulled free and shrugged out of my coat. "No time for that, my girl." *Now, now, now!* "The sun will be rising soon." In a trice I was naked. I ripped the shirt from her with my teeth.

She screamed when I entered her. She dug her fingernails into my hot skin, but I barely felt her struggle. She belonged to me and I would fuck her at my leisure, although there was nothing leisurely about the way I pounded into her. She screamed again and I came in a gasping, bucking two-minute interval, remaining hard and full inside her afterward.

I held her pinned to the sheets beneath me. She'd

stopped struggling. Her heart beat against my chest like pounding fists. Finally, she shifted.

"Let me," she said, pushing against my weight until I turned over. I brought her with me, still impaled. I pushed my hands upward along her belly and breasts, caressing the snake tattoo from tail to snout. I slid my fingers around her hips and tugged her downward. She squirmed and grimaced slightly before giving me a tentative smile, more like her old self. Shrugging out of my restraining grip she began her own rhythm, and soon we were both winded, straining toward another peak. With her hands flat on my shoulders she spiraled into a long back-arching orgasm, and I followed.

"Your skin is like fire," she managed as she slid off me.

I stared at the ornate crown molding along the ceiling. *It's the blood, it's the killing. It's who I really am.* Those words were not for her ears. But her body tensed as though the truth had passed from my hot skin to hers. I pushed up on one elbow and gazed down at her. "I've had an interesting evening," I remarked.

"I can see that," she said, as one finger slid across the already healing cut on my chest.

I could damn well guarantee she wouldn't want to know the details. In an effort to distract her, I ran a hand down her belly, sinking fingers between her thighs. I worked the wetness I found there before confessing, "I think I missed you."

"You th-think?" She sighed and opened her legs, an invitation for more exploration.

I sank my fingers deeper and looked downward to enjoy the sight of my hand fondling her sex. That's when I saw that the wetness I'd felt was blood. Her thighs were red with it. Something gripped my stomach. "I've hurt you," I said, unable to take my eyes off the sweet redness.

She slowly pushed herself up and followed my gaze. "Yes," she answered, dropping back to lie flat. "Don't really care—not now." She moved her hips against my hand.

"Let me make it better," I offered. Without waiting for a reply I grasped her hips and lifted her higher on the bed. Then I set my tongue to work on the blood. It tasted of her and of me. Perhaps I'd come blood after overfeeding. Whatever the case, she was soon moaning from my ministrations. In normal times this would have been a dangerous pastime for me—starved for human blood, this would have been the ultimate temptation. But tonight I was satiated, and the small amount of blood I licked and sucked from her skin seemed more like dessert after a twelve-course meal. Sweet and stimulating. Obviously, she agreed on the matter of stimulation, since she came hard once again, against my tongue.

Afterward, I carried her to the bath and we soaked for a short time. She still seemed a little wary of me, but not so much that she wasn't happy to wash away any signs of blood or dust from my skin. She washed my hair with her clever fingers and I was beginning to think of tumbling her again when I felt a presence near.

I rinsed quickly and snatched the towel Eleanor offered. But instead of letting her dry me, I went to the window and looked out. I could feel the sun, less than an hour away, rising to drive me back to the darkness. My sire came to mind, and I did my best to envision him burning to cinders under a bloodred sunrise. If there were any mercy in the universe he would die a miserable death and vanish into hell where he belonged. A chill ran through me like an ill-omened wind. His evil was close and choking. I scanned the shrubbery in the side yard, where I saw him, leaning on the wrought-iron fence. He was waiting for me.

Reedrek.

I pulled on my pants, prepared to go out and face him. Suddenly there was a knock downstairs on the front door.

"No!" I shouted. In my haste to prevent Reedrek from entering, I grasped Eleanor's locked bedroom door and yanked. The door burst from the hinges and I shoved it away, making it down the stairs in three long strides, just as one of Eleanor's girls sleepily reached the front entrance.

"Do not open that door," I ordered.

Her hands immediately fell back to her sides. The knock sounded again, more insistent. The girl, Tami I think, looked up at me, then up the stairs. I followed her gaze to find Eleanor, wrapped in one of her satin bed-sheets, standing on the first landing. It would do no good to try to keep him away from her now. The damage was done. I'd allowed my lust to disarm me. Could I have been a bigger fool?

"Back away," I said, and gave Tami a little shove before unlocking the door and swinging it open myself.

Reedrek smiled.

I turned to Eleanor and in my most persuasive, mind-shifting tone said, "This man is never to be invited into this house. Do you understand?" Both she and Tami nodded. "Warn all the others."

"Dear William, I thought we were just getting to be friends again and now this. You leave me out in the open with no care for my safety. You won't even introduce me to your playthings."

"We were *never* friends."

His smile and good manners disappeared. He reached

through the opening and dragged me outside. I could smell his skin smoking from the action. Having crossed an uninvited threshold, he was burning.

"Stay in this house!" I managed to shout back to Eleanor as I struggled with Reedrek. We rose into the air, him in his element, me grappling with my rising anger. Instead of helping my cause, leaving the ground only worked in Reedrek's favor. He dragged me, barefoot and shirtless, into the waning dark and all I could think about was what he would certainly do to Eleanor after he'd finished with me.

Jack

A shaft of light pierced my eyelids and I flung my forearm over my face. "Hey!" I protested. I squinted one eye open just enough to see who'd rudely awakened me. "Olivia. Where the hell have you been?"

"Cheers to you too," Olivia said airily. She wrapped her arms around Rehya—now in four-legged form, signaling that it was daytime—and dragged her from the coffin. "Out, Lassie," she said.

Reyha landed on her feet after a catlike save in midair. She whined and retreated to the ottoman where I had tried to finish vampirizing Shari the night before.

Rehya rested her sleek head on her paws and stared at me. The only thing that would distract her was if William came in, at which time she would shift her undivided attention to him.

Olivia had some kind of wild light in her eyes. It occurred to me that she might have come under Reedrek's thrall. I knew I couldn't trust her—not that I trusted her all that much to begin with—and I found myself wondering who would win a catfight (if you'll pardon the expression) between a two-thousand-year-old Egyptian mystic attack dog and a strong female vampire. I shuddered just thinking about the possibility of having to sic Reyha on Olivia. *When Supernaturals Attack*. Even Fox wouldn't put that show on television.

Olivia crawled into my coffin, a come-hither look on her face. She straddled me and began to massage my bare chest. "I guess since my box is occupied, you'll just have to share yours." She inclined her head toward the coffin that contained Shari's body. "I saw there's a Goldilocks in my bed. No matter. I'll play Mama Bear to your Papa Bear. Who is she, anyway?"

I swallowed hard as she tweaked my nipples none too gently. "Her name is Shari. I tried to make her into a vampire last night and it didn't work. She's dead. Really dead."

As quick as a flash Olivia's demeanor changed. Her flirtatious smile disappeared; her vermilion-painted mouth became a grim line. She sprang back onto the floor, landing on her high snakeskin heels. She walked over to her coffin and, taking a moment to steel herself, raised the lid. I went to stand beside her as she somberly studied Shari's body.

Shari's corpse was in slightly better condition than it had been when I'd last seen it, thanks to Melaphia's recent ministrations. Her chants and potions had had some restorative effects—short of actually bringing Shari back to life, of course. There were twigs and herbs scattered on Shari's body. I could see why Olivia had mistaken her for a sleeping vampire.

"Melaphia dressed her and did some kind of spells and incantations over her body while I was sleeping last night. I guess that's what the herbs are for. She said it would help keep Shari's body from being possessed or something."

Olivia picked up a sprig of what looked like lavender, sniffed it delicately, and then replaced it. "Yes. Melaphia is a good woman. There are things I will do for Shari as well. I must bleed for her, and . . . other things. I'll also document her brief half life. Later."

"Document?" I asked, confused.

"Never mind. I'll explain some other time."

I sighed. "I didn't mean to hurt her, honest. I did everything William said to do—to the letter. I can't figure out what happened. Melaphia said it just happens sometimes, but there must be more to it than that. Do you know anything about making female vampires? I mean, you are one, and you got made somehow. I don't remember my own making, so I was wondering—"

Olivia put her fingers to my lips. "No one remembers their own making. But in answer to your question, yes. I know a great deal about how female vampires are made, just as I know of their trials and tribulations once they become full-fledged blood drinkers. There are certain . . . difficulties involved at all levels. But Melaphia was right. There are many things that can go wrong in the process and none of them bear thinking about too closely at this point. I'm sure you did your best, so try not to dwell on it."

"She appeared to me as a ghost last night after her spirit had the time to leave her body."

"Really?" Olivia said, her eyes widening. "How extraordinary. You must be a sensate."

"Huh?"

"A blood drinker who has the power to communicate with the lower undeads—spirits and the like."

"You make it sound like there's a class system where dead people are concerned."

She didn't crack a smile. "There is."

"So I guess we're pretty high up in the pecking order?"

"Dead right," Olivia said. She did smile then. "We're the crème de la crème."

"That's French for top dog, right?"

"Like comparing crème brûlée to a tin of Alpo, but yes, something like that."

"You have to get up pretty early in the night to put one over on old Jack McShane." In actual fact, I felt about as ignorant as the night was long. There was an undead caste system, and we were at the top. There was a name for my ability to communicate with spirits—in addition to being a smart-ass dead white boy, I was also something called a sensate. Who knew?

"We vampires are like the rock stars of the dark realm," Olivia continued. "Royalty, if you will."

You learn something every day. Well actually, I didn't start learning anything until just lately. "You're just trying to cheer me up."

"Yes, I am. But that doesn't make it any less true."

"So, if we're such hot stuff, is there anything that you or I can do for Shari at this point? I mean besides the bleeding and documenting stuff you mentioned earlier?"

"I wish I could tell you there was. But the spells and treatments that Melaphia made, as well as the small gestures I will do, are the only things that can be done."

"Shari said she was in a bad place, a dark place, and there were some shadowy, scary things out there trying to get her."

"That concerns me. But if Melaphia did things correctly, it should prevent Shari's possession. I don't fully understand the source of Melaphia's abilities, but the methods she has used on Shari are very ancient indeed and have similarities to the ones I'm familiar with. They have much in common with the ways of the Druids."

"Aren't they the ones who dance around the maypole naked on moonlit nights?"

"It's a little more complicated than that."

My head was starting to hurt again, as if it were about to bust with all this new information. My mind turned back to the girl in the coffin. "Reedrek drained Shari to the point of death, so William asked Shari if she wanted to be one of us. She said she wanted to be a vampire. Where the hell is William anyway? Do you know?"

A strange look came over Olivia's face the instant I said the name *Reedrek*. It was like she'd just remembered something very important. She turned back to stare at Shari's face and reached out to smooth her hair, murmuring something to the dead girl. She seemed deeply moved by the death of Shari, a young woman she never even knew. After a while, she said to me, "If she chose to undergo the transformation from human to blood drinker, you can rest assured that you did the right thing, even though it was not to be." I barely noticed that she'd ignored my question about where William was.

"I just can't shake the feeling that I blew it." I put my elbows on my knees and my head in my hands. "I think there must be something wrong with me."

I felt her hands on my shoulders, kneading and massaging. "Poor Jack. Let me comfort you," she whispered in my ear. As her face brushed mine, I smelled it. Let me tell you, there's a reason that the women at the department store fragrance counters don't come up and spritz you with Eau de Evil Dead. Olivia had been with Reedrek. Now there was no doubt in my mind that she was dancing to his tune. Whatever happened next, I was going to have to be awfully careful.

I thought I heard Rehya growl from across the room. Olivia swung around in front of me and took my hands in hers, lifting up my arms so she could sit on my lap to face me. She kissed both my palms, after which she put them against either side of her face and looked deeply into my eyes. "You are such a lamb, aren't you? You dear, sweet, innocent lamb."

She emphasized the word *innocent*. I've been called a lot of things by women, let me tell you, but this was a brand-spanking-new accusation. I tried to think what she might mean by that—other than my failed vampire-making and my general ignorance—but she was starting to unbutton her shirt, so I pretty much stopped thinking about anything but the promise of boobs. "Mmm-hmm," I agreed. "That's me—baa-aaaah." I was vaguely aware that Reyha had hopped off the ottoman and gone under the leather chair. I couldn't see her face anymore and hoped she couldn't see me anymore either.

Olivia planted a kiss on me that would have made me swoon if I hadn't been sitting down. It was long and languorous and by the time it was over, her shirt was unbuttoned and her lace-clad breasts were in my face. She pushed her fingers into my hair as I nuzzled her cleavage.

"Speaking, as we were, of Melaphia's knowledge, what *is* her secret? Where did she learn to do what she did with Shari?"

"Hmm?" How could she expect me to talk at a time like this? My tongue was otherwise engaged, trying to snake its way under the top of the bra to get to the tender buds beneath. Why was she asking me about . . . what was she asking me about?

"Melaphia. Where does she get her know-how? Is it voodoo? I read that there's lots of that here in Savannah."

"Voodoo. Yeah. She knows about voodoo." Voodoo schmoodoo. Right then I was more interested in finding out whether Olivia's frilly little bra hooked in the front or the back.

"Is that where William's protective power comes from? That was quite an impressive display in the nightclub. Reedrek couldn't lay a hand on him."

I found the bra closure—eureka!—and flipped it apart with the dexterity only decades of practice can bring. The elastic let go with a snap and rode up around Olivia's neck. Her breasts sprang free and I pressed my face between them. It was then that the dirty old man vampire smell of Reedrek came back to my nostrils. My horniness got the best of me, though, pushing away the implications of that odor, and I ignored her question.

She went for my belt the way Shari had the night before, and I flashed back to just a few hours ago and what had happened after the first time I had wild sex with a fellow vampire. "Hey," I said, dragging my face away from her breasts, "the last time I did this with a girl vampire, she turned toes-up. What if it wasn't the vampire-making process? What if I'm cursed or some kind of poison to girl vampires or something?"

Olivia laughed harshly as she undid the belt. "Don't be ridiculous. You couldn't harm me if you tried."

Good enough for me. If something did go wrong she couldn't say I didn't warn her. I captured a nipple in my mouth right about that time anyway, and all rational thought left my brain. My body managed to make note of the fact that my jeans weren't between me and her anymore, and that she was hiking up the skirt that was barely there to begin with. I reached to cup her butt and found that her bottom was completely bare. I slid my fingers between her thighs.

"Not after I get done with you, that is," Olivia hissed. With that cryptic comment, she drove herself down on my erection with a force that made me yell. As I looked into her face, I could see her look of triumph turn to one of surprise. She looked searchingly into my eyes and put her hands on the back of the chair for leverage. At the same time, she toed off her high-heel boots and settled her feet firmly onto the spindles around the bottom of the chair. The look of confidence returned to her face and she kissed me again.

I began to squirm, seeking friction, and she complied by raising herself up and plunging back down once more. She groaned. "Tell me, Jack. Tell me what William's secret is. I have to know."

I put my hands underneath her bottom and tried to lift her for another stroke, but she hooked her feet under the spindles and didn't budge, determined to remain in control. If she didn't move again soon, I was prepared to beg for mercy, but that's not what she wanted. No, she wanted to know about William's power, and—now it was dawning on me, despite my growing physical need— she wanted to know for Reedrek, because Reedrek was controlling her.

I let my head loll back on my shoulders, closed my eyes, and took a deep breath. I would not give up William's secrets to Reedrek through Olivia, but I would make her work to try to drag it out of me. And I'd enjoy the hell out of it. She thought she was Mata Hari, did she? We'd see who'd control this little interrogation session. I opened my eyes and stared at her as calmly as I could. "I have no idea what you're talking about."

That wasn't what she wanted to hear. She raised herself up again and came back down. "You're lying." Her face was turning beet red, unheard of for a vampire who hadn't just fed. Point for Jack.

I tried to keep from moaning again. I was as hard as a sapphire, so hard I was half afraid of breaking off each time she came down on me. I wanted to scream, but I wouldn't give her the satisfaction. I said nothing as she seated herself on me, and me inside her, again.

"Why are you protecting William?" She was losing control, I could tell, and not just sexually. There was something else, too. "Look how he's treated you all these years. He's kept you ignorant of your power, withheld the glorious truths of your nature as a vampire. He didn't tell you about the splendor that can be yours. All he has shared is the dark side. It's a bloody shame. And still you serve him. You're a fool!"

I remembered something then. William had warned me not to have sex with Olivia. Then he'd told me that I *had* to have sex with Shari. Why? Was it really that making Shari would give her strength and make me stronger as well? Or was it that Shari couldn't give me knowledge—and Olivia could?

Olivia bucked and plunged again, making me grit my teeth. "Reedrek is the one to whom you should give your loyalty," she said. "He, not William, has your best interests at heart."

"Is that what Reedrek told you? Did he tell you to come here and fuck me into telling you William's secrets? Did he tell you to promise me a lesson on how to be a vampire for dummies?" She flexed her legs and tried to rise again, but I held her shoulders, letting her know who was in charge. Bad Daddy Jack was in the house.

She laughed, and the sound had a hysterical edge that gave me the creeps. "He tried to enthrall me. Oh yes, he tried. But I'm stronger than that. And I'm stronger than you, you bloody ignorant whelp."

"Oh yeah?" I took my hands from her shoulders and whipped my arms underneath her legs, dislodging her feet from the spindles. I raised her and brought her down on me with so much force that I winced. "We'll see about that."

I scooted my behind as far back in the chair as it would go and leaned forward, raising her legs high and bending her knees over the back of the chair. Her hands lost their grip on the chair back and flailed helplessly at our sides. I then wrapped my arms around her waist like a clamp.

"Tell . . . me . . . where . . . William . . . is!" I heard myself demand, working her torso up and down with every word I spat out. The position we were in narrowed her passage to a viselike grip. I thought I'd lose my mind.

"Go to hell!"

"You first!"

She screamed. I was beyond caring if it was from pleasure or pain—that's what she got for trying to play me. Besides, she was supposed to be sapping my strength, so she got the long end of the stick out of this deal in more ways than one.

She tried to find purchase with her hands to regain control or maybe free herself altogether, but instead she pawed uselessly against my outer thighs. She tried to counter my movements with her legs, but I'd pulled them off the chair and trapped them against my chest and shoulders. She seemed to be getting weaker.

"What's happening to me?" she whispered breathlessly. "This isn't how it's supposed to be. Something's not right."

Still working her up and down like I was churning butter, I looked at her. Her eyes were glassy and her face was going slack. She seemed on the verge of fainting. Her muscles—all but the ones that were gripping my shaft—were going limp. Was this one going to die on me, too? Damn, I didn't know my own strength. Time to wrap things up anyway. Just as I felt my release, Olivia's body shuddered and I could feel her muscles spasming rhythmically all around my shaft. She screamed again with what strength she had left, and I groaned and emptied myself into her.

The look in her eyes turned to horror and I could see Reedrek reflected in them. Not his image, but his presence. It was as if Olivia's orgasm had shattered her defenses and a barrier to her true state of mind came tumbling down. He'd been here, spying on us somehow through Olivia's mind. Still staring into her eyes, I knew the moment she snapped out of Reedrek's control and back to her senses.

I took a few seconds to get my breath before I loosened my grip on her waist. She fell backward, and I had to lurch for her to keep her head from hitting the floor. I picked her up and rose unsteadily with her, not knowing if she was strong enough to stand on her own.

After a few more moments, her lids fluttered and her eyes began to focus. She squirmed in my arms, so I set her on her feet. Her skirt settled down around her hips, but she was still topless and barefoot. She seemed to be gathering her strength and her thoughts.

It's always a little awkward right after your first round of wild, athletic sex with a woman, but this time took the cake. The encounter we just had felt like a to-the-death, no-holds-barred championship-title wrestling match from hell. Was that what sex with another vampire was like? Every time? Cool. I could do without the cloak-and-dagger stuff, though. Other than that . . .

The charged silence continued as Olivia wavered on her feet like a candle flame in a sudden breeze. I reached out to steady her, feeling the need to say something to break the tension. Being that it was a sensitive situation, and being that I'm a man and all, I chose something entirely inappropriate.

"Uh, was it as good for you as it was for me?"

For somebody who looked as washed out as a dishrag, she sure was fast. She drew back her arm and slapped me across the face with enough force to send me flying backward. My feet were still tangled up in my jeans so I couldn't land with any grace whatsoever. I just hit the wooden chair and went right on over, my feet shooting straight in the air.

"What are you, and what did you just do to me?" Olivia screeched.

"What are you talking about?" I put my hand to my stinging cheek. "And *ow*!"

Her face mottled with rage. "There *is* something wrong with you, something very wrong with you indeed!"

"Me?" I righted myself and the chair and struggled back into my jeans. "What about you? You were channeling Reedrek the whole time we were doing it." The meaning of that struck me like a hammer blow. "Gross!"

"Okay, maybe I was." Olivia corralled her bra, still dangling around her neck, and fastened it. "But I'm all better now. What I want to know is, why am I knackered?"

"What?"

Olivia rolled her eyes as she buttoned her shirt. "You weakened me, you wanker. I was supposed to be able to draw power from you. But instead I feel shattered . . . dazed."

"I'm sorry."

She gave me a murderous look. "Of course you are."

"I didn't do it on purpose. Honest."

Olivia smoothed down her hair and narrowed her eyes. "What exactly happened when you had sex with Shari last night? What was happening at the precise moment that she began to fail?"

A terrible realization began to sink in. "I—I guess it was the same thing that was happening right about the same time you started to get all weak."

Olivia studied me for a long moment. "How do you feel right now, Jack? Completely relaxed from a really good shag?"

I flexed my muscles, then stretched. "I feel great. Really great." The truth was, I felt strong. Superman strong. I peered at her boobs, trying to tell if I had the X-ray vision to see through her clothes. I almost thought I could. "Kind of like I could leap tall buildings in a single bound."

"I'll be damned." Olivia crossed her arms and stared at me like I was some new species of vampire. "In all the years I've been studying the effect of gender on vampirism, I've never seen anything like this."

Hell, maybe I *was* a new species of vampire. "What do you mean?"

"I didn't gain strength from you—you sapped nearly every bit of strength that I have. Even now I feel as if I could faint."

"You need to feed. Let me get you some blood. William keeps some human blood from a lab on hand for emergencies. That ought to help you get some of your strength back." I went to the little refrigerator under the bar, found the human blood tucked far in the back, and emptied a bag of it into a glass. Olivia walked slowly over to the bar and leaned against it. She took the blood and nearly gagged on her first deep swallow of it.

"Small sips. It's strong stuff," I said. I waited until she had finished the glass and poured her another round. It would probably take more than two to improve her mood. "Olivia," I began, hating to have to ask the question, but needing to know, "did I kill Shari last night?"

Olivia looked at the polished marble surface of the bar, as if searching for a reflection long gone. "Almost certainly," she said. "You have to promise me you will never attempt to make a female vampire again."

"Of course I won't." I leaned my elbows on the bar. As much as I wanted to drown my sorrows in more Scotch, I had to try to keep my wits about me. The world was spinning fast enough as it was. I refused to think about Shari. I'd make like Scarlett O'Hara and think about it another day. Right now, William was gone and I no longer knew if I could trust Olivia. She seemed to be thinking straight right now, but maybe Reedrek would be able to take control of her again. When she'd first shown up tonight, she'd seemed suitably concerned about Shari and perfectly normal. Then she'd changed. I couldn't afford to turn my back on her again.

Everything was so damned confusing. I didn't even know if I could trust William any longer. Maybe Olivia had been right when she said that I should go over to Reedrek's side. It would be a whole lot simpler. Why not just give in to the evil? I knew Olivia had been under

Reedrek's thrall when she'd suggested it, but that might not make it any less of a good idea.

Olivia was still steadying herself with one arm propped on the bar. "Do you feel any better?" I asked.

"Yes. Somewhat."

"Good. Now, where's William?"

Olivia couldn't meet my eyes. "He's with Reedrek."

"What? How?"

"Reedrek was holding me. William exchanged himself for me. He told me to come back here."

"Shit. Do you think you could get me back there?"

Olivia shook her head. "I got so confused in those damned tunnels. In this condition, I'll never find Reedrek unless he wants me to. Jack, what the hell do we do now?"

"You don't do anything. You're not going hunting for Reedrek in the shape you're in. He'd drain you in a heartbeat. You're staying here." I didn't tell her that the other reason she was staying here was that I couldn't afford to trust her. Not until I'd had a chance to figure things out, and maybe not even then.

"Like hell. If you're going out after William, I'm going with you." She slammed her glass down on the bar and thrust out her dainty chin.

"I'm not playing nursemaid to a sick vampire. It's daylight out. You get your restorative rest, and maybe— *maybe* I'll let you out when the sun goes back down." Olivia started to protest, but I skirted the bar and lifted her up again. She felt as light as a feather. I could have raised her above my head with one finger. I carried her to my coffin and laid her in it.

"Jack, don't you dare!"

Rehya came out from under the leather chair, wagging her tail and sporting a soppy, doggy grin.

I pressed Olivia back against the cushions, closed the lid, and locked it. I could hear her muffled curses from inside. "Let me out, you bastard! I've got to prepare Shari!"

"You can work with Shari after you've recovered. She's not going anywhere."

"Damn you, Jack."

"Nighty night. You've been a really good sport."

I jammed my boots back onto my feet and let Reyha out the vault door to the upstairs. "Go to Melaphia, girl." She licked my hand and did as I told her.

I went to the door to the tunnels and pushed it open, not knowing where I was going and not particularly caring either. I headed out in the general direction of the garage. I wanted the comfort of familiar surroundings—not to mention a shower and a shirt that wasn't ripped to shreds. If I took my time it might be dark by the time I got there. If not, hell, in the mood I was in maybe I'd just step on out into the sun and light myself up like a Christmas tree. Fa-la-la-la-freakin'-la.

At the first street grate I paused and looked up toward the world of the living. If I stood off to the side and avoided the shafts of light coming down, I could see a bit of the sidewalk and the feet and lengthening shadows of humans passing by on their way to work. More than ever I longed to be one of them again.

But here I was, Jack McShane: bloodsucker, murderer of wannabe female vampires, scourge to the true ladies of the night everywhere—a literal ladykiller. I hung my head and thought of Connie. A wave of longing rolled over me like the tide coming in on Tybee. My dark-haired Latin beauty. At least she had a beating heart, so I knew I couldn't kill her. Well, I *could,* but I wouldn't. I wouldn't harm a hair on her head in a million years.

An autumn leaf from one of the oak trees on the square blew across the grate, lodged briefly on the edge, and fell between the iron bars. It floated down to me like a gift from an unseen hand, and I reached out for its golden loveliness, forgetting about the shafts of morning sunlight. My flesh began to burn, and I pulled my fingers back and put them to my mouth to ease the pain.

As I stared at the leaf, it began to glow along the edge where I'd held it. By the time it landed, it was on fire, ignited by my oh-so-brief touch. It struck me then that I couldn't have Connie, not *really* have her till death do us part. If I were to ever win her living heart, if she ever came to love me as I now knew I loved her, my version of "eternally yours"—making her a vamp—would kill her as surely as I'd killed Shari and almost killed Olivia.

I watched the leaf in horrified fascination until there was nothing left but a wisp of smoke, which disappeared with a sudden downdraft from the grate leading to the living, sunlit world. Then I retreated into the shadows where I belonged.

Eleven

William

I awoke in the dark.

It's nearly impossible to knock a vampire unconscious, but then, Reedrek had had hundreds of years of practice. I kept still, taking stock of my situation. There were familiar tomb smells, along with tabby and brackish water. I could sense Reedrek nearby. His personal odor of grimy decay seemed to permeate my skin.

Have I mentioned that I cannot kill Reedrek? Not unless I'm willing to die in the effort. You see, there's this inconsequential, well-known rule, or custom, you might say: An offspring cannot kill its own sire. I imagine the rule evolved from that whole Oedipus incident a few thousand years back. Or perhaps it's a defense mechanism bred into the blood mutation of the species. Without it there would be precious few of us around. I am the perfect example of an offspring who would've happily killed my sire the first night I awoke as a blood drinker, if I could have.

Just then things didn't seem to be going well for me. I tried to move and found my arms pinned straight out to the sides, hands palm up. The only things missing were nails in my wrists. The rest of me seemed . . . contained, as if I'd been wrapped in a cocoon—a juicy bug caught by a spider. There was cold rock or concrete at my back and something extremely heavy—also rock or concrete— balanced on my chest. I felt like a vampire sandwich.

I almost smiled. Jack would have a fine laugh if he could see me now. But thinking of Jack sobered me. Where was he? What had Olivia done to him?

I stepped off the platform of my worry and focused my thoughts on more practical issues. I could feel the sun high somewhere out in the waking world. Perhaps Jack was being a good boy and sleeping. But Olivia had had a whole night to find and influence him. I truly believed Jack was clever and resourceful, but in my current situation I had little hope he could outsmart Reedrek. After all, I'd done such a spectacular job of outsmarting him myself.

And then there was the vision—of Jack betraying me. I'd thought to deal with Reedrek before that could occur. My only remaining hope rested on Jack's pure Irish pigheadedness. I could vouch for the fact that he rarely did what anyone tried to force him to do. Charming him was another thing altogether. Even so, the odds that Olivia would be able lead him astray were at best even.

The memory of her lusty ride in Eleanor's playroom surfaced. If my sire had set Olivia on a course of seducing Jack, she would weaken his natural power with every orgasm. That would make him easy prey.

Damn Reedrek. My chest expanded with my anger, and the bonds encircling me tightened.

"So you're awake." A rustle of movement—wading

through water—from an unseen part of the room heralded Reedrek's approach.

"No thanks to you," I managed through clenched teeth.

He made a sort of clucking sound, then, suddenly, there was light shining in my eyes. I could see part of a room. I was laid out on a stone table. We were in what I deemed to be one of the older family mausoleums near the center of the cemetery. Moldering bones littered the shelves built above the water line and a net of roots like spiderwebs clung to the damp rock. A human head, freshly harvested, stared down at me from an upper shelf. It seemed Reedrek had taken to heart the medieval custom of placing a skull on the dinner table. On the opposite wall were three sets of manacles and chains, two of which still had arm and hand bones hanging from the rusted circles. It seemed that some family members had been buried before they were completely dead—unlike the newly added headless human crumpled in the corner.

"We're in Bonaventure," I said.

"Yes. I brought you here for a little privacy." Reedrek gave me a sad look. "You should know by now, child, I will have what I want. There is nothing you can do to trick me or to stop me."

"I am not your child."

"Ah, but you are. And this is the time to put away childish games." He sat down next to my bare right arm. "Now we shall see about this voodoo blood. I wanted you to be awake for this. I intend to have a little taste," he said, then sank his fangs into my wrist like a ravenous dog.

Pain is a definite drawback to being one of the living, immortal or otherwise. Through the years I'd learned to deal with it, to block the worst of it. But this pain was like none I'd ever known—razor-sharp teeth on bone. The sensation scoured my body like a withering wind.

Where my body shrank away, my hate propelled me into motion. With a howl of pure fury that echoed off the walls, I gave one huge heave, arching my back against the weight holding me down. The stone teetered for a moment, then began to slide sideways.

Reedrek, forced to move or be crushed, hissed in aggravation, spraying my own blood across my arm and face as he braced the falling stone. I heaved again, but he held the slab in place. I thought he might curse me then, or kill me. I hoped for the latter. Instead I saw the fist-size rock in his hand as it descended toward my face. Then I saw nothing.

Bells were ringing. The sad clanging church bells of a funeral procession. Without the help of Lalee's shells, I floated above the scene like a bird gliding on a steady wind. An English wind. The smell of sun on grass and stone. As I looked out over the sunlit fields and rock-lined road, the tightness in my chest eased, and I drew in a deep breath of home. The mourners below me carried two wooden coffins toward open graves in a field across from a churchyard. *Unconsecrated ground,* I heard one woman whisper behind her hand. I swung lower and looked more closely as the priest hitched up his habit and followed the few mourners through the weeds. Something about him seemed familiar. Then I realized it was Father Gifford from my own parish in Derbyshire. This must be a vision of how they'd buried me, and my sweet Diana.

Her soul seemed very close as I bent over her coffin for one brief moment and touched the lone flower someone had placed on the lid. My heartfelt wish to see my beloved wife one more time lodged in my chest.

I'm so sorry I didn't save you, love. So sorry . . .

New grief seized me as though I hadn't spent five hundred years getting over the loss. Fierce tears burned my face. I wanted to pound on the coffin lid until it burst open and set my wife free. But it would do little good. She was dead—already, in a way, free. Not trapped in the dark like me.

"My wife—her soul is pure. She should've been buried in our family plot next to the church," I said, although no one could hear. They wasted little time lowering the coffins into the unmarked graves.

"May God have mercy on their souls," the priest said, then dusted his hands as though the pagan process had made them dirty. At least the villagers had not burned us like witches.

"I want my mother," I heard a child groan.

"Shush, dear. Your mum is dead and your da, too."

I glanced up as a woman hefted a young boy into her sturdy arms. Juney Cecil, she'd been Diana's maid-servant. "Don't fret," she crooned. "You're comin' to live wi' me and James now."

Surprise held me captive as I looked at my son, my living son, Will. Damaged—there was a crude bandage on his neck—but alive. Juney turned and started back down the path with Will crying in her arms. He'd survived after all. Thinking to help him, I followed them for several paces until I realized there was nothing I could offer him, not help, not comfort, not even explanations. With eyes that had lived too long and seen too much, I watched my son disappear once again out of my life. *Good-bye Will . . . Papa loves you still. I have not forgotten you through the empty years.*

Left among the grave diggers covering the graves, I searched for some sort of calm. Unless time was a twisted trickster, Will had long since lived whatever life he'd found and had died a normal human death. Whether this brief vision of him was granted by heaven or hell, I couldn't say. It felt like a glimpse of both. But if God truly existed, how had he let my family come to this un-natural end?

"No use putting too much care into it," I said to the grave digger covering my coffin. "I'll be digging through and out soon enough." The words may have sounded like the cry of a bird for all the attention he paid to them. I looked up toward the Godless sky and found myself high in the clouds again, among bright white, angel-hair clouds lit by the glorious setting sun. The beautiful sight seemed to squeeze my already bruised heart. Then, just as I imagined I'd finally escaped dark-ness, the ocean below me shifted to darker and darker blues until the clouds disappeared and stars twinkled above me. In the distance I spied a coastline, and as I ap-proached it I found a river that I followed to a harbor filled with ships.

Savannah.

Gone were the big hotels and the new convention cen-ter on Hutchinson Island. This was sometime in the past, when the docks on the river were smaller, the un-paved distance between the river road and the water less wide. When there were few streetlamps and more dark business was done in the open. I drifted over my own shipping yard, casually assessing the year. Since the outer dock had yet not been built, I had to guess it was sometime in the early 1930s—during what the humans called the Great Depression and before the Second World War. That war had changed the face of Savannah, espe-cially the docks. As I mused about ship building and war trade, my feet touched ground and I recognized a familiar face in the darkness.

Jack.

He and a partner in crime were unloading some sort of contraband from a rebuilt tug and putting it into another one of Jack's long string of behemoth automobiles. This one was black with running boards like the footboards of a horse-drawn hansom carriage.

"What are you doin' here?" he asked, obviously surprised to see me. I could understand his confusion. This out-of-body flight without the help of Lalee's shells seemed to have few rules and even fewer explanations. I had to assume it had something to do with the strength of my voodoo blood.

It was surprising that Jack *could* see me in this night vision. I'd settled into the part of invisible flyer. "I thought I might see how the other half lives," I answered. The man helping Jack stopped and set down his burden, staring at me as though he saw but didn't want to see a ghost.

"Well, you're scarin' the help," Jack said, then addressed the human. "It's all right, Leo, I can finish up here. Same place tomorrow night."

The man nodded, never taking his gaze from my vicinity.

"Pleasant dreams," I heard myself say. The man disappeared into the darkness. I touched the keg Leo had left behind. "And this would be?"

Jack stopped, his hands on his hips. "Surely you're not here to give me a lecture on breaking Prohibition. You know I run moonshine." He nudged the keg with his foot. "This would be it."

"Oh," I said. "Yes, of course I knew that. I just

haven't had the occasion to see you in the process of doing it."

He shrugged. "Not very glamorous but it does pay the bills. I have to run this batch up Charleston way." He continued loading his wares into the car. "So what brings your lordship down to the docks? Don't you and the other swells play cards over at the Desoto on Friday nights?"

"Ah yes, the Desoto. I miss that old hotel." I'd been one of the original investors. Let's see, that would've been 1890 or so.

"Whaddaya mean, you miss it? It's pretty hard to miss a hotel that takes up an entire city block. You know, the one with the verandas and stained-glass windows?" He peered at me in the dark. "Are you drunk or somethin'?"

" 'Or something' would probably be the case."

After a gesture of impatience with my answer, he put the last keg in the car. "You want me to drop you off around there?"

"Why don't I ride with you while you make your deliveries?"

"Now I know you're drunk. I can't take someone dressed like you to the places I go. It'd be like wearing a tuxedo to a craps game."

I looked down and saw that my imagination had dressed me in Armani again. I shrugged out of the jacket, loosened the cuffs, and rolled up the sleeves of my dress shirt. "This better?"

Jack rolled his eyes.

I ignored him and got into the car on the passenger side. There were two small kegs on the seat and I tossed them into the backseat. Jack's personal stash, no doubt. "Are you coming?"

We rode through the city in silence. I found it entertaining to see the old streets and buildings. For an immortal, time passes slowly, but even at a snail's pace it's difficult to notice every change that happens around me. To see this glimpse of the past was like watching the living history of the city I'd come to call my own. And the people I called my own as well.

Most humans romanticize the past as though life was simpler in bygone days. As one who has witnessed half a millennium I would beg to differ. Each decade and generation has its own peculiar opportunities or challenges, and the humans who populate those times believe their talents and failings are unique. The philosopher who said that history repeats itself is absolutely correct. The clothes, currencies, and top dogs may change but the underlying human nature remains constant. Thank goodness I am dead and have learned from my mistakes.

"Why the hell do you want to go with me, anyhow?" Jack asked just after we'd rumbled over a small bridge on our way out of town.

"It's difficult to explain."

"Try me."

"All right." It wouldn't hurt to tell him. He'd never believe me, anyway. "The William you're seeing is not the William you know."

"Huh?" Now he sounded annoyed rather than curious.

"The William that you know is probably at this very moment playing cards at the Desoto as you thought."

"Are you trying to tell me there're two of you?" He slowed the car as if he was thinking of leaving me there.

"I guess you could call this one a vision."

"Of Christmas past, I suppose," he scoffed, driving on.

"No," I said. "Of Christmas future."

We were flying along the tabby-paved road now—without the benefit of headlamps. Either Jack was in his usual hurry, or he was pressing the accelerator without realizing it. I looked out over the marsh but the darkness was nearly complete except for the moon rising through the trees. The warm breeze was musty with the smells of stagnant water and rotting vegetation.

"You're not real then? I mean this you, not the other one."

"Right." There were so many things I wanted to tell him. Things I should have said, should have shared. But first I needed to explain so he would believe me. "My mind is here but my body is—" A sudden weakness rocked my concentration. My body . . . was trapped in an underground mausoleum. Perhaps dying. Leaving something—my life—behind. Only this time was different, I realized. That was why my blood had brought me on this walkabout through time. Maybe I couldn't go back and hold Will or tell him his papa never forgot him. But I could try to save Jack. Give him enough to survive. All I had to do was say the words and make him believe them. I could feel time running out like grains through a hole in a sackful of sand. *There's no time.* "I want you to know Jack, that whatever happens in the future—that I'm sorry . . . that I truly—"

The car slowed. Jack had stopped looking at the road; he'd shifted his questioning gaze to me. My chest felt crushed. I found it hard to breathe. "Don't tru-ust Reedrek," I managed.

I heard Jack say, "Wait! Who? What's wrong?"

But I was too far away to hear. The pain returned like a tidal wave, not only flooding my head but the body I now inhabited again. My infernal luck had run out. I felt very near the end of my existence.

I worked to whisper, "Good-bye Jack," before opening my eyes. Then I was staring at Reedrek's smiling face. "Back again, are we?"

Jack

I carefully followed the tunnels, navigating by the street grates overhead, until I knew I was underneath the garage. Along the way I'd found an old pickax, which I now used to dig into what I was pretty sure was the oil pit under the first bay, near the center of the building, away from the front and side windows. I had a lot of energy, not all of it physical, to burn off. I used the strength I'd accidentally taken from Shari and Olivia to dig past the thin layer of concrete and into the pit where we stood to do lube jobs. It was a good way to blow off steam, too. I was still pissed at William for leaving me alone to make Shari and for not telling me about the tunnels.

Just as I was cracking the concrete lining of the pit, the half-rotted handle of the pickax broke. I gouged the rest of the way in with the blade. Was Olivia telling the truth when she said we'd be better off with Reedrek? Hell, maybe I should just go all evil and be done with it.

All of a sudden I sensed William. It wasn't as if I could tell that he was nearby or anything; it was just a feeling I can't explain. I also flashed back to the '32 Cadillac LaSalle I'd used to run liquor. The law in those days knew the car and my shady business, but when I hit the gas none of their rattletraps could catch me. The coincidence was weird because I don't ever remember William getting involved with my 'shine-running operation. He'd turned a blind eye to it . . . Then the flashback was gone as quickly as it had sprung to mind.

When I'd mined a hole big enough to crawl through, I stuck my arm in as far as it would go. It didn't catch fire so I stuck my head through and looked up. The sun coming from the windows did not reach the back corner of the pit where I was. Goody. I crawled through the hole—which I figured I could use from now on to access the tunnels from the garage whenever I needed—and came up the steel stairs to the main floor.

My office was in the interior of the building, so it had no windows. Neither did the bathroom and tiny shower I'd put in. I flipped on the light and made a beeline for the bathroom. I stood under the shower and let the hot water warm me. I had a lot to think about. If I'd been human I would have thrown my CD collection and some clothes into the 'Vette and just taken off for the West Coast. Always wanted to see California and the Pacific Ocean. But that was a little impractical for a vampire. I could just see myself driving down the Pacific Coast Highway with the top down. Besides, there was that troublesome vampire rule—one of the few William had actually told me about. A vampire must wait upward of two centuries before he can spend a night away from his sire. Sixty more years to go. Sighing, I turned my face up toward the soothing water.

Even with the water running, I heard the scratch of metal in the lock and the steel door creaking open. Shit. Had Reedrek done away with William and come to claim me? I shut the water off and shook myself like a spaniel. My hearing, extra sharp to begin with, seemed to be even finer. Since the power sex, all my senses had become stronger. I could probably hear hummingbird wings. Footsteps approached my office; by my reckoning they were just on the other side of the bathroom door.

I didn't have a weapon, but I knew I was strong enough to take almost anybody down with my bare hands, even a pretty strong vampire. Maybe even Reedrek. I took a deep breath, flung the door open, and leaped toward the sound of the footsteps.

And ran smack into Connie, knocking her up against my old metal desk.

She landed on it and her butt skidded across the slick surface, scattering my blotter, pencils, and pictures of Renee to the floor. She wound up sitting in the middle of the desk, feet apart, mouth open in a little o. During the slide, she'd managed to draw her service revolver, but luckily she recognized me before she pulled the trigger.

The gun pointed squarely at my chest. Her eyes rested squarely on my penis.

"Hmmm, hello there, Jack. You're looking . . . well."

"What . . . what are you doing here? Aren't you supposed to be off work by now?" I said as nonchalantly as I could. Just to be safe, I raised my hands. If she shot me she'd learn, faster than a speeding bullet, all there was to know about Jack, the immortal vampire. Not to mention really piss me off.

"I'm working a little overtime. I passed by here a while ago and the office light was off, and then when I came back by it was on. Rennie said you'd closed the shop for a few days so I thought I'd check on things for you." She finally looked me in the eye. "Don't you remember telling me where you hide the extra key?"

"Oh, yeah. Right. Well, thanks." I lowered my hands.

"You know, after we talked the other day, I figured I'd be seeing more of you." She looked back down at my privates, rather appreciatively if I do say so myself.

"And so I am, but I had a more romantic setting in mind. You never called."

"I know. And I'm sorry." I grabbed my pants off the doorknob where I'd left them and quickly stepped into them. It seemed like I'd been putting my pants on in front of a lot of different women lately. Five different women had seen me naked in the last couple of days, if you included Reyha. That was a record for me. "I think you can put that gun away now," I said, zipping my fly.

"I'll be the judge of that." She grinned and pointed the revolver at my feet. "Dance."

"What?" I froze.

"You're no fun." She sighed and holstered her weapon. "I always wanted to say that to somebody. This seemed like a good opportunity."

I grabbed the spare shirt I kept hanging on a peg behind the door. "Sorry. I'm not in the mood for jokes." And this was a really bad time to be playing the dating game. Although with the way things were shaping up in my world now, I might not get another chance.

She hopped off the desk and together we picked up the stuff that had slid off. "Had a bad couple of days?"

"You have no idea how much more complicated my life has gotten since I last talked to you."

"That helps my ego a little bit, I guess. I take it you've been too *busy* to call, even after that toe-curling kiss we shared."

"Oh, yeah. That."

"Yeah. That."

How could I tell Connie that right after we kissed and decided to date each other I'd discovered I was a menace to nonhuman women? If she was entirely human, she would not be subject to the power-draining phenomenon. After all, I'd had sex with more human women than I cared to count in my existence as a vampire. But with my heightened strength and senses, I was surer than ever that she was—not inhuman exactly . . . but somehow *extra*human. There was something other-worldly about her, and not just her overall hotness. It was a mystery—yet another thing to add to the growing list of stuff I had to figure out once all this trouble with Reedrek was over.

Or maybe I didn't have to wait. I suspected she didn't know what she was, but that was just an assumption. Maybe she did know, and maybe if I dropped a strong enough hint, she'd even tell me. I knew she wasn't a vampire, but she might be something, well, compatible. "Um, this thing with my uncle Reedr—I mean Fred—has been taking up a lot of my time. I haven't been able for us to get together like I've wanted. But I really do want to get to know you better. You know, you've never really told me about your background, where you're from, stuff like that."

Her eyebrows rose and her nose twitched like she smelled something fishy. "Huh? You want to know who my people are? I never figured you for a society guy like William Thorne."

"I'm not. I'm just interested, that's all." I sat on the edge of the desk and patted the spot beside me. "You told me one time that you grew up in Atlanta. Are you from there originally?"

She sat down. "No. I was born in Mexico City and adopted by a couple from Atlanta."

"No kidding. Do you know anything about your biological family?"

"Nope. Just that someone abandoned me when I was a few days old. A nun found me at the foot of a makeshift shrine to some pagan goddess or something and took me to an orphanage. Then it was off to Atlanta, going to private schools, playing sports and cheerleading—yada yada yada. I got a college degree in law enforcement, and, boom, I wound up here. That's about all there is to tell." She swept her hair off one shoulder and looked away.

"You were left at a shrine? Sounds like someone wanted to protect you from someone. Or something."

She shrugged. "Maybe."

"Now, why in the world would a nice cheerleader who went to private schools want to be a street cop? And why would they make you start at the bottom when you have a four-year degree? I mean, if you don't mind me asking."

"You're not the first who's asked." She brushed a wisp of blue-black hair off her cheek. "Let's just say I acquired an interest in addressing the problem of domestic violence, and where better to be than the front lines? I had a . . . good friend whose boyfriend was abusive. It's become a calling, I guess. As far as the rank issue is concerned, well, put it this way: the old-boy system lives."

Speaking as one of the oldest boys . . . she didn't know the half of it. "That's it, huh?"

"That's it." She didn't meet my eyes. There was more that she wasn't saying, much more. But I sensed she was telling the truth about the little she'd revealed.

"So what about you, Jack?"

"Me? Oh, there's not much to tell. What you see is what you get." I gestured around the shop with one arm.

"Where do you live, anyway? I don't believe I've ever heard you say."

Live? "Oh, nowhere." I pretty much stayed dead.

She socked me in the arm. "You're being evasive. I have ways of making you talk."

INSIGHT VACATIONS

The Art of Touring in Style

PREMIER PLUS MEMBER

Premier Plus

NAME:

INSIGHT VACATIONS
The Art of Touring in Style

MEMBERSHIP NUMBER:

50204553

www.insightvacations.com

"Do they involve those handcuffs you have fastened to your belt?" I reached out and tweaked them.

"Maybe. If you don't tell me where you live, I'll use all the interrogation techniques I know on you."

"I give. I live out by Bonaventure."

"Is Uncle Fred staying with you out there?"

"Mmm. I really don't know where Uncle Fred is right now. That's part of my problem."

"Why? Does he need a keeper or something? He seemed pretty spry the day I met him."

"Oh, he's spry all right." Spry enough to kill William, me, and most of the human residents of Savannah if the urge struck him.

"Speaking of Uncle Fred, I saw him with William Thorne last night in a bad part of town. Right out on the street on foot. We were called in—shots fired. Funny thing, when we got there a guy had his throat slit but there were no bullet wounds. What could Mr. Thorne have been doing there at that hour?"

I felt my mouth fall open. Olivia had made it sound like Reedrek was holding William somewhere. Now here Connie was telling me she'd seen William loitering on the street with his supposed arch-nemesis. "You're kidding. Tell me exactly where you saw him and what he was doing."

Connie told me the intersection nearest where she'd seen them. It was a bad part of town, all right. If I had to go and tow a car from there, I'd have to watch my back and be ready to sink fang into some gang member or drugged-out mugger.

"I think he saw me," Connie said. "But it's hard to be sure. They were just standing there. And then they walked away."

"There wasn't anything unusual about how they were acting?"

"No, not that I could tell. Nothing unusual except the time and place, of course."

That's right. She wouldn't have been able to tell unless she was close enough to see blood on them and then only if they'd been sloppy. There was only one reason for a vampire to go into a neighborhood like that.

. . . a guy had his throat slit but there were no bullet wounds.

To hunt.

A neighborhood full of homeless addicts and lowlifes meant easy pickings. And not only in terms of being able to find someone stoned or drunk who couldn't act fast enough to get away from you. In a neighborhood like that, life was cheap and even someone you knew might be willing to kill you if he were desperate enough for cash or for a high. The police knew that, and most of them wouldn't exactly bend over backward to find out who'd rid them and the town of another scumbag. Or they would just round up the usual suspects. Who wouldn't be vampires.

Yes, William—who knew the city better than anyone, having lived here for hundreds of years—had known just where to take Reedrek to hunt. Had William allowed himself to be enthralled by Reedrek? No. I couldn't believe it. William was too good at cloaking his feelings when he wanted. It made sense that he'd be able to cloak any incoming influences, too. Even Reedrek couldn't make him do something he didn't want to do. What the *hell* was going on?

"What's wrong, Jack? You've been staring off into space so long it's scaring me. Do you have a problem with Mr. Thorne? Something I should know about why he's taken to hanging out in high-crime areas after dark? Does this have anything to do with the trouble you keep talking about?"

I looked back at Connie. "No. Nothing that I know of. I think it's pretty strange, too. I'll ask him about it next time I see him." I'd find out, all right. Even if I had to beat it out of him. With my increased strength I might just be able to best William in a fair fight.

"So finish telling me about yourself, Jack. How long have you been in business here with the garage?"

"Uh, can we get into this later?"

"Yeah. I guess." She looked a little hurt.

"You know those complications I mentioned before? Well, they're really . . . complicated."

Connie looked at me evenly. "Mmm-hmm. And do they have anything to do with that platinum blonde who came into town a few days ago and is staying at Mr. Thorne's?"

Dang. Nothing got by this girl. I was surprised she hadn't figured out I was a vampire already. But I guess first you'd have to believe in vampires. "Well, yeah, but—"

"Good-bye, Jack. Let me know when your life gets less complicated."

With that she stood up and walked out. Just like that. I wanted to stop her, to run after her, to turn her around and hug her to me, but what was the use? How could things possibly work out for us? I was a damned vampire for pity's sake, a bloodsucking killer, and she was the law. Add to that the problem of her being not quite human, which could spell disaster, too. I mean, what if she was some kind of creature that clashed with vampires? We could be natural enemies or something.

If realizing all that weren't enough, I realized that I

had forgotten to ask her if she was still wearing the charm. Crap.

I sat down in the desk chair and tried to get my head together about this whole crazy mess. Okay. Olivia was back and going in and out of some kind of trance that Reedrek put her under. William was still AWOL, last seen hunting with Reedrek in a bad part of town. I was supposed to host William's big party, to make toasts as well as to glad-hand high-society people and aristocratic vamps who would barely speak to me if they saw me on the street. I'd accidentally killed a girl a few hours ago, I'd given another the vapors, and Connie hated my guts. A long drive to California was looking better and better, even if I was on fire the whole time.

I squeezed my eyes closed and rested my head on the back of the chair. "Could things *get* any weirder?" I muttered out loud to myself.

"I don't know, Jack. Could they?"

Double crap.

With my eyes still closed, I asked, "Is that you, Huey?" Of course it was. I recognized his voice, which was the same as always, even in death.

"Yep. It's me, Jack."

I opened my eyes. There he was, sitting in the metal chair against the far wall, a beer in his hand. I cleared my throat and blinked a few times. "How you doing, dude?"

"Can't complain." He took a sip of the beer and smiled contentedly.

"Is it . . . nice where you are?"

"Yeah. Right nice. There's no hard work to do, and . . ." He looked over both shoulders and then leaned forward. In a conspiratorial whisper, he said, "*She's* not here."

"Uh-huh." That would be his wife, the one who put a curse on him to keep him from drinking. "I see you've got some refreshment."

He held the bottle aloft. "Yep. Good brand, too. And all I can drink."

"Hmm. An import. Not bad." Good beer and no nagging. Huey had made it to heaven, or at least his version of it. Is everybody's heaven tailor-made for them? Guess I'd never know. The best I could hope for was some kind of benign dead end. Whatever it was would never be an improvement over what I had now. All the more reason to try to stay alive, even if that meant casting my lot in with an evil SOB. I found myself wishing that Shari had made it to a place as good as poor old Huey had.

"Don't feel bad for me, Jack. I'm doing real good. Now. The end there on earth was pretty bad, though. That mean, smelly guy cut my throat. He was awful strong. I couldn't get away from him to save my life." Huey belched to punctuate his narrative.

I wanted to tell Huey that I would find Reedrek and give him what was coming to him. But would I? Could I? I looked at Huey, sitting there in his work shirt and Dickies, drinking his name-brand beer. "Why did you decide to come back to see me, man?" I asked.

"Just to say hello. That's all right, isn't it?"

I sighed. "Sure it is, buddy. I'm glad to know that they're treating you good."

"Oh, yeah," he said. "I reckon I'll be going now. Thanks for the big send-off, by the way. It was real sweet of y'all to say all those nice things about me."

Now, there was another reason not to speak ill of the dead. They could still hear you. "You're welcome, Huey. Come back anytime."

Huey waved and gradually faded away, like an old

soldier. I guess he'd answered my question: No matter how weird things get, they can always get weirder.

I picked up the phone and called Rennie to tell him to bring my car to William's by sundown. Then I called Melaphia.

"Jack, what's happening? How did you get to the garage?" she said, having seen the garage number on the incoming call readout.

"Got here through those tunnels. The ones nobody ever told me about." I paused to see what she had to say for herself.

"Um. Sorry, Jack."

"We'll talk about that later. Has William come back yet?"

"No, not yet."

"Okay. I'm going to go out and look for him underground until sundown. Maybe I can sense something if I come near him. Then I'll check back in with you. Olivia is sleeping in my box, and I fastened her in so she wouldn't follow me. She was . . . weak, and she needed the rest. Check on her at sundown. She said she wanted to do something for Shari—register her, bless her, something. Between the two of you, do you think you could find a place to bury her in the tunnels somewhere?"

"No problem. I'll make sure it's unconsecrated ground."

"Huh?"

"If Shari was even partially transformed and is buried in consecrated ground, she'll suffer for all eternity. We'll be sure to stay away from the cemeteries, the church properties, and any of the war monuments, just to be safe."

Would the revelations never end? I had questions but now was not the time. "Thanks. Maybe William will be back by the time I check in with you at sundown. He's probably found somewhere to get his beauty sleep." I didn't tell her what I'd learned from Connie. It would only make her worry more. I knew that even if William had thrown in with Reedrek, he would never hurt Melaphia.

"Oh, and don't let Olivia wander off," I added. "She may be in Reedrek's thrall and I don't trust her. In fact, don't turn your back on her. Use one of your hexes or something to protect yourself. She was in her right mind when I left her, but . . ."

"Don't worry. I'll use a binding spell to make sure she doesn't, as you say, wander off, and you know I can protect myself from that skinny white girl, vampire or not. It's you I'm worried about. Promise me you'll take care of yourself. I don't know what I would do if you and William both disappeared on me."

"I'll be careful. I promise. Talk to you at sundown or before."

I jumped back down into the oil pit and squeezed through the opening into the tunnel. I set off in the opposite direction from which I'd come, not knowing where I was going or what I would do when I got there. It was hard to admit I was completely adrift without William. That was going to have to change.

William

I struggled briefly, trying to return to my vision, to Jack. I hadn't finished what I wanted to tell him. Wasn't that always the way? Hadn't I always been either interrupted or distracted from dealing with Jack's complete education? I suppose even being immortal was no excuse for thinking I could take care of Jack later. It didn't help that he was so self-sufficient. He'd seemed happy to remain as he was—strong, past the age of consent, and free. Of everyone except me, that is. At least telling him not to trust Reedrek was something. Unfortunately, I had no idea whether he would remember the encounter.

Or if the encounter had even taken place. Perhaps the whole thing had been an illusion. Even my mutated blood could propel me only so far. Maybe, with only hate to sustain me, I'd reached the end of my strength.

"You never told me what happened to your little swan. I haven't felt any power shift. Did you go all noble on us again and let her die?"

I had to fight a warped sense of time. Had hours passed in what seemed like seconds to me or was that an illusion as well? I gave up and concentrated on Reedrek's question.

"Yes," I hissed, straining at the bonds holding my arms down. With only one hand loose I could hurt him, even kill us both if I got the chance. The joy of knowing I'd sent him to hell wouldn't be lessened by the fact that I would be right there with him. As a matter of fact, being with Reedrek pretty much *was* my definition of hell.

Reedrek leaned on the rock holding me down and studied my face. "You know, there might be something about this bastardized blood of yours, because all of a sudden, I feel absolutely chipper. And, if I didn't know better, I'd think you were lying to me."

I stopped struggling and held his gaze while shoring up my inner defenses. I had no idea how my blood would affect Reedrek. It could hardly help but make him stronger, however. "You want to see inside my mind? Look again, *Father*." I concentrated on the image of Shari lying in the bathtub, pink-tinted water framing her pale, lifeless face. I had to do anything I could to block him from seeing Jack, who was, I hoped, making Shari. The deed should be done by now, though, and I hadn't felt any shift of strength, either. But then again, I had no way of knowing what had happened. My body was too busy processing twelve hours of intense sensations—feeding, fucking, and futility.

Reedrek frowned. "Perhaps I need to find one that you won't want to let go so easily. Such as those in the house you visited after leaving me."

I kept my thoughts on fire and blood—anything to block him from Eleanor.

"Perhaps this one, for a start."

The sound of someone being dragged forward shocked me. *No, not—*

Werm stood with Reedrek's fingers clamped around his neck. He looked scared but determined in a curiosity-killed-the-cat way.

"I called him here. We're going to have a little vampire-making party," Reedrek promised.

Begging for Werm's life would only increase Reedrek's lust to kill him. Reedrek's grip tightened on poor Werm; his fangs extended and Werm's look of surprise shifted to agony. He screamed, a long horrified sound. Another of Reedrek's little niceties—he did nothing to dull his victim's pain.

It didn't take long. Soon Werm's thin frame collapsed, empty and still. At least his tormentor propped him against the shelf near me instead of letting him fall into the dank water. Reedrek, grinning a bloody grin, plunged his thumbnail into the healing fang marks he'd made in my wrist and his fingers came back dripping. He used the blood to make the sign of the four winds on his newest convert.

"Call him," he ordered.

I remained silent. He could take my blood, but I wasn't going to offer anything else.

Reedrek turned to stare in my direction. "Call him, or on my word I will kill everyone in the house on River Street. They can't stay in there forever. I'll simply burn the house down . . . and kill them one by one as they come out. Call him, and I'll let them live."

Eleanor.

It wasn't as if his promise meant anything. He would kill who he wanted, when he wanted. If I called Werm, Reedrek would be sure of his "chip"—Eleanor's life— and use it against me later. But I was in no position to fight him. I could only delay—buy some time. As for Werm, he'd reaped his own reward. *If you play with fire . . . or vampires . . .*

"Werm—" My voice sounded more angry than seductive.

"Do it right, dear boy. You've always had a way with words."

Reedrek's sarcasm scalded me but I clamped down the response. Using my most persuasive tone I called again. "Werm. Come back to me. Come now."

One of his arms moved, trying to rise. Reedrek lifted him and brought him to my torn wrist. It took only a few seconds for him to smell blood and begin to suck.

Poor Werm, I thought, sinking into the oblivion of despair.

Poor Jack. He was about to lose another friend and gain . . . a brother.

Twelve

Jack

I searched the tunnels for hours, paying particular attention to nooks and crannies that nobody who wasn't a rodent had poked their noses into for decades. The passageways led to cellars of apartment buildings here, basements of office buildings there, as well as the occasional parking garage, manhole, or blind alley. I made mental notes of all of these outlets and inlets for future reference. You never knew when you'd need to duck quickly out of the way of the law, the sunrise, or some other creature of the night you didn't particularly want to deal with. Like that weasel Werm. Yes, the tunnels would come in very handy. If I lived long enough to use them.

The labyrinth wasn't without its interesting smells—I had a suspicion that homeless humans occasionally bedded down in the warmer corners—but I never got a whiff of William or Reedrek. As the last of the sun's rays were sinking, I made my way back to William's house, through the underground vault, and up to the kitchen.

Melaphia and Olivia were sipping tea companionably at the table.

Melaphia started when I came into the kitchen. "Did you find him?"

"No. I couldn't get a sense of him anywhere. I don't guess you've heard from him either?"

"No." Melaphia sat back and rubbed her forehead.

To my relief, Olivia looked pretty normal for a female vamp—not overly wan or woozy, and not under the influence of Reedrek. She was clear-eyed and serious. "How're you feeling, Olivia?" I asked her. "Better, I hope."

"Yes, much. Thanks," she said sourly. *No thanks to you* seemed to hang unspoken in the air.

The two of them looked downright chummy. So much so that I felt a little uncomfortable when both their gazes settled on me at once. I didn't have to wonder if Olivia had told Melaphia what had happened between us—the wild sex and how it had made her as weak as a limp noodle. I didn't have to wonder because of the way Melaphia's right eyebrow arched that certain way she had when she disapproved of something I'd done. It was the same sharp-sighted look that her mother had for me, and her mother before her, and so on as far back as I could remember. There were other, darker, looks as well, of course. Those were reserved for worse transgressions.

Embarrassed by having offended the sisterhood, I opened the fridge so I could hide my face for a spell pretending to look for a jar of blood. I found a pint jar of what looked like a good vintage (this week) and closed the refrigerator door.

I studied the jar lid as I opened it. "Good. I'm glad you're feeling dandy." *Don't everybody talk at once*, I thought, and started drinking. While wandering the tunnels I'd debated with myself whether I should tell Melaphia what Connie had seen. I didn't want to worry her, but I'd decided that she needed to know everything—if only because I didn't know what the hell to do and I needed her help to figure out our next move.

"Mel, I ran into Connie at the garage, and she told me something unbelievable." I told them what Connie had seen and described the neighborhood for Olivia's benefit. "William must've taken Reedrek there to hunt. There's no other explanation. But why? What the hell could he be up to? Do you think he's got William . . . enthralled, like he tried with Olivia here?"

"Bloody hell," Olivia muttered. She looked even more shaken by the news that William was hunting humans— even the criminal element—than Melaphia was. That was odd.

Melaphia pushed back from the table and began to pace, nervously twisting the fabric of her colorful broomstick skirt in her hands. "Okay, first let's look on the bright side. William's alive. He's probably just humoring Reedrek, maybe trying to con him by ingratiating himself with the old devil."

"That's the best-case scenario," Olivia agreed. "What if the worst should happen?"

Melaphia looked as if she'd been slapped. "Don't go there."

I finished draining the blood and set the jar on the counter a little too hard. Something told me that the worst that Olivia could think of happening was not necessarily the same worst that Melaphia could think of happening. It was as if I was developing a new and stronger sense of intuition since I'd powered up, so to speak.

I said, "If William doesn't come back soon we won't have to wonder 'what if?' Reedrek will come for me, and for you, Olivia. And God only knows what will happen then. Melaphia, I want you and Renee to get out of town for a while. I'm afraid—"

"I've already sent her to her aunt's in Brunswick. I'm not going anywhere while William and you might need me." Melaphia smoothed the wrinkles out of her skirt and set her jaw.

I held up my hands but then let them fall. "You're all Renee's got if something happens to us."

I could see the effort it took for her to pull herself together. William was the only father she'd ever known. "I'm a *mambo* of Savannah, remember? I can hold my own. Believe me when I tell you I can take care of myself and my daughter."

I knew it was useless to argue, and, besides, she was probably right. Melaphia's strength had never really been tested. Yes, she'd helped William and me through some difficult situations with the local ne'er-do-wells, and some of her accomplishments had taken considerable skill. But she'd never had to face anything like the evil that we knew as Reedrek. "All right, then. What do you suggest that we do now?"

"I think what we should do is take care of business and trust that William will come back as soon as he gets away from Reedrek," Melaphia said.

"What do you mean by 'take care of business'?"

"We've got a party to throw."

This damned party was something else I'd been thinking about as I searched the tunnels all day, and not only because I dreaded being in charge of it. "Look. What's the point of going ahead with this thing? The purpose of it was to introduce Alger to society, and now he's gone."

"I'm the new guest of honor," Olivia put in, standing

between me and Melaphia, her arms folded across her chest.

"No offense, darlin', but so what? We've got a crisis here."

Melaphia pinched the bridge of her nose as if to ward off a headache. "Jack, you're forgetting something. The party wasn't just to introduce Alger to Savannah, it's an opportunity for William to get him—and now Olivia—together with a few of the West Coast settlers that he brought over here earlier."

"Yeah, yeah, I know that. But again, so what?"

Olivia spoke up. "This is not a social visit. Before he left for America, Alger told me that he and William were to meet with some vampires who either led their own colonies or represent groups of vampires that have established themselves in the west. They were to discuss some important . . . issues."

If there was anything I didn't need to hear about right now, it was more freakin' *issues*. I'd had enough issues hit me in the last few days to last even a vampire's lifetime. "What kind of issues?"

"Of mutual protection. Ways to import more peaceful European vampires like me and Alger and the ones that William has already brought over here."

"Mutual protection?"

"Strength in numbers, Jack." Olivia looked uncomfortable, like something fearful had just walked across her grave, so to speak.

"Protection from what?"

"Demons like Reedrek."

"How many of him are there?" A tingly feeling was starting along my spine—the same feeling I got the time I walked by a wood chipper and narrowly missed getting staked by a large splinter from a used Christmas tree bound for somebody's mulch pile.

"Too bloody many," Olivia said, and rubbed her arms as if suddenly chilled.

"I thought this thing with Reedrek was some personal feud between him and William. Are you saying that there are other vampires like Reedrek coming over here to—to—do what exactly?"

"We don't know that yet. That's what the meeting is supposed to be about."

"How will I know the so-called peaceful vamps when they get here?"

Olivia shrugged. "That's hard to say."

"Well, you're just the Oracle of freakin' Delphi, aren't you?" I could tell there was more she wasn't saying. It was that intuition thing again. Part of me wanted to grab her and shake her until she told me everything, but another part was starting to wonder if I really gave a damn. This was William's deal, and he obviously hadn't meant to include me, so to hell with all of it. And to hell with William. About then I noticed the guilty look on Melaphia's face. She was toying with one of her dreadlocks and looking at the floor.

"I don't guess it would do any good to ask you what you know about this," I said to her.

"I'm sorry. He'll have to tell you himself." She looked up at me, her face strained. "When he gets back. Which brings me to the most important reason to go forward with the party."

"Which is?"

"Five vampires in one place would be a mighty temptation to a devil like Reedrek. I believe he will come out of hiding."

Olivia said, "Until then, Jack, you and I have to get

over to William's plantation. The other vampires have arrived and since William is out of pocket we have to greet them."

"Oh, we do, do we?" I picked up the empty blood jar again, wanting to hurl it against the expensive cabinetry. Instead I threw it in the air and caught it with one hand. "Well, who put you on the welcoming committee, blondie? I've got a better idea. Why don't you go on over there by yourself and play the good little hostess."

"I just want to help," Olivia said evenly. "We have to explain what happened to Alger."

"But don't tell them William is missing," Melaphia urged.

"Where the hell should I say he is? Skiing in Aspen? Snorkeling in Tahiti?"

"Tell them the truth," Melaphia said. "Tell them he's out looking for Alger's killer."

I turned toward the wall and set the jar in the sink. Still not used to my enhanced strength, I used too much force and it shattered, scattering glass and blood droplets out across the shiny stainless steel. "I don't even know what my role is in this mess and the two of you either can't or won't tell me. Give me one good reason why I shouldn't just walk out that door and never come back."

Melaphia's dark eyes grew shiny. "Because William's counting on you, Jack. And because he's your . . . family."

Aw, crap.

Melaphia knew I couldn't stand to see her cry. She'd known it since before she could talk. Olivia looked at me expectantly. What the hell. In for a penny, in for a pound. Where would I go, anyway? Something told me that even the California coast wasn't far enough to get away from what was brewing here in Savannah.

I nodded toward Olivia. "Get your fancy coat. Let's go."

On the way to the plantation, Olivia explained to me what she and Melaphia had done for Shari. She said that they'd found some incantation to get her to a better place, as well as a nice location to bury her body. I was glad for poor Shari, but to tell you the truth, most of it went in one ear and out the other. I couldn't get what Olivia had told me about all those other vampires out of my mind. I used to think I wanted to meet other blood drinkers. Be careful what you wish for.

I longed to go back to my normal world, the world of just a few days ago when William and I were the only bloodsucker act in town except for the occasional drifter or imported vamp that William introduced to society and then sent along his merry way. Yessir, Jackie-boy, welcome to the wide world of vampires, where you can't tell the good bloodsuckers from the bad ones without a program.

William's plantation was about a forty-five-minute drive outside Savannah, between the marsh and Isle of Hope. Well, forty-five minutes for most people, thirty for me. Olivia gasped as we drove down the driveway, or lane, as William liked to call it. It was something out of a picture book, with its long rows of live oaks lining both sides of the drive. I would have loved to have seen it in the daytime. Of course, there were lots of things I would have loved to have seen under the sun, but there's no use crying over spilled blood.

At the end of the long drive was a meticulously re-stored mansion that William used mostly for entertaining and as a retreat. He called it his country house. It was actually still a working plantation, though the human field hands had all been replaced by high-tech agricultural machinery. William had a professional farmer to handle the planting, dusting, and harvesting and a professional staff to maintain the mansion and make sure that guests were waited on hand and foot. He had a houseful of priceless antiques—silver, porcelain, and collectible gewgaws, along with a couple of classic cars in what used to be the carriage house. The dove gray Thunderbird was my own personal favorite.

When Olivia and I drove up, we were greeted by the estate's gardener/driver, whose job included parking your car when you drove under the porte cochere. Inside, I said hello to Chandler the butler and introduced him to Olivia.

"Mr. Thorne's guests are in the sitting room. I built a fire and served drinks. Will there be anything else right now, Mr. McShane?" Chandler took Olivia's leather coat and looked at me expectantly.

"No. That'll be it for a while. I'll ring if we need anything." Chandler nodded, hung Olivia's coat in the hall closet, and left. Like Melaphia, he was from another long line of loyal and well-paid family retainers. I used to wonder what kind of hereditary deal his family had made with William but I never got up the nerve to ask. It seemed too impolite. Chandler was the poster boy of polite. He served warm blood in fine crystal as smoothly as he served the expensive Bordeaux from the world-class wine cellar. A true gentleman's gentleman.

I took a deep breath as Olivia and I stood outside the closed double doors of the sitting room. "Is there anything I need to know before I meet these guys?" I probably had met them briefly when William had first smuggled them into the country, but since he didn't allow me any contact to speak of with Eurovamps, I figured I wouldn't recognize them and was pretty sure the rich, uppity farts wouldn't remember me either.

"Just be your sweet self, Jack," Olivia said, standing on tiptoe to kiss me on the cheek. Geez, what had gotten into her? Her mood had changed completely since we'd left William's house. Maybe she'd sensed how close I'd come to walking away.

I opened the doors and we walked in. Two guys of about my own human age were sitting in front of the fire chatting. One had dark hair, the other was blond. They stood up and stepped toward us.

The dark-haired one extended his hand and said, "I'm Iban. You must be Jack and Olivia. I spoke to Melaphia on the phone earlier and she said you'd be coming out." He was of medium height and slender build. Dressed in a loose-fitting (what Melaphia would call unstructured) black suit and expensive-looking black loafers with no socks, he looked a little bit like Antonio Banderas. His hair was long enough to curl up on his collar some, and he had a subtle, aristocratic-sounding Spanish accent. Think Ricardo Montalban and rich Corinthian leather.

His handshake was firm, his smile sincere. Despite myself, I liked him immediately. He kissed Olivia's hand and she gave a little mock curtsy.

"And this is Tobias," Iban said, raising his hand toward the blond guy in chinos and a Hawaiian shirt.

"My friends called me Tobey," the blond said. He gave Olivia and me a big smile and handshakes as well. "It's great to meet you guys." He seemed just as nice as Iban.

I scratched my head. "Tobey, you look familiar. Did I see you on your way through Savannah when William first brought you over?"

Tobey looked confused for a couple of seconds and then shook his head. "Oh, no. I'm not one of William's imports. I'm a native. I was sired by a vampire who was descended from an ancient clan out west."

I decided I wouldn't show my ignorance by admitting that I didn't know there *were* any ancient clans out west. Or anywhere else in North America for that matter. Ancient? Man, I had a lot to learn about vampires.

"And as for where you've seen him before," Iban said, "have you ever watched the racing they do under the lights in the desert? California and Nevada, isn't it? Tobey here is the reigning points champion."

Tobey waved his hand modestly. "They can't show it live on the East Coast 'cause it would come on so late at night. But you can see the taped version on ESPN4, Monday nights. It's no big deal."

My breath caught in my throat. No big deal? *No big deal?* To be a race car driver was only my life's ambition. Only my fondest dream in all the world. And this Tobey guy was living it. Why couldn't I have been made into a vampire out west where this was going on? But no, I had to have been made on the East Coast. Some bloodsuckers had all the luck.

"How do you do it? You—you don't have to practice or go to drivers' meetings or anything like that in the daytime?" I asked.

"Nah. I've got it all worked out. I have this recluse act going on. They call me the—"

"Nightflash," I said numbly. "I know. I'm a big fan."

Tobey grinned. "Hey, thanks. Yeah, we only practice and qualify at night because of the heat, so I've got it made. But William deserves a lot of the credit. He's the one who came up with the scheme. I met him right before he made you. Anyway, I was really into the railroad because it was the fastest thing that existed at the time. Later, I raced anything that moved at night. Like, uh, in the sixties, I was into moonlight surfing and midnight drag racing for a while."

"Isn't that how you met the Beach Boys?" Iban asked.

"Yeah. That was a blast. Legendary parties that lasted for days—uh, I mean nights. I even sang backup on a few of their tunes. William and I have kept in touch by phone, then on the Web. You know how he has his network of contacts he touches base with every now and then. The desert racing league was his idea, and the whole Nightflash thing. He's a real idea man, that William. Real resourceful."

I sighed. Man, what I wouldn't give to be in big-time racing. While Tobey got the big-time race car, the pit crew, the money, and the limelight, I got to race locally at dirt tracks under cheap, flickering stadium lights. Talk about a raw deal. Being a demon of Demolition Derbies was my only claim to fame. I felt Olivia's elbow nudging me in the rib region.

"Jack? Iban asked you a question," she said gently.

"Huh?"

"We were just talking about this portrait as you were coming in. There's nothing like the old masters. It has to be Dutch—such realism." He shrugged. "Look at the firelight on that face. I've tried for years to find someone with William's charisma to be in one of my movies. Don't tell me—I'll bet he passes the likeness off as one of his ancestors, right?"

"That's right," I said. I stared at the portrait of William hanging majestically above the marble fireplace as if I'd never seen it before. Yeah, no use crying over spilled blood. It wasn't William's fault that I'd missed opportunities in my life. He couldn't change the rules of vampire-hood, vampiredom, what-the-hell-ever it was. Them's the breaks, Jackie. The detour signs and out-and-out roadblocks of fate had curtailed all my dreams. I was stuck right here, stalled out in Savannah, G-A, with good old Daddy Dearest.

William

Werm made a gurgling sound and moaned as Reedrek fastened the manacles around his wrists. Chaining him was a kindness since there was no coffin to keep him immobile. In addition, I had the feeling that having him screaming and throwing himself against the walls would annoy Reedrek. As I knew well, annoying Reedrek could be hazardous to your health.

"That takes care of our little science experiment. We'll see exactly what more than a little taste of your bastardized blood can do." Reedrek dusted his hands together. "Now let's get down to business."

I twisted my arms against the ropes holding them down. "This isn't what I call business."

He gave me a sad look. "No, I suppose not. But I was referring to your little undead smuggling ring."

Now he had my full attention. I'd thought we were going to discuss my mixed blood again; Reedrek was famous for his thoroughness when his interest was piqued. His relentless predilection for secrets had translated into scores of people being tortured and killed throughout the millennium—until they gave Reedrek what he wanted.

I couldn't let him get what he wanted this time. It would mean the ending of everything I lived for, and the annihilation of my allies and friends, the creatures who inhabited my world, who knew me and trusted me— several of whom would be arriving in town to attend Alger's (now Olivia's) coming-out party. And, of course, it would also mean the entire mortal human population being translated into a vampire feed lot, women and children first. I gave up the effort to move the rock on my chest or break my bonds, deciding to save my strength. I'd need it even more desperately before Reedrek was through.

"I shut the whole operation down," I said, telling the temporary truth. "You killed Alger and I—"

"No!" He shoved a pile of bones farther against the wall and sat on the slab nearest my head. He leaned down close enough to hiss his awful breath in my face. "Don't even *try* to play me for a fool again. Tell me what I want to know and I'll leave you be."

He was lying. We both knew it.

A louder moan issued from Werm, our monster in the making, punctuated the horror of my sire and his empty promises. Then a plea: "Heeeelp meeee."

I could relate.

"Why would I believe you'd ever let me be?"

"Because it is what you wish for. Your entire life has been spent wishing for something other than what you are offered. I gave you immortality along with my blood and you only whine instead of taking your rightful place as a ruler of this mortal world. For two hundred years I showed you the haunts and pleasures of Europe and you wished for this new backward land of upstarts. I offered you a world full of willing women and you wished only for your mortal wife. Truly you are a sad case.

"Now, either speak up or suffer. How many have you helped? Where are they?" Reedrek persisted.

I composed myself as best I could, ready for pain, death, or both, and remained silent. He was right about my wishing. The only part he'd missed in my history was the wish to die. He had not freed me. He'd held me close to him for more than two hundred years until he'd had to let me go. Yet even putting an ocean between us had not freed me from the bonds of his blood. If I forced him to kill me I could take my secrets to oblivion, the only safe haven.

"I bet our young Master Jack could tell me everything," he said, like a snake striking close to my heart with his intent.

I forced myself to smile. "I kept him out of it. You can torture Jack all you like, he doesn't know anything."

Reedrek mimicked my smile, showing shreds of my flesh still caught in his teeth. "Who said anything about torture? I plan to offer Jack his own keys to the kingdom, if you will. He'll take your place and become the right arm of the most powerful master on the planet—me."

"Jack doesn't like you."

"Perhaps not. But he'll like what I can teach him."

Jack would *love* what Reedrek could teach him—most of it, anyway. Jack's softness for humanity would hold him back from the darker lessons of killing and torture, but Reedrek would overcome his humanness in time. My sire was not just the rotten apple in the barrel; he was the determined worm of utter destruction.

"What about your old rogue cronies on the Continent? Have they put you in charge of world domination, then? Did the majority vote to make you king of the planet?"

"Vote?" He looked disgusted. "You've been poisoned by this New World democracy crock of shit. Life and death are ruled by the strongest—not by some pap saying that everyone matters."

"There'll be hell to pay when they find out what you're doing."

"Maybe, but you have hell to pay before my turn arrives. Now, about Jack—"

"You won't have him. I'll kill him myself first."

Werm screamed as though he'd just discovered death and pain on a personal basis, then he fainted.

Reedrek laughed out loud. The show obviously amused him. "Now that's something I would like to witness—you, Mr. Wishful Thinking, killing your one and only offspring." He sighed. "I just don't believe you have the balls for it. Too bad you won't have the chance to prove yourself one way or the other. I would enjoy seeing you go against all your wishes—against your own blood. No matter, Jack is already half mine and the rest of him should belong to Olivia by now."

"He's smarter than you give him credit for," I said, more for my benefit than his. Now that Werm was once more awake, his screams were coming in closer succession, making it hard to hold a normal conversation. As if anything about this conversation was normal.

"No matter," Reedrek said finally. "Olivia knows how to handle him. I think it's time to call her back to me. She and Jack. But first . . ."

He left my line of sight and I heard him scrabbling with the lantern. The oily smell of kerosene wafted around me. I could feel him splashing it on my pant legs and feet. Then he lit a torch.

"While we're waiting, how about a little pain?"

Thirteen

Jack

I stared at the portrait of William. He looked only slightly older than I do, but by the time that portrait was painted he had already lived a hundred years. He was dressed up in some kind of uniform with a high collar and brass buttons, probably fresh from feeding off dying men on a foreign battlefield, the old war dog. Why me? I wondered, not for the first time. Why did he pass up all those other poor gutshot bastards on that and other battlefields and, a lifetime or two later, make me into a creature like himself? Did he give others the choice he'd given me? Did they all turn him down? Was I the only one who wanted to survive badly enough to sacrifice his very soul?

Or maybe he looked into my dying eyes and saw something different from the others. Maybe he saw something he knew he could control.

"So where is our host?" Iban said, raising his glass toward the portrait of William. "On the telephone, Melaphia was evasive when I asked her."

Olivia piped up, "He's got some business. Something that he had to take care of personally."

"Will he return later tonight? I'm looking forward to seeing him again, and I want to give him a tour of my new mobile home," Tobey said.

"Mobile home?" Olivia jumped on the chance to change the subject.

Tobey aimed his high-voltage beach bum grin at Olivia. "Yeah. It should be here any minute now."

Tobey didn't look like trailer park material. I was wondering what kind of nonsense he was talking when I heard the sound of a big truck horn. Understanding sank in. *That* kind of trailer.

"That must be my rig," Tobey said. "I gave my drivers a few days off to spend over in Tybee before we start back. Jack, Melaphia sent your friend Rennie over and I hired him to get it detailed for me. Want a tour?"

I nodded dumbly and followed him and the others through the front doors. An eighteen-wheel tractor-trailer rig was parked in the infield of the circular driveway since it was too tall to fit under the porte cochere. It was decorated all along its side with the Nightflash's black, gold, and red logo and several sponsor logos in paint that practically glowed in the dark. Rennie jumped down from the cab and came toward us, grinning like a mule eating briars.

"I got it all fixed up for you, Nightflash," Rennie said. "It's as clean as a pin." His black eyes, which always appeared magnified behind his thick glasses, looked particularly large and luminous. If I didn't know better, I would say he was in love.

"Thanks, man, and call me Tobey." The blond vampire pressed a wad of cash into Rennie's palm as my sawed-off partner handed him the keys.

"Okay . . . Tobey," Rennie said, a little breathlessly. "Hey . . ." He dragged his beat-up NASCAR cap from his greasy hair and whipped a Sharpie out of his shirt pocket. "Would you mind signing my cap? The guys will never believe this."

"Sure," Tobey the magnificent said. With a flick of his wrist he drew the stylized version of his logo, then scribbled his name.

"Thanks, man," Rennie mumbled, holding the hat like it was heavy or something.

As Tobey, Iban, and Olivia walked toward the trailer, I leaned in close to Rennie's ear. "You two wanna get a room there, Ren?"

"Aw, Jack, knock it off. How many Monday nights have you and me and the guys drunk beers and watched this guy race on cable and talked about how cool he was? I can't help but be a little starstruck. Besides, you should see inside that damned thing. Go on with ya."

I caught up with the others as Rennie walked toward the carriage house. I wondered if I should mention to him that hanging around William's famous freakin' fanged friends might be hazardous to his health. Look what happened to poor Huey. That's when I saw my own wrecker, parked like a forgotten one-night stand on the far side of the drive. Even my truck had another life beyond me.

Tobey put a key into a device on the back of the trailer and hydraulic doors slowly swung open. Then a stairway unfolded itself from the floor of the trailer as smoothly as those automatic ragtops come up and over the top of fancy convertibles. This guy was all about competition. We walked up the stairs and into a living room furnished with denim-covered sofas and chairs and a huge coffee table strewn with newspapers and magazines, as well as a small video camera and a couple of laptop computers with wireless network cards sticking out of their card slots. It was a portable office to compete with William's high-tech lair. A wide-screen HDTV sat against one wall and poster-size, framed racing photos covered the other. There were no windows, of course.

Tobey then showed us through the kitchen and dining room, drawing *oohs* and *aahs* from Olivia on account of all the gadgets and appliances, like an automatic wine cooler that had water swirling around the bottles to keep the temperature perfect for the fruit of the vine.

Then came the bedroom, decorated in the Nightflash colors, of course, with a king-size bed, a walk-in closet, and a bathroom. "Must be great for entertaining," Olivia speculated, emphasizing that last word with a wink. Tobey grinned and shrugged.

If my skin had turned as green as I felt, they'd be callin' me frog boy from now on. I wished somebody would gig me already, just stab me clean through the heart and be done with it. This guy was living the life of my dreams. Race cars and the supermodel-type babes who gave out the trophies at victory lane. Oh, yeah, somebody gig me now.

"Where's your coffin?" I asked sourly.

If Tobey picked up on my mood, he didn't let on. He nudged the far wall gently with the toe of his running shoe. "Hidden door," he said.

"Of course," I muttered.

"So you two rode out here from the West Coast in style," Olivia said as Tobey led the way back to the living room and plopped into one of the easy chairs.

"Sit," he suggested. "You bet. Me and Iban came out together. It takes a little longer this way, but with a couple of well-paid drivers you can trust, it's a lot easier and more comfortable than trying to fly."

"Or taking a train," Iban said, seating himself on one end of the long couch. "The railroad system in this country is a—how do you say?—a jest."

"A joke," Tobey corrected, and Iban nodded his thanks.

"I do not wish to wait on a side track for two or three days before moving. Anytime there are strangers around, there's too much potential for disaster to suit my taste." He leaned back in his chair. "I intend to sell my private shipping car and buy one of Tobey's *muy macho* trucks to take me to my locations."

"Wait just a moment." Olivia pointed to Iban, seating her leather-clad behind right next to him. "I just recognized you. Your last name is Cruz, isn't it? You're Iban Cruz, the film director!"

Iban smiled broadly, showing just a hint of fang. Guess he figured he could let his guard down since he was among regular folks. "Guilty as charged."

"I've seen all your films! My favorite is *After Dark, My Darling*. I think I've seen it four times."

Oh, great. A race car driver and a movie director. Wasn't this just a fabulous freakin' career day? Talk about your dream jobs. I plopped down into what turned out to be a recliner. My feet popped up in the air. It was the perfect metaphor for being cut off at the knees. Well, just, *damn*.

"How do you manage to make movies when you can only go out at night?" I asked.

Iban started to answer, but in her excitement, Olivia cut him off. "He only films at night," she said. "It's his trademark. It's the ultimate film noir, and it's a brilliant cover. Perfectly brilliant."

Iban just smiled and shrugged in a what-can-I-say? gesture.

Chandler's head loomed right outside the still-open door of the semi-trailer. He was standing on the bottom step, so his face looked eerily disembodied. Kind of matched the way I felt. "Mr. Bouchard is here, Mr. McShane."

"Say who?" I asked.

"He's the scientist," Olivia said.

"Great. Tell him to step on up," I said. A scientist. I hoped he was really nerdy. Chandler disappeared and a tall, thin vampire in a navy sport coat, white shirt, and dress pants came up the stairs. He ran a hand through longish graying hair. He looked distracted but unfortunately not nerdy. His human age was older than that of the rest of us; my guess was he was made in his mid-forties. He didn't seem to know which of us to speak to first.

I stood up and extended my hand. "I'm Jack McShane."

"Ah," he said, evidently recognizing my name. "William's man."

I felt myself flinch. He might as well have said, William's *boy*. I shook it off and introduced the others.

"My name is Gerard Bouchard," he said. "I am pleased to meet you."

He didn't look that pleased. All in all he looked like he'd rather be most anywhere else. I knew the feeling.

"So . . . what kind of scientist are you?" Olivia asked.

"I'm a geneticist. I study various aspects of vampirism."

That was nice and vague. To hell with him, too, if he wanted to be secretive. For all I cared, he could take his test tubes and put them where the sun didn't shine. I was starting to feel nervous and closed in. I'd never been in a room, or trailer, full of vampires before. For as long as I could remember, I'd longed for my own kind, but now that I was hanging with a bunch of vamps, they were collectively making me queasy. And substandard in the vampire pissing contest. I figured it was time to get down to brass tacks.

"Have a seat, Gerry. We need to catch you all up on some things." The scientist sat down, looking like he smelled something he wanted to scrape off of his Italian shoe. I remained standing. "I've got bad news and bad news.

"I don't know how much you knew about this Alger guy, Olivia's sire, who was going to be the guest of honor at the big party," I said. "In fact, I don't know why we don't know more about each other to begin with."

Iban looked around at the others before he answered, as if seeking a consensus. "It's a security precaution, Jack. None of us is supposed to know very much about the others, for our own protection. The only reason Tobey and I know each other is because we live in the same state and cross paths now and then. William and Alger are the only ones who hold all the pieces of the puzzle."

Gerard said, "William and Alger are the only vampires whom we know outside of our own colonies."

"Colonies?" I asked. I'd heard Olivia mention the word before, but I wasn't sure what that meant when it came to vamps.

"Each of these men represents a colony of vampires in another part of the country," Olivia said. "Alger told me a little about them, but I didn't know much more until tonight."

"Okay. Whatever." I looked at Olivia, who was steeling herself for what came next. "Alger's dead. He was murdered on William's boat, the *Alabaster,* before he reached Savannah."

The three newcomers gasped in horror and Olivia looked at the floor. "He was staked and burned on the deck, and the human crew was murdered along with him. We found one body; we assume that the others went overboard. William ordered me to scuttle the boat so the authorities wouldn't ask questions. When we told you earlier that William was out on personal business, that was, well, a lie. He's actually out looking for Alger's murderer." That was a lie, too, of course, but they'd already had enough to digest without the news that William was seen hunting with Reedrek.

"Do—do you know who killed him?" Tobey asked, his blue eyes round and troubled.

Olivia rose to stand beside me. "Yes. It was Reedrek— William's sire. He must have stowed away on the *Alabaster* or boarded it from another craft. In any case, he's definitely here in Savannah." She paused to look sidelong at me. "We've both seen him."

And one of us may be at least partly enthralled by him, I almost added. I still wasn't sure I could trust Olivia, but I didn't know if I trusted these guys either. By the looks on their faces, they already knew plenty about Reedrek. Better not to open my mouth about him and Olivia.

"It begins, then," Gerard said, his mouth set in a hard, thin line. Tobey and Iban exchanged worried glances.

"It?" I asked. "What 'it'?"

"Maybe not," Olivia said, ignoring me. "Right now he only seems interested in the voodoo blood."

"He knows about that?" Gerard demanded, alarmed.

And clearly so did they. I guessed William had managed to share the info with the rest of them at some time in the past. It made me feel less special, but there was a lot of that going around.

"I think so," Olivia said in a small voice.

"How?" Gerard said.

I just looked at her, wondering if she would 'fess up. After glancing at me again, she said, "He revealed himself to us at a nightclub. I was so enraged at him for murdering my sire that I followed him before William and Jack could talk sense into me. I don't remember much of what happened when I was with Reedrek, except that I couldn't kill him. And during the ordeal . . . I think I may have told him about the blood."

"You mean—he tortured you?" Iban asked, plainly outraged.

Olivia hugged herself and looked at the floor again, but said nothing, leaving them to assume Iban was right. This chick could be in one of his movies and win an Academy Award.

They were silent for a long moment and then Gerard asked her, "How long have you been in the U.S.?"

"Almost a week. Why?"

"If Reedrek only found out about the voodoo blood in the last few days, that is not why he came all the way over to America. Why did he come if not to destroy us?" Gerard asked.

"Who else came with him?" Tobey wanted to know.

I thought back to my earlier conversation with Olivia and Melaphia when they mentioned the bad vamps and how we needed "strength in numbers." This was some serious shit, by Ned. I answered Tobey, "Nobody that we know of. That is, we haven't seen anybody else."

"If he came to challenge us, why did he come alone?" Tobey said.

We all looked at one another. Silence. Finally, Iban asked, "What do we do now?"

Nobody said anything. I was getting more and more fed up with one crisis after another and no answers about any of them. Beside me, Olivia's body began to jerk. "You all right?" I asked. Stupid question. When people started to jump like somebody threw them into a hot, greased skillet, they're not all right.

"I—I have to go," Olivia said through clenched teeth. "It hurts!"

"What's happening?" I asked.

"I don't know. I just have to go." Olivia lurched toward the stairs.

Iban said, "It must be residual effects from the torture. She must have suffered some kind of neurological damage."

"She was fine a moment ago. It must be something else." Gerard narrowed his eyes.

I had my own theory—Reedrek's enthrallment kicking in again—but I decided to follow Olivia's lead and not mention it. "Probably just a reaction from that human blood she had this afternoon. Donor might've eaten some tainted oysters or something."

I caught her by the arm to steady her before she fell out of the trailer and down the stairs. She calmed immediately, so much so that she sagged against me, forcing me to wrap both arms around her to keep her from falling. "Your touch," she said, "has made it better. Just like that."

The three other males exchanged glances while I shifted my arms underneath Olivia's to support her better. "What?" I asked them.

Iban rubbed the back of his neck. "You seem to be giving her strength simply by touching her, Jack. Maybe you should, uh, you know . . ."

"Have sex with her," supplied Gerard. Leave it to the scientist to be clinical. "If you can make her stronger just by holding her, think what you can do with actual genital penetration."

"Dude, seriously," Tobey said, looking at Gerard, then Olivia. "Have some sensitivity."

"Thanks for spelling it out, Gerry. I'll take care of it." Absurdly, I flashed back to that old soul song "Sexual Healing." Olivia had had plenty of that for one day. She and I exchanged glances, silently agreeing it was not the time to share the results of our last encounter. "Okay, we're going, then. Stay put until you hear from either me or William."

"Shouldn't we help hunt for Reedrek?" Tobey asked as I led Olivia down the stairs. I could tell he didn't particularly want to but felt like he should at least offer.

"No. It's too dangerous. You don't know Savannah well enough. Just let Chandler know if you need anything. I'll be back in touch by tomorrow night, if not before. Can you guys take it if I wake you in the daytime?"

"By all means," Gerard said. "The butler said he would secure my coffin. I believe it will be in the cellar as usual." He had the same old-fashioned way of speaking that William sometimes fell back to. Plus the hint of a French accent.

"If you need to rouse Iban and me, just have someone thump real hard on that back wall," Tobey said. "I'm a light sleeper."

"Will do." On the middle step, I decided it would be easier just to carry Olivia rather than half-drag her along. I swung her into my arms as if she weighed nothing at all. My strength was still supersized and it seemed that my hearing was as well because halfway to the car, when I should have been out of earshot, I heard Tobey say, "Did you see that? What a stud! Man, just imagine what could happen when he puts it to her. She could go all Supergirl with the power he gives her."

So much for Mr. Sensitivity.

I set Olivia in the passenger seat. When I crossed in front of the car to get to the driver's side, she let out a wail. "Don't walk away! I'm in pain when you're not touching me!"

"Why is that?" I said, putting the Stingray in reverse but making no move to touch her. Let her suffer a little. Maybe she would come across with some information. "I have a feeling you know exactly what's going on with you right now, so spill it."

She scooted as close to me as she could get without actually being in my lap and clung to my right arm.

"I have to shift the damn gears, lady. Give me some room." I pushed her away and got the car headed back down the driveway. "What's happening?"

"He's calling me to him!"

She plastered herself to my side again, and this time I let her.

"Who? Reedrek?" I started to turn in the direction of the highway, but Olivia grabbed the wheel. "Hey!"

"Yessss." She drew the word out on a long painful breath. "He's that way." She pointed opposite the direction I'd been headed in.

I sucked in some air of my own when it hit me that this was how to find William. Reedrek would draw Olivia and me to both of them. As Olivia urged me on, past the turnoff to first one major road back to Savannah and then another, I realized where we were going.

Bonaventure.

William

The burning . . . the burning.

My mind flew deeper into the past to ward off the excruciating pain of the present.

Flames. The whole city seemed to be burning brightly. People screaming and running . . . some of them on fire.

Two great fires had devastated Savannah, one shortly after Georgia ratified the Constitution and another, larger one, twenty-four years later in January 1820. I had unfortunately been occupying my house in town for the second.

Agony.

Now, as I had that night, I staggered through the smoky, ember-filled streets, horrified. A screaming woman, skirts aflame, threw herself into my arms. The smell of burnt flesh filled my senses as I shoved her to the ground and rolled her to extinguish her clothes. But she was beyond help, even if there had been anyone to tend her. People were running past carrying children, belongings. One man had a dog in his arms, another a chamber pot filled with water. They were heading for the squares, away from the scorching heat of the burning buildings. There they stood, shivering in the hope that the blessed coolness of a well or a fountain might protect them.

But they had forgotten the trees. The great oaks, limbs weighted down with beards of moss, lit the sky like oiled torches, dropping flame and death on those below. I stood in the center of the street and howled into the night—for death, for pity's sake, for rain. Lalee had made certain I would not burn, nor would my holdings on the river. But the city—there was not enough magic in the old *orishas* to save the city.

I heard Lalee's chant over the roaring destruction. The words made little sense but the sound immediately calmed me. I looked down and saw that my legs and feet were wreathed in blue flame. But the pain had receded, the smell was far less choking. Lalee would keep me from wanting death. At least for a while. I would burn, but I would survive; I would heal yet one more time.

I had to save Jack—

Time shifted. Without warning I was standing outside Eleanor's house on River Street, looking up as ominous black smoke billowed from the third-story windows. Flames licked along the curtains of Eleanor's bedroom and I could see her face through the glass. She was screaming, her hands blistered, pushing outward. There were sirens in the distance, but I knew they would be too late. I had to save Eleanor, to break down the front door. To my horror I found that, as in a nightmare, I couldn't move. My feet seemed frozen to the ground, my chest tight with fear. All vampires dread fire, but Eleanor was mortal.

Eleanor.

I could only watch as the windows shattered from the heat, spraying the sidewalk with glass. Her beloved face disappeared as the inferno spread from room to room until the entire building was engulfed.

Jack

On our way to the cemetery, the more Olivia came in contact with my bare skin, the more she perked up. I'd heard of clingy females, but this was ridiculous. You couldn't pass a penny between us if your afterlife depended on it. She gathered her wits enough to form a theory about my effect on her.

"I know what it is," she said. "It was the sex earlier. You're backward. It bound me to you in the way it usually binds a male to a female—you got my power instead of me getting yours. And when Reedrek's thrall kicked in, my bond to you counteracted it. It made me feel like I was being pulled in half. But now that I'm close to you and we're headed toward where Reedrek is . . ." She craned her neck to look at the speedometer. ". . . and going really, really fast, I feel much better."

After suffering through California career envy, being called backward was just glaze on the stale doughnut of my night. But if in my *backward* sort of way I'd managed to get something over on Olivia—the know-it-all—then that was something. Might even come in handy with good old Uncle Reedrek. "What's going to happen when we're face-to-face with him?"

"I don't know."

"Great."

When we pulled into the cemetery, the gates were locked, but the chain was no match for my strength—well, and that of the bolt cutters in my trunk. You'd think they'd wise up. I'd cut the lock off the gates so many times the security guard had to think there was a crazy lock collector in the neighborhood. In the last few years I'd sent Rennie over to replace the hardware and leave the keys on the base of the stone lion just outside the gate.

Olivia guided me straight through the old part of the graveyard, past the Jewish section, with its Hebrew writing and Stars of David on the tombs, on to an even older part back near the edge of the marsh. Not far from where we'd found William's Jag and Shari. Twitching again, Olivia got out of the Corvette and hurried to an ancient-looking tomb covered by a slab of marble so old that the epitaph could have been read only by making a paper rubbing of it. She placed her hands flat against the worn surface.

"Under there," she said. "Hurry. I feel like I'm on fire."

I lifted the marble slab off the top of the tomb and set it aside. With my unusually sharp night vision, I saw a set of earthen steps leading straight downward. I took Olivia's hand and started down. By the time we reached bottom, there was no doubt which direction would lead us to William.

We would simply follow the screaming.

I knew this screaming. This was the pitiable, ungodly, otherworldly shrieking of a creature in the throes of becoming a vampire—or dying in agony in the attempt. What the hell was happening? *First Reedrek and William go hunting and now they're making vampires? What's next?* The image of the California coast came to me again. Maybe I could hijack Tobey's truck. Hell.

The shaft of moonlight behind us was gone, but up ahead a new light was feeding our eyes. A vampire's eyes are like a cat's. We can't see in complete darkness, but we can take the most feeble light source and multiply it like those night-vision goggles they show on TV. As we neared the source, I knew what it was. I could feel the heat from it: a torch. An actual old-fashioned torch, the kind the angry villagers carried in the Frankenstein movies. I don't know how I knew but I knew. It was like I was walking straight into a monster movie—the story of my life—and I didn't know if I was a good guy or one of the monsters.

Now that was just sad.

We found ourselves going around a bend in the passageway. A few steps later we were standing in an opening—a room for lack of a better word—one step above black oily water. My mouth went dry at what I saw, and something near my unbeating heart clenched. I instinctively began to take a step backward, but I made myself hold my ground and put myself between Olivia and . . . them.

William lay on a table, covered almost completely by a large block of stone, his mouth, neck, and chest caked with blood. His arms were tethered straight out from his shoulders. Behind him, sagging against the chains that fastened him to the stone wall, was my own personal little stalker, Werm, blessedly silent, but only for a short while I was sure. A severed head rested on a shelf like a mushy hood ornament. Whew! The combined smells of stagnant marsh water, ozone from Werm's changing corpse, and burnt flesh—vampire flesh—made my stomach do an uneasy flip-flop.

In the foreground, looking every bit the demon in his black suit with his bloody fangs standing out against a bone-white face, was Old Stinky himself, Reedrek. He swept his arm upward and outward, as if welcoming Olivia and me into a grand home instead of into a nightmare.

"My children," he said. "You have come to me at last."

William

"What in the living hell is going on here?"

The sound of Jack's voice, along with the dead weight of the stone on my chest, yanked me back from my misery. *I'm so sorry, Eleanor.* I kicked as though swimming against the ever-stronger current of pain and hopelessness. My strength, which I'd come to take for granted, seemed completely occupied with staying conscious and healing my scorched flesh.

My limited view consisted of Reedrek's backside and the unfortunate Werm, but I knew Jack was in the room. The implications were troubling. I'd hoped to be in a better position to stave off Reedrek's plan but now I had to trust Jack's rebellious nature. We'd plumbed the solidness of his hard head in the past.

"Welcome to my little party," my sire said. He sounded so gleeful I felt a twitch of anger. I did my best to fan the ember.

I heard splashing footsteps, then I could see Jack's horrified expression. "What the hell do you think you're doing?" he asked, staring at me as if I were already dead.

"I told you, I—"

Another of Werm's rattling screams interrupted Reedrek's welcome speech and must have annoyed the grand master.

"Silence!" he commanded. Werm's breath appeared to freeze in his throat, and he was left with one arm outstretched toward Jack—eyes wide and pleading.

Then I saw Olivia. Without a thought for her expensive leather boots and pants she shloshed through the water and wrapped herself around Jack's arm as though she belonged there. It wasn't a good sign.

"I'm having a little fun before I kill my kinsman here. I thought you might be interested in helping."

Jack still looked a little shell-shocked, but I could see him striving to overcome it. "And why would I want to do such as that?" he asked, falling back into his prevampire mode of speech: a sure sign of stress.

Reedrek turned so I could see him smile. "Why, so you can take his place as my heir, of course."

Before Jack could make a response, Olivia, with a mewling sound, winnowed her way even closer to him. The action drew Reedrek's gaze. He was used to having everyone's complete attention and he reached for her.

"Come, my dear. You've done well bringing him here, but now—"

Tiny blue sparks arched between his fingers and the skin of her arm. Reedrek snatched back his hand with a frown.

"Jack?" I managed. "Go home." It was all I could think of to say. I'd constructed block after block in my mind to keep Reedrek out. If I opened it now to Jack, Reedrek would win without a fight.

I intended to fight awhile longer.

"Just go and leave you here, huh? You don't need my help. As usual."

His bitterness surprised me.

"Of course he doesn't need your help," Reedrek said. "He hasn't taught you enough even to help yourself."

"That's for damn sure," Jack said under his breath.

Reedrek crossed his arms and leaned against the stone holding me down. "Well, I will teach you whatever you wish to know."

Jack slowly shifted his gaze from me to Reedrek. "In return for what?"

"Now see, William?" He poked my arm as if he was

about to tell a good joke. "He's not as stupid as you said he was."

Now it was Jack's turn to frown. He brought one hand up and rubbed his forehead. There was a sudden flash of light and Olivia fell away from him. She screamed as she collapsed to her knees in the black water.

"Defiance doesn't become you, my dear." Reedrek held out his hand to help her up.

Olivia cringed back. "Don't hurt me anymore."

Reedrek wiggled his fingers impatiently. "I'll do what I wish to you. Alger is dead, and as I am his sire, you are mine to do with as I please."

Jack dragged Olivia to her feet. She clung to him like her life depended on his touch. "Let her alone." He angled his head in my direction. "You can do what you want with him, but she's with me."

Things were not looking up.

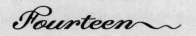

Fourteen

William

I could feel the riptide currents of Reedrek's mind rushing toward Jack. Relief, on my part, was instantaneous. My sire was so busy with his new recruit that he had momentarily forgotten about me. Jack squirmed as if he could feel invisible hands searching his clothes; then he glanced at Olivia, probably to see if the hands were hers. I mustered my strength and sent him my own sally of information.

He's lying, trying to enthrall you. Do your best to block your thoughts.

Jack's brows knit with a slight frown. His gaze flicked to me briefly, then returned to Reedrek.

"It seems as though you take after William here more than you realize," Reedrek said. "He is forever trying to save damsels in distress."

"Now it looks like he needs saving," Jack said.

I hoped it wasn't a rhetorical statement.

Jack untwined Olivia's grip and gave her a little push toward the stairs. "Wait for me outside."

Olivia's gaze shifted to Reedrek. She hesitated, unde-cided.

"Go on," Jack said. "He doesn't want you. He wants me." He turned to Reedrek and crossed his arms in defi-ance. "That right, old man?"

Reedrek was silent for several seconds, taking a new look at his potential convert, I would imagine. Thank-fully, Jack was beginning to show how stubborn he could be.

"Go," Reedrek ordered Olivia, as if it had been his idea in the first place. She didn't wait for more discus-sion. After the brief sound of her booted footsteps reced-ing up the stairs, silence returned.

"So. What's the deal?" Jack asked.

"I'll teach you everything I know, make you a prince among our kind. You'll be the monarch of your own destiny. Anything you can imagine, you will have."

Jack frowned at me as he asked Reedrek, "What do you want in return?"

"My dear boy . . ." Reedrek moved forward as though he would throw a companionable arm around Jack's shoulders. Jack stepped back out of reach. Reed-rek shrugged. "Well, there is the matter of this voodoo blood. I intend to learn everything about how it affects vampires. How it changes them."

"I don't know about any of that," Jack said.

"Of course you do. And if you tell me, I'll begin your education in other matters."

A pause.

"There's a vial of special blood, old blood that William keeps hidden."

I couldn't help myself. "Don't—" I said between clenched teeth.

Reedrek chuckled. "That's an excellent start. Bring it to me and we'll begin our association."

"What about William?" Jack asked.

"Oh, I intend to let my new"—he waved a hand in Werm's direction—"disciple finish him off when he's made."

He won't kill me until he has what he wants from you, I whispered in Jack's mind. *Werm cannot end me; I'm his sire.* Without opening my mind to him, I couldn't tell if Jack heard me or not. He started to look a little red in the face, the stress of both Reedrek and me trying to control his mind taking its toll.

"Why don't you bring him to his own fancy party he's been planning for weeks? All his society cronies will be there. A little public humiliation will do him good. We can show everyone how weak and toothless he is now." Jack looked at me. "Will you need a wheelchair"—he practically spit the word at me—"*boss?* Or can you walk?"

I wondered if Jack's show of hostility was for Reedrek's benefit or if he was truly furious with me. His suggestion indicated he had a plan. Unfortunately, no one knew better than I that Jack hadn't been taught how to use the talents he'd need to defeat Reedrek. I'd kept him ignorant and now he had no clue what he was up against.

"Cronies, you say?" Reedrek prodded me. "Are these people I should be acquainted with?"

I remained silent and his mind beat against my blocks like a battering ram. I wanted to scream *Noooooo!* But any reaction from me would only help Reedrek— although he seemed to be doing just fine with Jack without my assistance. My boy Jack was going to lead Reedrek right to the center of my secrets. Right to those who trusted me. Then we would all die.

"Tomorrow night," Jack said. "Eight o'clock at the Hamilton House on Lafayette Square. Be there or be square."

Jack

I staggered back the way Olivia and I had come, clutching my head. I was insane. What else would explain my leaving William there like that? My thoughts careened off William's and Reedrek's as they invaded my mind. If I couldn't recollect myself, I'd be totally screwed. They'd both tried to delve into my mind so deeply my head hurt with the effort to keep them out. It was like they were trying to force me out of my own brain and take over—the ultimate control. It seemed like whatever I chose to do somebody was always going to be controlling me. The question was, whoever I served, what was going to be in it for me? My only hope of sanity was to get as far away from them as possible. And away from Werm, who was more pathetic than ever as he writhed in agony, chains stretching his arms in opposite directions as if symbolizing his altered state: half in the human world and half in the world of the undead— and dying by inches between them.

But mostly I had to get away from the sight of William lying there, his flesh oozing from burns. Even in the pasageway I could still smell it, the same odor that had come off Alger's burned remains on the *Alabaster*. Burned vampire flesh smells like . . . hell. My first instinct had been to go to him, to throw that slab of rock off his chest and free him, but I didn't know who was the enemy anymore. Maybe it had been him all along.

I stumbled blindly down the passageway, knowing which way to go since I had already come this way once. I could smell my own tracks. As I made my way to fresh air I struggled to figure out what I should feel for William—rage, pity, resentment? I didn't know what I felt. I only knew I had to get away.

When I burst through the opening, Olivia was waiting for me. She wrung her hands as I replaced the marble slab. Ignoring her, ignoring the car, I struck out on foot toward home, *my* home. Confusion and fatigue were weighing on me now. I'd never been up this many hours straight. My undead body felt as if I'd been high on some powerful drug for days and was nearing a hard, hard crash.

I could hear Olivia following me. I didn't care what the hell she did or where the hell she went. At the storage facility that I called home, I walked through the gates with Olivia on my heels.

I dug my keys out of my jeans pocket and unlocked my room. Olivia stepped in beside me. I turned on a floor lamp as I made my way over to the refrigerator.

"Jack," Olivia said. "What are you going to do?"

"Fix myself a goddamn drink. You want one?"

"You know what I meant."

I took a half-full pint jar of blood out of the fridge, opened the cabinet above the sink, and pulled out a bottle. "Why the hell do I have to do anything? Why can't I just get as far away from here as possible?" I topped off the jar with Jack Daniel's.

Olivia ignored my questions. "Reedrek tried to get you to renounce William and follow him, didn't he? How did you leave things? *What are you going to do?*"

"What do you think I should do, *princess*?" I turned around and leaned on the sink as I sipped the spiked blood. "Behind door number one is Reedrek with the knowledge and ability to make me a goddamned vampire prince. Just like that." I snapped my fingers. "All I have to do is meet him at the party with a vial of voodoo blood. And behind door number two is my good old Daddy Dearest, William, who's treated me like a mushroom for more than a hundred years."

"A mushroom?" Olivia looked at me as if I'd turned psychotic.

"Kept me in the dark and fed me bullshit." I laughed harshly. "That's a joke, babe. Only it's also the truth." I took another long drink.

"Jack—" Olivia began, but I cut her off.

"Yeah, Reedrek can make me all that I can be, as that commercial says, a full-fledged vampire if I choose to follow him. Or I can save William and his merry band of race-car drivers, movie directors, and hell, ballerinas, cowboys, and rock stars for all I know, and risk getting killed by Reedrek and all his little helpers that I've only heard rumors about.

"So I find myself wondering, Hey, what's so bad about Reedrek anyway?"

I thought about my human father. He'd never promised me a damn thing. Even though I earned my keep and more, to him I was a burden, another mouth to feed.

At least Reedrek made me feel . . . wanted.

Olivia was indignant. "He killed Alger!"

So what? I wanted to ask. Both William and I had killed other vampires when they got out of hand. So Reedrek and Alger had some kind of dispute over feeding territory or whatever. What of it? Then I remembered what the other vamps had said about Reedrek's supposed evil minions.

"What's the deal about these dark sires?"

Olivia's face clouded over and she looked away, unable to meet my gaze. "Jack, I promised William that I wouldn't get into all that with you."

"Typical." I had always suspected William kept me in the dark to keep me in hand, but in the past few days I'd had it confirmed over and over. It made my fangs throb.

"You have to understand," Olivia pleaded. "When you break a promise you've made to a master vampire, there are . . . dire consequences."

Her words made my undead flesh tingle. Unbeknownst to her, I had almost made a promise to a master vampire myself—one a helluva lot more powerful than William. I could almost feel Reedrek's darkness enveloping me, and . . . I liked it. Olivia's voice sounded distant.

"Jack, you're looking strange. Are—are you enthralled?"

I set the empty jar on the counter and massaged my temples. Was I enthralled? At this point I couldn't say I cared. "They both tried to get in my brain," I admitted. "I don't know who's in there. I don't even know if I'm in there. I'm so . . . tired."

"Did you agree to give him the voodoo blood or not? And if you did, did you mean it or were you just humoring him?"

As if I owed her answers. She had an agenda just like the rest of them. Maybe I needed to play it close to the vest, like everybody else around here. "Wouldn't you like to know?"

"Don't play coy with me," she said coldly. "Reedrek wouldn't let us walk out of there without something in return. This is too big for you to handle. I think it's time we called on Tobey, Iban, and Gerard for help."

Everybody has their breaking point. Those words—coming from her—were mine.

I took a step toward her, grabbing the broom from where I kept it leaning against the wall between the sink and refrigerator. I brought the broom down onto the sink as hard as I could, breaking it. The brushy end went flying. Then I swung out with the handle, knocking over the floor lamp. The room plunged into darkness. "Play coy?" I exploded. I could hear her stumble over something as she backed away. "Play coy with you?" I repeated. "Who the hell are you to demand that I tell you my plans? If I remember right, you're the chick who tried to seduce me so you could drain my strength, without telling me the consequences. You're the one who left our protection to follow Reedrek on your own and got enthralled, which forced William to trade himself for you, and now he's being tortured. You know a lot more than I do about what's going on and yet even with William gone, you've only told me the bits you absolutely had to. And now, because I'm a little confused, you tell me *I can't handle the situation*?" I swung the broom handle, whiffing at empty air, my eyes still becoming accustomed to the darkness. "Fuck you. As I see it, you're part of the enemy."

I heard Olivia gasp and smelled the stink of her fear. My vampire eyes had gradually begun enhancing the tiny speck of light coming underneath the door from the security light outside to the point where I could see Olivia cowering against the far wall. I was on her in a second, one hand pinning her neck to the wall, the other poised to drive the jagged wooden broom handle through her heart. I brought my face close to hers and extended my fangs. My eyes dilated fully, making the room swim with otherworldly light.

"Don't you dare tell me not to play coy with you," I said. "I'll play with you however I like." I pressed the point of my makeshift stake into the flesh just beneath her left breast as I tightened my grip on her neck.

"I'm not the enemy," Olivia croaked. "Jack, Reedrek's got you. At least part of you. I can see him in your eyes, the way you could see him in mine when we were shagging."

She was right.

I dropped the broom handle and staggered to the nearby sofa. I could feel Reedrek inside and now it sickened me. And it scared the hell out of me.

Olivia followed and sat beside me. "Tell me what's happening to you right now."

Her kindness calmed me a little. I pointed to my forehead. "William . . . is telling me to block Reedrek's thoughts and to hide my own thoughts from Reedrek."

"Do you know how to do that? Protect your thoughts from your sire and anyone up past him in your bloodline?"

"Yeah, I think so. I've done it to William before. He never taught me, of course. I just figured it out for myself. I'm sure he sensed I could block him, but he never said anything. It's all so confusing and it hurts my head." I let my head loll onto the back of the sofa and closed my eyes.

"Do you think that Reedrek has been able to read anything from you so far?"

"What do you mean?"

"Can he tell there are other vampires here in Savannah?"

"I dunno. I don't think so."

"You need rest," Olivia said soothingly. She laid her cool-as-death fingers against my temple and smoothed back my hair. "We can't stay here. It's too close to Reedrek. Let's go back to William's."

"Okay," I said. Getting far away from Reedrek—and William—was the best idea I'd heard all night. "And yeah, I'm going to bring that voodoo blood to Reedrek. To get William back." Olivia seemed satisfied with that. She didn't ask me again if I had decided to follow Reedrek, and I saw no need to bring the subject up.

Reyha met us at the door. "What's that smell?" she said, bringing a hand up to cover her nose. "Not William—" she gasped, horrified. She stumbled back from me and buried her face against Deylaud's chest, her mournful howl muffled by his shirt. Across the kitchen Melaphia dropped the telephone receiver and left it where it fell.

"No," I said, almost too tired to explain. "I mean yes, and no. He's burned but still alive."

Deylaud ushered his sister into the other room as Melaphia bore down on me. "Where?" she asked, her mouth set in a grim line.

"Bonaventure—we just left there," Olivia said. She went directly to the top story of the night, failing to mention our broken-broomstick slow dance at my place. "We couldn't rescue him. But Jack has a plan. He made a deal to get William back. Tell her, Jack."

I knew Melaphia wouldn't like it. That blood was the most precious thing she had except for Renee. It was her ancestral gift. She knew something was up, because she gave me a look that burned my skin, making my dry eyes itch like I might go all girly-man. "I told Reedrek I'd give him that vial of old blood you hid on the altar if he'd bring William to the party tomorrow night." I didn't volunteer what Reedrek said he'd do for me.

"Lalee's blood . . ."

"Look," I said, too exasperated to feel guilty, "it was the only thing I could think of, all right?"

"No, it's not all right. But I can see you're past caring."

That surprised me, and it hurt. I wanted to swear that I would have taken another way if there had been one. But bottom line, I knew Melaphia would do anything to get William back. And she knew I knew.

"Have you heard from the others?" Olivia asked.

Melaphia was still staring at me. It took her a few seconds to register Olivia's question. "Yes, the phone has been busy all night. Iban is beginning to worry that things are worse than he thought. I promised them William would be in touch. And then there's Lady Eleanor. She's called at least five times."

Then Melaphia immediately turned her full attention back on me. She was another one who could read minds, and she was even better at reading body language. I was almost too tired to care, but it was still all I could do to keep from squirming.

"There's something else about this party deal that you're not telling me." She took a step closer. "Isn't that right, Jack? I feel it in my blood."

Melaphia's inner sight never failed. She must have picked up the fact that I stood to gain something in the blood transaction.

Well, she could just live with whatever suspicions she had. I was through spilling my guts. That old voodoo blood might be running in my veins but it hadn't made me any stronger or smarter. When it came down to give and take, I'd been taken.

A knock at the front door saved me from having to answer.

Both Rehya and Deylaud went for the door. Their otherworldly growls, even in human form, sent a creepy shiver down my back. I thought again that I wouldn't want to be on their bad side.

With his hand on the doorknob, Deylaud paused and looked at Melaphia. "It's a woman—mortal."

"It's almost sunrise. Who would be coming here this time of night?" Melaphia wondered aloud, but she nodded for Deylaud to open the door.

"Eleanor . . ." I said to the newcomer, surprised to see her. As far as I knew William had never brought her here. He always went to her house.

"Fire, fire, fire!" Reyha shouted. Everyone on our side of the threshold seemed to be waiting for me to do something.

Eleanor looked like she'd had one helluva night and would rather be anywhere but here. "I'm sorry to intrude—" she began, without stepping inside.

"Come in, child," Melaphia said, drawing her through the door and past a menacing Deylaud. "What has happened?" It's funny that she called Eleanor *child* considering that she was most likely the same age or even younger. Was that supposed to be a compliment? Reyha gave Eleanor one sniff then retreated, threw herself on the couch, and hid her face with a pillow. Then again, what did I know about how women thought?

Eleanor blinked and tears tumbled down her cheeks, but she dashed them away and straightened her spine. "I have to know if he's all right."

"Fire," Reyha said again from underneath her pillow. Melaphia kept her attention on Eleanor. "Tell me about the fire," she said soothingly, before looking at me. "Jack, I think you should go get cleaned up. You look like a raggedy man. I'll fix Lady Eleanor a cup of tea."

I was grateful Melaphia didn't mention what I smelled like. Olivia wasn't much better off. I was glad for an excuse to get out of Melaphia's sight. "Yeah, okay. I'll be right back." I nodded my head in the direction of the bathroom and Olivia followed.

"You'll have to wait your turn," I said to her as I twisted the knobs on the shower to hot.

"Don't be silly," she replied. "It's not as if you haven't seen me naked."

I stopped in the process of pulling my shirt over my head and gave her my best evil eye. "Look, don't get any ideas. I'm *not* in the mood."

That brought a laugh out of her. "Hey, that's my bloody line from now on. Sexing with you is off limits. It's too hard on a girl."

Great. Even in my grand opportunity to turn her down, she finds a way to get one over on me. I yanked my shirt over my head, dropped it, and then sat down on the closed commode to remove my boots. "Just stay away from me."

"Can't," she said, levering off one of her boots, then the other. "You have part of me now. When you need me, I have to be there."

I stood up again and, just for spite, unfastened my belt and jeans, pushing them down slowly to let her get a good look.

She took one—a good look that is, before meeting my eyes again. "Go ahead, get in. I'll wash your back."

And it was a damned good back wash, too. No sex, just a nice competent scrub—like she was my shower geisha or somethin'. She seemed to have forgotten all about my threat to broom her into the next dimension.

It was a good thing, too, 'cause if she pulled any funny business like trying to bite me, I was just in the mood to bang her head off the tile. I guess I was growing into my legacy—William's anger was legendary. And after all, I was his son. His heir. Reedrek's offer floated through my thoughts. I needed more info.

"Tell me about the vamps where you come from," I said as she scrubbed my shoulders.

"You mean in England or in the EU?"

Maybe this conversation was going to be too much for my overheated brain cells. "How many do you know personally?"

"Oh, in England . . . dozens, I suppose." She moved the bath sponge to the small of my back. "I don't necessarily like all of them though."

"Now there's a surprise."

She turned me around to wash my chest. Her silver eyes met my own. "Some of them belong to Reedrek."

Ah, there was my grandpappy again. Seemed like I couldn't escape him, no matter what.

"Okay, how about the ones you do like?"

"Most of them are women."

That got my attention. "How come the only ones William brings over here are male?"

"I'm not sure that's true. Perhaps you just haven't recognized the females. They have to be more secretive. Their lives depend on it."

"Why, 'cause they're weaker?"

"No, just the opposite—because they're stronger."

Rather than going into that whole Venus and Mars gobbledygook I stuck with "Why?"

"Because the way sex is supposed to work with vampires is akin to the mortal version. Sex between a mortal male and female is meant to be an exchange of power.

The male shares his ability to begin new life, and the female nurtures and grows that life. Afterward, they are permanently connected through the child. When one calls on the other for help or protection they have a tendency to comply because they are bound by the fruit of their union."

"But we vampires can't make babies."

"No shit." I hated when Olivia treated me like I had the IQ of a clam. "Go on."

"In our case, the males still contribute their creative potential, but instead of nurturing a new life, the female takes it as a surge of pure power, and it still binds the male to her."

"So the more sex a female vamp has with male vamps, the stronger she gets? That sucks."

Olivia smiled. "Sucking doesn't count." She tweaked my semi-hard unit. "Now you, as I said before, are backward. When we did it, I didn't gain your power; instead, you took some of mine and bound me to you."

"Really?" Now that was more like it. "So you have to do what I say?"

"Not hardly." Olivia sniffed. "We only did it once." When I didn't respond she added, "But it does connect us—that's why you could get me away from Reedrek." She kissed me sweetly on the lips but didn't touch me otherwise. "I thank you for that."

I didn't feel so bad about the backward thing anymore. But I never would've known any of this if William had had his way.

"So if the females are so powerful, why do they have to hide?"

Olivia's good humor disappeared. "Because sometimes a male will resent a female draining his power and will eventually kill her to be free. Unless she outsmarts

him. Luckily, males being how they are, this is not difficult."

"Oh" was all I could think of to say.

The hot water was beginning to cool.

Since Olivia didn't seem interested in washing the
family jewels, I removed the sponge from her hand and
took care of it myself. She washed her hair, then mine,
and in the process we both got lathered and cleaner than
we needed to be. It was almost a relief not to have to be
Romeo after the days and nights I'd had lately.

"There, don't you feel better now?" she asked as she
dried my back.

I did feel better but I was still pissed enough not to
want to admit it. "Maybe," I answered.

With a huff of a laugh she dried herself off and put on
the clothes Melaphia had set inside on the counter.
Eleanor was on her second cup of tea and looking a little more together when we reentered the kitchen. I could
feel the sun, less than an hour away. My mind buzzed
with new information. I could've fallen asleep on my
feet.

"Melaphia has explained that William is out of contact but he'll be at the hospital benefit ball," Eleanor
said, but a pained expression crossed her face. "After
what happened at my house I didn't know what to do.
That man—that terrible man took him. William told me
to stay inside but the fire has made that impossible."

"Fire?" I said.

"Her house is gone," Melaphia answered.

Eleanor left her tea at the counter and moved to stand
in front of me. "Please tell him—" In the rumor mill
she'd been painted as a woman who seldom lost control.
She had that whole dominatrix thing going for her. But

here, now, she drew in a shaky breath. "Please take care of him," she asked with pleading eyes.

Guilt felt like a fist in my throat before anger blotted it out. *Take care of him? Like he's taken care of me?* Of course, the sire I thought I knew had never asked for my help or care. Instead he'd practically treated me like a child.

I just nodded.

Melaphia took my arm and steered me toward the stairs to the vault. "I'll call Iban and tell him the news, and I'll send Reyha and Deylaud to walk Lady Eleanor back to her hotel as soon as the sun comes up. You need to get some sleep." She looked past me to Olivia. "You too. We all have to be prepared for tomorrow night."

I dreamed of sugar and spice and everything nice . . . meaning Connie. She was definitely spice. In the dream I was a vampire prince to her Cinderella Jones. We were dancing under a blood-colored hunter's moon; she was in my arms, smiling up at me as if she wanted to see nothing in the world but my face. To hell with William and the rest of the world. I pulled her closer to smell her hair and she nuzzled my neck. I felt the sharp sting of teeth and realized her intention. She belonged to William, not to me, and she wanted my blood. I was in just the mood to give her a little taste.

William

It seemed to take forever for Reedrek to drift off to sleep. Outwaiting him nearly did me in. Werm's transformation was complete and Reedrek had allowed him to feed from me before rechaining him to the wall. As a fledgling, he needed a real meal, and, because I was his sire, his first feeding would bolster us both. But we'd have to wait until the sun went down. Until Reedrek took Werm hunting.

For now, most of my newly acquired strength had been spent. Between healing my wounds and fighting for Jack's mind I'd used nearly everything. No holding back. But I hoped I had one more surge left, enough to go to Jack, at least to warn him.

Reedrek shifted, snoring, knocking a few old bones off the shelf he'd usurped from a long-dead human. The bones made a splash in the water and I waited. The snores continued. I settled my mind, calming my thoughts. With closed eyes and a deep breath I pictured the vault below my house, Jack's black-and-silver coffin.

Then I went in search of Jack.

The air shifted around me but I held my concentration. A jolt shuddered through my mind, and I found myself looking down at the number three painted on Jack's coffin. I seemed to be floating in the air above it.

"Jack?" In my out-of-body state I wasn't sure if I could wake him.

Nothing moved—no sounds came from within. I redoubled my effort. "Jack, where are you?" Another flurry rustled like wind in leaves through my mind. Then I saw him: he was dancing with a woman under a bright, bloodred moon.

"Jack!"

He looked up and the woman disappeared as though his will was the only thing that held her there. The music still played but Jack stood with open, empty arms, staring at the spot she'd occupied.

"What the hell?" He lowered his arms, then stomped over to me. "Why the hell are *you* here?" he asked. He looked back, checking to see if his partner had reappeared. "Why can't you leave me alone, even in my dreams?"

"We have to speak about Reedrek. He's lying to you, he'll—"

"Like you're always telling me the truth?"

"It's not the same—"

Jack laughed but more with disdain than with amusement. The music stopped. "So, your lies are okay and his are, what? Evil? Is it evil to give me what by rights should have been mine all along?"

I could feel my strength waning—the moon that had been flying high overhead had disappeared. "What do you mean?"

"I mean the knowledge of what I am, what I can do. And the support of a—of a friend."

I had to hurry. As I watched, Jack began to disappear, fading from the feet up. "No matter what he teaches you or offers you," I warned, "the one thing he won't give you is . . . freedom."

Jack evaporated. I opened my eyes to find Reedrek's unholy stare glowing through the dark as though he'd heard every word. He chuckled, rolled over, and went back to sleep.

Jack

William disappeared from my consciousness as quickly as the beautiful dream of Connie had. Then someone else knocked at the door of my mind. It was Reedrek. I saw him before me all cleaned up, if you can believe it. Thank goodness this dream wasn't in smellavision.

"Are you ready, Jack?"

"Ready for what?"

"I'm going to show you what could be if you pledge your loyalty to me."

"What if I don't want any more mind games?" I mentally steeled myself against him.

"Relax, my boy, you don't have a thing to lose. Not yet, anyway. This is just a little peep show into the world that could be yours. Enjoy it. Savor it. I'll be your guide. Think of me as St. Nick, the bringer of Christmas . . . possibilities."

I felt like I was caught up in a whirlwind, and before I knew it, I was standing on a platform in what looked like . . . Las Vegas. Neon was everywhere, flashing in endless cascading colors up and down the Strip. The lights hurt my sensitive vampiric eyes and I blinked. Behind me was a line of chorus girls decked out in G-strings and feathered, sequined bras. Their elaborate headdresses, not to mention their miles-long legs, made them look seven feet tall. The cleavage alone nearly made my eyes bug out. Reedrek had to grab me by the elbow to turn me toward the front of the platform.

"Behold, Jack." Reedrek was decked out in a tuxedo with a cape. An honest-to-Pete velvet vampire cape with gold braid and tassels. I had the momentary urge to laugh but the rest of what I saw brought me up short.

Next to us on the platform was a beautiful Chevy Monte Carlo, painted up in black, blue, and silver. With a big number three on the side.

"Dale's number," I breathed.

"Yes," Reedrek said smugly. "The Desert Racing League insisted that you should race with his number, since you're the DRL's equivalent of NASCAR's late, great Dale Earnhardt himself. Oh, and I took the liberty of selecting a nickname for you. What do you think of 'Dark Knight'? Too corny?"

I looked at the logo on the car. DARK KNIGHT was painted in blue Old English letters with a stylized silver knight's helmet beside it. Actually, it looked pretty hot. In fact, the whole scenario was making me hard. My own state-of-the-art racing setup. But it was impossible. William had told me from the beginning that I couldn't stay gone from him for any length of time until I reached two hundred. If I ever got that old.

"What are you?" I asked Reedrek. "Colonel Tom Parker to my Elvis?"

"Exactly," he said, looking delighted. "A particularly apt comparison since we're here in Las Vegas. I'll be your manager. I can make the arrangements in the blink of a mortal's eye. But there's more to see." Reedrek pointed toward street level. "I know your weakness for human females."

What arrangements? Was this guy so powerful he could break the vampire rules? As I looked down I realized that my eyes had become accustomed to the glare, and I saw them—heard them. A couple hundred women of every shape and size thronged below me, squealing my name. "Jaaaaack!" they shouted, looking pleadingly up at me. They were jumping up and down, waving outstretched arms, wiggling and jiggling invitingly. From my lofty vantage point it looked like a sea of painted lips, bouncing breasts, and restless thighs. They all wanted me. I could see it in their eyes. And these were quality women. Las Vegas by God women. Not the frustrated housewives on the make and honky-tonk angels that were my usual speed. There were plenty of those, mind you. But there's such a thing as quantity versus quality, and here there was plenty of both.

"Hey, now," I heard myself say. It was then I saw the outer circle just beyond the mob of women. Men standing two and three deep, looking at me with admiration, envy, awe. They wanted to *be* me. Hell, who wouldn't?

I felt Reedrek's hand on my shoulder and turned to face him and another man. "Jack, I'd like you to meet a representative from your main sponsor—Buster's Brewery. They're going to be working with you to formulate your own brand of beer, specifically tailored to your own tastes and marketed all over the world."

The man extended his hand and I shook it. "It's a thrill to meet you, Jack. On behalf of Buster's I want to welcome you to our corporate family. This is for you." He held out a sack as big as a pillowcase. Reedrek took it from him and opened it so I could see inside. It was cash. The biggest wad of cash I had ever seen in my life.

"Take it, boy," Reedrek said. "It's all for you. It's your signing bonus."

"Huh?" I said, stupefied. A closer look revealed that the cash was all in large bills. There must have been a million dollars in that sack.

"Your manager tells me he's had plans drawn up for your own personal eighteen-wheel motor home. Rumor has it that it's even fancier than your friend Nightflash's. Let us know if this isn't enough to cover it. There's plenty more where this came from."

"Over here, Knight!" Four photographers appeared just below us, gesturing for us to prepare for a picture. Reedrek thrust the money sack into my hand and the beer man stuck a cap, emblazoned with the beer company logo and my number, on my head. They positioned themselves on either side of me. "Smile," another of the shutterbugs said, and rapid-fire electronic flashes stung my eyes.

As the flashes receded, the truth exploded in my reeling head.

Reedrek knew about Tobey.

The beer man just mentioned the Nightflash, and Reedrek mentioned the DRL. The old demon had gotten into my head after all and I hadn't even realized it. Did that mean he knew about Iban and Gerard, too? I looked sideways at Reedrek. If he was reading my mind right now, he didn't show it—he was too busy leering at the showgirls and grinning for the camera. What had allowed him to enter my mind? The answer was all around me. It was my envy of Tobey and what he had that I didn't. It was the green-eyed monster within.

"Can we get a quote?" said a man standing behind the lensmen. He held up a tape recorder. Reedrek nudged me forward.

"I—I'm very happy to . . . to have this fine brewery as my sponsor. I look forward to a long and . . ." I caught the eye of a particularly stunning blonde right below me. She snaked her tongue all around the edge of a pair of perfectly painted, suckable lips. ". . . satisfying relationship," I finished.

The beer man shook my hand again and retreated to the back of the platform. Then Rennie came up the steps in a black, blue, and silver pit crew uniform, grinning from ear to ear. "Your crew chief has something for you," Reedrek said. Rennie held a matching driver's uniform and a racing helmet painted to look like the helm from a knight's silver suit of armor. I marveled not only at the outfit, but at the look of rapture on my best friend's face. What if somehow Reedrek could give me the power to make this happen for the little guy? To change his life.

Did Reedrek know how to push my buttons or what? Every single one of them. From my love of racing to my love of women to my love of my human friends. He'd taken these things from my mind when I wasn't looking.

"Thanks for naming me your crew chief," Rennie said. A tear of joy made its liquid way underneath one of the thick lenses of his glasses and down the stocky little man's chubby cheek. "You have no idea what it means to me." Rennie set the uniform and helmet down on the car and gave me a hug. I patted him awkwardly on his stubbly, crew-cut head. Then he left the platform, eyes streaming.

The beer man stepped forward again. "And now let me introduce you to the finalists for the title of Miss DRL. You'll be selecting the winner, Jack, and you have all weekend to make up your mind." The beer man winked at me lecherously and elbowed me in the ribs.

Sashaying up the platform steps in spike heels came three of the most beautiful women I'd ever seen in my life. Great goodness alive.

A blue-eyed blonde in a bolero top and short shorts came first. She slid her slender arms around my waist and pressed her breasts against me. "Pick me, Jack. I'll give you anything. And I mean anything." She pressed a kiss to my lips and I came away with the taste of honey-suckle on my mouth. Her lips puckered into a pout as she was forced to yield her place at my side to the second girl.

The green-eyed redhead, even hotter than the blonde, linked her arms around my neck, pressing herself more firmly against me, shoulder-to-thigh. She kissed me as well, opening her mouth slightly to greet my tongue with hers. She whispered throatily, "Pick me, Jack. And I *promise* you won't be sorry." I felt her body stiffen as the third girl pinched her shoulder in a signal to relinquish her place by my side.

The third beauty, a doe-eyed brunette, pressed herself to me and looked up into my eyes. Her gaze was full of adoration and desire. This dark beauty was familiar. Who did she remind me of? Catherine Zeta-Jones? Close, but not exactly. This girl was even hotter than the movie star. Who, I wondered, was she? She even felt familiar in my arms.

"All this can be yours, Jack," Reedrek intoned in my ear. "I can make it happen right now." He was standing right behind me, his hot breath on my neck. Ordinarily that would be quite a buzz kill. But what he'd said—that he could give me all this, that it was somehow possible . . . "All you have to do," he said, "is pledge your allegiance to me. And perform a . . . task now and then."

"What kind of task?" I asked. The woman stayed in my arms as if time had come to a standstill. If she heard Reedrek, she didn't show it.

"Oh, just enjoy some human blood from time to time. I promise you, there's nothing like it. When you give yourself over to your true nature, when you at last accept who and what you are, you will finally attain true happiness."

I didn't look at him, instead keeping my gaze locked on the liquid depths of the woman's coal black eyes. "And what am I exactly?"

"You're a monster, Jack. You're the offspring of the most ancient line of the most savage, merciless killers the world has ever known. You are the heir to a dynasty of blood. A prince among demons, a fledgling master vampire."

At any other time in my existence, I would have whipped a guy's ass for calling me a monster, even though it was technically true. But when Reedrek said it like that, it made me hard. I'd rebelled against my own demonic nature since the night I was made. But now everything looked different, and it wasn't just the neon. Was it time to embrace the darkness?

My mouth went dry with the thirst for blood. I saw the artery in the girl's neck pulsating. I now knew who she reminded me of. It was as if Reedrek had refocused my vision while he was speaking and I could see more clearly than ever.

Connie.

He'd picked up on my desire for her as he'd picked up on my other desires.

And it wasn't over yet. Great googly-moogly. My Connie grabbed me and suddenly we were rolling and tumbling across satin sheets, scattering rose petals to the hot desert wind. First time a woman had outclassed me in the sack. The more we fucked, the more otherworldly she seemed. Beyond me, above me—wild as a sex banshee.

I awoke bathed in blood-tinged sweat, staring at the black satin lining of my coffin lid.

Fifteen

Jack

The familiar dimness of my own coffin steadied me. It's not like anyone would know what I'd been up to all night/day—except maybe Reedrek. And I had to admit that if a dream could be good enough to practically make my hair stand on end with pleasure, then the real thing would have to be . . . awesome. My mouth went dry with the possibilities. I pushed the lid of my coffin open and immediately went for the wet bar.

For blood.

I felt parched—like Huey must have, suffering under his wife's curse, when he watched the rest of us guys slug back as many beers as we wanted—thirsty enough to risk death. The words *There are no limits* echoed through my body. *You can have all you want . . .*

My body didn't care who I betrayed or how I went about it—it only wanted blood. Human blood. I didn't bother emptying the IV bag into a glass. I simply bit and sucked. My hard-earned attempts at manners seemed stupid now. In midsuck a sound behind me turned me around.

Olivia, rising from William's coffin, watched me with questioning eyes. Reyha and Deylaud sat on the floor at either side of the coffin like living statues in a pharaoh's tomb. "Good morning," Olivia said. Reyha picked herself up and crossed the room to sit at my feet.

It's kind of hard to talk and suck at the same time so I just nodded. I was more interested in filling the emptiness inside me than in chitchatting with a houseguest. Even if we had bumped uglies the day before. I tossed the empty bag toward the trash can and ripped into another. Olivia sat cross-legged in William's coffin, all fresh-faced and pale. I found myself comparing her to Connie. The English chick came up pretty short, especially compared to the Connie I'd gotten to know in my dream. Hoo-ya.

As I ripped into a third bag of blood a wave of dizziness made me wobble on my feet. I suddenly realized what I was doing—gorging myself on human blood, forming a hard-as-rock erection on the memory of a dream. Connie wasn't really like that, was she? And she wasn't really *my* Connie, not yet anyway.

All this can be yours . . .

I stopped sucking, tore the bag open, and poured the remainder in a glass before offering it to Olivia. "Did you sleep okay?" I asked, trying to hide my hunger by wiping my mouth on the sleeve of my shirt. I still felt all caddy-wompuss.

She took the glass and sipped. The blood colored her lips a warm red, making my hands shake. I definitely needed to get a grip. "Yes, very well. No dreams." She slipped from the coffin and took a step in my direction. "How about you?"

No way was I answering that question. But as I tried

to think of something to head her off, I got a whiff of her. She smelled of William, from sleeping in his coffin, I guess. The familiar and mostly pleasant reminder of my maker wafted toward me like a comforting arm around my shoulders. Before I could get my mind around the effect, a hard pain struck me like a punch in the stomach from Evander Holyfield in the ninth round. I had to gasp in a breath.

"Are you all right?" Olivia asked, coming closer.

I straight-armed her to keep her away. "Yeah, just dandy," I managed before collapsing onto the ottoman with my head in my hands. "Drank a little too fast there . . ." Reyha padded over and rested her head on my knee. Her sympathetic eyes watched me with concern. I ran a hand over her soft, pale fur as I fought to keep from jumping up and running as fast as I could. Somewhere . . . anywhere but here.

"Good evening."

I looked up when I heard Melaphia's voice. The sight of her alarmed me even further. She looked like she'd gone native. Her coffee-colored feet were bare, but several gold and silver rings sparkled on her toes. Layers of thin, filmy, voodoo blue material fell in different lengths to form a sort of skirt, and her drawstring blouse was bloodred. A black spiderweb of a shawl draped over her shoulders, beads twinkling in its threads like dark stars when she breathed. And her beautiful hair—she'd twisted her soft chocolate dreads into clumps decorated with shells and bones. The whole package gave off a surge of power that a dead man could feel.

Dead man. That would be me.

"Come," she said in a commanding voice. "We have to get ready."

William

It took Reedrek two tries to shove the rock off my chest. I drew in several labored but deep breaths before trying to sit up. I could feel my strength growing, though. Not because of being released. Because of Werm.

Reedrek had taken Werm out for his first feeding right after sunset, and the both of us were stronger for it. Another severed head decorated Reedrek's makeshift trophy shelf. I was past the point of worrying who had been the unlucky donor. Any port in a storm, as they used to say in my sailing days—or rather nights. Difficult to be picky when I was so weak that I could be summarily dispatched—without the opportunity for revenge against my sire.

And I would have my revenge. I owed him for so many things—from the killing of my family to the fire at Eleanor's. The clock began ticking when Reedrek set me free. It only remained for me to choose my moment.

Werm, my new convert, lounged on one of the bone-covered slabs like a visiting film star. I had to say the change had improved him. His hair, formerly dyed purplish black, had reverted back to its original shade of whitish blond and shone with unnatural good health. His skin had lost any trace of adolescent pimples. His wiry body, still angular, had acquired some substance and certainly new vigor. I watched as he idly picked at the heavy stones lining the chamber, knocking them into the water with dollop-like splashes. Lizards slithered through the newly made holes in the wall.

"That's enough of that," Reedrek ordered, and Werm immediately turned his attention back to us.

"Looks like he's more yours than mine," I said, speaking the unfortunate truth.

"Well, what did you expect? More gifts when all you've done is cross me at every opportunity?"

"One can only hope."

"Hope?" Reedrek huffed. "You truly are a fool. I've given up on trying to convince you of anything. Tonight will be the end of your scheming . . . and of you. It's a pity Alger isn't here to see this. I should have waited. I would've found such pleasure in killing him before your eyes."

I ignored Reedrek and bent my mind toward Werm. *Come, shake the hand of your sire,* I whispered into his thoughts. After a surprised look, Werm got up, dusted himself off, and moved toward me. I held out my hand and he reached for it.

Reedrek struck before our hands met, faster than either of us at the moment. He grabbed Werm by the neck and thrust him against the stones he'd been picking at earlier. I felt the jolt of Werm's mindless fear.

"I'll tear off *your* head and feed your blood to the dogs!"

My own throat tightened, echoing the grip of Reedrek's fingers around Werm's neck.

"You don't speak or move unless I say. Do you have the wit to see who is giving the orders here?"

He won't kill you, I whispered. *He needs you.*

Werm tried to answer him but only gagged. Reedrek shoved him toward the door, then snatched up the closest intact human remains—mostly a pile of rotted clothes and bones—and threw them in Werm's direction to punctuate his order. "Now, go and do as I told you." Werm stood staring, stupefied for a moment. Perhaps his position in the undead food chain was beginning to sink in. "*Go!*" Reedrek shouted. My new convert brushed the dust of the moldy dead off the front of his leather jacket, remembered how to move his feet, and quickly left the tomb.

Jack

Melaphia led us into the corridor to her wall of altars. Each of the thirteen had been dusted and restocked with new candles and fresh flowers. There were fresh bowls of food, too, along with offerings of peacock feathers, African beads, and conch shells. I could smell the tangy odor of Jamaican rum and the still-warm splashes of chicken blood. It looked like every spirit, demon, and god had been called to attention. I wondered if Melaphia had slept even a little since she'd tucked me in at sunrise.

"On your knees, Jack."

I stared at Melaphia like my ears weren't working. "Huh?"

She put a strong hand on my shoulder, near my neck, and squeezed. "There are more powerful things in the world than vampires, boy. Do as I say."

The word *boy* registered just as my knees hit the floor. I was about to give her a hard time but when I looked up at her she was completely ignoring me. Her eyes were leveled on Olivia.

"I only protect those who help us. If you aren't friend then you're foe." Melaphia held Olivia's gaze like a snake holding a bird's. "Make a choice. And know that if you lie, the *orishas* will remember. The marks of protection can easily become marks of death."

Olivia nodded and slowly dropped to her knees.

Reyha and Deylaud, now in their human forms, hovered near the opening of the corridor. Melaphia pointed a finger at them and hissed like an angry cat. They quickly disappeared from the doorway. In human form Reyha wouldn't be able to fit in her usual hiding place between the ottoman and the recliner. I'd be willing to bet she was hiding in William's coffin instead.

"Now we begin." Melaphia moved to the altar at the center—the one holding the vial of Lalee's sacred blood—and began to light the candles. In the brighter light, I noticed a box that hadn't been there before. It seemed to be made of bone.

As she went about her business Melaphia hummed a strange tune under her breath and swayed, making the layers of her skirt lift and dance like flower petals in a nonexistent breeze. When all the candles were burning, she ran her fingers through the flames, bathing her hands in energy. Then she clapped her palms together in a rhythm only she understood before picking up a silver bowl of blood—fresh human blood.

"Take off your shirts."

For once, I didn't even bother to cop a peep at Olivia's chest. I didn't have time to think about sex; I was too busy calculating. Nothing and no one I knew would be the same after this night. Not Melaphia, not Connie, hell, not even the Rin Tin Twins. And then there was Renee. William had crashed and burned off his pedestal of vampire god. Whatever happened next was up to me.

If Melaphia had read my thoughts my ears would be blistered with threats. She considered William her true family—he carried the blood of her ancestors. Yet here she was, protecting me, the one who could betray William. The bowl in her hand was filled with her own blood. I could smell it. I gazed up at her as she plunged two fingers into the warm redness.

"I call on Ayizan, Maman Brigitte . . ." She rubbed the blood into my hair. My scalp twitched with power. It felt like my hair was dancing like marsh grass in a hurricane.

"I call on Ogoun Ge-Rouge," she muttered, and painted the blood on the center of my chest. "Warrior *loa* of blood, fire, lightning, and the sword. Bringer of vengeance."

A rush of wind followed by the loud bang of a slamming door made me jump. Suddenly, the skin she'd touched over my unbeating heart went cold. If the undead could experience death again it would feel like this. Personally, dying once had been enough for me—

"Laleeeeeeeee." Her chant echoed off the stone walls. "The daughter of your soul asks that you protect the sons of your family. Guard and guide, fulfill your oath." Melaphia threw her head back and wailed, "Maman Laleeeeeee."

The sound was downright creepy; hearing it, even a vampire like me didn't feel entirely safe. I squinted toward the altar and noticed that one of the statues had begun to drip bloody tears. Goose bumps rose on my chilled flesh and I couldn't resist glancing at Olivia.

Bare to the waist, she'd crossed her hands over her heart—but not in fear. Her eyes were closed, but she was smiling a secret-female-conspiracy smile. One gander at her enraptured face made me feel like an outsider again. If I didn't know better, I'd think she was praying. Even if I'd wanted to—pray, that is—I wouldn't have remembered how after all these years of unholiness.

Melaphia stopped wailing and put her hand on my shoulder once more. "Come." She helped me up before

I even realized I needed help. Then she walked me to the corner, where a large mahogany tub had been placed. It was half full of liquid. "Bathe your head in the water," she instructed.

Like the good boy I'd always been I kneeled in front of the basin, but then I had second thoughts. Just before I plunged my head under, I gave Melaphia a calculated grin. "I don't suppose this is holy water, now is it?"

She pinched my ear, hard. "Since when you don't trust me, boy?"

"Ow! Hey, the last time I trusted you I ended up locked in the vault. Olivia can go first."

With a *tsk* of annoyance, Melaphia motioned Olivia forward and watched her lower her head into the basin.

Then it was my turn. I took a breath and dunked up to my neck. As I came up spitting water, Melaphia used her hands to scrub my hair, shoulders, and chest. The water did burn, but it was a needles-and-pins kind of burn, annoying but not dangerous. As if I could do anything about Melaphia trying to hurt me if she decided to. But the thought did give me an idea—

"One more time."

Feeling really stupid didn't keep me from following her directions a second time. What the hell did I know about voodoo?

A moment later I was standing and dripping in front of her. She pulled my face down, smiled, and kissed me on each cheek. "All right. Go get dressed. I've put out your clothes." Then she turned her attention back to Olivia.

"Why do I have to wear this stupid jacket again? If I have to act like the lord of the manor at least let me dress like one." This was just too much. There were more than a hundred reasons I could bring up as to why wearing blue velvet wasn't a good fashion choice. And I wasn't beyond using every excuse before admitting the true reasons: It was William's jacket, the one he'd given me as protection, and the one I'd been wearing when I'd kissed Connie, what felt like centuries ago.

"It's clean, Jack, and it's a retro party. What's your problem?"

"Retro or not, cheesy is cheesy."

Melaphia gave me one of her you're-acting-like-a-child looks. "It's important. William wanted you to wear it."

William.

"You're going up against a master vampire to bring William back to us. This jacket is as strong as I can make it."

Olivia's entrance saved me from having to lie about who or what I was going up against. It wasn't just her arrival, but the way she looked.

"This is so beautiful," she said, twirling. The beaded fringe on her dress fluttered with a life of its own.

"It's from the 1920s. It belonged to a friend of William's."

"Makes me feel like a girl again." Olivia laughed. "What do you think, Jack?"

"I think I'd rather wear that dress than show up in this freakin' coat."

"Oh, don't be a spoilsport. Melaphia has her reasons. You should follow her advice."

I was about to tell her just how tired I was of advice when the front bell rang. I started for the living room, but Melaphia stopped me. "Wait."

Deylaud touched the doorknob, then looked to Melaphia. "Vampire, not one I know."

She moved to stand next to me, then nodded. "Open it."

"Werm," I said to our new guest, hardly able to believe my eyes. His hair had gone from inky black to nearly white. His skin had that pale, otherworldly glow that most of us vamps had, and he filled out his black leather a little better than the last time I'd seen his spindly self. "What are you doing here?"

"Well, hello to you, too, bro."

He looked as fit as a fiddle and downright pleased with himself. I took a step back and invited him to come inside. "You got what you wanted. You're a vampire. Bully for you."

"That's right, Jack. William did for me what you wouldn't. I'm now a badass blood drinker. Just like you."

Reyha giggled and covered her mouth—guess she could see actual horror on my face at being related to this weasel. "I can barely tell the two of you apart," Olivia deadpanned.

"Very funny," I said. "You're like me in your dreams, you little pissant. I can still break you in half as easily as I could before. Now, I'm really not in the mood for games, so what do you want?" I used to feel sorry for the guy, but that was over. When I'd chosen to walk in darkness, I hadn't had any idea what I was getting myself into. Werm, on the other hand, had sought out the life of a demon, knowing exactly what he would become. To hell with him.

"So this is it. William's house," he said, ignoring my question. He stretched his arms out expansively and looked all around. "The family home."

"Family?" Melaphia crossed her arms and eyed Werm.

"Jack, who is this skinny child? Did William really make him?"

"I'm afraid so," I said. "Everybody, this is—what the hell is your real name again?"

Werm looked hurt. "My name is Lamar Nathan Von Werm." He drew himself up to his full five-five. "But you can call me the Werminator."

Unbelievable. I rolled my eyes at the ceiling. Some nights it just didn't pay to get out of your coffin. "Call him Werm. I have no idea why William made him, but I think Reedrek had something to do with it."

"Maybe William didn't want you to grow up an only child, Jack," Werm said, laughing.

I didn't like being reminded of what I was trying not to think about. I was no longer William's lone offspring. Until today, I'd been the only vampire William ever made in his hundreds of years of existence, or so he'd said. I'd always been William's right hand, his enforcer, his only . . . son. Now, for whatever reason, he'd seen fit to create himself another offspring. Just in time for my own little graduation. Well, let Werm be his stooge from now on. That suited me just fine.

I reached out, grabbed Werm by his skinny neck, and raised him in the air nearly a foot off the ground. I flashed my fangs and snarled loudly, a sound so savage, so animalistic that I shocked even myself. Behind me I heard the women gasp and the dogs, even in their human forms, whine. "State your business," I said. My vampiric eyes burned into the fledgling's own and I could see the fear in his. About freakin' time I got some respect. "I ain't playin'."

"Clothes," he choked out. "Reedrek sent me for William's party clothes. And I'm supposed to say that they are coming, *as you wished.*"

"Yes!" Melaphia hissed. "I knew they would be there." I didn't take my eyes off Werm, but I could hear her feet beating a staccato path up the stairs toward the master suite.

"Jack," Olivia said gently. "I think you can put him down now."

"That's my call," I growled. I glared at him, realizing that I really did want to kill him—to drain him of the blood that my sire had given him and take it righteously for myself. My blood thirst made my fangs throb. I'd never tasted blood of my blood, and suddenly I desperately wanted to. Reedrek had said I was a monster, a born killer. Maybe I'd denied my true nature long enough. Bon appétit, Jackie. With a roar I brought Werm's throat to my mouth and sank my fangs into the cold flesh of his neck.

I vaguely heard screams as his blood began to flow into my mouth. I drew on whatever life force animated Werm's brand-new vampire body and bent it to my will, making it flow from him to me. I tasted my bloodline— Reedrek, William, Lalee, myself. It was intoxicating.

Werm flailed in my grip and Olivia screamed and tried to pull me off him. The dogs were howling eerily, their canine natures responding to the feeding, the blood-letting. Olivia wedged her arms between our chests to break my hold on the fledgling.

My fangs came away from his neck messily, leaking blood on my white shirt and leaving a raw gash on Werm's skin. I dropped Werm to the floor. Olivia caught him before he crumpled to the marble and helped him stand upright.

"Welcome to the—what did you call it when we first met? Brotherhood of the blood, was it? Well, you're at the bottom of the bloodsucker food chain, *little brother*."

Werm backed away, whimpering, until he was leaning against the door. Olivia put her hand on my shoulder. "Why don't you go change your shirt?" I faced her and she massaged my shoulder a little. Her visage was serene, and I knew she was trying to calm me. I let her.

"This is Reedrek's influence over you, Jack. His thrall doesn't wear off easily. Take it from someone who knows. You lost control for a moment, but it'll be all right."

"It's okay. I'm just mad because he wanted this. And then the little twerp had the nerve to—"

Just then Melaphia came downstairs carrying some kind of costume on a hanger. She studied Werm, who was holding his gaping wound together. It was already healing, but from the look on his face, he didn't know that. I hadn't sucked enough of his blood to slow down a vampire's natural regenerative power. He'd be fine in a few hours, assuming he first didn't die of fright from the knowledge of what he'd gotten himself into.

"I guess I don't have to ask what all the screaming was about," Melaphia said. I figured she would scold me, but instead she put a cautioning finger on Werm's ruined throat. "You're a demon now, boy. That means you're in a whole new world of darkness. Be smart and maybe you'll survive. Taunting a hundred-forty-year-old vampire, even one as tolerant as Jack, can get you dead real quick. If you don't show more brains than that, you won't live to see the winter solstice."

"Y—yes, ma'am," Werm rasped.

I started up the stairs, turning my back on them all, still thirsting for human blood even though I'd gorged myself earlier and had some Werm juice as a chaser. Usually I denied myself the pleasure of human blood unless I needed its rejuvenating effects to heal an injury. Biting Werm had felt good. Damn good. Was that because of Reedrek's influence? Or was it because I'd stopped fighting my instincts?

William's bedroom was immaculate, since he hardly ever used it except when he was entertaining women. In his cedar-lined walk-in closet I stood surrounded on all sides by expensive, custom-tailored clothing. I shucked the voodoo blue jacket and the stained dress shirt. Luckily William and I were nearly the same size. The variety of shirts was dizzying, most of them either of silk or the finest cotton. He was a little leaner than me, so I skipped past the fitted dress shirts and took down the next one I found. When I slipped it on, I discovered that it had French cuffs and tiny pleats down the front.

I lined up the cuffs and flipped open a velvet jewelry box sitting on the cabinet that was built into one wall. I saw his favorite pair of cuff links—silver, hand-forged by Paul Revere himself, and bearing the initials WCT. I worked them through the holes in the cuffs, put the jacket back on, and checked myself out. I didn't usually miss being able to see my own reflection, but now I did. As it was, I looked down at myself in the fancy threads and smoothed the nap of the velvet, enjoying the color of the material, the blue of the deepest mountain pond.

Not bad. I tugged at the shirtsleeves so that a half inch of snow white cuff as well as the cuff links showed beyond the deep blue of the jacket sleeves. Not bad at all. Connie's face floated through my thoughts and suddenly she seemed one step closer to being mine. I deserved to have her any way I wanted her.

I flung open the top drawer of the cabinet and sorted through the items, pocketing a monogrammed linen

handkerchief and casting aside bow ties and other doodads. I saw a white silk pocket square and tucked it into
the breast pocket of the jacket so that only about an inch
showed, just like William wore them. I studied myself
again. Maybe this jacket wasn't so bad after all. It would
bring out the blue in my eyes to impress the ladies. Yeah,
this jacket was growing on me. Why hadn't I liked it
from the beginning?

I reached for William's comb and brush, sitting beside
the jewelry box, and gave my hair the once-over. Then I
arranged the shirt collar against the jacket collar just so.
Just like William would've done. You don't practically
live with a Dapper Dan for a hundred years and not
learn a little something about grooming.

I stared down at my outfit again for a long moment.
Here I was, looking like the lord of the manor, wearing
his clothing and jewelry. Was it true what they said
about clothes making the man? If so, then I *was* the
man. What was the difference between William and me
when you came right down to it? He had more knowledge and money. That was it. According to my grandsire, I had the chance to seize the knowledge this very
night. And something told me that if I did, money would
become much less important. I could finally be my own
man, live on any terms I chose.

It would be easy.

I braced myself with one hand on the cabinet, the
gravity of the choice I faced hitting me like a sledge-
hammer in the brainpan. What was I thinking? The fact
that I was even tempted made me queasy. It had to be
Reedrek's thrall. To renounce William and go with Reedrek would mean giving up my family—not just William,
but Melaphia, Renee, Reyha, and Deylaud. It would
mean betraying the precious memories of Mel's mother

and grandmother, and the entire line of mystical women who were responsible for making me the man I'd become.

Man? I looked into the mirror, expecting just for a split second to see myself. Of course, there was no one there. I was not a man, did not possess the nature of a man, not anymore. I was a vampire. As William often said, sometimes I forgot that. I tried to have it both ways, with one foot in the world of humans and the other in our altered world, the world of eternal darkness. Maybe it was time to stop straddling the fence.

I remembered then that I had to get the king's ransom from Melaphia's precious subterranean altars. I slipped out of the closet and through the secret back door of the bedroom, taking the stairs downward to the darkness of the vault two at a time.

The weather and the moon seemed to have gotten the message to cooperate with William's shindig, or else. The night was cool but not cold and only a few clouds floated in the fall sky. The full hunter's moon hung like a fat party lantern, illuminating the courtyard of the Hamilton House along with twinkling man-made lights in the trees. Candles flickered on fine white tablecloths as white-shirted waiters circulated through the crowd. A string quartet, set up in one corner of the main ballroom, played softly—that kind of namby-pamby music William loved. Other than wishing for a little George Thorogood or even Tim McGraw, I felt the evening was going pretty well so far.

I'd taken my appointed place at the front door to greet the swells; Melaphia was a short ways away overseeing the help. I imagined she was also on the lookout for William.

"Hey, how y'all doing? How's your mama and them?" I pumped the hand of a stockbroker in a reasonable copy of a Confederate officer's uniform—the main anachronism being its lack of wear and dirt. After the first day of enlistment, I don't think I ever saw a clean or new-looking Sesesh uniform, officer's or otherwise. Losing a war has a way of roughing things up, both clothes and people. But then, this wasn't war. It was retro. The stockbroker's blond trophy wife gave me a semi-curtsy in her hoopskirts and a little wink from behind the vintage fan.

"Very well, thanks," the stockbroker replied. "Mother speaks highly of your front-end alignments. With all the curbs she runs over, I expect she brings her Caddy in pretty often."

"That she does. She's one of my favorite customers."

"Good. Good. Fantastic party. I'm sure y'all will make a lot of money for that new wing of the hospital."

"Thanks. I certainly hope so. The cornerstone is set to go in." I knew William's plans for the new wing included a new and improved blood bank. My mouth watered a little just thinking about it. In the past few days I'd rediscovered my taste for human blood. I also felt myself longing for the hunt again. It had been a long time.

"Tell me, Jack, where's William tonight, anyway?"

"The last I saw him, he was kind of weighed down. With work, you know. But we're expecting him to break free and join us any time now. In the meantime, I'm your host. The bar is right over there, so make yourselves at home." I clapped him on the back and headed him toward the hard liquor. Forget the sissy-boys passing out champagne. His wife followed, bringing her fist to her ear, thumb and pinky extended in the universal "call me" gesture. I gave her a nod and a little wave.

I'd had my fun with rich, bored society housewives, but they usually made me go out the servants' entrance, and not just because they didn't want to raise suspicions of an affair. They appreciated my talents in bed but wouldn't be seen rubbing elbows with me in public unless they came to the shop to pretend to talk about a car problem. Suddenly it seemed I was good enough to flirt with not only in public but at a high-falutin' soirée to boot. Wasn't that a fine howdy-do?

I was surprised at how comfortable I was with the society types once I changed my attitude. Maybe it wasn't them being uppity all these years that made them seem intimidating, but rather my own low opinion of myself, courtesy of my real human daddy. The man who predicted my future with the words "You ain't worth a half-cent copper." It seemed as if my insecurities had disappeared now that I was finally thinking straight after decades of being under the thumb of William, my vampire daddy. When I'd put on his clothes in his inner sanctum, it was as if I'd put on part of his power at the same time. Changing had been so easy. What else could I accomplish if I just set my mind to it?

Melaphia sauntered over in a traditional African ensemble, the kind black people used to wear in the sixties and seventies when "getting back to your roots" was fashionable. The colorful dashiki, matching headdress, and trade beads made her look like the African princess she was. She hadn't forgotten her voodoo blue, either—she wore a sky blue scarf tied around her neck. She was looking at me shrewdly, as if trying to figure out something.

"You seem to be the host with the most tonight. And here I thought you were dreading the social scene."

"Oh, well, you know. I can rise to the occasion as well as the next guy." I scanned the room, which was rapidly filling up with well-dressed socialites. Nothing but the best. Some of those retro designer outfits must've cost a pretty penny, even on eBay. I took another swig of my drink, which to the casual observer looked to be no more than a standard Bloody Mary. Little did they know how bloody it really was.

"Why can't I read you, Jack? Tonight of all nights, why can't I tell where your head is at?"

Probably 'cause I didn't know myself. I returned her level gaze. "Beats me."

"What are you not telling me, damn you?"

She said she couldn't read me, but the truth was that she just couldn't bear to admit what she knew: that I might actually break away from William.

After a quick greeting at the door, I'd deliberately avoided Iban, Tobey, and Gerard, who were scattered about the room, mixing and mingling easily with the other guests. I didn't want them to interfere when the time came to make my move. Whatever that move would be. Anticipation hummed inside me. A sea change was coming for old Jack. Tonight would be the first night of the rest of my life.

William

Even the undead have defining moments. Moments when the disparate *what if*s and *should have*s of half a millennium collide in one shocking instant.

This was one of those times for me. After my seemingly endless captivity, I was nearly overwhelmed by sensations, not the least of which was breathing the free air again. Wearing my own clothes felt luxurious. My old British naval uniform reminded me of England and home, of men in deadly earnest, of the storm-tossed ocean waves racing the moon.

There are few places, however, more beautiful than Bonaventure under a full moon. The lovely forest of artful stone built to honor the dead came to life when illuminated by light and shadow, reminding living souls of their rich lineage and of their final destination: peace. (What went on underground notwithstanding.) All in all, the old cemetery offered a place of reflection and calm among the daily breakneck pace of the living. But on All Saints' the place was transformed. From the worms in the sandy soil to the Spanish moss in the tops of the trees, many things besides us vampires were stirring in the moonlight.

Several buzzing trickster spirits circled around us like curious mosquitos. One of them kept tapping my sire on his shoulder, staying just out of reach when Reedrek turned to brush him off. Another maintained an ear-blistering stream of curses worthy of a victim of Tourette's. Knots of ghostly onlookers floated in the distance watching the show.

"Why did you leave the automobile at the gates?" Reedrek demanded, sounding peeved.

Werm, rather subdued after his trip across town to retrieve my clothes, looked confused. "They were locked," he answered.

"Don't be a fool, you're a vampire! No gate can shut you out! Why didn't you drive through them?"

"And dent my mom's Escalade? No way, man. She'd kill me."

Judging by the look Reedrek aimed at our new offspring, he might kill Werm out of sheer annoyance. I'd felt that way with Jack on many occasions.

The closer we got to the gates, the fewer spirits showed themselves. They took to the trees, faded into headstones, evaporated. Ahead I could see the reason why. There were groups of the living with flashlights, candles, and pumpkin lanterns on the sidewalk outside the wrought-iron fence. Trick-or-treaters mixed with curious teenagers and protective adults. Most of them probably thinking they wanted to see a ghost. It was Halloween, after all. The modern human version of All Saints'. In medieval times anyone wearing a mask and banging on doors would have been burned at the stake. Mutilating a perfectly good pumpkin—if we'd had them in Europe then—would have been heresy.

Seeing the younger ones daring one another to climb the fence reminded me of my Will teasing his mother from a tree limb. *I won't fall.* Diana and I hadn't known then that a tumble from a tree was the least of our future concerns. In the lull before the storm to come, I couldn't resist taunting Reedrek.

"I know now that you didn't kill Will," I said, looking sideways at him.

A curious mix of surprise and—something I didn't expect—mirth crossed his features. "Oh, really?" he said, recovering his sarcastic stance. "And how would you know that?"

I shrugged. "Doesn't matter. He lived. I might even have kin of my true blood somewhere in the world." I smiled my best mocking smile. "You didn't manage to destroy us all."

"Hey look! Ghosts!" someone shouted. We were close enough to be seen.

Werm, getting into the spirit, charged the fence. "Boooooo!" he bellowed.

Most of the crowd drew back in response, just in case. A few of them shouted back. "Boo yourself, you asshole!"

They quieted down as they watched us scale the fence, instinctively backing away.

"Hey, who are you guys?"

"We're vampires," Reedrek said with a toothy grin. "We've come to suuuuck your bloooood." With that, he shoved Werm toward the driver's side of his mother's automobile and opened the passenger-side door for me.

"I don't suppose any of you would happen to have a stout wooden stake handy, would you?" I asked the humans.

No one answered.

"After you," Reedrek said, making sure I went along for the ride.

The crowd gave us a round of applause as we pulled away.

Jack

"Ja-ack." Melaphia refused to give up. She sounded even more suspicious.

"Your imagination is running away with you," I lied. "William will be here soon, and then it'll all be . . . over."

She took a breath to reply, but it caught in her throat. I followed the direction of her stricken look. Renee had just walked through the double doors of the ballroom, looking small and vulnerable in her Catholic school uniform and white ankle socks. Melaphia and I met her in the middle of the room, and Mel grabbed her by the upper arms.

"What is wrong with you, child? How did you get here?" Melaphia was trying to keep her voice down because of the crowd, but the pitch rose in anger.

"I took the bus from the Greyhound station on Montgomery Street."

"You made your way here from Brunswick on your own?" I bent down so I was on her level. "By yourself? At night? You were supposed to stay with your aunt."

"You have pulled some crazy stunts in your time, you little rascal, but this takes the cake!" Melaphia railed at Renee. The child was as headstrong as she was precocious. If things weren't so dire, I would have laughed, remembering the day I told a tiny, glaring Melaphia that she would someday be paid back for own transgressions. Mel wound up her tirade by demanding, "Why would you do such a crazy thing?"

Renee crossed her arms over her narrow chest in the same gesture of mule-headed stubbornness I had seen her mother and grandmother make countless times. "There's going to be trouble. I can feel it."

Melaphia gasped and I straightened back to my full height. "And just what do you think you're going to do about it?" I looked around to see if anyone was in earshot. "Except get in the way?"

Renee balled up her little fists and said, "I'm not going to stay with crazy old auntie in silly old Brunswick when all y'all are fightin' something dangerous."

"Who said anything about a fight?" Melaphia glared at me.

"Not me," I said.

The truth was, I didn't know what was going to happen. Exactly. Best case, once Reedrek had what he wanted—the voodoo blood—there would be no reason for him to cause any more trouble. Sure, William had said Reedrek couldn't be trusted, but that was probably because he was afraid of losing me as a flunky. I figured I could talk Reedrek into leaving everybody else alone, including William. Still, I didn't particularly want Melaphia and Renee to witness whatever went down.

"Listen," I said, setting my empty glass down on a tray stand. "I think the two of you should go on back to the house and wait."

"So there *is* going to be a fight!" Renee declared.

"Speak up. I don't think everybody heard you," I hissed. I glanced around to see if anyone was staring and looked right into the eyes of Connie Jones.

"What's this about a fight? Do I need to get out my gun?" Connie smiled, and my long-dead heart did a flip-flop.

I took her in all at once, and then allowed myself a long, thorough look, starting with her gold strappy sandals and long skirt of gauzy off-white material shot through with gold threads. Above her small waist was a tight bodice with a gleaming brass breastplate. And above that were, well, breasts, cleavage, however you wanted to say it. The best view of Connie's I'd ever gotten outside my dreams. The real things were even better. But as much as I'd have liked to linger on her bosom, I couldn't help but stare at her face. She never used much makeup, and I liked that, but tonight she wore dark eyeliner that made her look like an Aztec or Inca goddess straight out of a picture book. I felt myself gaping.

And so, I noticed, were Melaphia and Renee. I found

my voice in time to make introductions before the silence became awkward. "Ladies, this is my friend Consuela Jones. She's a cop. Connie, this is Melaphia and her daughter, Renee. They're family."

"Do you really have a gun on you right now?" Renee looked up at her, wide-eyed.

"Yes," Connie said with a wink. "But I'm not telling you where."

Renee giggled and I noticed that Connie was wearing the charm I'd given her. The ugly-ass thing actually looked at home with the warrior woman outfit. "I'm glad to see that you're wearing my jewelry," I said. "After the last time we talked, I was afraid you might never speak to me again."

"I know. That's why I'm here. I felt bad about the way I left things. Especially after you'd indicated that . . . you might be going through some difficult times."

"Thanks. I'm glad you could make it. You look like a goddess."

Melaphia made a sputtering sound, even though she wasn't drinking anything. "You okay?" I asked. She had a weird look in her eye as if she'd been poleaxed. She hustled Renee away like she expected an explosion. Before I could ask what was wrong, Olivia walked up and extended her hand to Connie. "Olivia Spenser," she said. "Love the outfit." A little taller than Connie, she looked pointedly at the other woman's cleavage. "And the tits."

Connie shook hands with the vampire without missing a beat. "Consuela Jones. My friends call me Connie. You can call me Officer Jones. Your ass looks great in that dress, too, by the way."

Olivia laughed heartily. "Thanks. I work out. Isn't that right, Jack?"

I was in a field mined with estrogen bombs and didn't

know which way to run. Three and a half of the strongest women I'd ever known were facing me, and they were all looking to me for something different: Renee for security, Melaphia for loyalty to William, Connie and Olivia for territorial rights. Damn. As soon as I got over the shock, I might get to like all this feminine attention.

As if on cue, the crowd milling around the front door parted and in walked Reedrek, flanked by William and Werm. Werm, wide-eyed, looked as if he could jump out of his newly acquired vampire skin at any moment and desperately wanted to. Now that he was at a costume party, his leather, chains, and piercings looked appropriate at last—retro Billy Idol.

William's uniform, the one he'd posed in for his old portrait, was immaculate right down to the polished brass buttons, but he looked as if he'd been through the mill. Red welts stood out on his otherwise pale flesh. Some nameless emotion surged through me at the sight of his wounds.

Reedrek himself was dressed, ironically enough, in full-fledged movie vampire regalia. Just like in my vision, he wore a tuxedo, a white dress shirt, and a black velvet cape lined in red satin. You had to give some credit to an evil dead with a sense of humor.

When he stepped forward, all conversation, tinkling of fine crystal, and general crowd sounds ceased. With a prickle of excitement and a little fear I realized that he had enthralled everyone in the room at once. Damn, he was good. Could he teach *me* to do that? The very thought of it made me feel a surge of power in my blood, as if I'd grown an inch.

Reedrek extended his arms out to his sides, bringing the edges of the cape out until he looked like a giant, butt-ugly buzzard about to take flight. "There you are,

Jack, my boy!" He was actually talking in a Bela Lugosi accent. In addition to everything else, he was quite a showman.

"Tell, me, my son," he continued. "Is that a vial of voodoo blood in your pocket, or are you just glad to see me?"

Sixteen ～

William

Hamilton House had been decorated exactly as I'd specified, with candles and crystal, right down to the hothouse camellias and peonies flown in from Japan. And the music: Tchaikovsky. Since I chose to remain apart from most of the humans in Savannah, planning a party like this was not unlike the grand theater that was the rage in Europe during the monarchies. Glittering sophistication and opulence to dazzle. Impressing mortals amused me . . . and allowed me to pick their pockets for my pet causes.

Too bad my date for the night was Reedrek. Too bad this would be the last memory I took with me to hell.

I had to put away any enjoyment in the gracious surroundings and concentrate on stopping Reedrek. Either that, or watch everyone I cared for die . . . again. Standing in the foyer, I wondered what Jack had planned for the evening. What would his reaction to our sire be?

That's when my gaze found Eleanor, and the breath of free air I'd been savoring deserted me. She hadn't been burned after all. I'd suffered another of my sire's malicious games. A threat was as good as a nod when it came to evil, though. He would burn her if I failed.

She looked expectant and relieved, as though she'd waited all evening for me to walk through the door. Radiant, she was decked out in a cocktail dress that could have been part of Jackie O's fabled wardrobe, her long dark hair swept up into a smooth twist at the back of her head. Her demure attire might have fooled most of those in the room. I, however, remembered too many nights of that loose silken hair sliding over my chest and belly before Eleanor moved on to other pleasures. My pleasures.

Tonight she was transformed into a cool, sophisticated queen—except that this world, my world, was infinitely more savage than Camelot. Or perhaps not. Jackie had lost her Jack. As Eleanor held my gaze I could only say a silent good-bye before bringing my attention back to my sire.

With a wave of his hand, Reedrek calmed the room like a master hypnotist at work. The human guests were frozen with their last word or thought balanced between the past and the present. The musicians played on but the sound was discordant, off-kilter—the screeching of a note held too long. Even I was reluctantly impressed. With three of his offspring in the same room, Reedrek was on a power high.

In my weakened state, I had been careless. I knew better than to allow my gaze to stop at Eleanor, but my relief had overwhelmed me. In the next instant, Reedrek moved to hover near her like a bristling bee circling a dewy lily. He paused to smell her neck below her ear but kept his gaze on me.

"She smells of smoke. A pity her lovely pleasure house burned down." He sighed dramatically. "I believe I'll make this one when I'm done with you," he said. His tongue lolled out like a smiling dog before he licked her neck to mark the spot. "She'd make an excellent sex slave, don't you think?"

I could see confusion in Eleanor's eyes but she didn't move, couldn't move. She couldn't see the evil being, yet she knew something was wrong. I could have calmed her fears but I didn't. She needed to be afraid. I shut her out and locked my mind on Reedrek's as we moved into the house proper.

"If you're so good at creating offspring, why are you here alone?" I asked. "Why didn't you bring a gang of your thugs along?" There was only a slight hesitation in his reply but in between words I picked up a quick flash of raised voices in a lightless room.

Reedrek raised his head. "You belong to me. I don't need any help to get rid of you," he snarled.

"That may be true, but why not have an unimpeachable witness? Unless you want to do something in secret. If you're showboating for your friends, why would they believe what happens here?"

"Because your little smuggling venture will stop. Dead in the water, as they say."

And you will become king of the west, my mind taunted.

He didn't dispute me. His hand brushed Eleanor's breast as though he hadn't heard.

"Is it worth it?" I asked. "If you kill me, you'll lose the power of my lovely anger. You'll be stripped of one of your oldest assets."

My ploy paid dividends. He lost interest in Eleanor and moved back toward me. "As if you've been an asset to me since you moved to this godforsaken place. Have you ever heard of the law of diminishing returns? I invested in you for two hundred years. Every year since then, I get less and less back.

"Your time has come, as has that of your friends."

Friends.

I searched the room for Jack and Olivia. Then I saw Melaphia and Renee. I quickly looked past them, working to conceal my alarm. My gaze stopped briefly at Connie. They hadn't been frozen like the full humans in the room, although Connie moved extremely slowly, like a sleepwalker. Reedrek could hardly help but notice.

We met Jack, Melaphia, and Renee in the center of the room.

"Is that a vial of voodoo blood in your pocket, or are you just happy to see me?" Reedrek said to Jack with a chuckle.

Jack ignored him and stared at me. He was wearing the voodoo blue jacket that I'd given him, and one of my better shirts. Even as I had the thought, he self-consciously twitched the shirt's hand-sewn French cuffs, flashing my very own silver cuff links.

An obvious trespass. At any other time I might have laughed or even sparred a bit. But the time for sparring was over—the bell had sounded for the heavyweight bout.

"You look better than I expected," Jack said.

"So do you," I answered. "The shirt suits you."

He squirmed as though the material chafed his skin. Reedrek rested his hand on my shoulder before sliding it up to clamp his fingers around the back of my neck. A warning or preparation for the kill—either was possible. Reedrek had no more need of me if Jack gave him what he wanted. I shifted under his grip, moving one foot forward and slightly closer to his. I would not let him pull me into the air or spring forward at Jack. Not without a struggle.

"Where's the blood, Jack?"

"Right here in my pocket just like you said," Jack replied.

Reedrek held out his hand. "Well?"

"Uh, we have a couple of things to talk about first."

"We've already had our conversation." At that I could feel Reedrek's mind shifting again to assail Jack's. Only this time I went along for the ride. A vision of neon, car racing, and Jack's policewoman, Connie. Desert hot, screaming tires, and excuse the pun, *coming* attractions. All a boy could want.

Freedom.

So that was what he'd offered Jack. Something I'd been reluctant even to discuss with him. Temptation had always been Reedrek's strong suit. If he'd been around for more than a mere millennium I'd have sworn he was the model for the Christian belief in Satan. All myths have an origin.

Jack continued to look steadily into mid-distant space, outwardly seeing nothing. Inwardly, he watched Reedrek's highlight film in the theater of his own mind. And he wanted everything he saw. Of course he did.

Ice cold dread clenched my unbeating heart. Jack's eyes had gone reddish black with something akin to bloodlust. He'd kill for what he wanted. I wasn't worried for my own existence. I'd long since ceased caring about that. I feared for those I loved—Melaphia, Renee, Eleanor, even humanity itself because God only knew what destruction Reedrek and Jack, together, unbridled, could wreak. But most of all, I feared for Jack himself, the only offspring I'd known since I'd lost the first blood-of-my-blood, my beloved Will. Once I'd threatened to kill Jack myself rather than let Reedrek have him. Could I do it? Could I summon my strength of will to save Jack from what Reedrek would turn him into? If so, it was just as well the price of the effort would be my unnatural life. I had no intention of spending the rest of eternity with the grief of Jack's death by my own hand. The sorrow of what might be my only choice seared me more painfully than the flames of Reedrek's torture had.

Suddenly I heard urgent whispers, as if from a great distance, twining around me like smoke, tugging at my attention.

We are ready . . .

Not alone . . .

Kill him . . .

Reedrek must have heard them as well because the vision faltered. He released Jack's mind and searched the room. His gaze stopped on Tobey, who leaned against the courtyard doorway among three human women frozen mid-flirt. Producing a loud, menacing hiss, Reedrek bared his fangs and tightened the grip on my neck.

Tobey, dressed to kill as a Chinese martial arts master who'd walked straight out of a Shaolin temple, looked calmer than I would have expected. He placed his now-empty glass of champagne on a tray held by an immobilized waiter and sauntered toward the only movement in the room.

My second-worst nightmare about Reedrek and my friends was coming true. "Get out of here—"

"Oh, it's much too late for that. You're not going anywhere, isn't that right, Tobias?"

The whispers returned. *We can take him . . . Move away . . . Let us handle it . . .*

Reedrek glanced around at the sound. "Us?" He seemed more amused than worried.

Iban and Gerard appeared from other parts of the glittering crowd.

"Well, now isn't this gratifying? You've all turned out to greet me."

"Actually," Tobey answered. "We've all turned out to *eat* you."

Things happened very fast after that. Reedrek began to move and I stomped down on his foot before hooking my ankle around his. Instead of rising as he'd planned, he lost his grip on my neck, allowing me to push him forward. Momentum took him to the floor, where four vampires fell on him at once. Tobey bit savagely into Reedrek's jugular, then flipped him over so Iban and Gerard could each find a juicy spot. "Stay out of it!" Olivia said, shoving me backward before going for Reedrek's groin. With a whoop, Werm made it five by attaching himself to an ankle. The entire group grappled together, struggling and sucking. Reedrek's blood spurted and flowed, splashing fangs, faces, and party clothes. Olivia's silver hair was red with it. Jack himself seemed mesmerized—frozen like the humans in the room.

As I pushed myself up I felt the first hope I'd dared entertain. Olivia's suggestion was touching—meant to save me from the harm that would come to me for helping kill my sire—but I didn't intend to stay out of it. My bloodlust for revenge wouldn't be satisfied until my sire was dead. Past history should have taught me better: this victory was too easy and too soon.

Reedrek's scream of utter rage rattled the windows of the room. It appeared he wasn't ready to accommodate us. Two or three of the frozen humans nearest us were bowled over by the concussive force of the ear-cracking boom that followed. Alarms bleated from cars parked along the streets on the square, and a siren sounded in the distance. My ears were ringing like bloody cathedral bells as I reached for the back of Olivia's dress to pull her away. But Reedrek was faster. His body stiffened, rising off the floor even with the weight of the others on top of him. Then with a bucking spasm he produced his own personal lightning, a blinding flash of fiery voltage strong enough to burn my fingers through Olivia's clothes.

Everything went silent then, or perhaps I was struck deaf. Breathing hard, I could smell burnt flesh and scorched clothes. I watched in growing horror as my friends dropped away from Reedrek like dead bugs, their mouths burnt, their bodies limp. Anyplace his blood had touched them was blackened.

Reedrek pushed to his hands and knees, then to his feet. He was weakened but not, by any means, dead again. And that meant we were doomed—as, I finally realized, we'd been from the beginning.

The only members of our group left standing were those who hadn't attacked Reedrek: myself, Jack, Melaphia, and Renee, who was hiding, her fingers clutching the colorful material of her mother's skirt.

"Run!" I shouted. "Leave this place." I shoved Melaphia out of the way. Then, with a shriek born of soul-blackening hate, I launched myself at Reedrek. My fury reached him before my hands did. With a surprised look, he stared down at the red mist pelting his shirtfront like horizontal rain before my hands clamped on his throat. As I pulled him into the air, the chandeliers in the room began to sway and twirl. Safely away from those below, I bit down hard, tearing open Reedrek's neck but unable to stop him from sinking his fangs into my shoulder. Growling, we crashed into the barrier of the twelve-foot ceiling, rabid wolves in deadly earnest—sending the closest crystal chandelier plummeting amid the partygoers. Lath and plaster fell in a choking cloud around us as I did my worst to my sire.

His blood tasted like acid, burning me with the pure essence of long-fermented evil. No matter how much I drank, I would not kill him. I could, however, hurt him—slow him down. The red haze of my fury surrounded us and with the last of my strength I gave a gurgling howl and ripped again at his throat.

For a very brief moment, I tasted his fear. Looking for any advantage I shifted my grip to gouge at his eyes. A satisfying *pop* sent a gush of liquid over my right hand.

Reedrek's talons sank into my jacket, ripping wool and linen. He managed to bare my chest as he flung me away from his face. Loath to take any more chances, with one striking motion my sire slashed the skin over my heart with fingernails that were still hot from his surge of power, meaning to rip out my heart. I could feel his fingernails sink deep, slinging my blood over the still bodies on the floor. But I was on his now blinded side and managed to twist away. I fell to a place next to my friends and covered the wound with my hand, but blood still gushed between my fingers.

Melaphia, keeping Renee behind her, moved to my side. She yanked the blue scarf from around her neck and pushed it under my fingers to stanch the flow.

"Now, Jack. Give me the vial," Reedrek demanded.

The voodoo blood—Lalee's blood—would make Reedrek strong again, stronger than he'd even imagined. I watched my offspring calculate different outcomes.

"Don't you do it," Melaphia said to Jack. "That blood belongs to me, to my family. You have no right to give it away!"

"Quiet, woman!" Reedrek ordered. "You have no power here." As casually as one might swat a mosquito, Reedrek backhanded Melaphia. Then, to prove his point, he turned toward Renee. She made a small surprised sound as she rose into the air. Melaphia grasped for her hand but couldn't hold on. Renee didn't stop struggling until she hung suspended in the air in front of Reedrek.

He drew one edge of his cape forward to blot his bleeding, empty eye socket. "Your family, you say?" Reedrek asked, keeping his good eye on Renee with an unholy look of calculation.

"Here, take it." Jack withdrew the vial from his pocket.

Jack's mind telegraphed his alarm as he looked at tiny, helpless Renee. But he still lusted after the dark gifts Reedrek offered. I could taste the greed in his throat, and I could feel his remaining humanity, that which I treasured most in him, being shaken to its core.

My vision from the shells returned to haunt what would probably be the last moments of my overlong life. The vision of Jack, wearing my blue jacket, betraying me. Betraying us all. If Jack had had an alternate plan, he'd already failed.

"This is the real deal," Jack said. "You can kill them later."

So Jack thought to both claim his reward and have Reedrek spare his humans. Little did he know his grandsire had never kept a bargain. But then, I hadn't bothered to educate Jack in the ways of the truly evil, just as I'd neglected to tell him so much else. And my human family of the present would suffer the same fate as my Diana.

"Uncle Jack . . ." Renee's small plea seemed to please Reedrek.

"No, I think I will have the 'real deal,' as you say, and you can kill them now. It's time to put an end to this rebellion of blood. You were made to rule over mortals, to make them your minions. It's time for you to prove yourself worthy of the name *vampire*. Take the little one first. How is it the song goes? *You always hurt the one you love*." He reached for Renee's hand as though to help her, but instead, he casually ran his thumbnail along her wrist, opening the vein. Blood gushed, dripping down her fingers before falling through the air to splash on the floor. "Then I'll finish your sire."

Jack's fangs extended. His large black irises made his eyes look cold and doll-like as they fixed on Renee as if he'd never seen her before. Suddenly, my line of communication to his mind broke like a frayed violin string, and I couldn't tell what he was thinking, what he'd decided.

Then he blinked, and I knew. There had always been a chance he might betray me, but I would die with the conviction that he would never betray Renee and Melaphia.

I still trusted him.

With everything to lose, I used the dregs of my strength to reestablish the psychic connection with my offspring. I might help save him—or I might push him to become an evildoer worse than Reedrek.

Damn the consequences. I opened my mind to Jack.

Jack

The first explosion of William's thoughts rolled over me so fast I could only gasp like a swimmer pounded to the sand by a tidal wave. The force of it sent me back in time.

"Come on, Jack, you must bite deeper, harder." William's voice echoed through the flood of memories. Me, with my dead soldier's belly scrapin' my backbone. Him teaching me how to bite, how not to waste time or perfectly good blood by being weak-kneed about the killing. He gripped the dying soldier's hair and pulled his head back. "These poor souls are already suffering. You can release them."

Hell, I'd killed for the army, why not kill for myself? I bit down like a tiger, wanting to please my new savior and needing to cure my infernal hunger. I could see in his thoughts that he understood I'd been starving most of my years on earth. He'd promised me more.

"That's better," he said, unknowingly giving me more praise than my bastard of a father had uttered in his whole mean-spirited life.

Next I saw through William's gaze as he stood perched on the steeple of St. John's Cathedral. I felt his need to protect and guard this city from the monsters waiting in the darkness for their chance to take over new territory. And, more than this, I felt his need to protect me. Not just from the other vampires but from the knowledge that they even existed. How many battles had he fought to defend Savannah without even asking for my help? Without my even knowing? For a blessedly short time I saw fiery eyes filled with hate and bloody jaws snapping. I reeled backward from the power of William's concern for me and had to blink to focus on his living face.

Everything I'd ever wanted to know about when and why was staring back at me. There was too much to grasp all at once as it rushed into my mind. What came shining through the jumble of information the clearest was not a fact—but an emotion.

William's total trust.

Reedrek's voice fought for my attention. "He could have released you anytime he wanted. But he was determined to hold you for the entire two hundred years."

I lied to protect you, William whispered in my mind.

"What are you talking about?" A terrible realization teetered on the edge of my understanding. I wasn't sure I wanted it to sink in, but it did anyway. My sire had tricked me. All this time, he'd had me fooled into servitude when I could have been living out my dreams.

Unholy laughter came from a distance. Reedrek. "Oh, isn't this just too precious to bear." He made a mewling sound like a baby. "I only wanted to protect you," he mimicked in a high-pitched voice. "He plays the benevolent lord, but he's no better than me. All he had to do is declare your oath discharged. Then you could have traveled the world as a vested member of our little vampire club. Ask him the real reason why he didn't let you go to find your own destiny."

Visions of hot race cars and even hotter Vegas showgirls bombarded me. All my heart desired. I did my best to ignore him and concentrate on William.

Reedrek's mocking laughter hurt my ears. I battled both him and William for control of my mind. The part of my brain that was still Jack was trying to summon another memory—one of my own, not one that William had forced on me—to make sense of what was happening. A very old memory, one from my moonshine-runnin' days that had tried to surface the day I was diggin' into the oil pit. Back in the good old, bad old days, when I was happily unaware of anyone like my grandsire. William had come to me like a haint in the night, had warned me. What had he said?

William himself filled in the blanks. *I want you to know, Jack, that whatever happens in the future—that I'm sorry . . . that I truly . . . care about you.*

Don't trust Reedrek. Good-bye, Jack.

It finally made sense. William had visited me as a vision with a sentiment I had hungered to hear from my own father, but never had. I could feel the truth of the words, not like the poisonous lies Reedrek had told me. William had cared for me, and that was why he'd deceived me to keep me with him—to protect me. But there was one more thing I had to know.

"Why me, William?" I asked. "Of all the poor, dying bastards on all those bloody battlefields, why did you pick me to walk beside you?"

Reedrek stopped his braying laughter to hear the answer, making the silence in the great room seem like a living thing, a spectator as breathless for the truth as I was.

William appeared to be fighting for enough breath to answer. "Do you know what a gut-shot soldier always does, Jack?" he asked. "His last act on this earth is to use his ebbing strength to open his uniform and inspect his wound. That's why they are found on the battlefield with their clothing askew, as if trying to scratch an itch. But that's not what you were doing."

"I don't remember what I was doing," I heard myself say.

William smiled a weary smile. "You were propped on one elbow, using the last of your life to tend an old man dying beside you. As your blood drained away, you were trying to lift his upper body and head so he wouldn't drown in the mud hole where he'd fallen facedown."

William took a labored breath and continued, "That is how you would have died—in service to your fellow man. That is how I found you . . . why I wanted you. I thought the humanity in you could redeem any that might remain in myself. You and Lalee's spirit are all that has kept me on the side of the light for the past one hundred and forty years."

Holy crap. All this time I'd thought of myself as just a flunky. Now suddenly I was the savior. As I tried to absorb this, Reedrek shouted, "Of all the treacle-laced drivel I've ever heard—that is the frozen limit! It's time to shut you up for good." He dragged William from Melaphia's care and bit down with fangs already bloody from the fight.

William seemed to barely notice. His gaze held me prisoner. "Here's blood in your eye," he said.

Drink it, Jack, he said in my mind.

I pulled the vial from my pocket, popped the seal, and raised it in a toast to my sire and my grandsire. "Bottoms up." I'd swallowed half of it before Reedrek could react. He came up for air with an ungodly screech. "You will not!"

He flew at me as I stuck my thumb in the top and put my hand back in my pocket.

"Here, take it, then!" I flung the vial at his chest—not the voodoo blood, but the vial of holy water Connie had given me. His greedy fingers closed over it, breaking the glass, spraying him and William.

Father Murphy's law: It's hard to aim holy water. And this holy water seemed to be high-octane. Reedrek screeched and began to twirl in a hell of an imitation of one of those Tasmanian devils in Saturday morning cartoons. Only this devil was shrieking and smoking. William writhed on the polished oak floor at Reedrek's feet. I started forward to help him, but I didn't get more than a step. What happened next spooked me good. First the smell of cinnamon and vanilla bean spiced with rum.

Lalee.

As Lalee's pure blood mixed with my own, my arteries caught fire. If this was what happened to dopers when they stuck needles in their perfectly good veins, I finally understood what "getting high" meant. A soft chant followed the sizzle to calm my fear as what was left of my spirit grew taller. Like my body wasn't big enough to hold it. Higher, higher. Soon I was looking down at the top of Reedrek's spinning head. Shit. I'd faced all kinds of threats from some pretty nasty characters, but I'd never had to handle one on the inside before. One that could take me over, body and blighted soul, and literally make me ten feet tall.

But Lalee wouldn't hurt me. She whispered under my skin like the spirits of departed family members living in the walls of their great-great-great-grandchildren's houses. No, she wouldn't hurt me. But she would protect her own, even if it meant scaring me into the next dimension.

After traveling through every cell of my body, her low, eerie keening gained power and came blasting out of my mouth. The sound had a strange effect on the scene below. Renee's feet floated down to the ground and she ran to Melaphia. They both fell to their knees, looking up at me, their mouths moving like they were praying in church. William stopped writhing. I couldn't tell if he was dead or merely unconscious.

One thought clanged through my mind. *I have to stop him.*

I watched in awe as my own hand rose to point a finger at Reedrek. Greenish yellow fumes poured snakelike from the tip, twining around my grandsire head-to-foot as he twirled. The smell of sulfur—fire and brimstone— burned my nose. This voodoo stuff was pretty cool. Just as I was wondering what the smoke could do, a flame sparked from under my fingernail. Tiny flickering tongues of fire ignited along the rings of the circling smoke, surrounding Reedrek like a Christmas tree decorated with candles. His spinning slowed but the flames remained floating mere inches from his clothes. The warning was clear.

He was trapped.

I began to shrink down to regular size but still felt as supercharged as a fuely dragster revving for the green light.

I went to William first and raised him from the floor. *I have to help him. I only wanted to be like him— strong.* Suddenly the half-empty vial of blood floated before my eyes. I moved it to William's lips.

"Drink the rest," I said in a strange, French-tinged voice.

William's eyes opened, but he only stared at me. "You've come back," he mumbled, like a dying man seeing visions. I wasn't sure he was talking to me since I hadn't gone anywhere. And he was in bad shape. Half his face was melted from my bad holy-water aim, while his neck and chest oozed blood from Reedrek's attack.

"Come on," I coaxed in a voice closer to my own. "Drink it."

He let me hold it to his mouth but took only a sip. "All the rest," I ordered. Although I'd sort of enjoyed that whole ten-feet-tall thing, once was definitely enough. Let William see how he liked having someone as wild and powerful as Lalee inside his head.

I upended the vial to help him get it down. Then, as I watched, the damage from the holy water disappeared and the skin around his neck wound knitted together. A rushing sound came from his chest—flesh meeting flesh, healing. It was like an unholy miracle—if there is such a thing—a reversal of what William did for me on the battlefield that night. A repayment, a settling of scores. Blood for blood.

I propped him up against the closest piece of furniture before taking the dregs of blood left in the vial to Renee and Melaphia. As I squatted down, Renee and Melaphia both threw themselves into my arms, nearly knocking me over on my butt.

"Maman . . ." I heard Melaphia's joyful whisper as her sturdy arms held me prisoner. When she finally loosened her grip to meet my gaze I saw tears in her eyes. She drew in a deep breath of relief. "Maman, you and Jack have saved us all."

I didn't know what she was seeing inside my head but I had the uncomfortable notion that I should say something. "I—uh—" My voice cracked and left me. Renee's little arms stayed clamped around my neck.

"I am always about," we said in that strange patois. "Come, chile, let me see what the nasty one has done to my baby." With gentle hands I loosened Renee's hold on my neck and let Lalee do her thing.

The blood, she instructed. I ran a finger along the edge of the vial until it was wet and red. Then I smeared it on Renee's injured arm. The damage Reedrek had caused healed so quickly I jerked my finger back in surprise. The scent of cinnamon and ginger flowers rose around us.

"There, chère. It's all good now."

Renee laced her fingers into mine. "Thank you, Maman."

"I know you are a good girl—doing what your mama say. You'll be like me someday soon. Yes? And you will help the sleeping goddess find her way?"

"Yes, ma'am."

"That's right—nothing to fear. My blood guards you, as it guards those around you."

"Jack?" William was shaking my shoulder. "Get Reedrek below, into the tunnels. I'll clean up this mess and then we'll take him to the river warehouse." Before I could figure out how he supposed I could do that, he took the vial from my hand and moved over to the heap of five vampire bodies on the floor. One by one he painted their mouths and injuries with dabs of voodoo blood. They healed and began to revive.

I'd thought they were goners.

The tinkling of glass turned me around. The broken chandelier was rising, with William's help. When it floated near the damaged ceiling, William waved a hand, sort of like a better-dressed Reedrek, and the people in the room returned to normal. Just in time for the chandelier to crash to the floor for the second time. That was our signal to get out of Dodge.

Soon, with Melaphia leading, we were all, except William and Tobey, filing down the cellar stairs. I brought up the rear with Reedrek floating behind me like a tethered balloon. Showers of sparks crackled and fell anytime he floated too close to the ceiling or a wall. If we weren't careful, we might set the whole house on fire. It took only a few moments for me, using Lalee's second sight, to locate an entrance to the tunnels behind a dusty wine rack in the eastern wall of the cellar.

As we waited, Olivia touched my face as if she'd never

seen me before. "Wow. You feel like a bloody lightning storm is going on under your skin. I'm surprised you're not setting your clothes on fire." She bared her fangs in a half-serious way. "What I wouldn't give for a taste of that kind of power." Then her gaze moved to Reedrek where he hung unconscious and suspended. "Then again, I wasn't so lucky upstairs."

I felt Lalee rise inside me. "Keep your teeth to yourself. You were all foolish to take on one such as he," she said. "The blood the Captain gave you the night you set foot in Savannah is the only reason you survived. Don't try it again."

William

It required two hours and a great measure of Tobey's charm to calm the guests. While he entertained them with stories of great magicians and their most ambitious failures, I held quick conferences with the city officials present about faulty wiring and building-code violations. Since none of the mortals had been injured, they were willing, even eager, for the party to go on. But I did use the incident to educate them on the need for the new hospital emergency wing and blood bank we were there to support. Money and publicity—that was the name of this particular game. Jack could take up the plans where I left off.

Placating Eleanor was another matter altogether.

She who must be obeyed had felt the menace in the room and knew something threatening had taken place but remained as calm and serene as Aphrodite. She made a point to stay within touching distance as I soothed wealthy feathers and laughed off concerns, her gaze speaking volumes when our eyes met.

But I couldn't help her understand, or promise her any sort of tomorrow. I, a creature with unending patience and time, had a date with death. My fate waited below, in the tunnels.

Seventeen

Jack

When Melaphia was satisfied that Lalee had left the building, so to speak, and it was clear we vampires could take care of Reedrek from there, she left us at the entrance to the tunnels and took Renee home to bed.

By the time our little fang gang got Reedrek through the maze of tunnels to the warehouse, Lalee's magic was fading. Since I didn't know how to bring it back now that the voodoo blood was gone, we tied him up in a generous length of anchor chain with links as big as my fists put together and left him in a dark corner of the building behind some antique furniture—just in case any of William's workers came in before daylight and wondered why we had an old dude tied up on the floor. Weakened by the holy water and the other vamps' suck-fest, he'd be safe enough to handle for a while. He was still caterwauling about how if we managed to kill him, other vamps would come to kick our uppity New World asses when I stuffed an oily rag in his mouth and told him to suck on it.

"Is he telling the truth?" Werm asked.

The rest of us looked at one another. Finally Gerard, who seemed to know more about the global blood-sucker situation than the rest of us, said, "Almost certainly."

"You know what? I'm sick of worrying about tomorrow. Why don't we deal with right now?" I suggested. After the infusion of Lalee's blood, I was feeling like the Incredible Hulk on steroids, ready to take on Reedrek or anything else for that matter. And it wasn't just the physical strength talking. I had a brand-new sense of confidence, too. Whether it was from the voodoo blood, the rush of gaining William's trust, or my satisfaction in actually tricking Reedrek with the holy water, I didn't know. All I knew—it was coming from inside me, not from some damned sissy jacket.

Even the other vamps were looking at me like I was large and in charge. Olivia said, with something like awe in her voice, "Yes, Jack. Whatever you think we should do. Just tell us."

"Okay, y'all. Listen up. I'm not rattled by Reedrek's weird threats, but I'm getting the sun's-fixing-to-rise-so-get-me-the-hell-outta-here heebie-jeebies. It took so long to get Reedrek, with his personal version of hell swirling around him, through the tunnels that the party should be well over, so—"

Just then William and Tobey came through the passageway from the tunnels to the warehouse, interrupting me.

"We thought you'd never get here," Olivia declared, rubbing the tension from her crossed arms.

So much for *my* fifteen minutes of fame.

"We had to tie up some loose ends," William said. He looked toward the place where Reedrek was hidden, sensing him there. Then he turned to me with the barest hint of a smile. "Good work at the party, Jack. I knew all along you would have a plan."

I didn't get a hint of emotion from him. He was blocking me again. That was okay, though. He'd come through when it counted. I had a lot to sort through mentally and a lot of questions to ask once we'd done away with Grandpappy dearest. At least now I knew he'd give me the answers. I acknowledged William's compliment with a smile of my own. Even if he was back to lying, it was nice of him to say.

"What are we going to do with Reedrek?" Iban asked.

"We have to kill him," Olivia stated flatly. "William can't, and it would probably harm the others of us in Reedrek's bloodline. But Tobey could. Just stake him and be done with it."

"I wouldn't mind giving the old stinky dude a poke myself. But what if one stake isn't enough?" I said. I wasn't in the mood for taking any more chances. Lalee might not help save us a second time.

William was oddly silent. I expected him to be the man with the plan as always, but he stood back and let the others argue over Reedrek's fate—and argue they did.

"Okay. I'll do it," Tobey said. "How should I—"

"Wait. Why don't we just drag him out to the dock and leave him there for the sun?" Olivia suggested.

"Sure," Tobey said. "And who's going to stand there and watch to make sure he doesn't slip away instead? It's too close to water to take that chance—thirty feet down and he's safe from the sun. I know. I was a surfer."

"I have a better idea," Gerard said. "Help me get him

back to my laboratory. He's so ancient—if I could just study his genetic makeup—"

"No way!" Olivia said. "He killed my Alger. He has to burn in hell!"

"Hold on," Iban said. "There might be other advantages to keeping him alive. What if the other dark sires come looking for him. Perhaps we can use him as a bargaining chip. Who knows what they'd trade for him?"

Olivia's creamy skin began to redden. "And have Reedrek telepath them all our secrets? Like the potency of the voodoo blood and where the New World colonies are? I can vouch for the strength of his enthrallment. Who knows what kinds of information his mind can glean from us?"

The argument went on and on. I tried to jump in and point out *again* that the sun creeping toward the horizon was making my eyelids itch, but it was hard to get a word in edgewise. Finally, I looked toward William to see why he wasn't stepping in to settle all this, seeing that he was our leader. But—just like that—he wasn't there anymore.

"Where's William?" I interrupted. The others looked around and then at one another. We couldn't see William, and we could no longer smell Reedrek. I raced around to the spot where we'd left the old demon and, sure enough, he was gone, too.

"Why would William take him?" Tobey asked.

"*Where* would he take him?" said Gerard.

"I don't know," I said. "But wherever they went, it must be underground, because the sun's about to come up. You all go back to that last big intersection we came through in the tunnels. Split up and go in different directions. I'm going to check the waterfront and I'll join you if I don't find them. Go."

This time nobody argued. Only Werm gave me a last look back, for reassurance, I guess. I gave him a nod, and he turned and left with the others. I felt for the poor, confused little bastard for the first time since he'd been made. Who was going to teach him about being a vampire? He'd need my protection for the foreseeable future, and I'd give it, as William had given it to me.

Where the hell could William be?

I rushed out of the warehouse and onto the dock. In this small hour of the morning, a human being would have only heard silence, smelled nothing, felt only alone. My senses, already sharpened by my backward mating with Olivia, had exploded after I'd drunk the purest blood of the most powerful *mambo* who had ever drawn breath on these shores. Power rose inside me like oil through a wick. I heard the fish below me drawing water through their gills. Through the early-morning fog, I saw amphibians hibernating and felt the stubbly scrub grass on the far bank of the river. I could smell the catch of the nearest shrimp boat, four miles away.

And I knew by my mutated blood that if I gathered my concentration well enough, and if William let his guard down only slightly, I could get at his thoughts. I took a deep breath, closed my eyes, and called out to my sire, searching for him through the fog, feeling my way along the nerves and synapses of my mind for any path to him. The voodoo magic in my blood sought itself out in his. And I found him.

Take care of them, Jack. My humans and my city. They're yours now. You are my rightful heir. Good-bye.

My eyes sprang open. "Good-bye, hell."

William

As the bow of the motor launch cut through the glassy water of the river, headed for the sea, I felt elation rather than fear. The early-morning fog was thinning. I was about to see my first sunrise in more than five hundred years. Huzzah! It would be worth frying. Not only that, I would have the added bonus of watching my sire burn.

My blood war with Reedrek would finally be over. How much did I love that idea? Let me count the ways. No, it would take too long. The sun was flirting with the horizon. As Jack would say, within the hour I'd be toast.

Ah, I would miss Jack. If nothing else he amused me. That is, when he wasn't being his Irish-pigheaded self. At least by the end of our time together we'd come to a meeting of the minds of a sort. Melaphia and Renee would help him be a good steward of my legacy from the East Coast or the West. He would be free to choose.

Then there was Eleanor. Yes, I would miss she who must be obeyed. She'd given me too much pleasure for me to leave her behind without regret. I'd hated to part with her on a lie, but it couldn't be helped.

Last night at the party, after the battle, I'd promised to make her. Sworn to her on my honor as a gentleman and as a master vampire. I'd made the vow not only to give her what she thought she wanted—eternity with me—but to protect her. But I had found a better way. After this sunrise she would no longer be in danger. I glanced over at Reedrek, trussed up and gagged like an escapee from an asylum. He stared back at me in silence from his ruined face. I could feel his utter hatred mixed with his disbelief.

Once Reedrek was dead, all those I loved would be safe.

But I wasn't about to waste my last hour of consciousness on my evil maker. I felt like a runner on a downhill slope—running faster and with greater ease toward the end of a very long race. My gaze moved to the ever-lightening sky as I drew in a deep breath of ocean breeze. I'd missed the ocean, along with many other things.

Diana, my love. I'm sorry I failed you. I'm sorry I cannot be with you even in eternity. But, after all these years, you will finally be avenged.

Reedrek's ugly, poisonous voice broke into my silent communion with my wife's soul. *She lives still.*

First pain in the place where my heart used to be, then fury. I yanked the engine throttle back into neutral. The boat lowered and slowed as I swung around to face my tormentor.

"You are a bloody lying bastard!" I searched the closest cabinet for a weapon and found a steel gaff used to fend off other boats. "I won't listen to you sully her memory with your treachery." I plunged the sharp end of the gaff between the wraps of chain in the region of his shoulder.

He grimaced in pain but held my gaze. It was his only way to communicate. *I'm not lying, and if you kill me you'll never know where she is.*

I couldn't control myself. I pulled the gaff free and stabbed him again. "Liar!" Stab. "Liar!" Stab.

Lying in a pool of blood, he finally ceased his evil intrusion. I waited, standing over him like a whaler waiting for the catch to bleed out. When he shut his eyes rather than face my anger, I dropped the gaff and moved back to the controls of the boat. I didn't kill him. I was saving that for the sun.

Jack

I raced along in the Gladiator speedboat that William let me keep moored at his docks. I had tuned it up myself only the week before, and it was so fast no human could race it at top speed for fear of their mortal lives. It drove literally like the wind, becoming airborne every other second as it launched itself off the latest swell, flying low, fast enough to make me feel like I was alive again. Speed has always been my thing, but right then it was for more than recreation.

I had to catch William.

My eyes stung, not so much from the thinning darkness or the salt spray kicked up by the boat, but from the knowledge that William, my sire and only mentor, meant to sacrifice himself and leave me alone. I forced myself to concentrate again, searching for more understanding. William had spirited Reedrek away in his own boat and was heading out to sea—and to their deaths. But why? Was there no other way to kill the old bastard?

Speeding along, I reached out again with my mind. My sight focused tightly on the fog ahead of me and reverted to a kind of tunnel vision. And then I saw a scene that hurt my head—and my heart. Murder.

Reedrek murdering William's human family. Along with the vision came the rage. I felt as if I understood William and his sustaining, everlasting anger for the very first time. He'd loved the woman and the boy. And Reedrek had taken them away in a flash of fang and a slash of filthy claws. This was a real vampire, and it sickened me to know that I was a member of his clan. I felt William's need to kill the monster who'd destroyed his world, even though it meant his own final death and damnation.

Whoever said time healed all wounds was a liar.

I was getting closer. My supercharged blood felt William's nearby. My boat emerged from a fogbank and William's slower launch appeared ahead of me. It was a good thing no boat in Savannah could match mine for speed; I'd needed it, not only to catch up with William but to get us back to safety—that is, if I could talk William out of his suicidal scheme.

I maneuvered alongside and bumped him, a risky move that could've capsized us both, but it succeeded in forcing him so far toward the riverbank that he had to cut his engine to keep from crashing. I cut mine as well and steered hard into the other boat, sending both of us coasting to the marshy shoreline and effectively blocking William's escape.

"Stay out of this, Jack!" William shouted, his fangs extended. The force of his rage, now directed at me as well as Reedrek, almost blew me over backward. "I *order* you to go back to the warehouse."

"No," I said. I jumped into William's boat. "I know what you mean to do, and I'm not going to let you kill yourself." I glanced at Reedrek, still bound and bloody in the floor of the stern. He was watching us with beady, hawklike eyes. "He's not worth it."

William grabbed me by the collar of the blue jacket and brought us nose-to-nose. I'd never been so scared as I was at that moment, not even when I faced my mortal death on the battlefield. William's face was contorted, the flesh drawn back from his awful fangs. He was ready to do battle with anyone who got in the way of his lust for revenge. His irises were the gleaming, red-rimmed black of a creature with only death on its mind.

"His death is worth it to me," William hissed.

"I won't let you do this," I repeated. I drew back and

hit him squarely in the jaw, using all the strength of the voodoo blood, sending him sprawling against the far side of the boat. This was certainly a night of firsts for me. I'd never taken on William in combat, but sometimes a boy had to rise to the occasion. "We're taking him back to the warehouse and we're going to deal with him together—you and me. You're not going to kill him and die in the process. I won't allow it."

William rubbed his jaw and sat up. That's when I remembered that William had the strength of the voodoo blood as well. Oh, hell. I braced myself, feet apart, ready for the spring. But as usual, he surprised me.

"You're looking at this all wrong, Jack. Just think of it. You won't have me to boss you around, tell you what to do."

"Don't waste your breath on a psych job. It won't work." I crossed over to Reedrek and hauled him up, chains and all, ready to hoist him into my faster boat to race the sun back to the docks. But by the time I turned around, William was blocking my way.

"All the wealth, fame, and speed Reedrek promised you in the dream can be yours now. Just go and claim it and leave me to my destiny. You have your freedom. *Let me have mine.*"

We stood face-to-face now, with only Reedrek's squirming body in my arms between us. "No. If you're going to burn to a crisp getting rid of this guy, then so am I."

"You obstinate, mule-headed mick! What do I have to do to get through to you? I'm offering you everything I have, everything you've ever dreamed about. I'm offering you Savannah. And all without me in the picture to hold you back. Isn't that what you've always wanted?" William hauled off and punched me in the face with enough force to make my head snap back. I lost my grip on Reedrek, and he hit the deck so hard the boat rocked wildly.

"What I always wanted was just to know more, to do more, to . . . *be* more."

Reedrek tried to yell something, but the gag muffled the words; besides, I wasn't particularly interested. I gave him a hard warning kick in the mid-region and continued to concentrate on William. "But I never wanted to go it alone—not really. I just needed to know that you trusted me, that you needed me. We made a pretty good team last night. I don't want you to die.

"Please, please don't do this."

Every now and then in a man's life, whether you're human or vampire, you have to put your feelings on the line, let it all hang out. This was one of those times. "Aw hell," I muttered. "I love you, man." I put my arms around William and hugged him. Then I backed off and slapped him on the shoulder in a guy's guy kind of way, cleared my throat, and looked away. Sometimes what you learned from beer commercials comes in real handy.

William drew back and blinked. I felt the anger drain out of him like the outgoing tide. He looked more like I had slugged him again instead of given him a friendly hug. "Really?"

"Well . . . yeah. We'll figure out how to kill this buzzard together." I heard the buzzard's—I mean Reedrek's—bubbling howls and looked down to see what he was screaming about. His face was underwater. I looked back up at William. "Who punched holes in the deck? We're taking on water."

The cold water swirling around his ankles seemed to shock William back to reality. "Shit," he said. "Let's get out of here."

He helped me haul Reedrek into my boat. Since I was

driving, we set off for the safety of the warehouse. The first rays of the sun were creeping their way over the horizon, making the sky lighten with the softest shades of purple and pink. William found a tarp stowed with the life jackets and came to stand beside me at the wheel, pulling the covering over both our backs, leaving Reedrek squealing and squirming on the floor.

"Jack," William said, squinting against rays of the coming dawn.

"Yeah?"

"I love you, too."

"I know."

Eighteen

William

Rather than risk death ourselves, we decided to take a page from Reedrek's torture book. We'd bury him deep for a few hundred years, then decide what to do with him. If anything happened to Jack and me—the only ones with the information—Reedrek would stay buried forever. In the world war of the 1940s the Americans had a slogan: "Loose lips sink ships." Only in our case the ship (Reedrek) was already sunken, and we wanted it to stay on the bottom.

Just after sunset the next evening we transported my sire to the construction site of our new hospital wing. Since most of the money for the addition had come from my blood bank foundation, no one questioned my request to bury a time capsule underneath the twenty-ton Georgia granite cornerstone of the building. I told them the curious coffinlike steel box contained original plans for the building, photographs from the state archives, and a length of anchor chain used on the first ship launched from Thorne Marina in the 1800s. That was in case they heard something clank inside when the box was moved.

No pomp. Just two workers with a bulldozer and voilà, Reedrek was buried twenty feet down. After our own private voodoo ceremony, courtesy of Melaphia, to keep him down, concrete was poured and the cornerstone set in place. Jimmy Hoffa had nothing on my sire. Buried deep enough and dark enough to be forgotten. I didn't even bother saying good-bye. He'd wasted enough of my time.

As far as the rest of the vampire world knew, Reedrek died screaming at sunrise on November 1, 2005.

Since I'd been out of pocket for a few days I had other issues to attend. According to my list of waiting e-mails, Gaelan, the other missing offspring, had been found in Amsterdam, but in desperate condition. On Lillith's advice, the Abductors had buried Gaelan in her home ground for a rest of sorts. She would be safe there. As in the old days, a long cord with a bell at the end hung over her tomb. When she was ready she could ring her way out.

Another message held good news and bad, as well as an indirect answer as to why my sire had shown up in Savannah alone. Before traveling to the New World, he'd organized the killings of one of the stronger European clans in a grab for ultimate power. The killings had weakened him, so he'd come for me, thinking to force me to make offspring to help him regain his strength. Now the European clans were in factions, their treaties in ruins.

Good. Let them argue among themselves. It gave us more time to make our own plans. The time for hiding was at an end. We'd need a council of the New World clans and a plan of defense.

I had to admire Jack's loyalty and sense of timing. He'd talked me into staying around, just in time for a war.

Within a week, life had returned to somewhat normal. I'd shipped Olivia off, back to England carrying news and messages to those loyal to me. With my blessing she was to form a new group of vampires—those committed to peace—among her female friends. She'd even chosen a name, the Bonaventures, I believe. By eavesdropping on a conversation the night before she left, I found out more than I needed to know about the relationship between her and Jack.

"Hey now, are you sure you don't want to take another walk on the wild side? For old times' sake?" Jack had suggested. "You could rest up on the trip."

"No can do, Jackie-boy." Olivia sighed. I waited through a space of silence, politely refraining from tuning into Jack's thoughts. I'm sure some kind of bodily contact was proceeding. "I've got clan business to do. Can't afford to give any power away. Come and see me in London. We'll work something out."

I made a note that before Jack went anywhere, he and I needed to have a serious talk about sex among the undead. And the living. Jack was still moping about his policewoman, Connie. He knew there was no future for them and he was taking it hard. I didn't look forward to a lesson on the birds and the bees.

On the subject of sex: You'd think I'd lived long enough to learn that outsmarting a woman was nigh on to impossible.

In my rage-inspired insanity the night of the party, I'd promised to make Eleanor. Sworn it by my dead vampire heart. And now, since I was still around, she intended to hold me to it. We'd settled on a date in early December—her birthday. She'd decided that she would enjoy being thirty-nine eternally. I had already begun the process of having her lovely house rebuilt. She would reclaim her business and her life, but I would have all her nights.

The thought was downright stimulating, and I found myself rising to the occasion. A knock on my office door interrupted my contemplation of one good reason to stay alive.

It was Deylaud. I'd asked him to come down in human form to do some research and organizational work. In order to set about making alliances, I needed to know who stood on what side.

"Sit," I said, and he did.

"I'm making a list of potential allies. Do you remember the book you read—Olivia's book?"

He nodded.

"Tell me the names."

For a human, this request would have been impossible. But I knew Deylaud's first master had stored his entire library in Deylaud's mind. The only catch was that you had to know the title or the owner of the book to bring out the information.

"Miss Olivia's book—"

"Yes. The one you hid under the rug."

"The names. Living or dead?"

"Living."

His face pinkened but he entwined his fingers and began to recite.

"Lillith, Mesopotamia, 3000 B.C.; Aronica, Babylonia, 2800 B.C.; Boudicca, 1500 B.C.; Lisbet, 100 A.D.—"

"Move on to the later ones—after 1500." The old ones were less likely than the new to join Olivia's group.

Deylaud nodded, then continued, "Diana, England, 1528; Sarita, Andalusia, 1575—"

"What did you say?"

"Sarita, Andalusia, 15—"

"Before that—" I held my breath.

"Diana, England, 1528."

Deylaud watched me, politely waiting for my permission to continue. But I looked past him, unable to speak for a moment.

"Go back to the beginning. What's written on the first page of the book?"

Deylaud shut his eyes as though he had to turn pages in his mind.

"It says, Bloodline: A Lineage of the Female Vampire."

The old wound Reedrek had inflicted in my chest throbbed like a painful heartbeat. Could it be possible that my darling Diana, rather than resting in peace, had been alive all these years?

A vampire?

Letter from William, a Vampire

My name is William Cuyler Thorne, most recently of Savannah. Once, a very, very long time ago, I was a husband . . . a father. A mortal who lived and loved without thought of the evil creatures in the world.

Now I am one of those evil beings. A blood drinker.

A vampire.

Recently, after these many centuries, I've had to make good on my life's promise of revenge. Circumstances forced me to put up or shut up, as my offspring Jack would say. Presented with the chance to kill Reedrek, my villainous sire—and thus perhaps end my immortal existence in the bargain—I embraced it. But in our world, just as in the mortal one, things don't always go as planned. In my dash toward annihilation, I approached the finish line only to be pulled back to the unliving by Jack's inscrutable logic.

He needed me.

Now I have discovered a name in an ancient book. A name etched into my crowded memory like a ragged scar. A name that will forever raise the deepest love in my unbeating heart, drawing it up beside the hatred I feel for the monster whom I thought had stolen that love from me.

The book is a genealogy of Strigori—of vampires.

The entry is *Diana, England, 1528.*

My wife's image—Diana's lovely face—fills my thoughts, and for a moment I feel the tiniest hope that I might find her again. I've set Olivia to the task of tracking this undead

Diana. Yet it twists my gut to think that Reedrek might have made my guiltless love into a bereft creature like me. To complete the transformation, he would have had to mate with her, and the very possibility brings a surge of nausea. I would tear her tormentor limb from limb before allowing him to ravage her soul. It was unbearable enough to watch him kill her.

I cannot bear to think of it. By God, Reedrek couldn't have so complete a victory over me and mine.

Of course, if it is true, God had nothing whatsoever to do with it.

Letter from Jack, a Vampire

My name is Jack McShane and I'm a master mechanic, a ladies' man, a NASCAR fan, and a vampire—not necessarily in that order. Show me a car and I can fix it. Show me a woman, and I can seduce her. Show me a creature, human or not, that threatens my existence or the safety of my loved ones, and I will make sure it never leaves Savannah in one piece, at least not without that piece being chewed up and spit out. Literally.

They say you can't teach an old dog new tricks, but this dog's been kicking since the War Between the States and I've learned more about myself and my kind in the last few weeks than since I was made immortal. Turns out not all vampires are peace-loving types like me and my sire, William Thorne. Mind you, I've seen—and killed—my share of roving rogue vampires here and there, just to keep the peace. But I had no idea there were whole packs of evil ones in Europe—or that some of them would one day be coming for us.

But it all came out in the wash, as they say, and my sire no longer tries to keep me in the dark about such matters to protect me. He can't afford to. He needs me armed with the truth and ready to fight at his side if need be.

Now it turns out that William wants me to get all supercharged. See, I just got transfused with the blood of a powerful voodoo *mambo,* and William says I might now have powers I never dreamed of. Melaphia gave me some prayers and a whole laundry list of offerings for some voodoo deity so that he'll make me all the vampire I can be. She says I should be careful, though, because the voodoo gods are powerful, easily pissed off, and prone to retribution. Yeah, yeah, whatever. Voodoo shmoodoo. I'll light the candles and incense, say my spiel, and see what happens.

What could possibly go wrong?

William

Eleanor pounded on the lid of the coffin like a wild thing. Between guttural curses and terrified screams she frantically called my name as if something was eating her alive from the inside out.

I was helpless.

I could only sit and wait. Answering her did no good. She was writhing in some dark place, where neither my voice nor my mind could penetrate. There would be no comfort, no familiarity until it was over.

I'd reached out and banished Eleanor's mortal soul. Had I made a terrible mistake? Did having her permission make it any less heinous?

I shoved my hands through my hair and covered my ears. The screams led my long memory back through time like a broken record. Diana, Diana, Diana . . . I paced the room, doing my damnedest to leave the past behind. There had to be some way to soothe Eleanor, some way to ease her terror.

Then I heard the ocean, the calming call of the shells. It could have been a result of my distress, but more likely it was the new dose I'd taken of Lalee's ancient blood. The shells seemed to be summoning me of their own accord. As fast as my mind registered the need, the bone box appeared, floating before me. The shells could transport my waking mind through time and space much like a dream. But could they take me to the dark places where Eleanor lay trapped? And could I do anything once I got there? There was only one way to find out.

I retrieved the long, braided lock of hair Melaphia had cut from Eleanor and tied it around my wrist. Then I plucked the box from the air and cast the shells.

Eleanor . . . Closing my eyes I touched the soft strands, remnants of her mortal life, and waited for the sight of her.

I was transported to unnatural darkness.

As a night creature, my element is darkness. I can discern shapes in the deepest caves of the earth—even on the ocean floor if need be. But this darkness wasn't earthly. This was a suffocating, unnatural shadowness, the total absence of light or even its memory.

Yet there were sounds. The slither of scales on rock, the slow, sliding footsteps of bereft wandering creatures. With a low pitiful whine, something shivering cold brushed by me. Then in the distance came a guttural growl, followed by a shriek.

Was this some in-between dimension or had I been delivered to the dark side of hell? How would I find Eleanor here without sight?

"Eleanor?" I called, in case she was near and could hear my voice.

The sound echoed and set off a cacophony of noisy reactions. The beings inhabiting this damned place closed in around me, speaking, entreating, threatening all at once. The din was beyond alarming.

Even a vampire knows when to step back. Yet somewhere in the chaos I heard Eleanor's desperate whisper.

"William, I'm here. Don't leave me—"

For the first time in my overlong existence, I needed light.

"Stand back," I ordered to those clustered around me as I drew myself into a killing posture, calling on any power the shells could provide. If these creatures could hear my voice then they could be warned off. Let them come for me rather than Eleanor.

Let there be light . . .

I felt the spirit of Lalee rise through me, toes to ears, like oil through a lantern wick. As my being expanded, a brilliant wash of illumination lit the area. It took me several seconds to realize that the luminescence was emanating from my own skin. It took half that long to regret my request for vision. Some things are better left to the dark.

Here there be dragons.

There have been poems written to the velvet sky, but this place was of total, inky darkness. There were no stars—no light could penetrate the utter blackness above.

And there were many creatures around me. As far as my borrowed power could penetrate the gloom, there were beings: moving, searching, squirming in their dank bucket like mindless worms. Their howls and moans set my teeth on edge. Gerard, ever the scientist, would have had a field day with this supernatural evolution run amok.

I saw amorphous slugs leaving trails of slime. I saw zombielike humans, wild-eyed and witless, a primal forest of teeth, blood, lolling tongues, and blank, horrified eyes. I was trapped in a den of demons.

In the distance, Eleanor, or her essence, called to me, though ten thousand trapped souls stood between us. The demon closest to me drew back, driven by the unfamiliar light. But one of the larger ones growled and leaped toward me like an overgrown rabid dog. I braced myself for the attack, but as with Reedrek on the *Alabaster,* the snarling beast sailed through my insubstantial form without result, leaving behind an essence that smelled of ripe dead meat. As he continued past me, he crashed into more demons, who roared and proceeded to bite and tear at his body until all that remained was blood and gore . . . and teeth. Bon appétit.

Then they all fell silent, whether from shock or fury I could not say. Frankly, I didn't care. For this one moment, I had become the Lord of Light instead of darkness, and I intended to use it to my advantage. As I waded into the demons, they fell back before me, covering their eyes like pilgrims in the desert who'd found a flaming angel in their midst.

Hallelujah!

Finally I reached Eleanor, a press of demons silently at my heels. "William!" Eleanor flung herself at me with little more than a ripple. As our spirits joined, she smelled alternately of magnolia and fear. I tried to comfort her, but without touch it would be difficult. Our connection was rooted in the physical, in sex.

"I won't let them harm you." I moved toward her until our spirit forms overlapped and she stood inside the circle of light. She crossed her arms and hugged herself, perhaps imagining my not-so-human comfort.

"Why am I here? This isn't how you said it would be." Her voice shook with growing horror. "Am I dead?"

She wanted to know if she'd been sent to hell. I couldn't set her at ease, not without lying; there had always been the chance that she might be lost.

I raised a hand in her direction and pushed glowing fingers along her cheek. She closed her eyes and sighed as if she could feel the touch. "Help me."

"I won't leave you. I'll see you through it." And as easily as that I'd made another promise. One that might be an end for both of us and a bitter beginning for me. If Eleanor did not survive her making, then both of us would be trapped in the dark.

A buzz and hiss traveled through the throng pressing around us. There was movement, a shifting on one side. *William* . . . I heard my name again and glanced down toward Eleanor. She, however, was gazing at the crowd. There was a disturbance in the distance. A small glow seemed to be moving in our direction, the light pinkish white. The crowd parted and another angel stood before us.

No, not an angel.

Shari.

She looked very different than last I'd seen her. Her

honey blond hair had turned silvery white, her warm amber eyes were a glimmering gray. She was fey as the fabled Sidhe. Her burial clothes were torn at the sleeve and shredded at the hem; her bare feet were bloody.

"William?" This time she posed my name as a question, as though she couldn't believe her eyes. "You've come to save me?"

I couldn't bring myself to tell her otherwise. "I'll do my best."

Then her gaze passed from me to Eleanor. She moved forward and put out her hand as though we'd just arrived at a party and needed introductions. "I'm Shari," she said.

Without releasing contact with me, Eleanor made an effort to take Shari's insubstantial hand. "I'm Eleanor."

They both looked at me as if I should know what came next. Where was Jack when I truly needed him? "Are you all right?" I asked, ridiculous as it might seem.

Shari seemed to shrink inside her pale glow, then nervously glanced around the circle of hideous onlookers. "They don't bother me much, now that I have protection. The lady—Melaphia—told me what to do when they try to scare me."

"And what is that?"

Obediently, Shari bowed her head and began a low chant.

Jack

"Here are the printouts you wanted," Werm said. He had a sheaf of papers in one hand and a bunch of some kind of sticks in the other. "And the incense you asked for, from Spencer's at the mall."

All conversation among the irregulars had stopped as Otis, Rufus, Jerry, and Rennie took in the spectacle that was Lamar Nathan Von Werm. His silvery white hair was gummed up into little icicle spikes all over his head. His black leather jacket was too big and boxy, and his matching pants too tight. When the irregulars weren't loitering in my garage, they were hanging out at some real bad dives— if Werm even set foot in there, he'd get his ass kicked. And that's not even considering the eyeliner and black nail polish he was sporting.

"Boys, this here's Werm," I said.

Rufus and Jerry sniffed the air, making Werm for a vampire immediately. Shapeshifters and vampires can always spot each other, or smell each other. Rennie, who was human, wouldn't have been able to tell that Werm was undead if I hadn't already warned him. Otis, who wasn't a shifter but wasn't completely human either, was looking at Werm like he was from the planet What-in-the-Sam-Hill-Are-You?

I introduced the irregulars, who grunted their acknowledgment of Werm's presence but didn't offer to shake. I couldn't say as I blamed them. I had my hopes that Werm would grow out of his goth phase pretty soon. Goths made excellent dinner guests, when they *were* the dinner. It was damned embarrassing to be seen with one of them on a regular basis, though.

We were all standing around the card table. The boys had brought me the items I'd assigned each of them to get, since shopping is not easy for vampires. I don't always have time to get out to the all-night Wal-Mart, and besides, the flourescent lighting makes my skin look like I just stepped out of a wax museum. Makes those Wally-world "associates" a trifle nervous.

"Otis, what's that rusted grill for?" I asked.

Otis had rolled in a waist-high charcoal grill, the old round kind, painted in black enamel. "It's your altar," he said proudly. "You said you wanted something you could set up outside. You can burn your candles and incense inside this baby without starting any brush fires."

"You're nothing if not practical," I said. "And if I get hungry I can always roast some wieners."

"Or some wiener dogs," Jerry suggested. He shrugged

when nobody laughed. Nobody mentioned the V-word at the garage, not even Rennie, who'd known me longer than any human besides Mel. From time to time, Jerry referred to my nature indirectly, but I let him live. At least I have so far. Jerry handed over a pack of tea lights from Dollar Tree. "Nothing but the best for you, hoss."

"Thanks," I said. Jerry was tall and muscular, unlike Otis and Rufus, who were lanky and wiry. I could probably count on him in a fight but hadn't ever had to call on him to watch my back. I hoped I never would. For all I knew, he might owe more allegiance to a pack leader somewhere. He was big and strong, but I doubted he was alpha.

"What is all this stuff for again?" Rufus asked. He was a shapeshifter, too, although I had a feeling he was a different variety than Jerry. His ears weren't as pointy as Jerry's, and he never came around when the moon was full.

"Some voodoo ritual William's housekeeper wants me to do. It's supposed to make me stronger or something."

"I've got to do one, too," Werm said proudly, "to develop my own natural strengths."

"Yeah, well, you look like you need all the help you can get, sissy boy," said Jerry.

Werm reddened with anger, but he kept his mouth shut. I was sorry for the little whelp. He thought that becoming a vampire would make him an instant badass. No such luck. Poor little bastard was probably still getting sand kicked in his face down at the nightclubs. Since I'd made him swear not to bite humans, he complained of being a vampire in name only. Still, it was better than him winding up in the city lockup with sunshine streaming through the windows until he was cooked well done.

Werm put the incense on the card table, along with the other items that the gang had helped me gather up. It was like a messed-up redneck scavenger hunt. Rennie got the list Melaphia gave me and ticked off each item with a pencil. White rum, cigars, cedar sprigs, white candles, incense.

"Who's got the food offering?" Rennie said, and looked at the others over his Coke-bottle-thick glasses.

Otis stepped forward with a small bag. "It's a chicken leg from KFC," he said. "Extra Crispy."

"I'm an Original Recipe man myself," said Rufus.

"Me too," Rennie agreed solemnly, and handed the list over to me.

Jerry weighed in with an observation on the secret herbs and spices, and a debate broke out on the merits of pressure cooking versus slow roasting. While they were busy with their discussion, Werm sidled around the table and handed me the papers.

"And they think *I'm* a pussy," he muttered sullenly.

"Watch yourself," I said, folding the sheet from Rennie and stuffing it into the breast pocket of my chambray shirt in order to keep it separate from the other papers. "Three of them could probably eat you in a couple of bites and pick their teeth with your bones."

Werm must have thought I was speaking metaphorically because he only shrugged. "Why do guys like that always pick on me?"

I took the papers from him and began to scan them. "Have you looked in the mirror? Maybe it's the earbobs."

"Why do they smell funny? And why did my fangs tingle when I got within smelling range?"

"They're shapeshifters," I said. "Two of them, anyway. I don't know about the other one. That's one of the things I've got to teach you—how to recognize other nonhumans. Remind me to do that someday." I glanced at the papers before folding them and sticking them into my back pocket.

"You're shitting me, right?" said Werm. "You mean, like, werewolves?"

"Yeah. Like werewolves. Don't get your panties in a twist."

Werm stared at the irregulars with alarm. "How many other kinds of—of nonhumans are there out there?"

"Lots. Listen, you chose this existence, remember? Your

nice little sheltered human life is over. You're a creature of the night now, and you've only traded one set of guys who can kick your ass for a whole different set of guys who can kick your ass. Only this time, they're not going to have baseball bats. They're going to have long, pointy teeth. And you're going to have to learn to deal or die. Welcome to the dark side, pal."

Werm let this sink in, nodded, and drew himself up. Despite his appearance, the kid had heart. And brains. If he kept his nose clean, I actually thought he had a chance to survive. For a while at least.

Changing the subject, Werm asked, "Why did you want to know about Mayans?"

"Never you mind." I'd asked Werm to run an Internet search on the Loa Legba, who Mel had directed me to pray to. I also had him do a separate search on anything having to do with Mayan goddesses. I needed the voodoo lowdown to come up with my own spirit ceremony. The stuff for Connie I'd go over later in private.

"You run on along and pray to that herb god or whatever it is that Melaphia told you about."

He brightened a little. "The god of *really* secret herbs and spices. I've got some pretty good weed I can burn as an offering, maybe even get a good contact high. But first let me see how you do your ritual. Then I'll know more how to do my own."

I was going to tell him to shove off, but I already felt guilty for not having the time to teach him any more vampire stuff than I had. He'd just gotten a rude introduction to shapeshifters because I hadn't taken the time to prepare him for other creatures that went bump in the night.

"Follow me." I swept the items from the table into the grill, replaced the cover, and rolled the whole thing right past the ongoing fast-food argument and out the back door of the garage. I settled the grill onto a nice flat spot.

"First things first," I said. I screwed the cap off the bottle of rum and threw it aside. "Here's to the Loa Legba," I announced, drank, and passed the bottle to Werm.

He sniffed it prissily and said, "Don't you want me to get us some Coke to drink this with?"

"Son, that would be the ruination of two good drinks. You're a vampire now, a tough guy. Drink like one."

Werm glanced at me doubtfully and took a snip. He busted into a prolonged coughing fit and handed the bottle back to me, glad to get rid of it.

Werm opened the package of candles while I bit the end off the cigar Jerry had brought and spat it into the dirt. I lit it off one of the candles and drew on it until I got it going real good. Then, while Werm was lighting the rest of the candles, I tried to remember what Melaphia had told me to do. The first thing that came back to me when I thought about the meeting was the look on William's face when he'd kissed Eleanor's hand.

Hellfire and damnation. I took another long swig of the rum, feeling the burn all the way down into my guts. I had completely chickened out of telling William about Olivia's discovery of Diana's existence. But how could I tell him? In the days since Eleanor's making, he'd been a different man, er, vampire. His mood was more upbeat than I'd ever seen it. He'd even been patient with Werm at the meeting. If that didn't signal a sea change in William's attitude toward the universe I didn't know what did.

He was . . . happy.

I marveled at the thought. *William* and *happy* didn't belong in the same sentence, but it was right there in his eyes. How could I tell him something that was going to make his world fall apart? But I had to if I wanted to save myself. What was the rush, though? Diana and William had been separated for hundreds of years. What would another few days' difference make? If I thought about it long enough a solution would surely come to me. I took a long draw on the bottle, as if the answer to my problem was hidden at the bottom.

I drew the papers out of my pocket and handed them to Werm, who began to read about the Loa Legba by the light of the candles. "It says here that he is the great phallic deity."

"I'll drink to that," I said. "That's what the gals down at Eleanor's used to call *me*. Not in so many words, you understand." I raised the bottle high in salute and took still another drink. "To Loa Legba! My man! He can throw it over his shoulder like a Continental soldier." In my rapidly inebriated state, the words *shoulder* and *soldier* turned into a mouthful of slurred mush, making Werm giggle.

"Have you fed tonight?" Werm asked, taking the bottle from me.

"Nope. You?"

Werm screwed up his face, took a drink, and screwed up his face again. "No." Werm swayed a little as he handed the bottle back to me and peered at the papers. "The words are trying to swim away from my eyeballs. Hey, I didn't know vampires could get drunk."

"You bet your ass we can." I took another drink. "Over the fangs and through the gums."

Werm looked up at me in wonder. "Coooool," he slurred. He stared at the words as if he was trying to interpret hieroglyphics. "It says that the Loa Legba appears as an old man with a cane and a sack, and that he's the guardian of the gateway."

"What gateway is that?"

"The one from one world to another. That's all it says. My inkjet cartridge ran out." He shrugged. "Sorry."

"That's okay. I've got the prayer Melaphia wrote down for me right here." I took the list out of my shirt pocket and turned it over to the back. Melaphia's neat handwriting looked like gibberish. Some of the words were foreign, and even though she'd spelled them out phonetically, I still could make sense of only a few of them here and there. I was going to have to wing it. What could go wrong?

"Okay, gramps. This one's from the heart," I said. I handed the bottle to Werm, who took another drink, nodded approvingly, and handed it back. I raised the bottle and sprinkled a healthy shot or so over the altar.

"Uh, I salute you. I honor you. And I ask you to—" I stared at the paper again. "Open the gateway. Yeah, that's right, and I guess I'm supposed to ask you to make my natural vampire powers even stronger."

"I think that's the key," Werm said sagely. "That's what Willyum and Mela—Melaph—Mel said."

"Yeah," I said. I set the bottle down and made a sweeping gesture toward the other items on the grill. "All this stuff here is for you. The candles, the cedar, the incense, the chicken. So open that ol' gateway of yours and let the sun shine in." I snickered. Maman Lalee help me, but I did.

"We didn't know if you liked Original Recipe or Extra Crispy," Werm said and busted into a giggling fit.

I let the papers fall and grabbed onto Werm's shoulder for support, but we both collapsed, braying with laughter like a couple of jackasses. "Hey," Werm said. "Maybe you should see if you can fly now."

"Fly? Hell, I can barely stand up." I snorted again with laughter, and Werm shrieked in hysterics.

We were laughing so hard that I didn't feel the change in the atmosphere until the candles started to flicker. The wind had shifted, but there was something more. Something unnatural was in the air. Something unwholesome and thick with decay. I've said it before and I'll say it again. When a vampire gets creeped out, well, let's just say it's messed up. Seriously messed up.

Werm felt it, too. We stopped laughing at the same instant. We had both been doubled over, and at that level our vision was clouded by the smoke from the burning incense and flickering candles. We straightened up slowly, and when we did, we had a clear view of the relatively fresh earth a few feet away from us—it was shifting, and not because we'd had a couple snorts from the bottle. My supersensitive hearing picked up a scrabbling noise underground.

Werm heard it, too. "Jack, what's that?" he asked. "It's coming from that bare patch of dirt over there."

My boozy brain was trying to clear itself. "You mean that patch of dirt about the size of a Chevy Corsica?"

Werm just looked at me, not understanding. I didn't want to understand either, but I was beginning to all the same.

Oh, no.

"Werm, help me think. What did we just ask that voodoo spirit for? What did we ask him for *exactly*?"

"We—we asked him to make your vampire powers even stronger. What's wrong with that?"

"Oh, shit."

Since Werm was still staring at me, he didn't see the mottled hand burst out of the ground in the Savannah moonlight. He didn't see it grasp at the chill night air.

A little while back, my evil grandsire, Reedrek, made a big show of murdering my friend and employee Huey. The poor little simpleminded fellow had the misfortune of being at the wrong place at the wrong time and, long story short, kind of got gutted like a trout. Since we didn't want to get the police involved and since Huey didn't have any family, we decided to bury him behind the wheel of his beloved Chevy with a beer in his hand.

Now as I've explained before, I have what you'd call an affinity for the dead, even beyond the fact that I *are* one, as the old joke goes. I can barely walk through a cemetery without the passed-on wanting to get all chatty with me. In short, ghosts love ol' Jack. In fact, Huey had visited me once after he died, here in the garage, just to let me know that he was doing well in the afterworld. Then he went about his business. That was fine and dandy.

This wasn't.

What stood before Werm and me was not a ghost. It was a zombie. It was a full-bore *Night of the Living Dead* walking corpse. It was Huey in the flesh, you might say. Mottled, rotting, putrid flesh.

Werm walked stiffly to a clump of bushes and retched quietly.

It didn't take a rocket scientist to figure out what had happened. My powers where the dead were concerned—those that were previously limited mostly to communication—had blossomed into full-fledged corpse reanimation. Yes indeedy. Thanks to a well-hung voodoo deity, I was now the proud owner of a bouncing baby zombie. Ask and ye shall receive.

Huey raised his hand, one of the hands that he'd just used to claw his way out of the earth. "Hey, Jack."

"Hey, Huey."

Werm appeared at my side. *"That's Huey?"*

"That's him," I said. "Huey, this is Werm."

"Hey, Werm."

"Hey, Huey," Werm said wanly. "Jack, I think I know what must've—"

"Yeah, me too."

Werm and I walked back into the garage, Huey shuffling along behind us. The irregulars were playing cards now, like they did most nights. Jerry, who'd brought the cigars for the ritual, had evidently purchased enough for everybody, because there they sat, puffing away and sipping their beers as pretty as you please. Because Werm and I had come in ahead of him, they didn't notice Huey until he sat down at his usual place at the table.

What little action there was at the table froze solid, as if, ironically, the living men had gone into suspended animation and only the dead man showed any sign of life. The only movement they displayed was the downward trajectory of their cigars, which now hung limply from the corners of their mouths.

For a moment I was reminded of that famous old painting of the dogs playing poker. That's how still they were, as still as the dogs in the painting, until Huey grinned, showing a mouthful of greenish teeth and rotting gums.

"Deal me in, boys," he said.